Some Girls Bite

'... Chloe Neill owes me a good night's sleep! With her ...erfully compelling reluctant vampire heroine, and her careful world building, I was drawn into *Some Girls Bite* from page one, and kept reading into the night. I love Merit and can't wait for the next book in this fabulous new series'

Julie Kenner, *USA Today* bestselling author

'There's a new talent in town, and if this debut is any indication, she's here to stay! Not only does Neill introduce an indomitable and funny heroine; her secondary characters are enormously intriguing . . . truly excellent!' *Romantic Times*

Friday Night Bites

'Ms Neill has created an urban fantasy world that's easily believed and a pleasure to visit. *Friday Night Bites* is wonderfully entertaining and impossible to set down' *Darque Reviews*

Twice Bitten

'Neill continues to hit the sweet spot with her blend of high-stakes drama, romantic entanglements and a touch of humour . . . certain to whet readers' appetites for more in this entertaining series!'

Romantic Times

Hard Bitten

'A fast and exciting read' *Fresh Fiction*

Drink Deep

'Neill has another powerhouse entry to this series with *Drink Deep*, and her legions of fans are sure to be delighted' *SFRevu*

Biting Cold

'Chloe Neill keeps readers right on the precipice of anticipation'

Fresh Fiction

House Rules

'Rising star Neill has made the learning curve for her gutsy heroine, Merit, quite steep, which means the journey is all the more sp... ...antic Times*

By Chloe Neill

Chicagoland Vampires series

Some Girls Bite

Friday Night Bites

Twice Bitten

Hard Bitten

Drink Deep

Biting Cold

House Rules

Biting Bad

Wild Things

Blood Games

Dark Debt

Howling for You (eBook only novella)

Lucky Break (eBook only novella)

Dark Elite series

Firespell

Hexbound

Charmfall

A CHICAGOLAND VAMPIRES NOVEL

MIDNIGHT MARKED

CHLOE NEILL

First published in Great Britain in 2016
by Gollancz
An imprint of the Orion Publishing Group
Carmelite House, 50 Victoria Embankment,
London EC4Y 0DZ
An Hachette UK Company

This edition published in Great Britain in 2016
by Gollancz

1 3 5 7 9 10 8 6 4 2

A CIP catalogue record for this book
is available from the British Library

ISBN 978 1 473 20851 3

All characters and events in this publication are fictitious and any resemblance to real persons, living of dead, is purely coincidental.

Printed in Great Britain by Clays Ltd, St Ives plc

The Orion Publishing Group's policy is to use papers that are natural, renewable and recyclable products and made from wood grown in sustainable forests. The logging and manufacturing processes are expected to conform to the environmental regulations of the country of origin.

"Kings fight for empires, madmen for applause."

John Dryden

CHAPTER ONE

THE DEVIL'S EYE

Late April
Chicago, Illinois

I stood at the corner of Clark and Addison in jeans and a Cubs T-shirt, my long hair pulled into a ponytail through a vintage Cubs cap.

At a quick glance, I probably didn't look much different from the thousands of humans around me. But I was a vampire, and I'd caught the devil's eye. So there was a House medal around my neck, a Master vampire beside me, and a dagger tucked into one of my boots.

I stared up at the building, excited as a kid at her first baseball game. The famous red marquee glowed over the hologram of Harry Caray smiling behind thick black glasses that was projected onto the sidewalk.

I'd been a vampire for three hundred and eighty-four days. This was going to be one of the best of those, because I was home.

For the first time since becoming a vampire, I was at Wrigley Field.

"Do you need to take a moment, Sentinel?"

I ignored the teasing tone of the man who stood beside me, the four-hundred-year-old Master vampire who ruled Chicago's Cadogan House and the parts of my heart that weren't devoted to great books and good pizza.

I turned to give him a pithy look, expecting to see sarcasm on his face. But there was something softer in those deep-set green eyes. Love tinged with amusement. His hair, thick and gold like summer silk, was tied at the nape of his neck, showing off knife's-edge cheekbones and a square chin. And although he wasn't much of a baseball fan, and even though we lived on Chicago's South Side, he wore a vintage Cubbies shirt that fit his lean body like a very fortunate glove. Ethan Sullivan didn't wear casual clothes very often, but he wore them as well as he did his bespoke, thousand-dollar suits.

"I *am* taking a moment," I said with a grin. "Quit distracting me."

"Heaven forbid I should do that," he said knowingly, putting a hand at my back.

"Could you possibly goggle from a booth? I am absolutely starving."

For once, I wasn't the one asking to eat. That honor belonged to my best friend, newlywed Mallory Carmichael Bell.

I was still getting used to the name change.

I glanced back at her, her hair as deeply blue as the Cubs logo, her petite frame tucked into skinny jeans and a snug blue and red Save Ferris T-shirt. "Didn't you eat a granola bar in the car?"

"I did," she said, "but it's the only thing I've eaten today. I spent half the day bitching at the Order for its record-keeping failure," she grumbled. "Anyway, I'm starving."

The Order was the official, if surprisingly incompetent, union of American sorcerers. It wasn't the kind of complaint you'd expect to hear in front of Wrigley Field, but it wasn't unusual for our group. Two vampires, two sorcerers, and all four of us trying to nail the city's most powerful financial and political mogul, who also happened to be the leader of the city's criminal underground. Our enemy was Adrien Reed, and his organization was known as the Circle. He had supernatural minions, including a sorcerer of his own who'd used his impressive power to transform a vampire into the Master whom Ethan had believed was long dead.

"Let's discuss the details away from the crowd," said the sorcerer beside Mallory. Her husband, Catcher Bell, was tall and leanly muscular, with shorn hair, green eyes, and a generous mouth currently pulled into a line as he scanned the crowd for threats.

He wasn't the only one looking. Ethan had informed the Cubs we'd be attending the game, and given the WELCOME CADOGAN HOUSE! message on the marquee, they'd decided not to be shy about it. We had to be on our best behavior—and our highest alert.

The evening at the ballpark had been Ethan's idea—a few hours of normalcy in a month that had involved a mysterious evildoer from Ethan's past and a new evildoer who believed he could lie, cheat, and steal with impunity. We'd temporarily thwarted Reed, but he'd promised us another round. We were looking forward to the battle, and we were determined this inning would be the last.

Also, my birthday was in a few days. I'd officially turn twenty-nine, although I still looked twenty-seven and three-quarters and would for the rest of my potentially immortal life. There'd been a time when I wasn't comfortable with the fact that Ethan had made me a vampire—it had been necessary because of a violent attack by another vampire, and not of my choosing—but I'd worked through those issues.

My vampire senses were strong. I'd filtered them heavily because we were surrounded by so many people, but I still heard my name and Ethan's whispered around us by humans who recognized us from newspaper articles and Internet sites. Ethan had his own fandom; EthanSullivanIsMyMaster.net was a very real thing. Given the e-mails the House's Initiate Liaison and social secretary, Helen, had intercepted on my behalf, he wasn't the only one with fans. Personally, I found all of it unnerving. Flattering, but unnerving.

As to the real-world threats, Ethan had ordered me not to be brave, not to engage anyone unless absolutely necessary. Since protecting him and the House was my solemn responsibility as Sentinel, we undoubtedly had different definitions of "absolutely necessary."

"Where are we eating?" Mallory asked, glancing at the restaurants arranged around the ballpark. The neighborhood had always been crowded on game day, but recent renovations had spawned more bars and pubs and brought out more people.

"Someplace familiar," Ethan said, then glanced at me. "If you're ready?"

I grabbed Ethan's wrist, checked his gleaming steel watch. Tonight's game was a rare late-night matchup at Wrigley sponsored by a battery company that was giving away Cubs flashlights.

"We've got an hour and a half," I said as Ethan adjusted his watch again. "And I'm going to get one of those damn flashlights." Since we were awake only at night and usually on a Mission to Save the Vampires and Humans of Chicago Even if They Didn't Appreciate It, a flashlight would most certainly come in handy. And a Cubs light? Total score.

"I'll do everything in my power to get you one," Ethan said. "We're going to Temple Bar."

I brightened. Temple Bar was Cadogan's official watering hole and only a couple of blocks away from Wrigley. I hadn't had a chance to visit in months.

"They have food?" Catcher asked.

Ethan smiled knowingly. "They've ordered pizza in the event

Merit was hungry. I understand cream cheese and double bacon is on the menu."

"You know me too well," I said. I really wanted one of those flashlights, but I could still appreciate an hour of deep dish with friends. Besides, cream cheese and double bacon was my favorite topping combination—a culinary concoction that could cure most ills, at least in my bacon-addled opinion.

"Let's get moving," Mallory said. "Because God forbid Merit doesn't get her flashlight."

"They sell flashlights everywhere," Catcher muttered as Mallory slipped her arm into his and we crossed the street toward the bar.

"You don't get it," she said, patting his arm, then glanced over her shoulder. "Husbands. Am I right?"

God, it was weird to hear her say that.

Temple Bar was a narrow building full of brass, wood, and Cubs memorabilia. The paneled walls were lined with vintage pennants, T-shirts, and game balls, and bleacher seats scavenged from Wrigley during the renovation. High-top tables and leather booths filled the space, and they'd added a pool table. The bar was packed with vampires in Cubs gear, their supernaturalness obvious from the buzz of magic that electrified the air.

Sean, one of the two vampire brothers who managed the place, rang the brass bell that hung behind the bar. The patrons turned their heads toward the sound.

"Master on the premises!" Sean yelled cheerfully, pointing toward Ethan with his free hand.

The bar exploded with cheers and applause as vampires turned in their seats, craning to get a look at their Master. I took for granted how often I saw Ethan, whether personally or professionally. To the other Cadogan Novitiates, being near him socially was a rarity, a treat.

They smiled as we walked in, their gazes still slightly suspicious when they got to Mallory. She'd mostly redeemed herself to the House after a troubling history, but vampires had long memories.

We headed to a four-top. Sean's brother, Colin, came around the bar, white towel slung over his shoulder. Sean was younger than his brother, but both looked as if they'd stepped out of an Irish travel brochure: tall and lanky, with red hair, blue eyes, and ruddy complexions.

"Liege," Colin said, giving Ethan a little bow, then smiling at me. "It's been too long," he added, playfully squeezing my shoulder. "What's the occasion?"

"Merit's first post-fang game at Wrigley," Sean said, setting a pizza box, paper plates, and napkins in the middle of the table. The scents of spicy sauce, smoky bacon, and cheese filled the air, and the box had one of my favorite words printed across it in bold red letters—SAUL'S. Not just my favorite kind of pizza, but from my favorite pizza place in Chicago. Ethan had really gone above and beyond.

Thank you, I said silently, activating the telepathic link between us. *I appreciate the effort.*

You'll appreciate it more later, he said, with a wickedness in his eyes that promised delightful things to come—even if the Cubs didn't pull out a win.

"Well, well," Colin said, glancing at me. "That's worth a drink on the house. You're a gin-and-tonic girl, right?"

"I am," I agreed. "And that sounds great."

"Done," he said, and looked at Ethan. "Sire?"

Ethan had gotten an upgrade, at least in title, when he became a member of the Assembly of American Masters, a newly created organization intended to give American vampires control of their futures. So far, they'd been very low-drama, which was a nice change from their predecessor.

"I'll have what she's having."

"I knew you'd trust my judgment eventually."

Catcher snorted. "About food pairings, anyway."

"A Novitiate takes what a Novitiate can get," Colin said with a wink. He took Catcher's and Mallory's orders, left us with pizza. We exchanged shrewd looks, waiting for someone to make the first move toward a slice.

"Well, I'm not waiting for your people to play supernatural rock-paper-scissors," Mallory said, spinning the box so its maw opened toward her, and sliding a piece onto a plate.

"Which would be what, exactly?" Ethan wondered.

She paused, chewed contemplatively, then raised two fingers in a "V," curled them into would-be claws, and wiggled them like she was sprinkling a spell over us. "Vampire-shifter-sorcerer," she said. "You can call it 'VSS.'"

"I think you just invented a meme," I said, impressed.

"Of course I did. I'm awesome. Pass me the cheese."

We'd nearly finished the pizza when Catcher gestured toward the pool table. "You play?" he asked Ethan.

"Every now and again."

"You up for a match?"

Ethan glanced back at me, eyebrows lifted.

I looked at the clock. We'd eaten quickly, still had time before the game started. I would have been perfectly fine getting to the stadium early, watching players warm up and fans file in, balancing Chicago dogs and phones and beers as they did so. But when Ethan glanced longingly at the table's immaculate green felt and curvy baroque legs, I knew I was lost.

"Go for it," I said, then cocked my head. "Although I didn't know you played."

"I'm not a hustler," he said, with a smidge of indignation. "But I play as well as I Master."

Insecurity was not a trait Ethan was familiar with. "In that case, have fun."

"You think he's going to school Catcher?" Mallory asked as they made their way through the crowd to the pool table.

"I don't know," I said. That was true enough, although Ethan didn't do much without a plan for victory—or at least an exit strategy.

I watched him, tall and rangy, select a pool cue, test its weight, and check its flexibility. A pair of vampires rose from their seats near the bar, wandered over to say hello. Blond hair tucked behind his ears, the cue he'd selected in hand, Ethan shook the vampires' hands, then introduced Catcher. They chatted as Catcher racked the balls, and they prepared to play.

"Will Catcher throw a fit if he loses?" I asked. He was the generally grouchy type. I liked him very much.

"Catcher thrives on moderation and reasoned action."

I snorted. "And Ethan is humble and operates the House as a democracy."

"So we're both full of shit," she said, then cast her gaze toward her well-toned husband. "If he loses, it serves him right for challenging a vampire in his own place."

"Maybe not the wisest move," I agreed.

"Anyway," she said, scooting closer, "I'm glad they're gone. Now we can talk."

Given the drama of the last few weeks, I assumed she had bad news about evil or magic, and prepared myself for the worst.

"I'm afraid the sex is going to become stale."

Colin arrived with fresh drinks—a Manhattan for Mallory, another G&T for me. For one last, peaceful moment, I squeezed the lime into the glass, licked lip-puckering juice from my thumb. And then I took a drink, put the glass down on the table again, and did what I had to do. I invited her to talk to me about sex with Catcher.

"Why do you think it's going to become stale?"

She leaned toward me, arms folded on the table. "I mean, I don't know. We're married, and it's good. It's really good. And frequent."

I knew I'd regret it, but couldn't help asking. "How frequent?"

"At least daily. Sometimes more so. We're naked a lot," she said matter-of-factly.

"I would guess so." And I was doubly glad I didn't share her town house anymore. Mallory owned the place, and I'd been her roommate before I moved into Cadogan House. When Catcher moved in, there'd been a lot of naked canoodling in the public areas, including the kitchen. I, for one, hadn't needed to see Omelet à la Catcher's Naked Ass. "So, it sounds like things are fine right now?"

"They totally are. I guess that's the part that worries me. It's just, I love who we are right now. And I know part of being married is becoming 'comfortable' with each other. I just don't want us to become so comfortable that we're basically just roommates or something. I want to keep that spark alive." She looked over at him, her eyes shining with love—and a little glazed with lust. And Catcher was alpha male in and out, front and back, and all the way through to the other side.

"Yeah, I don't think that will be a problem," I concluded.

"I mean, we can't keep our hands off each other. That's why we were late," she said, winging up her eyebrows.

We'd picked up Mallory and Catcher in one of the House's enormous black SUVs, since Ethan's personal vehicle—a sleek black Ferrari—had been destroyed in a car chase with one of Reed's cronies.

So they'd been at it while we were sitting outside on the curb, completely unaware.

"Well," I said after a stiff drink, "even if the pace, let's say, does slow down, being comfortable with each other is awesome."

I glanced at Ethan, who was standing on the other side of the table, cue in hand like the pike his Swedish countrymen might have used. "Having someone get you is pretty amazing."

"He does get you, and that's important." She grinned. "But you can't tell me Darth Sullivan doesn't show you his 'Dark Side' regularly."

"You're ruining *Star Wars* for me. But to your point, yeah." I grinned. "He's plenty skilled with his, you know—"

"You're trying not to say 'lightsaber,' but you really want to."

"I really do." I waved my hands for finality. "Let's just say he's got one and he knows how to use it."

"Katana. Broadsword. Saber."

"We were supposed to be discussing Catcher," I reminded her. "And since I've seen his, *ahem*, broadsword plenty of times, I can verify he's got one. I think every relationship has its ups and downs, its arcs. Sometimes rampant nakedness while a girl is trying to prep her damn ramen noodles."

Mallory snorted into her drink. "They aren't good for you anyway. Too much sodium."

"I'm immortal," I pointed out.

"You are that," she said. "I hope you're right. Do you think you and Darth Sullivan will be able to keep the spark alive six or seven hundred years from now?"

Immortality wasn't something I thought about often, mostly because I couldn't really imagine it. Ethan had been alive for nearly four hundred years. He'd seen war, violence, famine, and empires come and go. Assuming I stayed away from the business end of an aspen stake, I could see all that and more. But the expanse of time wasn't something I could easily wrap my mind around.

"I don't know," I said honestly. "I can't imagine not wanting him, but immortality is a long time."

"And if he proposes?"

He'd hinted about it enough, preparing me for its inevitability, that "if" was really a conservative estimate. "*When* he proposes," I said, "and *if* I say yes, then the decision is made. The deal is done, and there's no going back."

I smiled at that. Immortality intimidated me; commitment did not.

"Good," Mallory said, then clinked her glass against mine in a toast. "Let's drink to commitment. To the grouchy-ass men we love, who really should worship at our feet." She grinned wickedly. "And do, when the incentive's right."

"I feel like we're getting dangerously close to naked Catcher territory again."

"We're only territory *adjacent*," she said with a wink. She put her glass down, looked at me for a few seconds. She smiled softly, as if she knew all the world's secrets.

"What?" I asked.

"Nothing. Just thinking about how much we've changed. Vampires, sorcerers, two sexy-as-hell and utterly egotistical men. An awkward adjustment for you, and a detour into darkness for me. And yet here we are, having a drink and preparing to go see the Cubbies." She clinked her glass against mine. "I'd say we turned out pretty good."

I couldn't argue with that.

Ethan came out strong from the break and nearly ran the table. It was an inadvertent cue bump by a Novitiate who'd had a little too much to drink that spoiled the plan. The Novitiate was apologetic, but what was done was done. Her slip gave Catcher control of the table, and control it he did. He called each shot, nailed each shot, and when he was done, left Ethan staring at the wreckage.

Or so Catcher told the story. Given that his ego nearly matched Ethan's in size and strength, I guessed the truth was somewhere in between.

When we'd wrapped up and were prepared to (finally!) head to the stadium, Colin refused Ethan's money and tried to shoo us out of the bar; Ethan, ever strategic, managed to slip bills to Sean on the sly. He preferred to pay his debts.

We emerged into the glorious spring night, the crowd bristling with energy and the sheer joy of being outside after a hard Midwestern winter. And, of course, the possibility of destroying the Cardinals on our home turf.

Ethan held my hand as we followed Catcher and Mallory through the crowd to the gate. Our seats were on the third-base side, which had been my favorite spot for an afternoon of baseball.

Ethan glanced back at me, green eyes glowing. I didn't think he was much of a baseball fan. Maybe it was vicarious excitement, because I was probably elated enough for both of us. Or maybe he was pumped about the free flashlights. Because I certainly was.

Are you ready for this, Sentinel? Ethan asked silently, using the telepathic link between us, forged when he'd made me a vampire that night a year ago.

I smiled back at him. *I am bursting with excitement.*

He took my hand, and we walked down the street just like two humans, a couple on their way to a night at the ballpark.

Mallory stopped short and turned back toward us, her expression tight, her gaze focused on something behind us. People grunted and cursed as the stream of people was forced to divert around her, and then us, when we reached her.

"Did you feel that?" she asked.

"Feel what?" Catcher said, looking around to find the threat she'd seemed to identify.

"Something magic. Something bad." Without another word, she began walking away from the stadium. We fell into step behind her, dodging through the stream of fans headed into the stadium as we moved toward Temple Bar.

But she passed the bar, kept going until she turned in to the wide alley that ran beneath the trestle that held up the tracks for the Red Line.

"Mallory!" Catcher called out, and we darted after her into the alley.

The smell of death—overripe and cruel and undeniable—spilled out from the darkness. Something had met a very ugly end here.

Or someone, I realized, glancing at the body on the ground.

CHAPTER TWO

BAD BITE

The man was young, maybe twenty-five or twenty-six. He had rough, tanned skin, brown eyes, and deep lines around his mouth. His body was whipcord lean beneath jeans and a T-shirt, and thatchy brown hair stood in mussed spikes on his head.

Magic still lingered in the air above him like heavy fog waiting to settle. And it carried with it the faint sense of animal.

He was dead . . . and a shifter.

His face was horribly swollen and bloody, his hands ripped at the knuckles. But that wasn't the worst of it. The left neck and shoulder of his T-shirt was saturated with blood that had drained from the puncture wounds on his neck. More had spilled on the ground around him.

He hadn't just been killed. He'd been murdered . . . by one of us.

I felt a sick twist of guilt. The North American Central Pack was our ally and many of its members were our friends. But they wouldn't take kindly to the death of their own by one of ours.

A second man in jeans and a dark, long-sleeved shirt burst out of the alley, ramming into Mallory and throwing her to the ground.

In that fraction of a second while he stumbled forward, he turned toward me. There was something familiar in the scent and magic that surrounded him, but nothing I could place. The bill of his cap shaded his face, showed only the thick, dark beard above pale skin. And the scent of the blood he'd stolen still clung to him.

The moment passed. The vampire—the apparent murderer—caught himself with a hand on the sidewalk before bolting to his feet again and taking off.

I didn't stop to think. I tore after him, heard Ethan fall into step behind me, his footfalls light and fast.

The vampire darted through the alley across the street, disappearing into shadow. He was twenty feet in front of me, but when the alley dead-ended, he dodged into the street and the glow of overhead lights. He darted between buildings with rooftop views of Wrigley, and then onto Sheffield on the stadium's east side.

Music blaring in the bars around us, Ethan and I kept pace with each other, our gazes on the perpetrator, who still trailed the magic of the murder he'd wrought.

I doubted any Housed vampire would take out a shifter on the street, at least not one from Chicago. He was most likely a Rogue, a vampire who lived outside the House system. Or maybe a vampire from another city on some kind of mission to take out a shifter. Either way, there'd be hell to pay with the Pack.

We dodged through a group of girls in pink Cubs T-shirts, one of them wearing a veil. Probably a bachelorette party, and from the curses they hurled after us, they'd been partying for a while.

The vampire neared the intersection with Waveland. He glanced back to check his lead, nearly ran into a group of guys and girls heading across the street from bar to stadium.

"What the hell?" yelled one of the men, tall and skinny with shoulder-length cornrows, neatly sidestepping to avoid getting mowed down by our runner.

"Sorry!" I offered as we slid through the gap he'd created.

We need to cut him off, Sentinel. He killed and he ran, and I doubt he'll stop.

No argument there. I mentally pictured the neighborhood, tried to guess where he might go. But since I didn't know him—or where he'd come from, or where he was going, or what kind of transportation he might get into—I really didn't have anything to go on. He'd been in Wrigleyville, and he'd done murder in Wrigleyville. And now, with two vampires on his tail, he was probably hoping to get out again.

Right, Ethan said as the vampire turned and dodged back toward the El.

Maybe he'd taken the Red Line to get down here, and was planning to take the same route home again.

Stay on him, I told Ethan, and dodged across the street. If I could make headway, I could cut him off before he dodged into the alley again.

"Cubs hats!"

A man stepped in front of me from out of nowhere, wearing a column of stacked baseball caps on his head, a dozen more hanging from his fingers. "You need a Cubs hat?"

He was enormous. A red-and-blue-clad wall of a man. "Not tonight, pal," I said, and tried to pivot around him, but instead we did the awkward left-or-right dance as he swung his hats back and forth, tried to get a bite.

I finally managed to slip around him, but the effort had slowed me down. The vampire darted across the street and into the shadows under the tracks again. I hit the shadows only seconds before Ethan . . . and nearly too late to hear the engine race. The driver's door still open, a beat-up Trans Am barreled toward us. The door slammed, the vampire's face shadowed in the vehicle, but I could see—and sense—perfectly well the handgun that pointed out the window.

I moved with only instinct, and without thought.

"Move!" I told Ethan, and turned in front of him, pushing him to the ground as the shot rang out, the sound slapping off brick and concrete and steel. Tires squealed as the car jerked forward, turned onto the street, and screamed into the night.

I rolled off Ethan. "Are you all right?"

"I'm fine," he said testily. "You stepped in front of me."

"I will always step in front of you. You named me Sentinel."

"In the larger scheme, not my wisest decision."

I wasn't going to argue with that admission of fallibility, even if I disagreed with the sentiment. "You can't take it back now. I'm finally getting good at it."

"Jesus, Merit."

"What? Are you hurt?" I didn't see blood, so I looked around, then back at Ethan. "Is he back?"

"No," he said, with silvering eyes that shone in the dark. "You've been shot."

"No, I haven't." I glanced down at my arm, saw the crimson rivulets that flowed down my arm and now pooled into my open palm. Adrenaline faded, and I felt the spear of fire that lanced through my biceps.

"Damn it," I said, my vision dimming at the edges. The world began to spin, but I gritted my teeth. I was a goddamn vampire, and I was absolutely not going to pass out. Not after chasing a murderer and taking a bullet for my Master.

"It looks like I took another bullet for you," I said.

Ethan grunted, ripped off the bottom hem of his shirt, and pulled a handkerchief from his pocket. He folded and pressed the handkerchief to my arm, then used the hem to secure the handkerchief in place and create a make-do bandage.

"*Ow,*" I said when he secured it a little more snugly than he should have. Fast healing was one of our better biological advantages, but we still felt pain, and this hurt like a son of a bitch.

"You did that on purpose," I said as he tucked the ends of the fabric into place.

"You did *that* on purpose. It's your fault you got shot."

"Technically, it's the vampire's fault. And I'd still rather be shot than listen to Luc harangue me because I let *you* get shot."

Ethan just growled. He was so adorable in ultra-alpha protective Master mode, with his blond hair and green eyes, and a slightly murderous expression on his face.

I frowned. "I think blood loss is making me loopy."

"Well, this isn't exactly how I thought the evening would go, either." The bandage assembled, he sat back on his heels, brushed the hair from my face. "Could you try not to get shot again? I believe this is your third time."

"Fourth," I said, wincing as pain waved across my arm. "And I promise to try not to get shot again. Because it really does hurt."

He leaned forward, pressed a soft kiss to my lips. "Steady on, my brave Sentinel."

Brave . . . and slightly bullet-ridden.

Ethan grabbed water and aspirin from a corner store, which he administered as well as any experienced nurse.

We waited until my dizziness had passed; then we walked back toward the alley. Mallory and Catcher stood beside a peeling pier that supported the tracks, staring down at the body. Humans had already begun to gather on the sidewalk, trying to get a glimpse of the man on the ground.

Catcher's eyes narrowed in concern at my bandaged arm. "What the hell happened to you?"

"Vampire, Trans Am, handgun."

"He shot you?" Mallory said, horror on her face.

"That was the handgun part. And I'm fine. Nurse Sullivan fixed it up." Nurse *Darth* Sullivan, I thought, wondering if he'd pulled the fabric tight enough to cut off my circulation completely. But since I didn't think I was playing my best snark game at this point, I kept the insult to myself.

"Are you all right?" I asked her.

She showed me her skinned elbow. "And sore rump, but otherwise fine. It's not every day you get elbowed by a murderer."

"He got away?" Catcher asked.

"That was the Trans Am part," Ethan said. "I can describe the vehicle, but it didn't have plates, so there won't be much to go on. And we didn't get a good look at his face. White male, probably six feet tall. Slender. Dark hair, thick beard."

Mallory must have noticed my worried expression. "You sure you're all right?" she asked.

"I'm fine," I assured her. Or would be, as soon as my arm began to heal. The pain had already changed, from a sharp-edged sting to a throbbing, dull ache.

We turned our attention to the man on the ground.

Shifters could heal human injuries if they shifted into their respective animal forms. If they were *capable* of shifting. I guessed the victim hadn't been able to manage it.

"He wasn't here very long before you left," Catcher said. "He was still warm."

"I felt some kind of magic," Mallory said, looking down at him. "I don't know what it was, but there was something here."

There was no outward sign of magic here—just the shifter

and the vampire. Ethan looked at her quizzically. "Have you ever felt anything like that before?"

She shook her head, blew out a breath through pursed lips. "No. Never. And I gotta say, it's freaking me out a little bit. I'm not sure I want to be the girl who can suddenly sense death." She put a hand on her chest, her mouth screwed into an "O" of horror. "Oh my God, what if I'm the new Grim Reaper?"

"You aren't the new Grim Reaper," I said. "And not to be more grim, but there are a lot of people on the planet, and I'm pretty sure someone is always dying. Can you feel anybody else?"

Mallory blinked. "Well, no, now that you mention it. Which is a relief."

"So you felt it because of this shifter's proximity," Ethan said, "or his magic." He glanced at Catcher. "Did you feel anything?"

He shook his head. "I didn't. But she's more sensitive than I am that way. Which is fine by me. We called Chuck," he added.

My grandfather, Chuck Merit, was Chicago's supernatural Ombudsman, a human who acted as a liaison between the Chicago Police Department and the city's magical populations. Catcher was one of his employees, as was Jeff Christopher, a tech-savvy shifter and mostly white-hat hacker.

"We called Gabriel, too," Catcher added. "That seemed like the best thing to do, all things considered."

Ethan nodded. Gabriel Keene was the Apex of the North America Central Pack of shifters. This shifter was in his territory, so he was most likely one of Gabe's people.

As if sensing the direction of my thoughts, Catcher put a protective arm around Mallory, pulled her closer. But she wouldn't have anything to fear from Gabe. He'd sheltered her, retrained her, after her addiction to black magic threatened to destroy her.

Sorcerer and shifter had become allies, too. And now a vampire threatened to strain the Pack's relationship with all of us.

I'd like to have a look around the alley, I told Ethan. *Why don't you stay here with them?* I glanced back at the ever-growing crowd. *The fewer people milling around in whatever evidence is around here, the better.*

That's a good thought, Ethan said with a nod, and pulled a pocket-sized black flashlight from his pocket, handed it to me. It wasn't a Cubs flashlight, but it would do.

"I'm going to check things out," I said to Mallory and Catcher. At their nods, I switched on the flashlight and moved into the darkness of the alley.

I walked slowly forward, flipping the small but powerful beam back and forth across the ground. Most of it was paved, except for a short stretch behind a row of town houses. Their back doors opened onto a small strip of grass, just enough space for a barbecue grill or an area for pets to take care of business.

The usual suspects were stuck to the broken and stained concrete. Discarded paper, gum, empty plastic bottles. Farther down the alley, cars were wedged into slots only an automotive savant could squeeze into. Bikes were locked onto a forest green rack bolted into the ground, and the smell of beer and fried food lingered above the insistent smell of death.

The railroad trestles rested on square concrete pedestals. The beam of light flickered across one, highlighting what, at first glance, I'd thought was a graffiti tag. But there seemed to be more letters than the few that usually made up a sprayed tag.

I stopped and swung the light back again.

The entire pedestal, probably two-and-a-half-feet tall and just as wide, was covered by lines of characters drawn in black. Row after row of them. Most were symbols—circles and triangles and squares with lines and marks through them, half circles, arrows and squares. Some looked like tiny hieroglyphs—a dragon here, a tiny skeleton there, drawn with a surprisingly careful hand.

They buzzed with a faint and tinny magic, which explained the care—or vice versa. I didn't recognize the flavor of the magic; it was sharper and more metallic than any I'd run across before, and a sharp contrast to the earthier scent of shifters.

Magic symbols twenty feet away from a shifter's death. That couldn't have been a coincidence.

I knelt down, shone light across the pedestal. I knew what these were. They were alchemy symbols, marks used by practitioners who'd believed they could transmute lead into gold, or create a philosopher's stone that would allow them immortality. I'd studied medieval literature in graduate school. I hadn't studied magical texts per se, but they'd occasionally appear in a manuscript or the gilded marginalia of a carefully copied text.

Still, while I recognized them for what they were, I didn't have the knowledge to decipher them. That was a job for people with substantive knowledge about magical languages. Catcher or Mallory, or maybe Paige. She was a sorcerer, formally the Order's archivist and at present the girlfriend of the Cadogan House Librarian.

I scanned the rest of the pedestal, and the beam flashed across something on the ground—drops of blood. Blood had been shed here, and plenty of it. But why? Because of the vampire? Because of the markings?

I've got something, I told Ethan, and waited until he and Mallory gathered beside me. Catcher stayed back with the shifter.

I kept the light trained on the pedestal so they could review the markings, then shifted the circle of light to the blood on the ground below.

"Part of the attack took place here," Ethan said. "And the symbols?"

"They look alchemical to me," I said.

Mallory's gaze tracked back and forth across the lines. "Agreed. Symbols of alchemical elements, built into an equation. That's why they're in rows."

"Wait," Ethan said. "You mean alchemy, as in changing lead into gold?"

"That's the most well-known transmutation," Mallory said, hands on her hips as she leaned over beside him, peered at the magic. "But folks try to do all sorts of things with the practice. Healing, communicating with the spiritual realm, balancing the elements, distilling something down to its true essence."

Ethan frowned, looked down at the pedestal again. "So what's the purpose of this?"

"I had to study alchemy when I took my exams. Although I didn't use them." She added that quickly, as if to remind us she hadn't made use of all the magical Keys in existence to create her black magic. Although she'd certainly used enough of them. "I also watched a lot of *Fullmetal Alchemist*. Quality show. Quality."

"There are television shows about alchemy?" Ethan asked.

"It's anime."

Ethan's expression stayed blank.

"Never mind," she said, waving it away. "We'll have a marathon later. But for now"—she pointed to one symbol, a circle with a dot in the middle—"that's the sun. And that's Taurus," she added, pointing to a small circle topped by a semicircle of horns. "Merit's astrological sign, as it turns out. It's probably not related to you," she said, glancing at me. "It's just part of the equation related to the positions of the stars. That's one of the things that makes the alchemy work, at least theoretically." She put her hands on her hips. "If we want to know why this is here, we need to translate all the symbols and figure out what they mean together, in context."

We walked back to Catcher, and Mallory explained what we'd seen.

"How does alchemy match up against the Keys?" I asked them. The Keys were the building blocks of magic, at least in Catcher's particular philosophy.

"It's just a different way to approach the energy, the power." He shrugged. "You might say a language different from mine, but a language all the same."

Mallory looked at him, nodded. "With rules, just like any language would follow."

"So, who put them here?" Ethan asked. "And why are they near the scene of a shifter's death by a vampire?"

Mallory looked at Catcher. "I don't know anyone who practices alchemy, not even through SWOB." Sorcerers Without Borders was an organization Mallory had created to help newbie sorcerers in the Midwest. It was help she hadn't gotten when she first learned she had magic—but that she definitely could have used.

"It would have to be a sorcerer, right?" I asked. Everyone looked back at the concrete. We'd been looking for a sorcerer, after all. This wasn't the kind of magic that Adrien Reed had dabbled in, at least as far as we knew, and there was nothing to tie him to this. That meant we had another sorcerer, another potential enemy, and this one involved in the death of a shifter.

"Yeah," Mallory said. "These would have been made by a sorcerer."

"Is it dark magic?"

She opened her mouth, closed it again. "I was going to give you a trite answer. A quick no so everybody would feel better." She looked back at the pedestal, considered. "Yeah. There's some darkness there. Not entirely surprising, considering the bloodshed, the murder. Even if the magic didn't cause them, there's clearly some kind of relationship.

"But it won't affect me," she added. "Dark magic affects the maker and the recipient. I didn't make it, and there's no reason to believe it's supposed to affect us. So you don't have to worry about me."

"We aren't worried," Ethan said, and the confidence in his voice made her relax a little.

"Okay," she said. "Okay."

She said the first one for us; I was pretty sure she said the second one for herself.

"So we've got a sorcerer, a shifter, and a vampire here together," Catcher said. "And the shifter ends up dead."

"VSS," Mallory said, the acronym for the "game" she'd invented earlier. "And the first round is a dead loss."

Chapter Three

RED FLAG

My grandfather appeared a few minutes later, pulling over to the curb in his official white van. He wore a short-sleeve plaid shirt, slacks, and thickly soled shoes. He still used the cane he'd needed since he was trapped in a house fire caused by anti-vampire malcontents, but moved spryly with it.

Jeff Christopher, brown-haired and lanky, climbed out of the car's passenger side, waited while my grandfather gave instructions to the officers who'd pulled up behind him in two CPD cruisers. When my grandfather finished his instructions and moved toward us, the cops turned to the crowd, creating a barricade to control the gathering people.

"Merit, Ethan," my grandfather said, then nodded to Mallory and Catcher. His expression was serious and slightly sympathetic, not an uncommon expression for a man who, more often than not, was dealing with supernatural fallout.

"Sorry it took so long," my grandfather said. "There's an accident on Lake Shore Drive. Traffic was moving at a crawl."

Not an unusual circumstance for Chicago.

"We're sorry you had to drive out all this way," I said. My

grandfather's office was on the city's South Side, relocated from the basement of his house after the firebombing.

My grandfather looked around. "You reached Gabriel?"

"Should be here anytime," Catcher said with a nod.

And so they were. The rhythmic thunder of bikes roared as the shifters moved into the alley. Seven traveled together tonight, and they slipped around my grandfather's car in a line of chrome and black leather.

Their arrival made me nervous—not because I feared shifters, but because I regretted what had gone on here and knew some blamed all vampires equally, including us. It hadn't been that long ago that we were in Colorado, watching animosity between shifter and vampire bubble up.

Ethan reached out, put a hand at the small of my back, a reminder that he was there. He couldn't change the circumstances—death, murder, bitter magic—but he'd remind me that I wouldn't face them alone.

Gabriel rode in front, an imposing figure on a long bike with wide handles, every inch of the chrome gleaming to a mirrored perfection. He stopped his bike ten feet away, pulled off his helmet, and ran a hand through his shoulder-length mane of tousled golden-brown hair. His eyes were the same tawny gold, his shoulders broad beneath a snug black V-neck T-shirt that he'd paired with jeans and intimidating black leather boots. He hung the helmet on a gleaming handlebar, swung a strong thigh over the back of the bike, and walked toward us, followed by his only sister, Fallon.

She was Jeff's girlfriend, a slight woman of surprising strength, with warm eyes and long, wavy hair in the same multihued shades as her brother. She rode the bike directly behind his, wore a skirt with boots and tights, a gray tank under a short-sleeved leather top with lots of pleats and zippers.

The other shifters were male, with broad shoulders, plenty of leather, and generally dour looks.

Gabriel nodded at my grandfather, at Jeff, then looked at Ethan.

"Sullivan," he said, then glanced at me. "Kitten. He's one of ours?"

"We don't know if he's one of the Pack's," Ethan said. "But he's definitely a shifter, so we wanted to give you the opportunity to find out."

We escorted him to the body, and Gabriel crouched by the fallen shifter, his leather boots creaking with the movement. Elbows on his knees, hands linked together, he looked slowly and carefully over the body, his gaze finally settling on the wounds at his throat.

The silence was thick and to my mind, threatening.

"His name was Caleb Franklin," Gabe said. "He was a Pack member—a soldier. A shifter who helped keep order in the territory. He'd go on runs with Damien, actually."

Damien Garza was a tall, dark, and handsome shifter with a quiet personality, a dry wit, and an exceptional hand with an omelet.

Gabriel stood up. "But Caleb's not a Pack member anymore. He defected."

Ethan's eyebrows lifted. "He left the Pack by choice?"

"He did."

"Why?" Ethan asked.

"He wanted more freedom."

Since the Pack was all about freedom—the open road, communing with nature, good food, and good drink—I guessed we weren't getting the full story. The look on Ethan's face said he didn't entirely buy it, either. But this wasn't the setting for an interrogation of the Pack Apex.

"The vampire?" Gabriel asked.

"We gave chase, but he got away."

Gabriel nodded, noticed the bandage on my arm. "And got you in the process."

"Handgun through the window of a beat-up Trans Am. I don't suppose that vehicle rings any bells?"

He shook his head, glanced at Fallon. She shook her head, too.

"He did this in a relatively public space," my grandfather said, "but he was eager to get away."

"We found something else," I said, gesturing down the alley.

We walked toward the pedestal—a human, two vampires, three shifters, and two sorcerers, all of us impotent in the face of death.

Fallon, Gabriel, and my grandfather studied the pedestal.

"Alchemical," my grandfather said.

"And the Merits are two for two," Catcher said. "That's as far as we've gotten. We can pick out individual symbols, but we don't know what they mean in context." He glanced at Gabriel. "This mean anything to you?"

Gabe shook his head. "I can feel the magic but don't recognize it."

"It's weird, isn't it?" All eyes turned to me. "I mean, it has a weird edge. A sharp edge."

"Metallic," Mallory said, nodding. "That's the nature of alchemy."

"And there's one more thing," Catcher said. "Mallory felt something. Some kind of magic."

All eyes shifted to her now.

"That's how I found him," she told Gabriel. "I felt—I don't know how else to describe it—like a magical pulse. And then we looked for him, found him."

Gabriel cocked his head at her. "You haven't sensed anything like that before?"

"No," she said. "And God knows I've been around enough bad magic in my time."

I reached out and squeezed her hand, found it a little clammy. She gripped mine hard and didn't let go.

Jeff and Catcher took photographs of the symbols. My and Mallory's hands were still linked when we walked back toward the body. Three more of the shifters had dismounted, and they stood around him protectively.

"We'll want to take him home tonight," Gabriel said.

"You know that won't be possible." My grandfather's tone was polite but firm. "We'll release him to his family, but not until the postmortem is complete."

"We're his family," Gabriel said gruffly. "Or the closest thing to it. The Pack doesn't give two shits what Cook County has to say about cause of death. Especially since that cause should be brutally obvious to anyone with a brain."

"Gabriel," Ethan said, the word as much warning as name.

"Don't start with me, Sullivan." Magic began to rise in the air, peppery and dangerous. "He may not have been mine when he was alive, but he's mine now."

He and Ethan might have been friends and colleagues, but they were also leaders with people to protect, and very little tolerance for those who challenged them.

"And you watch your tone, Keene. I recognize your people have endured a tragedy, but we are not your enemy. And you are not immune to the rules of the city in which you live."

Gabriel growled, and his eyes lit with the promise of anger, of fighting, of action. "A vampire killed one of my people."

Ethan, who had his own steam to work off, stepped forward. "Not one of my vampires."

I considered pushing between them, demanding they separate and calm down. But I wasn't about to incur Ethan's wrath by playing that card again. Besides, it wasn't the first time they'd nearly come to blows; maybe their beating the crap out of each other would clear the air.

Fallon apparently decided she wasn't having any of it. She nudged her way between them, both towering over her by five or six inches.

"Stop being assholes," she said, her voice quiet but firm. "We've made enough of a scene as it is, and have enough tragedy to deal with. You two want to beat the shit out of each other? Fine. But do it out of sight, when the humans can't see and we don't have to waste time watching."

Biting back a smile, I glanced at Jeff, saw his eyes light with appreciation and pride.

Gabriel's position didn't change. Shoulders high and stiff, chest forward, hands balled into fists, his tensed body speaking of barely banked rage. He slid his gaze to his sister, nailed her with a look that would have made me nervous if directed at me.

But Fallon Keene just rolled her eyes. "That look hasn't worked on me since I was seven." She pointed a finger—the nail painted matte navy—at Gabriel and Ethan in turn. "Get. Your shit. Together."

Fallon turned on her heel and walked back to the other shifters, whispered something to them. They seemed to relax but kept their wary gazes on their alpha and the alpha he stared down.

"Goddamn murder," Gabriel said, running a hand through his hair again. "Waste of life, waste of energy."

"You'll get no argument there from me," Ethan said. "And perhaps she's right. That we shouldn't waste any more time."

Gabriel made a sound that was half grunt, half growl. "I find the vampire first, he's mine."

Ethan was quiet for a moment, no doubt evaluating his strategy, his best play. He wasn't one to take advantage of murder, but he rarely made a move without thinking it through.

"All right," he finally said. "But before you take care of him in whatever method you deem appropriate, we want a chance to question him."

"Because?"

"Because he's killed a shifter and attempted to kill Merit. That's more than enough reason for me."

Gabriel considered it silently. "Rest of your people going to be so easygoing about his fate? The other Masters?"

Ethan's expression flattened. He liked Scott Grey, the Master of Grey House, and he tolerated Morgan Greer, the Master of Navarre House. "Should this atrocity prove to have been committed by one of their vampires, I suspect they will want to handle his punishment. That would be an issue for you to take up with them. But there's no reason to believe he was a Navarre or Grey House vampire, either. I've been in Chicago a long time, and there was nothing about him that was familiar to me."

Gabriel looked at my grandfather. "We will have to mourn him."

My grandfather nodded. "We can give you space if you want to do it here. We'll have to request you not touch him, if that's possible."

Gabriel didn't seem to like the answer but didn't argue with it. "Give us space," he said, and if operating by an unspoken command, his people clustered around Caleb.

Ethan put a hand at my back, and we walked back toward the street.

"Give them a wall," my grandfather said. And however weird the uniforms might have thought the request, they obeyed it. They moved to stand shoulder to shoulder facing the crowd, giving the Pack some privacy. We took places beside them, the line stretching all the way across the alley.

Gabriel spoke first, a whisper that put magic into the air, a song that rose and fell like a winter's tide. I couldn't distinguish the words. He'd disguised them somehow, muffling vowels and consonants, perhaps so they could be shared only by the Pack. But the point of the song was clear enough. It was a dirge, a song of mourning for their former Pack member.

I let myself drift on the rise and fall of the song. It told of blue skies and rolling green hills, dark and deep waters and mountains that pitched toward a dark blanket of sky scattered with stars. It told of birth and living and death, of the Pack's connection to wildness, and of the reunion of loved ones. The tone momentarily darkened, unity giving way to struggle, to war.

The hairs at the back of my neck lifted. Ethan moved incrementally closer, pressing his shoulder into mine as if to protect me, just in case.

The tone changed again, fear and loss evolving into understanding, acceptance. And then the song ended, and the magic faded again, faded back into darkness.

I opened my eyes and glanced back, meeting Gabriel's gaze.

I dipped my head, nodding, acknowledging that which he'd allowed me to share. And when I looked back at him, I realized he wasn't looking at me, but past me, into some time or space long past, into memory or recollection. And from his expression, not an especially happy one.

"We'll take care of him," my grandfather promised when the shifters had moved back to their bikes. "I'll accompany him personally to the morgue, speak to the medical examiner personally. You'll remember they have protocols in place."

It wasn't the first time a shifter had died in Chicago. There'd been several killed in a botched attempt by Gabriel's brother, Adam, to take over the Pack.

Gabriel picked up his helmet. "I know you do what you can, within the parameters you've got. I'm in the same position."

"Then we understand each other," my grandfather said. A van

from the Cook County Medical Examiner's Office pulled up to the alley entrance. "I'm going to go have that talk," he said, then squeezed my hand. "Get home safely."

"We will," I promised, and he made his way to the van.

"We should probably talk tomorrow," Gabriel said. "We'll host a wake at the bar, and you'll want to wait until after. It wouldn't be the best time for vampires to show up."

Little Red was the Pack's official bar in Ukrainian Village. It was a well-worn dive but served some of the best fare I'd ever tasted.

"I appreciate the warning," Ethan said.

Gabriel pulled on his helmet, clipped it, then slung a leg over his bike. He started it with a rumble, then turned the bike back onto the street. Fallon followed him, then the rest of the shifters. And then silence fell again.

Ethan put a hand on the back of my neck, rubbed. "Not exactly the evening I had planned, Sentinel."

"You hardly could have predicted this."

"No, not the particulars. But that trouble would find us, even in Wrigleyville? That, I should have predicted."

"You can owe me a Cubs game," I said.

I was lucky to be alive. But I still hadn't gotten my flashlight.

It was past midnight by the time we dropped off Mallory and Catcher in Wicker Park. She and Catcher stood on the sidewalk with their fingers linked. But for the evening of supernatural mayhem, they could have been just another couple heading home after a night on the town.

Mallory covered a yawn. "I'll get started on the symbols tomorrow, although Catcher's pretty swamped at work." She looked at Ethan. "Maybe you could talk to Paige? See if she's got time to help?"

Ethan nodded. "I'd had the same thought," he said, which made three of us. "And we should have alchemical texts in the library to assist with the translation."

"I'll talk to Jeff," Catcher said. "Maybe there's something he can work up from a programming standpoint—something to speed the translation along."

"Oh, good idea," Mallory said. "There were a lot of symbols."

Catcher glanced at me. "I'm sorry the night didn't turn out like we'd planned. I know you were looking forward to an evening at the ballpark."

I nodded. "There will be other nights. Bigger things to worry about right now anyway."

"Yeah," Catcher said ruefully. "That's beginning to feel more and more common."

He and Mallory walked inside, closed the door, turned off the light above their small porch, a signal that they were locked safely inside.

"Let's go home, Sentinel."

I'd been excited to leave the House earlier in the evening, eager to get to Wrigley, enjoy a beer, and watch some baseball. And now, with the evening having taken such an ugly turn, I couldn't wait to get home again.

CHAPTER FOUR

A DOCTOR IN THE HOUSE

Traffic on the Kennedy hadn't been any better than Lake Shore Drive. We'd avoided the accident, but not the three-mile backup that kept traffic at a crawl, so it took an hour to get back to Hyde Park.

Cadogan House glowed in the darkness, a beacon of warm light and white stone. The House was three stories of imposing French architecture surrounded by rolling lawns and an enormous wrought-iron fence meant to keep out enemies, paparazzi, and curious passersby.

There was a gate in front, recently upgraded by Ethan and at present guarded by humans. Two at the door, and four more patrolling the House's perimeter. Both were insurance against whatever mischief Adrien Reed might have planned.

We drove the SUV back into the House's underground parking lot, entered the code on the door that led into the House's basement floor.

"Ops Room to update Luc?" I asked. The House's security operations room, along with the arsenal and training room, was located in the basement.

"You will. After you've been treated."

"Treated?"

"Your arm," he said.

Those two words were enough to remind me of the wound and send it throbbing again.

"Ah. Right."

He crooked a finger at me, and I fell into step behind him as we took the stairs to the House's first floor.

The first floor was as lush as the basement was utilitarian. The scent of peonies and roses filled the air from an arrangement on a gorgeous antique table, which complemented the gorgeous woodwork, expensive rugs, and priceless artwork.

There was a desk in the foyer now, where a Novitiate vampire dealt with the supplicants who now requested an audience with Ethan. As one of the twelve members of the Assembly of American Masters, they looked to him for help, advice, and arbitration of disputes.

Ethan acknowledged them before directing me to his office, which was as luxe as the rest of the House. There was thick carpet, an imposing desk, and a comfortable sitting area with leather club chairs. Bookshelves lined the left side of the room, and an enormous conference table spread across the back in front of a bank of windows. They were open now, and would be shuttered automatically when the sun began to rise.

At the moment, the room was full of vampires. Malik, Ethan's second-in-command, leaned against Ethan's desk. He was dressed in the Cadogan uniform—fitted black suit, white button-down shirt that contrasted against his dark skin and pale green eyes.

Luc, the House's guard captain, had tousled blond hair and the face and body of a well-practiced cowboy. He'd been excused from the House's black-suit dress code. He wore jeans, boots, and a T-shirt with CADOGAN HOUSE GUARD CORPS printed in a circle across the front, the image of a bacon rasher in the middle. SAVIN'

YOUR BACON SINCE 1883 was printed across it. He'd created the design because, to quote him, "nothing fuels a vampire like a good rasher."

His girlfriend and fellow guard, Lindsey, stood beside him. She was pretty, blond, fashion-conscious, and a very good friend. Tonight, she'd paired neon yellow stilettos with her House uniform. Matched with the jaunty high ponytail and small neon earrings, she added a little flair to the otherwise unrelieved black.

Juliet, another House guard, stood nearby with a bottle of green juice in hand. She was petite and looked delicate, with cream and roses skin and red hair, but she was a ferocious and determined fighter.

She'd recently decided "juicing" would further enhance her butt-kicking abilities, and she'd tried to foist one of her liquid kale concoctions on me. I declined to drink anything that looked like lawn clippings. Besides, if I wasn't pumping my body with trans fats, I wasn't fully utilizing my immortality.

When we stepped into the doorway, the vampires took in my blood-spattered T-shirt and bandage and Ethan's own ripped and bloodied T-shirt.

"You two can't even go to a damn sporting event without trouble," Luc said.

"I grabbed shirts for you," Lindsey said, offering folded black cotton to me and Ethan. "Fresh from the swag room."

"You aren't technically a Guard," Luc said to me, "but since you just took another shot on behalf of your House and Master, we figured you deserved one."

"That, and the fact that I train and work with you guys?"

Luc winked at me. "That helps."

"What's the House record for gunshots?" I asked.

"Five," Ethan said. He'd walked behind his desk, was scanning his computer screen. "Peter had that prize. Would that he'd been here for a sixth," he muttered, undoubtedly angry that he couldn't deliver that sixth shot.

Peter was a former Cadogan Guard who'd betrayed the House for Celina Desaulniers, the former Master of Navarre House.

Given the night we'd had, I was determined to keep the mood light. "And what's the prize for beating the record?"

"House arrest," Ethan said. He glanced up, smiled thinly. "And you wouldn't enjoy that, Sentinel."

No argument there.

"Am I late?" A woman with dark skin and dark hair pulled back in a ponytail and wearing pink scrubs stood in the doorway. Delia was the House's doctor.

"You're right on time," Ethan said. "Your patient awaits."

"Patient?" I asked.

"Treatment, Sentinel. Your wound should be addressed."

I didn't like the way that sounded, especially since my arm was already itchy with healing. "I'm fine."

Delia walked toward me, a tray in her hands. "Hello, Merit. How are you?"

"Hello, Delia. I'm fine."

"Got shot again, did you?"

"I did. Although I didn't pass out this time." The last time, I'd hit my head and been knocked unconscious.

"That's something at least." She put the tray on Ethan's desk, then walked to the sink in the small bar in the bookshelves, washed her hands to the elbow. I appreciated the effort, even if it seemed unlikely a vampire would die of sepsis.

With cool and careful fingers, she lifted my arm, surveyed the bandage before glancing back at Ethan, taking in the ripped shirt. "Homemade bandage?"

"Make-do," he agreed. "We were chasing a suspect."

"Again," Luc said, "only you, too."

Delia looked at me. "Pulling away the bandage might hurt, so let's get it over with." Without waiting for me to object, she released my arm. "Would you mind stripping her?"

Lindsey winked at me. "Of course not."

I pushed away her hands. "Hey, I don't need stripping. It's my arm that's damaged."

"The shirt is filthy," Delia said. "It looks like you scraped off a few layers of a dirty street."

That wasn't far from the truth.

"Take it off, or I'll cut it off."

"Hard-ass."

She snorted. "You deal with a few dozen humans in an emergency room in an evening and see how much of a hard-ass you become. Gentlemen, if you would, please turn away so that our impressively modest Sentinel can get momentarily naked."

"Awwww," Luc said pitifully, but he and Malik turned their backs. Ethan didn't bother. He watched us, concern in his expression, as Lindsey helped me pull the shirt over my head, then over each arm in turn. She tossed it onto the floor.

"Bandage?" she asked, and at Delia's nod, pulled away the fabric Ethan had used to keep the handkerchief in place, tossed it aside with the T-shirt.

"You can burn that when you're ready," Delia said with a smile, stepping forward to palpate my arm, inspect the remaining bandage from each angle. "Or keep it as a souvenir of your fourth bullet for the House."

"Being shot four times isn't such a big deal," I muttered.

"Certainly not for people who've been shot five times," she said with a grin. She picked up a pair of blunt-ended scissors from the tray she'd brought in. "You ready for this? I'll be as careful as I can."

I blew out a breath, nodded. And as I stood in Ethan's office in jeans and a bra, I reached out for Lindsey's hand. She took mine, squeezed it.

"On three," Delia said. "One . . . two . . ."

As I tensed, waiting for three, she ripped the fabric away.

I nearly hit my knees from the rush of bright, naked pain. "Damn! I thought you were going on three!"

"Two gets you done faster," she said, and began inspecting my arm. "Good. It's a through-and-through, so we won't have to drag fragments out of you."

"There's no way I'd let you come at me with a scalpel."

"If I had a quarter," she muttered, gaze narrowed as she poked and prodded. "The bullet damaged your muscle, tendon, but missed the bone. Might be sore for a couple of days, but you're used to that."

"You're a cruel woman."

She looked up at me and grinned. "I know. I'm a much better doctor." She gently patted on a cooling gel, then turned me toward the light and inspected the arm she'd cleaned and medicated. "Much better. Let's get the clean T-shirt on you, and you'll want to keep that uncovered and clear for a little while. It's nearly healed, and you don't want to have to deal with this again."

"No," I said, wincing as Lindsey helped me pull the shirt over my head. "I do not. And thank you for the help. Even if I'd like to punch you a little bit right now."

"I can't say I blame you."

Delia's phone rang, and she pulled it from her pocket and glanced at the screen. "And duty calls again. I need to run." She glanced at Ethan and got his nod of approval.

"Thank you for the help," I called out as she hurried toward the door. I looked back at Ethan. "In case that didn't register, will you please thank her for me?"

"I will," he said. "And she's happy to help." He smiled slyly. "But you should probably work on not getting shot again."

It was on my agenda.

"Now that we've addressed Merit's injury," Ethan said, when we'd reset from a medical discussion to a strategic one, "she also made a rather significant discovery."

"That's why I brought that up here," Luc said, pointing behind me. I followed the direction of his gesture, saw the enormous, wheeled whiteboard near the wall behind us. We used it when we needed to do investigating, identify facts, formulate theories. And lately, we'd been doing a lot of it. My grandfather's influence, maybe.

"Two new marker colors, too," Luc said, eyes gleaming. "So we can color-code as necessary."

Ethan gestured the group to the sitting area while Luc arranged the board in front of the bookshelves and uncapped a marker, the scent of solvent filling the room.

"Also strong colors," Lindsey said, wrinkling her nose as she sat in one of the club chairs in the sitting area. Malik took the other chair after offering it to Juliet. She declined with a wave of her hand, sat down on the floor, crossing her slender legs in front of her.

Ethan walked to the small refrigerator tucked into the bookshelves, pulled out two bottles of blood. He handed me one, then took a seat on the leather couch beside me.

I opened the blood, took a satisfying drink. In the company of vampires, it was a perfectly normal thing to do.

"Seriously," Juliet said, waving a hand in front of her face, "that marker could clear a room."

"Good," Luc said, positioning himself in front of the board, marker in his fist like an expensive, bladed weapon.

"What am I always telling you about weaponry?" Luc asked, scanning the faces of the guards.

"*Anything is a weapon, and a weapon is anything,*" we parroted back like perfect pupils. But with more sarcasm.

"Good," Luc said with an approving nod. "You need to clear a room, you now know how to do it."

"Committed to memory," Lindsey said, tapping a nail against her temple.

Luc grunted doubtfully but looked at us. "All right, Sentinel. You've got our attention. Give us the details of tonight's trouble."

"Dead shifter," I said, "apparently killed by a vampire under the El tracks at the Addison Station. And nearby, alchemical symbols written on a concrete pedestal."

Luc nodded, wrote the three headlines at the top of the board: vampire, shifter, sorcerer. Then he marked a line through "shifter," killing him symbolically.

"That's quite a variety of supernaturals in one place," Malik said.

"No argument there," Ethan said.

"Shifter had puncture marks on his left-hand side," I said. "Blood near the body, blood near the pedestal."

"The shifter's name was Caleb Franklin," Ethan put in. "An NAC member who defected."

Malik's eyebrows rose, and he looked up from the tablet on which he'd been writing notes. "Defected?"

"Defected," Ethan confirmed. "Keene didn't provide details, only said Franklin wanted more 'freedom.'" Ethan used air quotes, which meant he'd found the excuse as questionable as I had.

"You buy that?" Luc asked, arms crossed.

"I do not," Ethan said. "But one does not interrogate the Apex of the NAC Pack near the scene of his dead, if former, Pack mate and in front of several of his comrades."

"A wise political course," Malik said.

"What about the vampire?" Luc asked.

I gave them his description. "I didn't see his full face, but what I did see didn't look familiar."

"Me, neither," Ethan said.

But he might, I thought, look familiar to someone else. I pulled out my phone. "I'm going to see if Jeff can check security cams in the area. Maybe we can get at least a partial still of his face."

"Good," Luc said, and wrote *Need photograph* on the board. "We can send that to Scott and Morgan, see if he's familiar to them."

"I'll also send it to Noah," I said. Noah Beck was the unofficial leader of the city's Rogue vampires. He'd hooked me up with the Red Guard, a secret vampire corps, and was a member himself, but I hadn't seen him in a while.

"And the alchemy?" Luc asked, after adding Noah's name to the board.

"There were a lot of symbols," I said. "Jeff and Catcher took pictures, and they're working on an analysis. Mallory and Catcher think it's some kind of equation based on the way it's written—neat rows and columns—but they've got to translate in order to know what kind."

Luc glanced at Ethan. "Paige?"

"That's what I was thinking," Ethan said with a nod. "When we receive the photographs, will you see if she can help? Mallory will assist, but there's a lot to translate in order to figure out what was written there."

"And that's our biggest question," Luc said, writing *ALCHEMY* in all caps across the board with a bright green marker even stinkier than the first.

"This reminds me that I knew an alchemist once upon a time," Ethan said, his gaze on the board. "Or a man who called himself an alchemist, at any rate. He was in Munich in the employ of a baron who wanted more wealth. He was convinced turning lead into gold was possible."

"When was this?" I asked. Ethan had nearly four hundred years under his belt, after all.

He frowned. "Mid–seventeen hundreds, I believe. Alchemy had its run, but as far as I'm aware, it hasn't been popular in magical circles in a very long time."

"I assume the purported alchemist wasn't successful?" Malik asked.

"He was not. He supposedly had success using a meteorite discovered in the Carpathian Mountains, but, to no one's surprise, he wasn't able to repeat the results for an audience." Ethan lifted a shoulder. "He was a charlatan. He lived off the baron for nine or ten years before the baron grew tired of tricks."

"What did he do?" I asked.

"Put the alchemist's head on a pike to warn away anyone else who might have hoped to deceive him."

Juliet glanced back at me. "Any chance this alchemy was practice, scribbles, the ravings of a madman, anything like that?"

"It was awfully precise to be scribbles," Ethan said, glancing at me. "There were, what, a few hundred symbols there?"

I nodded. "At least that."

"Someone has magic planned," Malik said, and a heaviness fell over the room.

Luc tapped the plastic marker against the board. "Let's talk through what that magic might be."

"It was close to Wrigley Field," I said, and all eyes turned to me. "Maybe the geography matters. Maybe they plan to hit it."

"On the night of a game," Juliet said, and I nodded, anger bristling beneath my skin. Supernaturals being violent toward one another was one thing. But targeting humans—those who didn't have their strength, their power, their immortality—was something else entirely. It was a breach of the rules, whatever that game might have been.

Luc blew out a breath, wrote the idea on the board. "What else?"

"The El," Ethan said. "The symbols were written on the trestle. Perhaps the magic was intended to disrupt service, to knock out a pedestal and derail the cars."

"Like an explosion," Luc said, and added that possibility to the list. He glanced back at me. "Only the one pedestal?"

"Yeah. We don't know if he or she only meant to prep one and got interrupted, or only needed one in the first place."

Luc uncapped the marker, drew three enormous question marks in the middle of the board. "So we need intel there. Translating the equation, hopefully, will fill in some of it."

"We can also check the chatter," Juliet said. "If it's a big operation, there's a chance someone is talking about it on the Web."

"Good," Luc said, adding the strategy to the board. "And how do the shifter and vampire fit into this?"

"If they're friends with the sorcerer," Juliet said, "they could have been entourage, buddy, bodyguard. Maybe a disagreement broke out."

"Or, if not friends," Lindsey said, glancing at Juliet, "maybe a rival or personal disagreement. Maybe the shifter was trying to interrupt the sorcerer."

Lindsey nodded. "Doesn't like what the sorcerer's doing, doesn't like how he's doing it, so the vampire takes him out."

"Or maybe the vampire was the antagonist," Luc said. "Shifter and sorcerer are working together, vampire shows up, tries to head off the magic. Takes out the shifter, but the sorcerer gets away."

"If that's true," I said, "and the vampire's trying to avoid some big alchemical whatsit, why would he run away from us?"

"Maybe he's on our side, relatively speaking, but didn't want to be identified." Luc glanced at Ethan. "Could have been a Red Guard member." Luc was one of the few Cadogan vampires who knew I was involved in activities outside the House; he didn't know that activity was the Red Guard or that Jonah, the Guard captain of Grey House, was my partner.

Or had been, anyway. Things were tense between us at present because I was sleeping with the presumed "enemy," whom I refused to spy on.

"Could have been," Ethan said with a slow nod. "But murder isn't typically the RG's MO. They aren't normally that violent or that proactive. And killing with a bite isn't their style."

I'll ask, I told Ethan silently, already brainstorming how, exactly, I was going to do that without making things worse. ("Hey, Jonah. I know we aren't really talking right now, but did one of our RG colleagues kill a shifter near Grey House earlier tonight?")

Ethan looked at Luc. "The shifter is our best lead at the moment. We have a name, a position, and a Pack. Find out what you can about his defection, and we'll talk to Gabriel. He said they'll host a wake tomorrow."

Luc's eyebrows lifted with surprise. "Even though he defected?"

"That was my question, too," I said.

Luc nodded thoughtfully, considered. "We'll do the research."

"Discreetly," Ethan said.

"I am nothing if not discreet."

Lindsey snorted. "You walked down the hallway wearing nothing but a towel the other day."

Luc grinned, stretched his arms. "I was hungry."

"Mmm-hmm," she said. "You were showing off."

Ethan laughed lightly, but then closed his eyes, rubbed his temples. Here, in front of his trusted staff, he could be vulnerable. "Alert the House just in case. If an unknown sorcerer is spreading magic around the city, and a vampire is killing shifters, that kind of trouble could find its way here."

"Already has, arguably," Luc said.

Ethan nodded. "Nothing so far indicates the man or woman who wrote these symbols is known to us. Until we figure out the reason for the magic, we treat it as antagonistic. We don't need to lock down the House, but I want everyone on alert."

"The House is already prepared because of Reed," Malik said, comforting. "They'll be careful."

Ethan nodded at Malik, then looked around the room, meeting the gaze of each vampire in turn. "A shifter was killed by a vampire tonight. Gabriel trusts us to a point, but that trust will only extend so far. We don't want to put our alliance at risk." He rose. "I'd like a report at dusk with what we've learned about the defection, the shifter, the symbols."

The other vampires understood the meaning of Ethan's change in position, and they rose, too.

"On it, hoss," Luc said, then nodded at me and headed toward the door, his guards behind him.

I rose to follow Luc, but Ethan put a hand on my arm. "Go upstairs. Take the rest of the night off." He glanced at the clock on the wall. "We've only a few hours before dawn in any event, and tomorrow promises to be busy. I'd like you to help Mallory and Paige with the translation. I'll clear it with Luc."

He wouldn't, actually. As Master, he'd inform Luc, which was a very different thing.

"I'm not sure how much help I can be," I said. "I don't really know much about alchemy, just recognized the symbols."

"That's why you'll be their minion, and not the other way around."

"Ha-ha."

He pressed his mouth to mine. "I'm going to take care of a few issues here, including updating the AAM, and then I'll join you in the apartments. Perhaps we'll enjoy some wine in front of the fire."

The AAM was the Assembly of American Masters.

"Is dealing with Nicole going to put you in the mood for wine drinking?" Nicole Heart was the Master of Atlanta's Heart House, and the vampire who'd been elected leader of the AAM.

He chuckled. "It will certainly put me in the mood to want a drink." He pressed his lips to mine, softly, tenderly. "Have a rest, Sentinel. I'll see you soon."

The Masters' apartments were on the third floor of Cadogan House and were composed of a suite of rooms: sitting room, bedroom, bathroom, and enormous closet that held Ethan's collection of suits and my leather fighting ensemble.

The rooms were as luxurious as the rest of the House, with beautiful furniture and art, fresh flowers, and, since the night was waning, the silver tray of snacks that Margot, the House chef, left for us every night. Tonight, it was here earlier than usual, but Ethan had probably told her how our evening had gone, requested she prepare it.

When I'd closed the door and kicked off my shoes, I unwrapped one of the gold-foiled chocolates she'd taken to leaving lately, a mix of chocolate, hazelnuts, and toffee that hit the spot.

As carefully as I could, I stripped off the rest of my clothes and headed for the shower. Ethan hadn't spared any expense in the bathroom, with lots of marble, gleaming fixtures, and the fluffiest towels I'd ever used. And of course they were monogrammed with a curvaceous "C" in rich navy blue.

I turned on the enormous shower, let the water warm and the steam rise, and stepped inside. Eyes closed, I dunked my head and let the heat roll over me until I felt soothed again.

When I was dry and robed, I surveyed my pajama options in the bedroom's chest of drawers. I usually opted for a tank or T-shirt and patterned shorts or bottoms. It was unlikely an emergency would occur during daylight hours—what could we do about it anyway?—but I liked being dressed just in case.

There were fancier things in the drawers—silk lingerie so delicate it felt like liquid between my fingertips, lacy and strappy things that weren't built for comfort, but to excite. I couldn't say I was feeling especially amorous, not with Caleb Franklin on my mind. I was feeling emotionally exhausted by supernatural drama.

The apartment door opened, closed, locked. Ethan appeared around the doorway, a leather portfolio in hand. He put it on the desk and glanced through the apartment, looking for me.

"Feeling indecisive?" he asked with a smile.

"Unsettled." I pulled out a Cadogan tank, matching bottoms, placed them on the bed. Ethan had branded the House from top to bottom and everywhere in between. It wouldn't have surprised me much to wake up one evening and find an inked "C" on my biceps. "I didn't expect you to come up so early."

"I decided I could also use a break." Ethan walked closer, eyebrows drawn together in concern. "You're all right?"

"I'm fine. Just tired and frustrated."

His body tensed. Not much, but then I was attuned to it—and his moods—more than most. "Frustrated? About what?"

"About everything." I walked back to the bed, sat down. "Ethan, every time we turn around, somebody wants to kill us, control us, put us out of business, put the Pack out of business. I guess I'm feeling burned out."

He walked closer, pressed a kiss to my forehead. "You aren't the only vampire to have these feelings."

I looked up at him. "Oh?"

"Many Novitiates, many staff, have talked to me about their

frustration, their fear, their stress." He sat beside me, hands clasped in his lap. "We lived unmolested for many years before Celina decided to announce us. If we'd stayed quiet and let others handle the problems that arose, we wouldn't have drawn as much attention. But we did. And so we face the consequences of our caring."

And wasn't that a kick in the ass? "I know," I said. "It's just . . ." I groped for words, pulled up my legs to sit cross-legged, and glanced at him. "I don't want our child to grow up in a world like the one we're facing right now. Where every night is a new battle."

No vampire child had ever been carried to term, but Gabriel believed Ethan and I would change that, but only after we suffered some kind of unspoken "testing."

Ethan's expression went hot with protectiveness. "When the time comes, he or she will want for nothing, will know no fear, and will be protected by both of us."

There was a ferocity in his eyes that surprised me. Not because I doubted he'd be a good father; to the contrary, it was easy to imagine him holding a child, protecting a child. But he'd been as surprised as I was when I told him about Gabriel's prophecy. He'd come around.

And speaking of the prophecy, I leaned forward and pressed my lips to his. "We've got an hour before dawn. What would you like to do?"

My seduction game was on point.

"Fantasy football?"

Before I could even blink at the suggestion, which was bizarre coming from him, he pounced, covering my body with his and pinning me onto the mattress. The weight of him, of his sculpted and toned body, felt like a miracle.

"I don't actually plan to immerse you in fantasy football," he whispered, his lips tracing a line across my neck, his long and skilled fingers becoming acquainted with the knot in my robe.

"No," I said, while I could still form words. "I don't imagine you did."

"Although the fantasy part—" he began, but before he could finish, his mouth was on mine again, teasing and inciting, igniting the slow burn that sent magic trickling across my skin and seemed to electrify the air.

"The fantasy part is well within my wheelhouse," he finished, and set out to prove it.

CHAPTER FIVE

TO THE VICTOR GO THE SPOILS

We'd developed a dusk routine. Ethan would wake first and get ready for his day; I'd wake groggily to find him in an immaculate suit, already groomed and golden and ready to take on the night. We were both vampires and should have had the same reaction to the sun's setting, but he always managed to wake before I did.

Tonight, the bathroom door was closed, the shower running. Maybe he hadn't completely beaten me this evening.

I stretched and sat up, reached out to check my phone, and found a waiting message from my grandfather: DNA CHECK OF FRANKLIN WOUNDS—NO MATCH IN SYSTEM.

So our bearded vampire wasn't a known criminal, or at least not one who'd ended up with his biological bar code in the CPD's databases.

There was also a message from Luc confirming that Jeff had sent the photographs of the alchemical symbols, and one from Mallory confirming that she and Catcher had enjoyed a night of raucous monkey sex. So no backsliding there, however unlikely that might have been. Good for them.

The final message was directly from Jeff—a grainy image of the vampire who'd killed Caleb Franklin. You couldn't see his face, but his approximate height, weight, color, and build were clear enough, as was the beard that covered the lower half of his face. Again, I had the sense of vague familiarity but still couldn't place him. I'd run into hundreds of vampires in the year I'd been one; it could have been anyone.

As much as I wanted to avoid it, because I had responsibilities, I sent the photograph to Jonah. It was the first communication I'd had with him in a couple of weeks, since the party at Cadogan House we'd used to trap the vampire pretending to be Balthasar, the monster who'd made Ethan. He'd been edgy then, so I hadn't followed up. As far as I was concerned, he and the RG were the ones with the issues. If they wanted to talk to me, they knew where to find me.

But in the meantime, a mystery was a mystery. PHOTO OF VAMPIRE THAT KILLED CALEB FRANKLIN, I explained. KNOW HIM? OR DOES NOAH?

He'd respond even if he was pissed at me, because that was the kind of guy he was. Or the kind of guy I thought he was. We'd see either way.

With that done, I stretched, climbed out of bed, and shuffled to the apartment door, where Margot left our dusk tray.

Ethan wasn't the only perk to life in the Master's suite. On a tray lined with linen, the smell of coffee wafted from a silver carafe. There were croissants in a basket, cubes of fruit in a bowl, and a folded copy of the day's *Tribune*.

I brought the tray and unfolded the paper, even as dread settled in my belly. The headline above the fold read, in enormous black letters: SUPERNATURAL CHAOS AT WRIGLEY. There were color photographs of cops, of shifters on their bikes, and of the line of cops and supernaturals who'd protected them while they sang for Caleb. I was in the center of that photograph, my eyes closed and my skin paler than usual. I'd bet money they'd Photoshopped the picture to make me look more supernatural. Tricksy of them, but a good bet financially. Vampires had been a hot commodity since Celina dragged us out of the dark.

I sighed and folded the paper again, realizing we weren't the only ones to have made it onto the front page in color. Beneath the fold was a photograph of Adrien Reed and his wife, Sorcha, standing in the large, granite plaza in front of the Towerline construction site. A white banner behind them bore the Reed Industries logo in dark green, the dark, pointed spire of a building spearing up between the words. They'd stripped an existing skyscraper nearly down to its steel frame, and had begun to rebuild the new facade around it, layering new steel and glass in alternating stripes up its sides.

Towerline had been spearheaded by my father, Joshua Merit, one of the most powerful real estate developers in Chicago. He'd given Towerline to Reed to cancel a debt owed by Navarre House; Reed apparently planned to take full advantage of the windfall.

Reed cut a fine form—if you ignored the ego, manipulation, and misanthropy. He was tall and broad-shouldered, his dark, waving hair perfectly cut. His tailored suit was deep gray, his tie bottle green. His features were strong—square jaw, straight mouth, gray eyes. He was in his forties, and wore his age and experience well, his salt-and-pepper goatee giving an edge of danger.

His wife, Sorcha, was equally arresting. Tall, thick blond hair, green eyes. She was perfectly slender—and I meant that literally. I wasn't sure if her body had been created by good genes, hard work, excellent surgery, or some combination of the three. Either way, it was remarkable. Each muscle was defined just enough, her skin smoothly golden. Her fitted green dress, which fell to just below the knee, had an asymmetrical neckline that dipped sideways toward her left arm before rising again to form a cap sleeve. The fit was immaculate. Nary a wrinkle. If I hadn't seen her in the flesh, I might have guessed her a cyborg with perfectly plasticized skin.

She smiled at the camera, but the smile didn't reach her eyes. She had the same slightly vacant expression she'd worn the night I met her. I still wasn't sure if she wasn't interested in what was going on around her, or just didn't understand it.

MOGUL BREAKS CEREMONIAL GROUND ON MONUMENTAL DEVELOPMENT, read this headline.

My father and I weren't close, but I still felt a stab of anger at Reed's self-righteous smile. He hadn't worked for Towerline; he'd stolen it with violence and manipulation, just like the gangster he was.

I looked at Sorcha again and wondered what she and her gangster talked about at the end of the day. Did she meet him at the door of their mansion with a Manhattan in hand and ask about work? And was she oblivious of the crime that had paid for the luxury in which she lived, or did she just not care?

Frustration giving me a headache, I put the paper back on the tray. A small white card fluttered to the floor.

For a moment, I thought Margot had left a note with the tray to say good evening or make a snarky comment about the headline. I should have known better.

I crouched, picked it up, and went deathly still, the thick cardstock in my hand.

The note wasn't from Margot or anyone else in the House. There was no name on the paper, but we'd seen the thick cardstock before, the familiar handwriting. It was from Adrien Reed.

I return to Chicago to find you in the news again, Caroline. An interesting tactic in our continuing game, but rest assured—I will have the victory.

I am curious—will he weep when he loses everything? Will he weep when he loses you? I look forward to finding out.

Frustration boiled into anger, so fierce that my hand shook with it. That would have been Reed's plan. He loved these notes, these intrusions, these reminders that he could get to us anywhere.

How had he gotten the card into the House?

I glanced at the tray. The paper. It was the only thing that wouldn't have come directly from the House's kitchen, and it probably would have been easy to convince the delivery person to slip the note inside. He couldn't have been sure I'd see it before Ethan, but that hardly mattered. Directing the card to me, implicitly threatening me, was exactly the kind of thing that would get Ethan's goat.

The shower shut off.

It was easy to see exactly what Adrien Reed had wanted to do—manipulate, irritate, inflame.

"Sentinel?"

Instinct had me crumpling the card into the palm of my hand.

Ethan stood in the doorway, one towel wrapped low around his lean hips, his muscles gleaming with water. "Are you all right? I felt"—he looked around the room, searching for a threat—"magic."

Thinking fast, I picked up the rest of the paper while tossing the note into the trash can beneath the desk, slick as a Vegas illusionist.

My heart pounding at the deception, I showed him the headline and photographs. Ethan walked forward, took the paper from me, flipped it open. His eyes tracked our story, then the one on the Reeds.

"Reed's put in a 'community safety center' in a building across the street from Towerline."

"What?"

Ethan glanced at me. "Too irate to read the article?"

"Towerline belongs to my father."

"You'll get no argument from me, Sentinel." His eyes scanned the story. "Reed has also rehabbed a building across the street from Towerline that will serve as the headquarters for the renovation activities. He's also announced it's home to an enterprise dedicated to bringing law enforcement and business interests together to reduce crime in Chicago."

"Reduce crime, my ass," I muttered. "That will give Reed access to every law enforcement plan in the city. It won't help reduce crime; he'll just be able to plan around it."

"Perhaps," Ethan said, refolding the paper. "But then again, he is meticulous in keeping those aspects of his life separate."

Instead of putting the paper back on the tray, Ethan tossed it into the trash beside the note that had accompanied it. Which was fine by me.

"As to the article about Wrigley, supernaturals are fodder for the press. There's little reporters love more than seeding dissent: *Are supernaturals really your friends? Are you sure? Did you see what they did this time?* They love to paint us with the same broad strokes."

"We are nothing like the vampire who murdered Caleb Franklin," I said with a huff. "He had no honor."

"No, he didn't," Ethan said. "Because if he'd had an excuse for the murder, some reason for it beyond self-interest or greed, he needn't have run from us."

"Yeah. Although that doesn't really make me feel better."

"I know something that would make you feel much better," he said, his tone all wickedness.

I poked him on the arm, which did make me feel a little better.

He grabbed his arm, doubled over in mock pain. "It seems your arm is in working order."

"Good enough to punch a vampire with a bad attitude."

He slapped my butt. "Get dressed, Sentinel. Let us show the *Tribune*, and our doubters, what vampires have to offer the world."

Thinking the night might call for action, I skipped the Cadogan uniform and pulled on my leathers. The black motorcycle-style jacket and pants were segmented just enough that I could fight if necessary. I wore a pale blue tank beneath the jacket, and black high-heeled boots beneath the pants. I added my Cadogan necklace, an inscribed silver teardrop, then pulled my long, dark hair into a high pony, straightening the bangs that fell across my forehead.

"Exactly what I had in mind, Sentinel."

I met Ethan's gaze in the mirror as I straightened out the ponytail. "I suspect there will be tension tonight. Seemed best to be prepared."

"I don't disagree," he said. And he certainly looked his best. He wore the Cadogan uniform: a fitted black suit jacket over an immaculate white button-down, the top button open to reveal his own Cadogan medal. Fitted black suit pants, and he'd left his hair down, and it shone around his beautiful face like a gilded frame.

I sighed. "You are just too handsome."

He arched a single eyebrow. "That doesn't sound like a compliment."

I turned around to face him, leaned back against the bathroom's marble counter. "It's part compliment, and part jealousy," I said with a smile. "Were your sisters as beautiful as you?"

Ethan had had three sisters, Elisa, Annika, and Berit, in Sweden before he nearly died in battle and was made a vampire. His expression softened as he remembered. "They were lovely. Elisa and Annika were twins. Both blond, with blue eyes and pale skin. Rosy cheeks. Berit was shorter and more playful. They'd all been of an age to discuss weddings when I was killed. But, of course, I didn't go back."

Because he'd imagined himself a monster. "You miss them."

He glanced at me. "It is a curse and blessing of immortality that you remember those who are gone even long after they are gone."

I took his hand, squeezed it. "They would have been so happy, Ethan, to know that you're alive. That you weren't killed in battle and are thriving centuries later and keeping their memories alive. Leading your vampires with honor, working for peace."

He tugged my ponytail, pulling me toward him, then pressed his lips to mine. "Thank you for that, Merit."

"It's the truth. They'd probably also be pleased that you're famous and rich and have a smokin' girlfriend."

He snorted. "And there, you've taken it just one step too far. I'm hardly rich," he added with a wink. "I've got some business to address tonight, supplicants who've been waiting, and I'd like to get you to help Paige with the translation."

I nodded. "I'd planned that after grabbing a bite. Oh, and my grandfather sent a message—said the vampire's DNA isn't in the system. So he's an unknown."

"Then we'll need to get to work." He held out a hand. "Let's get you fed and watered and into the library."

Cadogan House was a lovely dame, with beautiful art, antiques, and vampires. But there was one room that outclassed them all.

The library—two stories of books, all meticulously organized and cataloged. The first floor featured dozens of shelves and tables for studying. The second was a balcony of more shelves ringed by red iron railings and accessible by an equally red spiral staircase.

One of the oak tables in the middle of the first floor had been piled with books. *An Encyclopedia of Modern Alchemy, Alchemy and Hermeticism: A Primer,* and *Transmutations and Distillations for the Common Sorcerer* were atop the stacks.

"Don't get those out of order."

I yanked back my hand, glanced behind me. A man on the shorter side, pale skin, dark hair, was rolling toward us a brass cart filled with a dozen more books. Also an exception to the Cadogan uniform rule, he wore jeans and a black Polo shirt with a small Cadogan seal embroidered on the chest.

"Sire," he said. "Merit."

"Librarian," Ethan said. His name was Arthur, but everyone except Paige used his title. The Librarian was the master of this two-story kingdom within a kingdom and the books within it, including the *Canon*, the laws that governed vampires, at least for now. The AAM was still working out the legal situation.

"I found one more," said the startlingly beautiful woman who emerged from between two rows of shelves. She was tall and slender, with pale skin, green eyes, and a wavy head of red curls. She wore jeans, leopard-print flats, and a simple white T-shirt that still managed to look elegant and refined.

This was Paige Martin, a sorcerer and former Order Archivist. We'd brought her back from Nebraska after Mallory absconded with a book of evil magic. Paige and the Librarian had hit it off immediately.

She stood beside him, a good four inches taller, and passed him the books. "Merit, Ethan. I was just about to get started."

"Jeff sent you the pictures?" Ethan asked.

"He did," she said, and there was no denying the excitement in her eyes. She put a hand on her chest. "I don't want to make light of what happened to Caleb. It's just—I've never actually seen alchemy in practice. It's such a rare specialty. I'm—I guess 'intellectually intrigued' would be the best phrase."

She walked around the table, picked up a large poster that had been mounted to a sheet of foam board. It was at least four feet long and covered in rows of symbols.

"I just need to grab an easel from the storage room. Jeff figured out a way to blow up the symbols so they're clearer and easier for us to read. And he's divided them into two sets—one for me and one for Mallory."

"How can I help?" I asked, not entirely sure that I could.

"Alchemical equations typically have their own architecture. I'm hoping this one does, too. If that's right, and I can break the equations into their subparts, I'm going to give you some of the subparts for translation using these." She tapped a finger on the books.

"Do you have any idea what the alchemy might be used for?" Ethan asked.

"Not without translating," she said. "But I can tell you this—whatever it is, it's big. Most alchemical equations are pretty simple; that's the nature of alchemy. Right or wrong, alchemists believed you could change matter—change one thing into another, realize the true 'essence' of something—if you applied the right kind of solvent at the correct time of year, under the influence of the right heavenly bodies. It can get more complicated, sure." She gestured to the board. "But this? This is a lot of symbols, plus pictographs—the hand-drawn elements. And there's no explanatory text whatsoever. I think that's the point of the pictographs—concealing the instructions. As far as I'm aware, they're unique to the sorcerer, in which case the puzzle will be even harder to solve."

"Bottom-line it for me," Ethan said.

"Someone cared enough to be very careful and very specific

about the thing addressed here. I'm just not yet sure what that 'thing' is. But you'll be the first one to know."

Ethan's phone rang, and he pulled it out, checked the screen. "Give us a minute, would you?" he asked, and Paige and the Librarian nodded and disappeared into a row.

"It's Gabriel," Ethan said when we were alone, and pressed a button. "Ethan and Merit."

Gabe didn't waste any time. "I need a favor."

Ethan's brows lifted, and he put his hands on his hips. "I'm listening."

"I've got an address for Caleb, but I can't get away to check it out. I've got obligations as Apex related to the death, the wake."

Ethan lifted his brows again, and I could guess the line of his thoughts: Why did an Apex have obligations to a member who'd defected? I didn't doubt Gabriel was grieving; we'd seen it last night. But the Pack prided itself on loyalty. We simply didn't have the entire story.

"If you could take a look, or get your people to take a look, maybe you'll find something that ties him to the sorcerer, to the vampire. Something that explains why he was killed."

"We'll take a look," Ethan said, nodding at me. "The address?"

Gabriel read it off. "I understand it's near Hellriver. So be careful."

In the 1950s, Hellriver had been "Belle River," a pretty suburb near the Des Plaines River. That changed forty years ago, when an ugly chemical spill sent most of the neighborhood packing. The houses, churches, and stores were still there, but Chicago hadn't been able to get the funds for a cleanup, and nobody wanted to live in still-toxic Hellriver.

"We always are. How did you find the address?"

"Damien made some calls. Caleb may not have been a Pack

member, but he still had friends inside. It's not supposed to work that way—defection is defection—but I can't stop what I don't see."

"And now you can see it," Ethan said.

"Yeah. We'll be having some discussions about that."

"Good luck to you," Ethan said. "We'll take a look and let you know what we find."

"Appreciate it." There was a *thunk* on Gabriel's end. "God-damn whelps. *Somebody pull those assholes apart!* Later," he said into the phone, and the call ended.

"Sounds like he's having fun."

"If Mastering vampires is akin to herding cats, mastering shifters is akin to herding bull elephants."

"So you're saying you don't envy him."

"Not in the slightest." He put his phone away, looked at me. "Are you up for a field trip?"

I smiled. "As long as I can take my sword. I'm curious to learn more about our defecting shifter."

"You aren't the only one, Sentinel," Ethan murmured. "We should probably warn Luc we're going."

"Why? What could happen at the house of a dead shifter beside a toxic neighborhood? I'm sure everything will be fine." I didn't bother to hide my sarcasm.

"We're clear," he called out, and Paige came back with a thin black easel. She set it up, then placed the poster in the crossbar.

"Unfortunately," Ethan said, "I won't be able to volunteer Merit quite as early as I'd imagined. Gabriel has a lead on the shifter who was killed, and he's asked us to check it out."

"No worries," Paige said with a smile, and she probably meant it. "I'd like the chance to take a look before I assign anything to Merit."

The Librarian came back to us with a tablet and cord in hand. He plugged it in, arranged it on the tabletop for Paige to use. "Thank you, Arthur."

His cheeks flushed with pleasure. "You're welcome," he said, then put his hands on his hips, surveyed the setup.

"I think we're good to go here," Paige said.

"Excellent," Ethan said, putting a hand at my back. "We'll get to our business with the shifters. If there are any developments—if you learn anything—please let us know."

"We will," Paige said, settling herself into a chair. "And good luck."

"I'll grab my sword," I said when we'd left the library and were back in the hallway again.

"I'll advise Luc of the call, the trip. Meet you in the basement."

And we went our separate ways.

CHAPTER SIX

FOUR ON THE FLOOR

Despite our plan, I met him on the first floor near the staircase, just leaving his office, a glossy box in hand. "What's that?"

"A gift for Gabriel, should we end up at Little Red." He opened the tabs on the box, showed me the neck of a bottle of what looked like good Scotch.

"Excellent. This is random, but don't you think Paige is just gorgeous?"

We took the stairs to the basement. "I don't think there's a way I can answer that question without incurring your wrath."

I smiled at him. "As long as you don't touch her, I've got no problem with your agreement. I don't think her attractiveness is debatable. And if you do touch her, I'll slice your fingers off and feed them to a River troll."

"River trolls are fruitarians."

"Not the point."

He chuckled, keyed in his code, opened the door to the garage. "No, I suppose not. Regardless, I only have eyes for you, Sentinel. Well, you . . . and her."

I looked in the direction of his gaze, half expecting to find a beautiful woman in the garage.

But there was no woman. Instead there was a gleaming white, two-door convertible with sporty wheels, deep vents in the doors, and another vent across the back.

Hands on my hips, I glanced at him. "And what is this?"

"This, Sentinel, is an Audi."

"Yeah, I can see that." I could appreciate good steel, fine leather, and impressive horsepower, but I recognized the model for one singular and important reason. "You bought Iron Man's car."

"He's not even immortal." The clear disdain in Ethan's voice made me snort.

"He's a fictional superhero. You aren't in competition."

"He's a very *mortal* superhero outside that suit," he said, looking over his car with an appraiser's eye.

"You've apparently put some thought into that."

"A man carefully considers his ride, Sentinel. And his rivals. This car will get us where we need to go, and it will do so very, very quickly."

There was hardly a point in arguing with that. It certainly looked like a fast car, so I let the comment pass and walked around the vehicle, gave it a once-over. The car absolutely gleamed, its interior deep crimson leather, its soft roof made of fabric in the same shade.

I looked at him over the car from the passenger side. "You do have good taste."

"Of course I do," he said. "Shall we go for a ride?"

"I mean, I'm not going to say no." I grinned at him. "Have you named her yet?"

The faintest flush of crimson rode his cheeks. I wasn't sure I'd ever seen him blush before. "Sophia," he said.

"A lovely name for a lovely woman," I said, without much jealousy, and sank down into buttery crimson leather. "Let's see what she can do."

It would have been simpler to wonder what she *couldn't* do.

Her engine rumbled like hollow thunder, and she practically flew down the streets of Hyde Park. I wouldn't call myself a car person, but it was impossible not to appreciate the ride.

We drove northwest from Hyde Park to Hellriver, crossing the Des Plaines River and moving west.

Ethan had turned on a talk radio station, but switched it off again after a ten-minute dissertation on the Problems With Vampires. They included, to quote the speaker: (1) their penchant for violence; (2) their disdain for human authority; (3) their refusal to acknowledge humanity's innate superiority; and (4) their lack of temperance.

I wasn't entirely sure what the last one was about. Prohibition hadn't worked in Chicago in the twenties, and it certainly wasn't the law now.

Gabriel had been right about the shifter's location. Caleb Franklin's former home was only a few houses down from the broken chain-link fence intended to block access to Hellriver. Not that there seemed to be much improvement on this side of the barrier. The homes were dilapidated, the businesses boarded up.

"Here we are," Ethan said, pointing to a single-story house. It was yellow, the small porch white. The paint on both was peeling, and the concrete sidewalk outside jumbled and split. The yard wasn't fancy, but it was tidy.

We climbed out of the car, belted on our swords, and took the steps to the front porch. The neighborhood was quiet. I hadn't seen a single human, or supernatural, but a dog barked in the distance, warning its owner of something ominous in the dark.

The building was completely dark, utterly quiet. I closed my eyes, let my guards drop just long enough to check for signs of life inside. But there was nothing, supernatural or otherwise.

"There's no one in there," I said after a moment, opening my eyes again. "No sound, no magic."

"My conclusion as well," Ethan whispered, then turned the knob.

The unlocked door opened easily into a small living room that smelled of must and animal.

We walked inside, and I pulled the door nearly closed behind us. "Nearly" so that passersby wouldn't decide to investigate, but we could still make a quick exit.

The living room was marked by an enormous couch on the opposite wall. It was what I'd call the "Official Couch of the Seventies"—long, ruffled, and covered in cream velveteen fabric with orange and brown flowers.

There was a matching love seat, an end table, a lamp. No photographs, no curtains, no television or stereo.

"Not much here," I whispered.

"Or maybe our shifter wasn't into décor."

The living room led into a dining room that was empty but for a small table with four chairs and two more doorways—a kitchen straight back, and what I guessed was a bedroom to the side.

"I'll take the bedroom," I said.

"Passing up the kitchen?" Ethan asked with a chuckle. "How novel."

"As is that joke. Check the refrigerator."

My excellent suggestion was met by an arched eyebrow. "He's a shifter," I reminded Ethan. "If he's been here lately, he'll have food."

Ethan opened his mouth, closed it again. "That's a good suggestion."

I glanced back at him, winked. "It's not my first night on the job, sunshine."

Ethan humphed but walked into the kitchen while I slipped into the bedroom, a hand on the pommel of my sword. That the house seemed empty didn't mean we shouldn't be cautious.

The bedroom held a matching set of white children's furniture—lots of curlicues and gilded accents. Probably from the same era as the couch in the front room. The mattress was bare, and there were no ribbons or mementos tucked into the corners of the mirror that topped the chest of drawers. Furniture or not, no child lived here.

The bedroom led to a short hallway. Closet on one side, Jack and Jill bathroom on the other with avocado green fixtures. No toothbrushes, no towels, no shampoo bottle in the shower. There was a spider the size of a smallish Buick, and I gave him or her a wide berth.

The next door, probably another bedroom, was nearly closed, and a soft mechanical throb seeped through the crack. I flicked the thumb guard on my sword, just in case, and pushed the door open with the toe of my boot.

It was another small bedroom. A ceiling fan whirred above a black double bed with more gilded accents, the mattress covered by a rumpled duvet and thick pillows. This was Caleb Franklin's bedroom. And if the fan was any indication, he'd been here recently.

There was a closet in the far corner. It was empty but for a pile of dirty clothes on the floor. No shoes, no hangers.

I opened the drawers of the bureau and nightstand that matched the bed. The nightstand was empty; the bureau held a few changes of clothes. T-shirts, jeans, a couple of hoodies.

Had this been the freedom Caleb had wanted? The freedom to not care about material possessions? Had he found peace in this desolate neighborhood? And if so, why would anyone have bothered to kill him?

The bedroom's second door led into the kitchen, completing the circle through the interior. I walked through, found a small storage closet behind it that led to an exterior door. There was a mop, a bucket, and a worn pair of snow boots.

I felt Ethan come in behind me.

"Some clothes in the bedroom," I said, pulling open the door of a metal cabinet, finding it empty. "That's about all I've found. What about you?"

In the answering silence, I turned around. Ethan had walked to the refrigerator, opened it.

It was absolutely stocked.

There were bundles of produce—carrots with the green tops still attached, glossy eggplants, heads of cabbage—besides piles of steaks and dozens of brown eggs in a carefully placed pyramid. There were blocks of cheese, a dozen bottles of water, a plate of what looked like profiteroles, and several bundles wrapped in aluminum foil. The scent of spiced meat wafted out. I'd have bet good money they'd been prepared by Berna, Gabe's strong-willed and culinarily skilled relative.

"No processed foods in this man's diet," Ethan said.

"And a big appetite. Of course, he's a shifter." That meant he was an animal of some type, although we wouldn't ask Gabriel. The animal variety was considered very personal among Pack members.

"So we have an empty house and a stocked fridge," I said. "By all accounts, Caleb Franklin slept here, ate here, stored the barest necessities here. Didn't seem to do much else here."

"No," he didn't," Ethan agreed.

I looked around. "Whatever got him killed, there's no evidence of it inside." I glanced back at Ethan. "You want to finish up in here? I want to take a walk around the yard."

Ethan nodded. "I'll take a pass. Be careful out there."

I promised I would and walked back to the front door, then outside. I needed to think like him. He might not have had a Pack, but as the stocked fridge showed, he was still a shifter.

I hopped down the steps, walked around the house. There were shrubs in front of the foundation every few feet, and a few trees just beginning to bud around the edge of the narrow lot.

The backyard was small, bordered by the back neighbor's chain-link fence, which was covered in brambles and vines. There were a couple more trees back here, as well as a cracked and peeling red-wood picnic table. A swing hung from one tree, a simple wooden plank attached to an overhanging branch by a thick, braided rope, probably hung for the same child who'd once owned the white bedroom furniture.

I tugged on the ropes to check they were solid, knocked on the wooden seat. I gingerly sat down, pushed back in the soft earth with the toes of my boots. The swing moved back, then forward, then back again, the rope creaking with effort. I stretched out my arms and leaned back to look up at the tree limbs overhead.

The child would have played out here, the trees creating the walls of the castle only she could save. That was how I would have played, anyway. Our backyard had been empty of fun—no trees, no swings, no sandbox. Just the lawn my father paid some-one to trim into a perfectly manicured rectangle.

I sat up again, head buzzing from the motion. That was when I saw it—a square piece of plywood stuck over the painted brick foundation. The plywood was new, still showing its price in bright orange paint.

Maybe our shifter had a den, I thought. I walked toward it, knelt in front in the soft, new grass. There were no screws or locks; it had merely been set in place, propped up by a concrete block. I moved away the block, then the plywood, and peered into the crawl space. The ground beneath the house was packed dirt and dotted here and there with rocks and broken bricks. It smelled of wet earth.

The plywood had been larger than the void it covered, which was only about sixteen inches square. Big enough for pests to crawl into, but Caleb Franklin didn't strike me as the type to care overmuch about something nesting down there.

The hole wouldn't have been big enough for him to slip through. But maybe it was big enough for him to reach into.

With a silent prayer to whatever gods would keep the rest of the house's spiders out of my hair, I braced my hands on the foundation and poked my head inside.

It took a moment for my eyes to adjust to darkness-inside-darkness—and just a moment more to spy the metal cashbox just inside the foundation.

If I'd been a child in my imaginary castle, this would have been my long-lost treasure.

I reached inside, fingers grasping at something stringy before my fingertips landed on cold metal. I found the handle and pulled it out just as footsteps echoed behind me.

I stood, dusted the dirt from my knees with one hand, and walked to the picnic table. I set the cashbox on top of it.

"And what do we have here?"

"There was new plywood," I said. "I was hoping I'd find a hidey-hole, and it looks like I did. Or found something, anyway."

The box was rectangular, closed with a metal latch. I unhooked it and flipped open the lid.

There was a small manila envelope inside, the flap still gummed and open. I picked it up and emptied into my palm a small brass key. Its working end didn't have the typical angular hills and valleys; instead there were square notches. A number, 425, was inscribed on the head.

"Well, well, well, Sentinel. Look what you have there."

I glanced at him. "I'm looking but have no idea what it's for. Do you?"

Ethan smiled. "That is a key for a safe-deposit box."

A hidden box that led to a vaulted box. That was a pretty interesting find.

"So our murdered shifter, who defected from the Pack, has a hidden cashbox and a key to a safe-deposit box." I glanced at Ethan. "What does an unaffiliated shifter keep in a safe-deposit box?"

"I've no idea," Ethan said, eyes gleaming with interest, "but I'm eager to find out."

I slid the key back into the envelope and put the envelope in my pocket. Then I put the cashbox back where I'd found it, pulled the plywood and brick back into place.

And realized we weren't the only ones to have been here. The ground here was as soft as it was near the swing, so it had saved the impressions of the large, rough footprints.

I pointed them out to Ethan. "We aren't the only ones poking around out here."

"Then we'd best be the first to solve the mystery."

We made a final pass through the house, looking for information that might identify the bank Caleb had used, the location of the box. But we found nothing.

We turned off all the lights and walked outside, setting the lock on the doorknob to deter intruders. We were on our way back to the car when I heard a faint murmur of sound, a voice carried on the wind. And with that voice came the buzz of magic.

"Listen," I said quietly, when Ethan joined me on the sidewalk.

He tilted his head, and when he caught the sound, alarm crossed his face. "Magic," he said.

"Our sorcerer?"

He flipped the thumb guard on his katana. "Someone is doing magic in this neighborhood. Let us be prepared either way."

I nodded, kept my hand on my katana's handle as we walked across the street and down the block, pausing every few yards to check our position in relation to the sound. Silently, I touched Ethan's hand, nodded toward a small cemetery, the graves surrounded by a chain-link fence. Unlike much of the rest of the neighborhood, the fence and grass beyond it looked well tended.

"Longwood Cemetery," Ethan whispered as we reached the front gate. It was a double gate and standing open, large enough for cars to drive through.

I stopped at the entrance, gathered up my courage. I didn't like cemeteries. My brother, Robert, and sister, Charlotte, and I had held our breath when we passed them on car trips as kids. I was the youngest and always held my breath the longest. I had been completely terrified by the thought of all those people underground waiting, *Thriller*-like, to thrust out their dirty hands and grab my ankles. If I stayed quiet and still, they'd stay happily asleep beneath the earth.

The wind shifted and moved, directing the clear sound of a voice on the wind. We were looking for a sorcerer, and this definitely seemed like a potential hit. That meant I had to suck it up and walk into Longwood like the goddamn Sentinel of Cadogan House, with my head held high, my senses on alert, and my bravery intact.

But even still, and knowing what I knew now, I decided to take exceptionally quiet steps.

The gate led to a crushed-stone path that led straight through the cemetery and branched off to secondary trails.

The cemetery wasn't very large, but it was well kept. Marble gravestones sat at perfect intervals along shorter rows, and there were neatly pruned peonies and rosebushes every dozen yards or so.

I stayed close enough to Ethan that our arms brushed when we walked. "Freaking *Thriller*," I murmured.

"What was that?" Ethan whispered.

"Nothing," I said, and stopped short when a figure became visible in the darkness. *There,* I said silently, gesturing toward her.

A woman stood in front of a grave, silhouetted in the moonlight. She was tall, slender, and pretty, with dark skin, high cheekbones, and dark, braided hair pulled into a knot atop her head. She wore a cropped white cardigan, white sneakers, and a long, pale pink dress of sharp, narrow pleats that fell over her swollen abdomen.

Ethan stepped forward, broke a twig in the process. The crack was as loud as a gunshot. She turned around, one hand on her belly, fingers splayed in protection, another in front of her, threatening magic.

I'd seen Catcher and Mallory throw fireballs before, and didn't want any part of that. I put my hands in the air, and Ethan did the same.

The woman stared at us for a moment. "You don't look like ghouls," she said, but didn't seem entirely sure about it.

"We are not," Ethan said. "And you don't look to be an evil sorceress."

She snorted. "I most definitely am not. Could you move forward, into the moonlight?"

We did, hands still lifted in the air. It seemed safe enough movement; I'd yet to meet an evil, gestating supernatural.

"You're vampires," she said after a moment. "I recognize you. You're Ethan and Merit, right?"

Ethan nodded, but his gaze stayed wary. "We are. How do you know us?"

She smiled guiltily. "Gossip magazines. They're my guilty pleasure." She cocked her head at us. "You're in them a lot."

We couldn't argue with that.

She glanced at me. "And Chuck Merit's your grandfather, right?"

That was a much better reason to be famous. "Yes, he is."

"I'm sorry, I'm being rude," she said, putting a hand on her chest. "You startled me. Sorry about that, everyone," she added, looking around, hands patting the air like the simple movement was the thing that would keep the bodies in the ground.

Fear speared me, and I tried to logic through it. Surely her petite hands weren't the only thing keeping not-yet-walking dead from rising. Still, just in case, I moved a little closer to Ethan, ever the brave Sentinel.

He was going to give me so much crap about this.

"I'm Annabelle Shaw," she said. "I'm a necromancer."

"*Mortui vivos docent?*" Ethan asked.

"Very good," she agreed with a smile, and must have caught my look of confusion. "The phrase means, roughly, 'the dead teach the living.' In this case, the dead speak, I listen."

"I didn't know that was possible," I said, thinking of Ethan's temporary death and the possibility we might have communicated during it. "Necromancy, I mean."

"There aren't many of us," she said. "It's a pretty rare magic, which is probably a good thing. The dead are talkers."

Dread skittered along my spine.

Annabelle winced suddenly, lifted a hand to her belly. I caught the flash of concern on Ethan's face. He stepped forward and gripped her elbow to help keep her steady.

"I'm okay," she said, and patted his arm. She smiled a little. "Thank you. Peanut kicks like a mule. If I wasn't certain her father was human, I'd wonder. And I'm still fairly sure she's destined to be a kickboxer." She winced again, staring down at her belly as if her narrowed gaze could penetrate to the kicking child within. "You know, we'll both be better off if I have a functioning bladder.

She rolled her eyes, blew out a breath, seemed to settle herself. "Anyway," she said, "I'm a registered necromancer, affiliated with the Illinois MVD Association."

If there was anything I'd learned about supernaturals, it was that they loved bureaucracy. Magic wasn't worth doing unless a supernatural could throw a council or code of conduct at it, slap it on a T-shirt, and charge a due. And supernatural bureaucracy was just about as effective as the human version.

"How does that work, exactly?" I couldn't resist asking.

"Well, I take commissions, usually work on retainer. People have questions—they want to know if the deceased was faithful, where they put the garage key, whatever. Or they have things they want to tell the deceased that they didn't get to say while they were living."

"That's nice," I said, trying to unknot the tension at the base of my spine.

"Sometimes," she agreed, resting her linked hands on her belly. "And sometimes they just want to tell off the—and I'm quoting—'rotting, whoremongering, philandering, dickless bastard who, if all is right and just in the world, is spending his days in the embrace of Satan's eternal hellfire.'" She grinned. "I memorized that one."

"People are people," Ethan said.

"All day every day. Anyway, I try to balance out the commissions with public service. Sometimes I get a vibe that the deceased have things to say, like Mr. Leeds here, even if nobody's requested a commission. I give them time to get it out so they can rest peacefully."

If there was anything I wanted, it was a peaceful ghost.

"You were singing to him?" Ethan asked.

"I was." She lifted a shoulder. "Every 'mancer has his or her own style. I like to sing. It calms them, makes them a little more cooperative. And that means I don't need to use as much magic to keep them in check."

"What do you sing?" I asked, fascinated despite myself.

"I generally use slow jams," she said. "Classic R and B from the eighties, nineties has a nice, relaxed rhythm and sets a nice tone." She leaned forward conspiratorially. "Just don't tell my grandmother that. She's in the business, too, and she'd be pissed if she learned I was singing Luther Vandross to clients. She says gospel's the only way to go."

"We'll keep your secret," Ethan said. "And sorry we interrupted you."

She waved it off. "No worries. Some of them like to listen in, and cemetery conversations are usually pretty morose."

"Do you do a lot of work in this neighborhood?" I asked, thinking again of Caleb Franklin.

"We work territories. Not many want to work this close to Hellriver." She shrugged. "I don't tend to get bothered. And if I do, I know how to protect myself."

"Fireballs?" I asked, thinking of Catcher.

"Screaming ghouls," she said, her expression so serious I had to choke back a silent, horrified scream.

She must have sensed my concern. "It's not as bad as it sounds. They don't typically manifest physically, so they don't usually cause any physical harm."

"I'm stuck on 'typically' and 'usually.'"

She smiled. "Job hazard. And speaking of which, did you say earlier I didn't look like an evil sorcerer?"

"That's actually why we're here," Ethan said. "We're looking for a sorcerer—someone not of the Order, but actively practicing. The magic is likely to be dark, or at least unusual."

"What kind of unusual?"

"Alchemy."

Annabelle's eyebrows lifted. "Alchemy. That's not a word you hear very often." She frowned. "I'm doing the darkest magic around here that I'm aware of, and that's only because it's literally dark," she said, waving a hand in the air to indicate the nighttime. "You've checked with the Order?"

"One of our colleagues is doing so," Ethan said. "Although we've found them to be relatively useless."

"No argument there. The MVD Association exists because the Order didn't consider us sorcerers. In Europe, in Asia, India, magic-doers of all types are part of the same conglomeration. But in the good ol' U.S. of A., we are not good enough to join their party."

"Supernaturals pick the oddest swords to fall upon," Ethan said.

"You are preaching to the choir."

"What about a shifter named Caleb Franklin?" I asked. "He lived nearby. Did you happen to know him?"

She pursed her lips as she considered. "Caleb Franklin." She shook her head. "No, that doesn't ring a bell, either. And I don't think I know any shifters."

"How about this man?" I asked, pulling out my phone and showing her the grainy photograph Jeff had captured.

She frowned. "Hard to tell from the picture, but I don't think so. I feel like I'd have remembered the beard." Her eyes widened, and she lifted her gaze to mine. "Is this about what happened to that poor shifter at Wrigley? I mean, they didn't release his name, but a vampire and shifter were involved, right?"

"Caleb Franklin is that shifter," Ethan confirmed. "We believe he was killed by a vampire, and may have been involved in the alchemy. Alchemical symbols were found nearby."

"I'd have liked to have seen them," she said. "I mean, I'm sorry for his death, but it's interesting the way that rare magic is. Like walking down the street and seeing, I don't know, a diplodocus or something."

It was the kind of joke I'd have appreciated, if a concussion hadn't immediately shaken the ground beneath us. I gripped Ethan's arm with clawed fingers.

What. The. Hell?

He patted my hand supportively, but I could tell he'd gone on full alert.

"And that's my cue," Annabelle said, moving closer to the gravestone and resting a hand on a marble curlicue. "Mr. Leeds knows I'm here and thinks I'm ignoring him, so I need to let him talk. I don't, he'll get angrier and angrier. And that's when ghouls become a real possibility."

I managed a weak smile. "That must keep your dance card full."

"It does."

"Do you mind if we observe?" Ethan asked. "And please say no if it would disrupt your process."

"Or add to their potential ghoulishness," I added. "Because we don't want to do that." God, did we not want that!

Annabelle smiled. "I don't mind at all. But you'll want to take a step back and cover your ears. Sometimes they come up screaming."

Every cell in my body shuddered in simultaneous horror.

CHAPTER SEVEN

SHAKE THE BONES

I took several steps back, working carefully to stay in the aisle and avoid stepping on anyone else's plot. When Ethan moved beside me, I gripped his hand, unashamed.

Be still, Sentinel, he said. Those were the first words he'd said to me, and words I usually loved to hear. But here, in this graveyard, while waiting for a necromancer to commune with the dead, I wasn't loving it.

Annabelle moved to stand at the end of the grave, facing the stretch of grass and gravestone. She closed her eyes, blew out a breath, seemed to center herself.

The earth shook again, the concussion like a strike on a timpani drum.

I cursed *Thriller* silently again.

Seemingly oblivious to Mr. Leeds's irritation, or maybe because she was trained to deal with it, Annabelle held out her hands, palms down, over the grass.

"Harold Parcevius Leeds, I am Annabelle Shaw. I am here to help you speak. Please comport yourself respectfully."

Another tremor.

Eyes still closed, she shook her head, breathed through her

nose in what looked like irritated resignation. "Mr. Leeds, I am not interested in taking abuse from you. I am here voluntarily to help you communicate. If you can't be pleasant about it, I'll leave you to silence. Neither of us wants that. You want peace, and I want to help you find it."

She paused, waiting, as Ethan and I stood behind her, watching, and then she nodded.

"Thank you, sir. I appreciate your cooperation and acknowledge it. I can assist you in momentarily revisiting this plane, which will allow me to hear your claim or your confession. Do you acknowledge?"

Consent, it seemed, was important for all sorts of supernatural creatures. Mr. Leeds consented with another concussion, this one different from the others. It wasn't made in anger by a pounded fist. It was more like a desperate bellow, the plea of a man who needed to be heard. Pity spilled in to replace my fear, and I unclenched the fingers I'd wrapped around Ethan's.

Thank you, Sentinel. I was hoping to use those fingers again.

Magic began to shimmer through the air.

"Very well," Annabelle said as the magic grew around us. It wasn't painful, but it was unnerving. It was different from Mallory's or Catcher's magic—and it didn't escape my notice that it was also different from the tinny magic I'd felt in Wrigleyville. This magic felt tangible and real, as if our skin were being brushed by hanks of silk. Instinctively, I reached out to touch it, but my fingers grasped nothing more than air.

Electricity popped around Annabelle, magic sparking through the air like forks of lightning. The power grew fiercer, stronger, until the magic seemed to coalesce atop the grass into the outline of a man lying on his back, arms at his sides. His figure seemed built solely of light and shadow, like an X-ray in three dimensions.

I was actually looking at a ghost, and despite my deep-seated horror, I couldn't look away.

And then he sat straight up, opened his mouth, and screamed.

I clamped my hands over my ears, but it didn't help. The sound pounded through my head like it had mass, like it was beating through my skull and filling my body with noise. My eyes watered against the sudden pain and pressure, and still I couldn't look away.

Apparently used to the noise, or maybe immune to it, Annabelle held out a hand, utterly calm and composed. "I'm here, Mr. Leeds."

When the screaming didn't stop, Annabelle stamped a sneakered foot atop his grave, sending a wave rippling through grass and dirt as if she'd skipped a pebble across a glassy lake.

"Mr. Leeds."

Her words sliced through his anger like a honed katana, and the world fell suddenly silent. Slowly, I removed my hands again, my ears still buzzing from the magic or noise or whatever had assaulted them.

"Thank you, Mr. Leeds. I'm here for you, to hear whatever you'd like to tell me. You don't need to raise your voice. I can hear you. That's my particular gift."

The ghost seemed to stare at her, his expression unreadable. And then he clasped his hands together prayerfully and began to speak. The words were fuzzy, garbled, like a distant station on a radio, albeit with the volume maxed out. But the earnestness in his eyes, the pleading in his expression, was clear enough.

"I understand," Annabelle said. "I can provide a message to them, if you'd like. You only need to tell me what you'd like to say, and I will do my best to find them and see that they hear it."

He spoke again. This time he was calmer, which made his magic less chaotic... and some of his words understandable. "Wife...

Wrong . . . Unfaithful . . . Wasn't . . . *Wasn't* . . . Design . . . Please tell her . . ."

Tears gathered at Annabelle's lashes, slipped down her cheeks. But she didn't take her eyes off the man in front of her.

"I'll tell her, Mr. Leeds," she said, voice quiet but earnest. "I'll make sure she understands. That's my solemn oath to you."

And then she reached forward and held out a hand, grasping his translucent one in hers, small sparks of lightning traveling between them. If the sensation hurt, she didn't show it.

"Let your soul rest, Mr. Leeds. Let your mind and heart calm. Your message has been heard, and will be delivered, and you can depart from his earth and seek your rest. You can sleep now."

The magic shifted, softened. By listening to this man, by doing that simplest and most important of favors, she'd changed him. Even as he drew his hand away, his image began to fade, the hazy magic diffusing into the darkness. He lay down on the grass again, and drifted away.

Silence fell, and we honored it long enough that crickets began to chirp nearby.

After a moment, Annabelle wiped her cheeks and turned back to us.

"Thank you for sharing that with us," Ethan said, breaking the silence. "It was . . ." He seemed to struggle for words. "Quite a thing to see."

"You're welcome. They aren't often as visible. He was trying really, really hard to talk."

"Can we ask what he told you?"

She started to speak, but stopped and pressed her lips together, working to control her emotions. "He died after a car accident. Earlier that day, his wife had seen him with another woman. When he was in the hospital, before he passed, he heard her say she believed he was having an affair. But he wasn't. The woman was a jewelry designer. Her name was Rosa de Santos, and he was having a special necklace made for his wife. He asked me to tell her all that. To tell her that Rosa has her necklace."

"Oh, damn," I said quietly, tears threatening me as well. We worried about our own, our Novitiates, our House, when there were a million tiny tragedies every day. And as Annabelle's work tonight had proven, a million tiny miracles.

"Yeah," she said. "I have a lot of nights like this. But I'll call Mrs. Leeds, and tell her about Rosa and the necklace. She'll grieve again; it's inevitable. But now the fog across her memories, the fear of infidelity, will be gone."

"We'll let you get to that," Ethan said. "And we'll get back to our search."

"You know," she said, glancing toward the south, "if there are any maverick supernaturals around here, you might find them in Hellriver. The chemicals shouldn't hurt immortals, and there are plenty of sups who just don't care about that kind of thing. Where better to wheel and deal than in a neighborhood like Hellriver?"

"And since the CPD doesn't risk its officers' health by sending them into Hellriver," Ethan said, "there's protection for them."

Annabelle nodded. "They do sweeps once a year or so. Usually around Christmas. Charitable types will come around, shuffle any remaining humans into shelters, and the cops will follow, round up any stragglers. But when the holidays pass, there's not so much goodwill, and temps get cold again, people find their way back into the houses."

Living on the edge, Ethan said silently to me. *Much like Caleb Franklin.* He glanced at Annabelle. "How do you know so much about it?"

She smiled. "I come across all types, and I pick up information here and there, file it away. Context is important in my business. You never know what information you'll need. The folks who request my services aren't always on the up-and-up. And, frankly, 'mancers like to talk. This job can be dangerous. We try to keep each other aware."

"Any idea where in Hellriver the sups might be?"

"No, sorry. I stay out of there physically." She patted her belly, as if her touch would protect her child from the darkness around her. "Especially with Peanut, who is currently again kickboxing my internal organs. Enough already, kid."

"We'll let you get back to work," Ethan said. "If you do hear anything, could you let us know?"

"Of course," she said with a smile, and we exchanged numbers.

"It was a pleasure meeting you." Annabelle smiled and offered a hand.

I looked instinctively down, realized the skin of her palm was dotted with hundreds of black dots the size of pinpricks. When I looked at them, she looked down, squeezed her fingers.

"Each handshake with a client leaves a mark," she explained. "Not all 'mancers do it; they don't like the permanent reminder of death. But it's important for me to keep a memento of the ones I've spoken to. They trust me, and I take that trust very seriously."

I had no doubt of that. I took her hand, shook it. "I'm really glad we got to meet you, Annabelle."

"I'm glad you did, too. Be safe. And stay away from ghouls if you can."

I intended to, absolutely.

"Where to now?" I asked Ethan when we made our way to the sidewalk again.

"I suppose we should take a look at Hellriver. See if we can find alchemy or other sorcery."

I nodded, and we walked south toward the broken fence that marked the boundary between Franklin's neighborhood and Hellriver.

"We've discovered something our stalwart Sentinel is squeamish about," Ethan said. "Dead things."

"Dead things should stay that way. Present company excluded," I added at his arch look. "Because you're the most handsome ghoul of them all."

He snorted.

"Annabelle seems cool. Very levelheaded for a woman who does what she does for a living. She seems like the type who gets the job done, takes care of her family, fries up the bacon or whatever."

"Are you casting a sitcom?"

"It certainly sounds like it."

We reached the chain-link fence that separated Hellriver from the rest of the world, which still bore enormous yellow signs warning of the chemical spill. We walked over a section of fence that had been flattened against pavement, passed a peeling billboard of the neighborhood's once-famous dogwood trees. FOR BACKYARDS, FOR COMMUNITY, FOR YOUR FAMILY, it read.

Belle River hadn't made good on the promise.

The houses beyond the billboard were nearly identical—one-story rectangles with overgrown shrubs and attached, single-car garages. Their bright pastel paint had faded and chipped, yards were full of last year's dead weeds, and the asphalt was pitted and buckled. Streetlights had pitched over across sidewalks. The spill and evacuation had happened during the summer months, and lawn mowers still sat abandoned in the middle of several yards. Their owners had picked up and walked away from their lives.

Much like Caleb's, this neighborhood was utterly silent, which added to the sensation that we'd fallen into an alternative, dystopian universe.

"Is it just me, or is this just . . . wrong?" Ethan asked.

"You're not wrong, and it is."

If there were supernaturals or anybody else currently living in the neighborhood, they weren't showing themselves. The houses were dark, and nothing but dead weeds in the light breeze.

But there was something else, I thought, as the hair on the back of my neck lifted. There was magic.

You feel that? I asked him, switching to silent communication.

Ethan nodded, coming to a stop. *Look,* he said, and I followed his gaze to two images stenciled in dark paint onto the sidewalk. The alchemical symbols for the sun and moon—a circle with a dot inside, and a thin sliver of crescent moon.

I didn't think this was supposed to be part of an equation. It didn't feel like that, didn't have the same number of symbols or breadth of magic, of energy. It seemed more like a calling card. The demarcation of territory.

He's been here, Ethan said.

Yeah. He has.

Annabelle's instincts had been right. Hellriver was the type of neighborhood for a maverick supernatural. And more specifically, for an alchemical sorcerer. It also meant Caleb Franklin lived only a few blocks away from what seemed to be the sorcerer's territory. And wasn't that interesting?

Be ready, Ethan said as we moved forward again.

I nodded, my fingers already on the handle of my katana.

We reached a four-way stop, reviewed our options. Belle River was built to be a self-contained neighborhood. The houses surrounded a small commercial area—shops and diners around a central square. It was supposed to simulate a New England village, like

Stars Hollow come to Illinois. Houses stretched to our left, the square to our right.

Right, Ethan suggested, and I nodded my agreement, fell into step beside him.

The square was one block over, with ornate streetlamps and reaching trees around the edge, the remains of a gazebo now a tinder pile in the middle. On the other side of the gazebo was a small stream topped by a wooden bridge, the water still gurgling merrily after all these years. I wondered if it, too, had been spoiled by the chemical release.

The houses might have been empty, or seemingly so, but there was visible activity here—flickering lights in some of the narrow buildings that surrounded the square. Candles, I guessed, unless the users had brought their own generators.

We crept into the square, hiding in the penumbras of trees to stay as invisible as possible. We still hadn't actually seen anyone, but the sense that we were being watched hadn't yet faded.

Ethan stopped and glanced up at the building across the street.

It was a slim, three-story building. The windows had been painted black, but slivers of light shone through the glass where the color had been scraped away. LA DOULEUR was painted in gold letters across the sidewalk in front of it.

Well, well, Ethan said.

La Douleur, I said. *That's French for "pain."*

La Douleur is a supernatural bordello that caters to a very particular audience. Sex is one of the tamer things on the menu. It must have moved; it had been in Little Italy.

I slid my gaze to him. *And you're familiar with this particular supernatural bordello with "pain" in its name?*

I'm Master of my House, and I've been in Chicago for many, many years. It behooves me to be aware of my vampires' surroundings.

Mm-hmm, I said noncommittally, but was secretly intrigued. If

Ethan was familiar with a place like La Douleur, I wondered what else he'd "mastered" before we met.

His eyebrows lifted. *Are you implying something?*

I smiled slyly at him. *Not at all. At a more appropriate time, however, I will be questioning you about the depth of your knowledge of La Douleur.* For now, we were on an op and need to stay focused. *There's magic in the neighborhood,* I said. *A supernatural bordello might be the type of place a sorcerer would enjoy.*

Ethan narrowed his eyes at me, probably skeptical that I was really changing the focus. But I was. For now.

Yes, it does, he finally agreed, and we surveyed the building.

They'll recognize us if we just walk in, I said. There were probably few supernaturals in Chicago who wouldn't have recognized Ethan as the Master of Cadogan House. And my photograph in the *Tribune* wouldn't have helped, either.

Likely. Although . . . , he added, and glanced at me, giving me an up-and-down appraisal. I wasn't sure I'd like whatever he had in mind.

"Although" what?

I can use glamour.

Glamour was the classic vampiric power, a way of inducing someone else to do or see what you intended. You couldn't convince someone to do something they wouldn't otherwise do, but you could encourage them to see things your way. Glamour was, to my mind, one of the primary reasons vampires had been feared throughout history—because they could unlock a human's deepest desires.

I'd initially had immunity to glamour. Faux Balthasar had managed to knock that loose. Like a hound toying with its prey, he'd terrorized me with my newfound sensitivity.

I'd lost that defense, but I'd gained something, too. Glamour was part of the intimate psychic connection between vampires, and something Ethan and I hadn't been able to share before. When he was finally able to "call" me, to reach inside with that powerful magic, it had been one of the most stirring experiences of my life.

It had also been one of the few times since Balthasar that I'd come into contact with glamour without panic.

I looked back at Ethan, realized he'd been watching me. Probably working through the same mental gymnastics, and wondering how I'd handle it.

How, exactly, could you do that? I asked him.

He glanced at the building. *I believe I'd create a band of magic around us.*

I didn't know that was possible.

Frankly, I hadn't thought of it before. His gaze narrowed. *The Imposter showed it was possible.*

That was what Ethan had taken to calling Faux Balthasar—the Imposter. He could rot in hell, by whichever name.

Ethan glanced back at me. *Do you think you could handle it?*

Maybe. Maybe not. But I wasn't going to say no. There was too much on the line, and we'd come this far already. *Yes.*

Ethan watched me, brow furrowed as if he was debating whether I was telling him the truth.

All right, he finally said. *If you change your mind, you need only tell me.*

Before I could argue that I wouldn't change my mind, he leaned in and kissed me softly and, with his lips on mine, began to work his magic.

When he'd called me, I felt the pull in my gut, as if he'd reached into my soul and drawn it toward him, tugged on the emotional and biological connection between us. Ethan's magic had been both a comfort . . . and an enticement.

The point of this magic was different—he sought to tie us together in a cloud of glamour that would fool others—but the effect was nearly identical. Desire grew as his magic bloomed and enveloped us, pushing heat through my limbs and filling my body with need, with arousal and desire for him.

I dropped my head to his chest, clenched fingers into his shirt as the magic burned through me. *Ethan.*

You're making this difficult, he said. Even in silence, his voice was hoarse with desire, his body hard with it.

You're making it difficult, I retorted. *It's your magic.*

It's responding to you. His lips fell to my neck, traced a line against the soft skin there, drawing goose bumps along my arms.

Maybe this is a bad idea, I said, tilting my head to give him better access. *We won't be able to get anything done if we can't keep our hands off each other.*

Considering where we're going, I expect we'll fit right in. His lips found mine, his mouth firm and insistent, driving me forward into pleasure, his hands drawing me toward him, closer.

Moved by magic, I slid my hands into his hair. If only we weren't standing in a creepily abandoned park, in an even creepier abandoned neighborhood, and on the trail of a killer.

Nearly there, Ethan said, and I hoped that wasn't a euphemism. Not that I'd deny him pleasure, but I didn't want to be the only one left wanting.

Suddenly, like tumblers clicking into place, the magic firmed and settled. Relief replaced impatience, and the breeze cooled our heated skin. Still, we didn't move for a full minute.

"I believe that will do it," Ethan whispered, his arms banded around me, his head resting atop mine. "And as for the rest of it . . ."

"Later," I promised.

"Oh, most definitely, Sentinel."

"Did you manage it?"

Ethan squinted into the darkness around us, as if checking the outlines of the zone of magic he'd created. "I believe I did." There was quiet amazement in his voice. Perhaps there'd been some silver lining from the trouble the Imposter had caused.

"What will they see when they look at me?"

"Marilyn Monroe."

His answer was remarkably quick. "I wouldn't have figured you for a Marilyn type."

"I'm joking. I haven't changed your appearance. Merely softened it so you're unrecognizable."

"These are not the vampires you're looking for."

Ethan just looked at me. "I don't know what that means."

"For a man we call Darth Sullivan, you know surprisingly little about *Star Wars*."

"I don't know why I'd need to."

"Yeah, that's part of the problem."

"At any rate," Ethan said, a little bit testily, "they'll know you're female and that you're with me. They won't know you have a weapon, but to be safe, try not to bring unnecessary attention to it. Unless, of course, I have to drop the glamour. In which case, be prepared to fight."

I smiled at him. "I'm always prepared."

"That's my girl," he said with no little pride. "And while it will go against every instinct in your body, you'll need to pretend to be biddable."

"Biddable?" Every syllable of the word left a bad taste.

At least he looked marginally apologetic. "It will be expected," he said, "and we'll attract less unwanted attention that way."

"Why can't you play biddable?"

His smile was pure Sullivan. "Because I'm the Master."

I supposed I had that coming. "So, to review, you want me to play submissive Marilyn Monroe?"

Ethan paused. "That's a loaded question with several appropriate answers."

"Let's focus on the one pertinent to this job."

"You know what I'm asking, and why I'm asking it. And I'd like your word on it, Merit."

I knew why he asked for my promise—not because he doubted me, but because he trusted me. Because he knew if someone threatened him, I'd step in.

"You know what you're asking me to do," I said.

"I do. And that's why I'm asking you, instead of ordering you."

It was a bitter pill to swallow, but I didn't see that I had a choice. I batted my eyelashes, tried to Gratefully Condescend, as archaic vampire *Canon* required of Novitiates. "All right," I said. "Anything else, my lord and Master?"

"Yes. Try not to use that tone."

I couldn't make any promises about that one.

CHAPTER EIGHT

EASY LOVER

There was no bouncer, no line of supernaturals behind a velvet rope. There was only a door, solid and metal.

We walked toward it, Ethan's magic shifting around us as we moved. I was only a secondary recipient of his glamour—he wasn't trying to make me do anything—but I could still feel the breadth of its undulating power. A powerful vampire was Ethan Sullivan.

He rapped on the door with the heel of his hand, two hard strikes. Five seconds passed, and a small panel slid open with the grating sound of metal on metal.

A man's face appeared—pale skin, large eyes, and a flattened nose with a mole at one corner. If he was supernatural, I couldn't tell. At least, not through the door. Other than Ethan's, I couldn't feel any magic at all, and I'd have expected plenty to have seeped from a building full of aroused supernaturals. Maybe the building had been warded.

The man looked at Ethan, then me. "What?"

"*Sésame, ouvre-toi,*" Ethan said in melodious French.

I bit back a smile. The password was literally "open sesame," albeit in French. Supernaturals loved a bad joke.

The doorman's caterpillar-thick unibrow dipped low between his eyes. He bared large teeth. "That's an old password."

His tone threatened a violent response, and I had to stop myself from touching my sword. But I'd given Ethan my word, and I kept my composure.

Ethan managed a tone of mild boredom. "It's an old password because I'm an old client. I'm not going to explain myself to you. Get approval if you must, but open the door or I'll do it myself."

The bouncer stared at us for another ten seconds before slamming the grate closed again.

An old client? I repeated. *Add that to the list of things we'll discuss later.*

I have nothing to hide, Ethan said.

Why did hearing that make me think exactly the opposite?

It took a full minute before the door was wrenched open. We joined the bouncer in a box of a room barely large enough to fit the three of us.

The bouncer slammed the front door shut, which made the urge to grab my katana even stronger. No time for that now. We were in, and we were committed.

When the exterior door locked, the door on the opposite side of the room opened with a *click*, revealing a long hallway with oak floors, pale yellow walls, and a dozen more doors. Each door was wooden and unremarkable and looked exactly the same.

And we've officially gone through the looking glass, I said silently.

You might reserve that judgment, until we're actually in there, Ethan suggested.

Right on cue, a door on the right side of the hallway opened, and magic flowed out like water. More evidence, I thought, that the building had been warded, and that a sorcerer was at work in the neighborhood.

A vampire stepped into the hallway. Tall, thin, with remarkably pale skin. He wore an old-fashioned tux, spats, and white kid gloves fastened with pearl buttons.

"This way, sir," the vampire said in a crisp English accent, bowing slightly as he stepped back from the door and motioned us inside.

And away we go, Sentinel.

We walked inside.

When I thought "supernatural bordello," I imagined hunky elfish guys in tight leather pants with white hair and pointed ears, vampy women with corsets and long nails, their eyes silvered with lust and emotion. I always imagined anything with vampires would be heavy on Goth, lace, and candles, but it never was. I'd been in all three of the city's Houses—Cadogan, Navarre, and Grey—and I didn't think I'd seen anything mildly gothic in any of them.

There also wasn't anything gothic in here.

The large room, lit by wavering hurricane lamps, had wooden floors that were covered with expensive rugs and groupings of large leather furniture outlined with brass tacks. There were two walls of floor-to-ceiling bookshelves stacked with leather and gilt volumes. The room smelled of leather and fragrant smoke.

It took me a moment to realize what I was supposed to be seeing—an English gentlemen's club, or La Douleur's version of it.

There were, at my guess, a dozen supernaturals, mostly men. I looked for familiar faces first—Reed or his cronies, supernaturals I knew, the bearded vampire who'd killed Caleb Franklin. No one looked familiar. But they did look as old-fashioned as their surroundings. They'd adopted the dress, Victorian suits or dresses with pinched waists and high necks. They generally sat in couples or groups, chatting, kissing, or sharing blood.

We followed the would-be butler, who escorted us to a high-backed settee and gestured to it. "Please."

Sit at my feet, Ethan said, before I could move.

He must have felt my hesitation.

It is part of the illusion, of the theme of this particular room. Remember your word.

Since I'd given it, I bit back a sneer and sank to the floor at the edge of Ethan's chair as graciously as possible.

He stroked a hand over my head. "Very good," he said, signaling to the room that I'd pleased him.

I'd learned to bluff a long time ago, and if ever there'd been a time to use the skill, this was it. Dutifully, I rested my cheek on his knee.

"What may I obtain for you, sir?" the butler asked.

"Cognac, for the moment. We'll see how well my pet behaves."

I began to make very specific plans for Ethan's quid pro quo. If I had to sit at Ethan's feet, he'd damn well better be prepared to sit at mine.

The butler nodded, walked to a brass cart, poured liquid from a cut-crystal decanter. He brought it back to Ethan and then began checking with the other sups.

Do you recognize anyone? Ethan asked.

I trailed my fingers up and down his leg. *I don't. I count several vampires and shifters, but no sorcerers.*

Caleb Franklin's killer?

I looked them over. None had a beard, although that could have been removed easily enough. But the killer had also been tall and well muscled, and none of the vampires here seemed to have the right proportions, Ethan excluded.

I don't see him, I said.

Me, neither.

But there'd been other doors in the hallway. *There are other rooms? Themes?*

Yes. All varied in the degree of their explicitness.

Do any of them have black lace and candles?

Goth, Sentinel? Really?

Someday, I was going to wander into a lair of *Underworld* look-alikes and my prejudice would be rewarded. Until then, *Is there any way we can get to them? Inspect them?*

Likely not without a fight.

I have no objection to a good fight. Especially since I'd come out on the losing end of my last one.

The butler carried a drink to a female vamp with pale skin and long, dark curls. She wore a scarlet bustier and a fluid skirt in a matching fabric, her lithe form draped across a chaise longue. A male vampire, naked but for his spill of long, dark hair and snug, hip-hugging leather pants, stood like a statue behind her. He stared at nothing in particular, seemingly waiting for her command.

There were bruises across his face, across his collarbone.

The butler spoke quietly to the woman, but she shook her head, waved him away.

Across the room, a slender man in a three-piece suit, a fedora pulled low over his head and a slim leather book in hand, lifted his hand to signal for service. The butler moved to him, bent slightly at the man's words, then nodded, disappeared from the room.

Neither of them had looked at us, so it didn't seem likely that had been a signal about us. But one could never be too careful.

Fedora, two o'clock, I told Ethan, nipping lightly at the fingers he brushed against my cheek.

I'm watching, Ethan said.

I turned my attention to the rest of the room, searching for magic, a forgotten alchemical symbol, some hint of that metallic magic. But there was nothing. Just the prickly air of excitement, of sensual anticipation. Considering the number of vampires in the room, I presumed there would be blood.

I looked up at Ethan, working my features into an expression of total adoration. *If this is the appetizer, what's the main course?*

Ethan sipped at his cognac, kept a hand on my hair, stroking, his eyes on the room. The hallway door opened, and the butler escorted a young man inside. He was tall and leanly built, with dark skin and hair in short braids. He wore black slacks and a white button-down shirt, and his eyes glimmered with excitement.

I believe he would be the entrée, Ethan said.

Two female vampires with tan skin, high cheekbones, and straight hair pulled into high knots rose together from a sofa with an ornate back. They wore black silk dresses that snugged their bodies to midcalf, where the fabric pooled around their bare feet as they walked toward the young man. They were beautiful, and the man stared at them with obvious desire.

They took his hands, guided him toward a round, tufted ottoman in the middle of the room. They unfastened the buttons on his shirt, let it fall to the floor.

His neck and arms were dotted with scars, which the women caressed and flicked with eager tongues. It wasn't hard to guess the scars' origins; he'd given blood before, many times.

As the women lowered the donor to the ottoman, the butler appeared at our side. "If you'd come with me?"

Ethan kept his eyes on the ottoman. "And why would I want to do that?"

"Because Cyrius wishes to have a word with you."

Ethan rolled his eyes, playing at a man unaccustomed to being beckoned, which wasn't much of a stretch. But I caught the tightening of his jaw.

"I'm trying to relax, and I don't know who Cyrius is. If he wants to speak with me, he can do so here."

Trouble?

Cyrius runs La Douleur, Ethan said. *I've not met him, but I know his name.*

Another vampire entered the room—an enormous woman with freckles, brown hair, and silvered eyes that were focused on us. A katana in a lacquered black sheath was belted at her waist, and she probably had five inches and eighty pounds on me.

Good, I thought, as I met her threatening gaze. *That might make us even.*

Steady, now, Sentinel.

I won't move unless I have to, I assured him. But I hoped that I'd have to. Even vampires bored of posturing.

"*Now,*" the butler insisted, all pretense of politeness—and the British accent—gone. "Or we do this here."

Ethan rolled his eyes. "This was once an establishment of some gentility." But he put aside his drink, rose, held up a hand for me.

I nodded, rose obediently, and followed Ethan and the butler to the door where the vampire waited. When I looked back, the vampires had descended on the man on the ottoman, and the scent of blood rose in the air.

The man in the fedora was gone.

We were marched into the hallway again, then through the open door at the far end into an enormous concrete room, probably a dock for the store that had once filled the slip. A rolling overhead door was open, letting in an astringent, chemical breeze.

There was a desk in the middle of the space piled with papers, and white cardboard file boxes lined the walls, some bursting with paper.

"Excuse the mess." A man emerged from columns of boxes. A human of medium height, with pale skin, a round belly that hung over camouflage pants, and a gleaming head bounded by a perfect semicircle of dark hair. "We moved recently. Still organizing our inventory and whatnot."

Ethan and I didn't respond, but we watched him walk to the desk, pull out an army green chair, and take a seat. It creaked with his formidable weight.

He linked his hands on the table, looked up at us. His eyes were gray, and they narrowed as they took us in.

"Let's start at the beginning," he said. "You're Ethan and, whatsit, Merit? From Cadogan House? Glamour don't work on me," he explained, "which makes me perfect for this job."

So our cover was blown, and thank God for it. Playing meek was absolutely exhausting.

Ethan let the glamour slowly dissolve and flutter away. I rolled my shoulders with relief. The magic might not have had mass, but it still weighed heavily on my psyche.

I felt the vampire move closer, and I slipped a hand to my katana. The feel of the corded handle beneath my fingers was comforting.

"I wouldn't, if I were you," he said, gesturing to the vampire behind us. "She's very good with that steel."

There were many ways to bluff. You could preen and exaggerate your strengths, or you could let others believe you were less than you were. I opted for the latter, and managed to stir up a worried glance as I looked at the vampire over my shoulder.

She unsheathed her katana and smiled at me, lifting her chin defiantly. The steel of her sword was smeared and cloudy. She hadn't cleaned it recently. Catcher, who'd given me the sword I carried, would have my ass in a sling for that.

I swallowed heavily, playing up my fear, then looked back at the man again. He looked very pleased.

"I'm afraid you have us at a disadvantage," Ethan said, understanding exactly the game to be played. "I take it you're Cyrius?"

"Cyrius Lore. I manage this club."

"For who?"

"For whoever the fuck I want. It's no business of yours. The fact is, you came into my club with an old password. I don't like interlopers in my club."

"Surprising, since you'll allow virtually anything else."

Ethan's words were slow and dangerous, but Cyrius snorted. "You think I'm intimidated by you because you're head of some vamp house? No. I manage a club; you manage a club. That makes us equals, far as I'm concerned."

"I don't allow my vampires to harm innocents in my 'club.'"

Cyrius held up his hands defensively. "What happens among consenting adults is their business, not mine. I don't police what happens here."

I didn't buy that everyone here was consenting, or that Cyrius didn't know exactly what went on in his club.

But that was irrelevant, because he'd just shown us the only bit of business that mattered. On the inside of his right forearm was a forest green tattoo—an ouroboros, an old and circular symbol made up of a snake eating its tail.

It was the symbol of the Circle . . . and therefore of Adrien Reed.

Son of a bitch. *Cyrius's ink,* I said to Ethan, and watched his gaze slip discreetly from Cyrius's face to the symbol on his arm.

Cyrius Lore managed La Douleur, and the Circle managed Cyrius Lore. If we were right about the alchemical symbols, this was part of the sorcerer's territory. We had a link between Adrian Reed and the sorcerer, the alchemy. Reed's sorcerer and the alchemy sorcerer weren't two different people. They were one and the same, part of his criminal organization. I wasn't sure if that made me feel better or worse.

And once again, it raised questions about Caleb Franklin. Had he known about the Circle? About Reed?

Probably sensing our magic, Cyrius nodded and the vamp stepped closer, unsheathed her katana with a dull whistle of sound. I'd bet the edge was dull, too. She really needed to take better care of her blade.

She stepped forward, put the blade against my neck.

Maybe it was the place, maybe it was Reed. Maybe it was the residual effect of Ethan's magic. Whatever the reason, my blood began to hum beneath the cold steel, aching to fight. Ethan tensed with concern, but my adrenaline was already flowing.

Focus on him, I said silently. *She's mine.*

"Now," Cyrius said. "Why don't you tell me why the fuck you're in my place when you weren't invited?"

"We want information about Caleb Franklin."

Cyrius frowned, which didn't do his mug any favors. "The fuck is Caleb Franklin?"

"A shifter under the protection of Gabriel Keene," Ethan said. Not entirely the truth, given the defection, but true enough for our purposes. "He's dead."

"I don't know shit about him or who killed him."

"He lived nearby," Ethan said.

"We're in Chicagoland. Few million people live nearby. I know nothing about him, which means you've wasted your time and mine." Ugly or not, Cyrius's face didn't show any hint he was lying. Maybe he was just a good liar.

But the vampire was another matter. I didn't need to see her face to know she had knowledge; the fizz of magic in the air was enough.

"What makes you think you have the right to walk into my place, disrupt my club, and ask me questions about anything?"

The vampire adjusted her position. Her sword was still at my neck, but she'd moved closer to Ethan, and her eyes were on him. In lust, in fascination, in hope. Maybe she had a crush on our photogenic Master. I could probably use that. And considering the current position of her sword, wouldn't feel bad about exploiting it.

"I had the password," Ethan said drolly.

"Your password is garbage." Cyrius linked his hands on the table. "You know the penalty for trespassing?"

Ethan's gaze flicked to the tattoo, up again. "For trespassing on Reed's land, you mean?"

Cyrius shifted his arm to hide his ink, and his face went beet red. Maybe because of anger he'd been challenged, but more likely because of fear. Reed wouldn't be happy that we'd discovered his bordello.

He offered a mirthless laugh, full of false confidence. "You don't know shit about shit. But you just wrote your ticket out of here in a body bag."

It was the kind of lead-in I'd probably heard a dozen times. The prelude to a command of violence to be meted out by someone else, by their weapon and their sweat.

And I was ready for it.

Cyrius signaled the vampire with a flick of his finger, a death penalty handed down with no effort on his part. I understood he believed us a threat—and he was right about that—but I didn't have respect for people too lazy to fight their own battles.

Duck, I told Ethan, and when the vampire shifted her weight to bring the sword to bear, I moved. I put my hands on the arm of the chair, pushed up my weight, and as Ethan dodged, twisted and kicked. I caught her shoulder, sent her stumbling backward.

Ethan vaulted from his seat, jumped toward Cyrius, who'd pulled open a desk drawer. I caught the glint of metal, felt the buzz of steel in my bones. He had a gun.

Damn it. My arm had only just stopped aching. I did not want to get shot again this week. I'd let Ethan handle that one.

You got him? I asked Ethan.

I've got him. She's yours.

Damn right she was.

I unsheathed my katana as the vampire regained her footing. I could give credit where credit was due: She'd held on to her sword, and was resetting to face me again.

Good. That would make the fight more interesting.

"You should tell me your name," I said, raising my blade so it hovered in the air between us. "I mean, if we're going to fight like this."

She lifted her chin. "Leona."

"Merit," I said.

"I know who you are. The spoiled little rich girl."

There weren't many insults that would hit me dead-on, but that was one of them. I felt the sting, opened my mouth to argue that I wasn't spoiled. And while I was mentally trying to justify my existence, she moved.

She wasn't as fast as me, but she was big, all of it muscle that gave her plenty of power. Smiling, she moved forward, holding the sword aloft the way a knight might have carried a broadsword. She sliced down, the katana whistling by my head as I ducked away.

I'd barely pivoted when she tried another strike. Her arms were long, and she had a lengthy reach. I hopped onto a stack of the file boxes, jumped over the arc of the katana she swung at my feet. That made three strikes in a row for her, whereas I hadn't managed one since my initial kick.

I considered using that as strategy—letting her wear herself out while I tried to stay in front of her. But that wouldn't be much fun.

I bounced up and flipped over her head, spun my katana horizontal, and sliced across her torso. The blade caught leather, carved right through it, and stripped a line of crimson across pale skin.

She roared with agony and fury, brought the katana's pommel down hard onto the arm I'd injured the night before. Pain jolted through my arm—a needle-sharp stab surrounded by a column of deep, dull ache. Tears sprang to my eyes, an involuntary reaction, and my knees went wobbly.

"Little rich girl," she said, fairly singing it as I groped for the nearest column of boxes, tried to keep myself upright while my brain struggled back against pain.

Sentinel?

I'm fine, I said, risking a glance at him and Cyrius. Ethan had gotten the gun away; it was tucked into his jeans. But Cyrius had found a pearl-handled knife and was thrusting it toward Ethan.

You could use the gun on him, I pointed out.

How dull that would be, Ethan said, dodging a thrust. *You need help?*

That question was enough to have me rolling my shoulder, demanding my brain ignore the pain. I adjusted my fingers around the katana's handle.

"It's my father's money," I said. "Not mine."

"Like it matters. All you Housed vampires are the same. You think you're better than everyone else."

This time, I wasn't going to wait for her to nail me again. I took the offensive, moving forward, setting the pace and driving her back. I sliced horizontally, and she met my sword, blade against blade, the strike of steel against steel *clanging* through the air. I struck again, switching up my positions and direction.

Leona was bigger than me. I wouldn't beat her with sheer strength, and maybe not with stamina. But I was faster and better trained, and could probably force her into a bad move.

"You know," I said, "Reed's got plenty of money, too. It doesn't make sense you hate me, but work for him."

Leona scoffed, spittle at the corners of her mouth as she worked to counter my strikes. "I don't work for Adrien Reed. He's a *businessman*."

She used the world like a shield. "Yeah, keep saying that if it eases your conscience. But you know it's only half right." I switched up my attack, went for my favorite shot—a side kick that she batted away with an enormous hand. She tried to grab my ankle, but I cleared her, then spun and brought the katana around again.

Another clang of metal against metal. The sound made my teeth ache and my chest tighten with concern. The katana's cutting edge was sharp, hard steel. It was designed to slice and too brittle for prolonged blade-on-blade strikes.

Another overhead strike—one of her favorites. This time, I spun the blade in my hand to raise the spine, which was less brittle, into the blow to protect the sword's integrity. I still had to deal with Catcher, after all.

The woman had power, and the shock of impact passed through me like one of Mr. Leeds's concussions. But it must have passed through her, too. When she raised the sword again, her muscles quivered with effort.

We'd reached the desk again, and I jumped onto one of the chairs, then over it, putting space between us.

She kicked the chair out of the way, stalked forward, spinning the katana in her hand.

"Did you know who killed Caleb Franklin?" I asked her.

"No," she said, but the answer was belied by her fumble with the katana.

"Was he murdered to protect the alchemy?" Or given what we'd learned tonight, "Or to protect Reed?"

That was enough to have her lunging forward, the sword raised again.

Leona might not have been as good at bluffing as Cyrius was, but she was a hell of a lot braver and probably more loyal. I wasn't sure I'd actually be able to get any information out of her.

Darling?

Ethan's question, polite and casually curious, had me biting back a smile. He might as well have asked when I'd be home for dinner.

In front of me, Leona swayed side to side, shifting her body weight as she prepared to move. She looked tired, and I'd managed to get in a couple of deeper cuts. They'd heal, but use precious resources in the meantime.

Nearly done, I said, and glanced left, as if accidentally signaling my next move.

She took the bait, dodging left. I spun into a low kick and this time nailed my target. I kicked her legs out from under her. She hit the floor hard enough to make the building shake, her head bouncing once against concrete, her eyes rolling back.

I snatched up her katana, pointed both swords at her. Her chest rose and fell slowly. She was out cold.

My enemy vanquished, I glanced back at Ethan, found him standing over Cyrius. This time, Ethan had both the gun and the dagger. Cyrius sat on the floor, legs splayed in front of him, holding his arm at an awkward angle. Ethan looked healthy enough.

I walked to Cyrius's desk, pulled open a drawer, found exactly what I'd expected to find: a pair of silver handcuffs.

It seemed likely I'd find some in a place dedicated to kink. But I decided not to think too carefully about how they'd been used before.

I walked back to Leona, pulled her hands in front of her, and cuffed her. She was too heavy to flip over; besides, I planned to be long gone before she woke.

"He answer your questions?" I asked, when I'd blown the bangs out of my eyes and walked back to Ethan.

"He did not."

I grinned predatorily at Cyrius. "Can I have him?"

"No!" Cyrius said, which made Ethan grin.

"Not yet, Sentinel. Let's see, first, if he'll identify our murderer. Cyrius?"

When the man didn't answer, I knelt in front of him, rested my elbows on my knees. "He asked you a question. Answer him, or he'll give you to me. And you don't want that."

"That good-cop, bad-cop shit don't work on me," Cyrius said. But beads of sweat had popped across his forehead, and the words seemed to stick in his throat.

Ethan kept his expression mild. "You don't get it, Cyrius. We're *both* bad cops." He held up the weapons he'd confiscated from Cyrius, gestured toward my swords. "Tell me about Reed."

"He'll kill me."

"No, he *might* kill you," Ethan said with a terrifying smile. "We definitely will."

We wouldn't, of course. Not a man unarmed, who'd been no real threat to us even when he'd been pretending otherwise. But he didn't need to know that.

Cyrius wet his lips.

"You only get one chance to answer," I warned him, patting his knee collegially before I rose again. "So choose that answer carefully."

"He's right," Cyrius muttered, wiping his face with the forearm of his uninjured hand. "You're monsters. No better than anyone else. He'll fix it. He'll fix all this. Bring some goddamn order to the world. Make things right again."

Ethan's brows lifted. "Is that the story Reed's been telling you? That if he was dictator, if he ruled Chicago, life would be better for you?"

"He'll clean up the streets."

"He'll continue to *pollute* the streets," Ethan said. "He's a crime lord, for God's sake. He doesn't belong in charge any more than Capone did."

But Cyrius just shook his head. Whatever nonsense Reed had been spouting about his new world order, Lore seemed to earnestly believe it.

I stepped forward again and lifted the point of Leona's katana to his neck.

"Who killed Caleb Franklin?" I asked him.

"I don't know!" Spit accompanied the frantic words. "I don't know."

I pressed incrementally forward, until a droplet of crimson rolled down the blade.

"I don't know!" Cyrius yelled. "I don't know who he is. I've never met him or Franklin. I just know the vamp belongs to Reed."

"And the sorcerer?" Ethan asked.

"I don't know!"

"I'm tired of hearing that answer," I said, adding a little crazy to my voice for impact and digging the point a millimeter deeper.

Cyrius lifted his eyes to Ethan. "Stop her. For Christ's sake, stop her."

Ethan looked unmoved by the pleading. "Why should I? You said we'd leave here in body bags."

Cyrius didn't have a good answer to that. "I swear to God I don't know who the sorcerer is. Just that Reed's got one. We aren't allowed to know. We aren't allowed to get close."

Now, that was interesting. "Why?" I asked, pulling back on the blade, just a little. Cyrius's gaze flicked to me again.

"He's off-limits." He swallowed, now all cooperation. "The sorcerer's got something big planned with Reed. Something really big."

Reed, the alchemy, the sorcerer. All of them part of something bigger. And confirmation, again, of something I didn't really want to discover.

"Is the plan to do with the alchemy?" Ethan asked.

Cyrius's expression seemed genuinely blank. "The fuck is alchemy?"

Ethan shook off the question. "What big thing does he have planned?"

"I don't know. I just know we aren't supposed to bother him with mundane shit. Not right now. Not while he's focused."

Ethan considered the answer for a moment, then crouched down in front of Cyrius. "I'm going to do you a favor, Cyrius Lore. Before I call the CPD, I'm going to give you time to get out of here." He took Cyrius's chin in his hand. "Tell him what happened here tonight. And tell him we're coming for him."

"He'll kill me."

"You lie down with dogs," Ethan said, rising again, "you risk a bite." He looked back at me. "Let's get the hell out of here, Sentinel."

When we stepped into the hallway again, La Douleur was in chaos. They'd either heard the fight or word had traveled. Doors were open, sups in costume—black latex, sexy nurse, eighteenth-century French aristocracy (which was so very vampire)—hustling toward the front door and the cover of darkness. I felt momentarily bad about interrupting consensual activities, but that guilt was erased when a woman with bruised eyes, tears streaming down her face, pushed through the crowd to the door.

We stepped into darkness with the rest of them, threw into the stream the weapons we'd confiscated. And, like the rest of the supernaturals hurrying out of the club, we disappeared into the night.

Chapter Nine

SHAKE IT OFF

Gabriel had left us a message advising that most of the shifters had dispersed, and inviting us to stop by Little Red.

We'd get there, but first we had more immediate concerns—namely, my ravenous hunger. It felt like there were gears in my abdomen grinding angrily against one another. I was dizzy, lightheaded, and aching with need.

That I ached with other needs, too, would have to wait for a more opportune moment.

Super Thai was a hole in the wall in West Town, not far from Little Red. A tiny woman escorted us to a plastic-lined booth, where I ordered pad Thai. Whatever the fight had done to me, I needed peanuts and noodles, and I needed them now.

I only barely managed to wait until the waitress put the plate in front of me. I mixed peanuts and cilantro into noodles, doused my food with chili sauce, and dug in.

"I'm sorry," I said when I'd inhaled two enormous forkfuls. "I can't stop myself. I feel like I haven't eaten in a month."

"It might have been my glamour," Ethan said. He'd declined

food, and now watched me like a scientist. "Perhaps because your susceptibility came online late, and you're still adjusting to it."

"That and the fact that I just battled a two-hundred-pound warrior queen with a personal vendetta. But as for the glamour, yeah, that seems to be the way of things."

It was another reason a vampire in the making shouldn't get drugs to ease the process. Ethan had administered them out of guilt that I hadn't been able to consent to my transition because I was bloodied and unconscious at the time.

"Again," Ethan said, and I saw the quick flash of regret in his eyes. Pointless, since he'd saved my life.

"You did what you thought best to save me pain," I said, and saw his expression soften. I paused long enough to drink from the small glass of ice water that had accompanied my food. The hotter the food, the smaller the glass. Why was that?

"How do you want to deal with La Douleur?"

"We'll talk to Luc, add the club to the information we're compiling about the Circle, about Reed."

"We need to tell my grandfather. Make an anonymous report tomorrow, if you want. Give Cyrius time to report back to Reed first. But he's still part of the Circle, and the CPD should know it."

Ethan smiled, lifted his phone. "I submitted an anonymous tip to the CPD via the Web site while you were inspecting the menu. I also sent your grandfather a message, said we wanted to get clear before the CPD came rolling along, just in case."

Relief flowed through me. I didn't want my grandfather walking into a doubly hazardous neighborhood, but neither did I want to hold back information. "Good."

"I mean, I had plenty of time," Ethan snarked. "Between the spring rolls, the curry, and the pad Thai, you gave that menu a thorough inspection."

I made a juvenile face. Ethan's expression sobered. "You saw the woman leaving?"

"The one with the black eyes?"

He nodded. "I wanted to give her a chance to get away. She can report to the CPD if she chooses to, tell them what's happened to her. But that should be her choice, not a decision forced on her by a police raid."

"That was a good call." I plucked a peanut from my plate, crunched it. "Speaking of the CPD, I think they'll find more than they bargain for."

Ethan frowned. "Oh?"

"Let's say, hypothetically, that you previously visited La Douleur. In said hypothetical visits, did you ever see paper exchange hands?"

He smiled slyly. "Of course not. No one who visits that particular establishment wants a paper trail."

"Precisely. So why were there so many file boxes in the back room?"

Ethan opened his mouth, closed it again.

"Exactly," I said. "I'd also bet running a criminal empire requires plenty of paper. Even if Reed's gone digital now, he'd still have decades of paper. Hell, the tax evasion alone would require boxes of it. And where better to stash it than a neighborhood too polluted to visit?"

Ethan smiled warmly. "My, my, Sentinel. We might have to increase your stipend."

Every Cadogan Novitiate received a stipend for their contributions to the House. I didn't really need the money—not with the Master's apartments and a Margot to boot. But I appreciated the approbation.

"I'm sure you can think of a more interesting reward for a job well done. Or a clue well located." I speared a chunk of fried egg. "We put the CPD onto Cyrius Lore and La Douleur, and we're one step closer to bringing down Adrien Reed." I looked up at Ethan. "He's going to be pissed about that. He's also going to know that we know about Hellriver and La Douleur, that the alchemy and sorcerer are his, that he's responsible for Caleb Franklin's death, and that he has something big planned."

"Perhaps," Ethan said. "Although I wouldn't put it past Cyrius to avoid telling him, take whatever emergency cache he's squirreled away and leave town. He doesn't seem like the brave type. Either way, Reed will know we are on his path, and not afraid to get our hands dirty. I think that's a fairly good play."

"It's a good start," I agreed. Bringing down an enormous criminal organization was going to take a lot more than that.

"It's been a good night for you," Ethan said warmly. "You found a necromancer, kicked some fairly significant ass, and discovered some very good information."

I mimicked a microphone drop.

Surprising no one, Ethan didn't get it.

"If you keep me in Thai food, I'll try to come up with more good information."

"Let's start with the one plate, Nancy Drew, and see where it goes from there."

Little Red took up a corner in Ukrainian Village and was bounded by an alley on the other side. The walls were brick, and the front featured an enormous plate-glass window beneath a glowing sign.

When Ethan opened the door, the scents of meat, cigar smoke, and beer wafted out. The linoleum was dark, warped, and worn, the walls were dingy, and the tables were uneven, with wads of napkin stuck beneath too-short legs. It looked the same as it had the last time I'd been there; it was good to know some things didn't change.

Shifters sat at the tables, talking quietly, drinking beer, playing cards, and sending us distrustful looks as we walked across the room. We'd worked hard to make allies of the North American Central Pack. Yes, the shifters were in mourning and entitled to their feelings. I just wished they hadn't been so negatively directed at us.

Chin up, Ethan soothed as we made our way to the bar, where a short woman with bottle-bleached hair flipped through a magazine.

She looked up, gave us a once-over, and slapped the cover of the magazine closed with a powerful *thwack* that made some of the shifters sit up and take notice.

Steady, Sentinel, Ethan said.

I could be steady; I was trained for it. I just didn't want to be on the outs with Berna. She was pushy, abrasive, nosy, and had a wonderful hand at grilled meats. I liked her a lot.

"What is this?" she asked, in a voice heavily accented with Eastern Europe. Her eyebrows, slender drawn-on arches, were furrowed with irritation.

"Gabriel asked us to come by," Ethan said.

But Berna dismissed the sentiment with a swat of her hand "No. This." She pointed an arthritic finger back and forth at us. "You must be marry."

"We must be merry?" Ethan asked, obviously confused.

But I understood exactly what she meant.

"We aren't *Twilight*, Berna." She had a thing for the books, and seemed to think—or maybe hope—that Chicago's vampires had something in common with the fictional ones.

She made a *pfff*ing sound. "Vampires. Sparkle. If you are in love, you marry. This is life. This is way."

"Ah," Ethan said, his lips spreading with amusement. "I do intend to make an honest woman of her."

Berna snorted, held out a hand, waggled her fingers. I put my hand in hers, thinking she meant to check me for a ring, proof of Ethan's promise. Instead she flipped my hand over, traced a cracked and calloused thumb over my palm as she inspected it like a jeweler checking for flaws.

"Good line of life. Good line of love. There is no problem here." She turned my hand over again, patted it with affection. "You are good girl. Skinny, but good girl."

"She was a dancer, you know."

Berna looked over at Ethan, her eyebrows arching so high they nearly disappeared into her hair. "Oh?"

"She danced ballet for many years."

Berna looked me up and down, seemed to reach a new kind of acceptance of my frame. Not that I needed Berna's approval—my body was my body—but at least I wouldn't have to hear about it anymore.

"Ah," she said with a nod. "You know Bronislava Nijinska?"

I smiled. "I do. I've seen video of her dancing. She was very beautiful."

"She is epitome of beauty. That is the word? Epitome?"

"That's the word," I agreed with a smile.

"Good. She is this." Her measuring stick reconfigured, she looked me up and down. "You still dance."

"Informally," I said. "I train, and sometimes that means dancing."

"Mmm-hmm. I know teacher."

"I don't need a teacher."

She just lifted her sketched-on eyebrows. Berna wasn't a woman who took no for an answer.

"Vampires don't have time for ballet," I insisted.

"Vampires immortal. Vampires have time for all things, including dance."

She's got you there, Ethan said. *I'd love to watch you dance again.*

There is not enough money in the world to get me into toe shoes, I decided. I'd tortured my feet enough. Not that taking bullets was much of an improvement.

Clearly disappointed, Berna pointed to the padded leather door that led to the bar's back room. "Gabriel in back. You can go," she said, without so much as an offer of cabbage rolls or stewed meats.

I didn't want Berna angry at me. "I could probably practice more," I said, a peace offering.

She nodded. "Good. You practice, and we will talk."

That would have to do for now.

Little Red's back room was small but surprisingly cheery. There was a retro table that seated four, mismatched chairs on top of more warped linoleum, and old movie posters on the walls. Gabriel sat at the table with Fallon and a couple of male shifters I hadn't seen before. One had sunburned skin, bleached hair. The other had dark skin and straight, dark hair that was slicked back on top, shaved on the sides.

Gabriel looked at us, nodded. The other shifters must have taken that as their cue to exit, as they rose and disappeared into the bar.

"What's in the bag?" Gabriel asked.

Ethan slipped out the bottle, passed it over.

"GlenDronach," Gabe said, in what sounded to my ear like a pretty good Gaelic accent.

Ethan nodded. "A token in sympathy of Caleb Franklin's death."

"Thank you. We'll toast him with this."

Ethan inclined his head.

"You two hungry?"

Ethan glanced at me.

"Oh, that's a joke that never gets old," I said. In fact, my metabolism was a diesel engine; it rarely stopped running. But even I didn't think it was wise to pile rich Eastern European fare atop spicy Thai.

"No, thank you."

Gabriel's eyebrows lifted in surprise. "Well. Not an answer I'd have ever expected from you." He wiggled the bottle. "In that unusual case, how about a drink?"

"I wouldn't say no to that," Ethan said.

"Me, neither," I said.

Gabriel nodded, rose. There was a small refrigerator in a corner of the room beside a skinny rattan cabinet. Gabriel pulled out three glasses and brought them back, then poured a finger of Glen-Dronach for each of us.

"You find Franklin's house?" Gabe asked.

"We did," Ethan said, accepting the glass with a nod. "No one was there, and there weren't many personal effects as far as we could tell. A few pieces of furniture, probably came with the house, a few articles of clothing. No vehicle, no paper. Plenty of food in the fridge and freezer, so he was definitely staying there. We didn't find anything that indicated why he'd ended up dead."

All that was entirely correct, if not the entire truth. Ethan didn't mention the cashbox we'd found or the key. He must have had a reason for the omission, even if he hadn't shared it with me.

I took a sip, let whiskey burn down my throat. It was strong, but smoky and smooth.

Gabriel nodded his head back and forth, back and forth, as if considering the information, debating whether we told the entire truth. Or maybe that was just my conscience talking.

"Have you learned anything?" Ethan asked.

"Not really. There are a couple of shifters he's stayed in contact with, but they haven't seen him in several weeks."

Because he was involved in something big, I suspected.

"I managed to get the address, and that's it. They knew it by sight, but neither had been in. Caleb kept to himself."

Ethan nodded. "You mentioned Franklin's neighborhood was

at the edge of Hellriver. La Douleur has relocated there. We paid it a visit."

Gabriel's eyes lifted to Ethan, then me. "Now, that's a side of you I didn't expect to see, Kitten."

"And you never will see it," Ethan said with a mirthless smile, then glanced at me. "Would you mind showing him the tattoo?"

I nodded, pulled up the picture of Cyrius's ouroboros I'd snapped before we left, passed it to Gabriel.

"The Circle controls the Hellriver," Ethan said, "and Reed controls the Circle. Therefore, Reed controls Hellriver. It also appears Reed owned the vampire who killed your shifter."

Gabriel's expression tightened. But I wouldn't say he looked especially surprised.

"Would you like to tell us why you don't look at all shocked to learn this? And perhaps, while you're at it, why don't you tell us the truth about Caleb Franklin and why he left the Pack?" Ethan's words were carefully strung and mildly threatening.

In silence, Gabriel finished his whiskey and poured another finger, but didn't offer one to me or Ethan. He pivoted sideways in the chair, pulled out the chair beside it, and crossed his ankles over the empty seat. Free arm on the table, the other holding his glass.

I wasn't sure if we were watching him prepare to tell us a story or give us a dressing-down. Either way, he was setting the scene for something.

"Caleb Franklin was my half brother," Gabriel said.

That explained why Gabriel had nearly come to blows over a man who'd voluntarily abandoned the Pack. On the other hand, Gabriel was the oldest of the Keene siblings, who were named in reverse alphabetical order—Gabriel, Fallon, Eli, and so on. There was no "Caleb" in that list. Caleb's relationship with the Keene family must have had its own complications.

"Which side?" Ethan asked.

"My father's. He was unfaithful to my mother. Caleb Franklin was the result of it. My mother was a kind woman, but she drew the line at acknowledging my father's infidelity. So Caleb Franklin was a member of the Pack, but considered a bastard.

"My mother was adamant, so I didn't know him growing up. I learned about him later, met him later. He definitely had a chip on his shoulder. Hell, I'd have had one, too, under the circumstances. It certainly changed my perception of the old man."

Gabriel finished his whiskey. "Caleb came to me about two years ago. He'd gotten an opportunity—that's what he called it: an opportunity—to do some high-value, if questionable, work for a human. Not a big deal, he'd said. Just a contract. I said no. Humans didn't know about us then, and I gauged it too risky. The little shit did it anyway, and that was, of course, just the beginning.

"About a year ago, he was making a run of contraband, invited Eli to come along. Eli had no idea what Caleb was running, and they both got caught. They both ended up doing time for it. I was pissed. I confronted Caleb, reminded him that I'd given him an order. I could tell he was scared, and I thought, in the moment, that he'd been scared of me."

Gabriel put his glass on the table again, and silence fell over the room. And even with the door closed, I'd have sworn every movement in the bar outside had stopped, too, that all eyes were on the closed door and the magic that was beginning to rise within it.

"Caleb wasn't scared of me. He was scared of the people he'd been working for." Gabriel lifted his gaze to Ethan's. "They called themselves the Circle."

Ethan went very still, and this time it was vampire magic that lifted into the air.

"He'd been running contraband for them—drugs, weapons, and occasionally people, from Texas to Chicago." Gabe traced a finger across the table like the route on an invisible map. "I gave

Caleb two options: Leave the Circle and accept my punishment, or defect and lose all claim to the Pack."

"Adam was your brother, too," I said. "He betrayed you, and he wasn't allowed to live."

"Adam was responsible for the deaths of shifters; Caleb wasn't. Maybe I should have taken him out. But he had a hard run of it. Was in a shitty position. Had no claim to a throne he probably had some right to, even if a small one. Maybe that would have been enough to keep him on the straight and narrow. Or maybe he was just a bad seed. I don't know."

"He made his own choices," I said.

"We all do that," Gabriel said.

"So Franklin defected," Ethan said. "He picked the Circle. Why?"

"Because soldiers didn't leave the Circle unless they go out in a body bag. Because the man who controls the Circle is merciless."

Ethan's eyes had gone silver and cold and hard as steel, just like the words that punched through the air.

"You knew Reed controlled the Circle. You knew, and despite all the shit we've gone through in the last few weeks, the work we put in to proving that connection, you didn't lift a finger to help."

Gabriel's jaw stiffened, as did his bulky shoulders. Very slowly, he slid a glance to Ethan. "You'll want to watch your tone in my place."

Ethan was unmoved. "Fuck your place. Navarre is in financial shambles. Merit was stalked. My House was threatened. All because it took time for us to prove that connection."

Gabriel linked his hands over the table, leaned his chest over it, toward Ethan. "You think you're the only sup in this city allowed to take care of his own? You think your House is more important than any other family in this city? Then you've got it wrong. You got the information you needed. You didn't need me to volunteer it."

"You didn't want the Circle's eyes on you," I put in.

Gabriel slid his gaze to me. "Like I said, I protect my own."

"Your place or not, Keene, you are a son of a bitch." Ethan rose, chair scraping across the floor.

I heard similar movements from the bar, wished I'd brought my sword inside. I hadn't expected things to turn in this particular direction.

"That's rich coming from you, Sullivan. Every war creates victims. You know it as well as I do. We stayed here, in Chicago, instead of going back to Aurora. That doesn't mean I'm going to let a human piece of shit like Adrien Reed use my people against each other."

I could see the war in Ethan's eyes—his desire to slap Gabriel back for putting us in danger, for holding back crucial information, matched against his need to preserve whatever alliance remained between Cadogan and the NAC.

"We are allies," Ethan said, the words slashing the air like the sharpened blade of a katana. "Or so I was led to believe."

"My brother is dead," Gabriel gritted out, rising to stand over the table, his fingers still splayed across it. "Which proves this asshole is as dangerous as I imagined him to be. And he was killed by a vampire. You want contrition? Think again."

"What I want is to be able to trust someone in this goddamn town. What I want is for my vampires to have some peace and goddamn quiet. What I want is to not be stabbed in the goddamn back every time I turn around." Ethan reached out and, with a seemingly effortless flick of his hand, tossed a chair across the room.

The door shoved open, and a very large man filled the doorway. A shifter, with thick silver hair and a scar across his left cheek. He ignored me and Ethan, looked immediately to Gabriel—to his Apex.

Gabriel's gaze was on Ethan, and it didn't waver.

For a full minute, they stared at each other.

"Stop! You are stopping!" The words punched through the silence, followed by a rush of Ukrainian as Berna squeezed beneath the tree-trunk arm the shifter had stretched across the doorway.

She had a white bar towel in the hand she used to point at Ethan, then Gabriel. "No fighting here. No fighting. Is rule."

Gabriel's gaze snapped to her. Obviously angry, he muttered something low in Ukrainian. I hadn't heard him speak it before, and it sounded vaguely menacing in his growly and gravelly voice.

If Berna was intimidated, she hid it well. She pitched her head to the left and right, made a spitting sound that I was pretty sure was an insult. And then she leveled that gaze at Ethan.

"You make trouble in our house. Get out now before you make worse." And then she looked at me, flipped her fingers back and forth to shoo us out of the back room. "Both of you. Out. Now."

Ethan took a step toward the door, but glanced back at Gabriel. "We aren't done with this conversation."

Gabriel spread his hands, smiled toothily. "Anytime, Sullivan."

We walked out of the bar, leaving Gabriel Keene in Little Red, and our alliance on a knife's edge.

Chapter Ten

THE DECIDER

Ethan fumed in silence as we walked back to the car and drove back to Hyde Park.

His hands were white-knuckled on the steering wheel, and he pushed the car to the absolute limit. He'd taken surface streets, tested the length of every yellow light between Ukrainian Village and Hyde Park, and had nearly raced a small car with a spoiler off the line at a stoplight. The car's driver looked at the Audi the way a man might look at a beautiful woman—with lust and wanting.

Ethan was still fuming when we pulled into the House's parking garage. He slid the car into its slot, slammed out of the car.

"Would you like to talk before you take that enormous magical chip on your shoulder into the House?"

He turned on me. "Would I like to *talk* about it? Talk about what, precisely, Sentinel? The fact that our 'ally' knew about Reed, knew about his connection to supernaturals, and ignored it?"

"He wasn't an ally at the time—not when Caleb joined Reed."

"He's a goddamn ally now," Ethan said, "and he's been one for months."

"You didn't tell him what we found at Caleb Franklin's house. You didn't tell him about the key."

"And why should I? Caleb Franklin defected, and there's no evidence the key belonged to him or, even if it did, that it has any bearing here."

"So it's all right if you withhold information strategically, but not if he does it?"

I knew I was getting perilously close to insubordination. But that was the point.

"I'm not in the mood for games, Sentinel." Ethan stalked into the House, let the basement door slam behind us. The House seemed to shudder from the impact of anger, magic, and brute force.

He strode down the hall toward the Ops Room, temper flaring. If he wasn't careful, he'd spill that fury out on people who didn't deserve it. Not when it was really about the Pack.

And there were certainly better ways to work out his aggression.

"Actually, I think that's exactly what you're in the mood for." I grabbed his arm and, when he turned back to glower, met his stare head-on.

"Let go of me."

I didn't. "You want to go a round? We're yards away from the training room. If you want to hit something, you can try to hit me."

His eyes narrowed. "Don't push me, Sentinel."

It was too late for that. I'd been with this man for a year, and I knew exactly what buttons to push. "Oh, I'll push you, and I'll probably win. You want an invitation you can't refuse? Fine. Ethan Sullivan, I challenge you."

A single eyebrow arched. "Those are serious words, Sentinel, with serious implications."

"I'm well aware, *Sire*."

Ethan pivoted, strode like a warrior in the heat of battle to the training room, pushed open the doors. It was one of the larger rooms in Cadogan House, with tatami mats across the floor, weapons hanging from the wood-paneled walls, and a balcony ringing the room to allow vampires to watch whatever battle was taking place.

Tonight, there were guards in the room—Luc, Kelley, Brody, and a few of the temps—practicing basic throws and falls. They all looked up in alarm when the door swung open, slammed back against the wall.

"Out!" Ethan bellowed.

The temps jumped. Ever cool, Luc's gaze flicked to me, and I nodded infinitesimally. It was safe for him to leave; I'd handle this. I'd handle Ethan.

"You heard your Sire and Master," Luc said, walking over to pick up a clipboard and his shoes. "Everybody out."

They filed out in silence but didn't bother to hide the curious looks they threw at me, at Ethan. They knew something was wrong; they just didn't know what that was. Let the speculation begin.

When they were gone, Ethan closed the door firmly, locked it, then walked to a nearby bench. He pulled off his suit coat, tossed it aside. Unbuttoned the first button on his shirt, pulled it over his head. His belt, shoes followed. Without a word, wearing only his suit pants, he stepped into the middle of the mat, stretched his arms over his head.

Normally, I'd have admired the long, strong lines of his body, the stretch of smooth skin over muscle as he warmed up. But this time I was thinking about strategy, about how I could keep him from doing something he'd regret later, at least politically. About how best to channel his mountain of energy. And possibly, when all was said and done, about having my way with him.

I pulled off my shoes, dropped my jacket onto the floor, and strode forward in bare feet. I glanced around at the weapons that hung from the room's paneled walls. Pikes, swords, maces, axes. "Do you prefer weapon or hand-to-hand?"

Ethan's eyes were still silver with emotion. "Either is fine by me."

"Excellent," I said, mirroring the cockiness in his stance.

Music filled the room, a Muse song about fighting, combat, and victory. That would have been Luc's or Lindsey's doing. And since the scene had been set, I didn't waste any time. I feinted left, and when Ethan began to pivot, I executed a side kick that he only just managed to block with a forearm.

Ethan used the arm to push me off. I spun down, then around, and faced him from a low position. I tried a strike at his shin, but he jumped, managed a back flip that put him a few feet away.

His anger was still hot. Time to let him burn some of it off.

"Are you afraid I'm going to kick your ass? Because you seem to be holding back," I said.

Ethan's lip curled.

"That's not an answer," I said, "but it is a pretty good Elvis impersonation." I gestured him forward with a crooked finger.

We moved toward each other, meeting in the middle of the mats. He struck out with his right elbow, but he was angry and telegraphed his move. I saw it coming, spun, and came up behind him, kicked him gently in the ass. "A point for me. Quit holding back."

He turned around, hands raised to block my next strike. "I'm not holding back. I'm trying not to take my seething rage out on you."

"Why? You think I can't handle you?"

He offered a crescent kick, which I avoided by leaning back just in time. He struck again, and I kept the momentum, putting out my hands into a back bend, then flipping over.

"Better," I said when I was upright. "But you're still only barely trying."

I meant to piss him off. Meant to make him face that betrayal, the fact that shifters weren't really all that different from vampires when it came to playing politics.

Ethan growled deep in his throat, a predator preparing to take his prey.

I shivered, but there was no fear in it. My body reacted to his power and his confidence, even if his emotions were masked by frustration. Since he still needed to work through that frustration, I tried another side kick.

This time, Ethan managed to catch my leg. He twisted, sending me off balance. I hit the floor on my back, stared up at him . . . and felt my eyes go silver.

I saw the flare of panic in his eyes—that he'd hurt me—but I kept my gaze steady on his as I rose to my feet. "Do that again."

My voice sounded rough, breathy. A woman on the edge of arousal. Not because he'd gotten me on the floor, but because of his strength and power. Beneath the expensive suits, the imperious nature, Ethan was a soldier. He'd lived as one, nearly died as one. And in becoming a vampire, had been reborn as one.

Didn't that make us one and the same—two people who'd been clothed in something other than what they were? Me, before. Ethan, now. But nevertheless, at heart, warriors always ready for battle.

"*Again,*" I repeated, and assumed the fighting position, beckoning him forward.

He watched me, evaluated, took in the flush in my cheeks, the silver of my eyes, the intensity of my expression. I watched his recognition bloom—that he hadn't hurt me. That he'd thrilled me and was fully capable of doing it again. As his understanding bloomed, his frustration eased.

"Very well, Sentinel," he said, and this time his voice was silky. He reset, arms bent, fingers loosely fisted.

I went in high with an uppercut. He dodged to the side, tried a low punch that nearly landed. But this time, I flipped backward into a handspring, popping up a few feet away, my ponytail bouncing with the motion.

Ethan didn't waste any time.

He vaulted forward with a spinning kick that I'd have sworn whistled through the air. The kick was shallow, glancing off my arm as I blocked. I aimed a low kick at his balancing foot when he settled to knock him off-kilter. Like a practiced gymnast, he jumped over my kick, then spun backward over me.

I turned to face him again, and we stared at each other like raging animals, chests heaving, hearts racing. Ethan moved first, nipping at my bottom lip, tugging nearly hard enough to draw blood.

I dug fingers into his shoulders, pulled him toward me.

"*Ethan,*" was all I managed to say before the door opened, before we were thwarted for the second time tonight.

"This is becoming a really bad joke," I muttered.

A white flag slipped through the door, waved for detente. No, not a flag—a paper towel taped to a plastic-wrapped stick of beef jerky. I didn't appreciate the interruption, but I could appreciation the symbolism: peace via dried meats.

Luc's head popped inside, a hand slapped over his eyes. "I don't want to see what's happening in here, although if the magic is any indication, it's illegal in at least a couple of states. Liege, Nicole's on the phone for you. She wants to talk about Caleb Franklin's death, and Malik thought you'd want to take it."

Ethan ran a hand through his hair, settling himself. "And why didn't Malik deliver the message?"

"Because I lost the bet."

Ethan held back a snicker, but something relaxed in his expression. If nothing else, he was home among friends. "I'll be right up. Shut the door, please."

"Nothing would please me more," Luc assured him, and slipped out again, pulling the door closed behind him.

"Well," Ethan said, glancing down at me, "I guess that brings this experiment to an end."

"Temporarily," I said. "Temporarily."

His eyes gleamed with appreciation. Without a word, he pressed his mouth to mine, a promise of things to come. "I need to take the call."

"Take it," I said. "I believe my work here is done."

Ethan snickered, picked up shirt and shoes. "Feeling cocky, are you, Sentinel?"

"Are you going to drive back to Little Red and challenge Gabriel to a duel?"

"Not in the next several minutes."

"Then, like I said, my work here is done." I picked up my own clothes, met him at the door. "Sometimes you just gotta dance it out."

He smiled, and this time, he looked relaxed. "I guess, sometimes, you do."

"And one more thought, Ethan."

His eyebrows lifted. "Yes?"

"Gabriel knew about Reed and the Circle. He sent us into that neighborhood, had to know we'd find something. At least notice the geographical connection, maybe do some exploring."

"What are you suggesting, Sentinel?"

"He may not have wanted to tell us about Reed. Maybe didn't feel like he could. But he wanted us to know."

With that, I left him to his call.

I waited until Ethan had cleared the stairs before opening the Ops Room door. And when I did, all eyes jumped to me.

Luc, Juliet, and Lindsey stood together in a huddle. They separated and walked toward me.

"He's going upstairs," I said.

"What was that about?" Luc asked when they reached me. "And who won?"

"It was a draw, as you probably figured out when you opened the door."

Luc managed a blush.

I didn't figure there was any point in hiding the truth of the rest of it. "We went to see Caleb Franklin's house, found a secret hidey-hole and a safe-deposit box key." I pulled out the envelope, set it on the table. "We met a necromancer in Longwood Cemetery. Then we took a little visit to Hellriver. Discovered La Douleur had moved there—"

"Wait, La Douleur is in Hellriver now?"

We all looked at sweet and innocent Juliet, who was grinning wickedly. "What? I like cosplay. And you can't beat La Douleur for cosplay."

So many things I'd learned tonight. So many things I didn't need to know. And yet I was compelled to ask. "English club?"

She grinned. "Sexy anime."

Luc flicked away a fake tear. "Our baby girl is growing up. And she's growing up weird."

I smiled, appreciating the levity. "Anyway, La Douleur is in Hellriver," I confirmed. "Run by a guy named Cyrius Lore, who's got the Circle ouroboros tattooed on his arm. The Circle owns La Douleur, and they own Hellriver. Cyrius sicced a vampire on us, a battle ensued, which we won, at the point of a gun, a dagger, and two katanas. He admitted Reed's got something big planned, something the sorcerer is involved in, something that's got the sorcerer under wraps working on it. But that's all we got out of him."

Luc whistled. "That's enough for one night."

"Oh, but that's only half of it. We then went to Little Red to talk to Gabe about Caleb Franklin. Long story short, Caleb Franklin was an enforcer for the Pack. Changed his mind, went to work for the Circle and Adrien Reed. He's also Gabe's illegitimate half brother, so Gabe let him defect from the Pack."

Luc's anger fired. "Gabriel Keene's half goddamn brother worked for Adrien Reed? And he knew Reed's connected to the Circle?"

"And has done not one thing about it."

"No wonder Sullivan's pissed," Juliet said, and Luc nodded.

"Do you know what we could have done with that information?"

"I do," I said. "And for his side, there's loyalty and guilt in there. Gabriel would say he made the best decision for the Pack by kicking Franklin out, staying out of Circle business. Said it was a strategic decision just like the kind Ethan often makes."

Lindsey winced. "Unfortunately, I can sympathize with that argument."

"Yeah," I said, pulling out a chair and sitting down. "That's what I thought, too. Ethan's as strategic as they come, and he'd be perfectly fine keeping information from the Pack if it suited his interests." Hell, he'd kept information from me because he thought he'd been protecting me.

"Damn," Luc said, looking at the ceiling as he thought it through. "Where did they leave it?"

"I don't know. Ethan threw a chair, shifter threw open the door, Berna pretty much threw us out."

Luc's gaze dropped to me again. "No shit?"

"No shit. They left on bad terms, but nothing specific was said about the alliance or whatever. I don't know if this is a lovers' spat or a total fork in the road."

Lindsey smiled sympathetically, rubbed my back. "You're mixing metaphors, English major."

"The night has fried my brain," I said, crossing my arms. "Quite a damn situation."

"Yeah," Luc agreed. "And as much as it sucks, we're going to have to wait to see how it resolves. Puts Jeff in a helluva spot."

"It does," I agreed. "Right between the Pack and the Ombuddies. He won't want to disappoint Gabe or my grandfather."

Luc scratched his cheek absently. "I wish there was a flowers-and-candy equivalent of fixing supernatural disputes."

"Ethan took Gabe a bottle of Scotch. But that was before his confession."

Luc nodded. "We'll have to let that be for the time being. Let's get back to Franklin, Reed, the Circle, the alchemy." He gestured toward the conference table, and we took seats.

"We don't know who killed Caleb Franklin," I said. "We know it was one of Reed's vampires." I slid the key from the envelope, placed it on the table. "We need to figure out, if we can, which bank this came from."

"And that would normally be a job for Jeff," Luc said, tracing a finger around the key's square teeth. "Checking bank records for deposit box rentals in Caleb's name."

"Yeah," I said. "Bad enough that it's hacking, much less that our bosses are on the outs. But that can't be helped. He's the best guy for the job. Maybe go through Catcher?"

Luc nodded. "I can try that. You give him the details about what went on tonight?"

"Not all of them," I said. "Just what went on in Hellriver. Ethan sent my grandfather a message. You want to fill him in?"

"I can do that."

"What about Reed?" Juliet asked. "Any sense of what his plan might be?"

"None." I crossed my arms. "Cyrius Lore said something

about Reed bringing order to Chicago. 'Fixing' things. He's been living two lives for a long time—the businessman and the criminal. Maybe he wants to consolidate his kingdoms."

"How?" Luc asked. "He can't just declare himself king. People would think he's a lunatic. And running for office wouldn't work, either. People may not connect him to the criminal when he's running his business, but if he puts himself up for election, it's gonna come out. His opponents will look for it, and they'll capitalize on it."

"Maybe that's our best-case scenario," Juliet said. "They can do the work for us."

Luc snorted. "No kidding. The public won't believe vampires, because, what, we're biased? But they'll believe politicians and negative ads. *Humans*," he spat, not a compliment, even though we'd all been humans once upon a time.

"If Cyrius was telling the truth, and Reed really does have a big plan, I can't imagine bigger than trying to get Chicago. I just don't know how he thinks he could do it."

"Alchemically," Lindsey said, and we all looked at her, the room silent but for the humming of equipment. "I mean, it's out there for a reason, right? And Reed's connected to it."

Luc frowned, leaned back in this chair, and crossed his hands behind his head. "How could a few square feet of symbols help him win Chicago?"

When none of us had an answer, Luc looked at us. "Seriously? Nothing?"

"Not until we know more about the equation," I said. "And I don't suppose Paige has had a brainstorm in the last few hours?"

"Not that I'm aware of." He glanced at his watch. "I know it's getting late, but can you go up and give her a hand? I think Lindsey's right. That's where we have to focus."

"Sure," I said, rising.

The Ops Room door opened, and we all looked back. I'd half expected Ethan to walk in. But instead it was Kelley, with an armful of paper bags from SuperDawg.

"Hey, Mer." She looked at me cautiously, turning slightly so her body was an obstacle between me and the bags. "I didn't know you were back."

"I'm not going to grab those right out of your hands," I promised, although she looked dubious about the promise.

"I'm not sure I believe you." And to prove it, she walked around the table, put the bags down on the other side. The other guards hopped up, began distributing the grub until the only thing left was a single, floppy fry abandoned in the bottom of a greasy bag.

Beggars couldn't be choosers.

I popped the fry and enjoyed the hell out of it.

I didn't need dogs or fries. Not really. I was a vampire. And after a night of fighting Leona, Warrior Princess, and Ethan, Master of Vampires, I needed blood.

I went to the cafeteria at the back of the House, passing Ethan's closed office door along the way.

Dawn wasn't far off, and the cafeteria was dark but for the glow of a glass-doored refrigerator that held Blood4You products. The enterprising company had been expanding its menu lately, offering more types of flavored and carbonated blood. From the variety in the case, it looked like I'd missed a few recent announcements. "Taco Fiesta," "Cajun Heat," and "Farmer's Market" were now on the shelves.

"Oh, hey, Mer."

I glanced back, found Margot in the doorway. She was beautiful and curvy, with a gleaming bowl of dark hair and bangs that fell to a perfect point in the middle of her forehead. She wore a black dress over black leggings and sandals, a white Cadogan House apron over the dress. She cradled half a dozen bottles of blood against her chest.

"You look like you're in deep thought," she said, walking toward me. "Keep that door open, will you?"

"Sure." I held the door, took an armful of the bottles so she'd have a free hand to load Cajun Heat and Beach Bum.

"These flavors are crazy," she said, "but the House seems to be enjoying them." When that was done, she wiped her hands on her apron and glanced at me. "You all right? You look a little peaked."

"Long night," I said, and took a bottle of Classic from the fridge.

"Anything I want to know about? Or more drama that would give me the heebie-jeebies?"

"Heebie-jeebies," I said. Margot reached in, grabbed a bottle of Beach Bum for herself.

"Mind if I join you? I taught a merengue class tonight, and I am beat."

"Please do. Although I may not be very good company."

She grinned. "As long as you aren't going to spatter me with steaming egg whites, you're good. I could use some peace and quiet."

We took a seat at the nearest table, drank our blood contemplatively. The effect was nearly instantaneous, as if I'd been drinking pure energy.

"The House seems nervous," she said after a few minutes, picking at the label on her bottle.

I nodded. "Reed puts everyone on edge."

"Asshole," she said, and took another drink. "There's always one, ruining it for everyone. Ego validation, projection, whatever. I was a therapist in a past life," she explained with a downcast smile. "Realized offering therapy just made me need more of it, and needed my own outlet."

"Cooking?"

Margot smiled. "And baking, especially. Instincts are helpful, but it's really all about chemistry. Precision. It's hard to half-ass. You have to pay attention. Concentrate. It tends to"—she paused, seeming to grasp for the right words—"blank out the rest of the mind. The worries. The anxiety. Those thoughts that roll around, over and over." She glanced at me. "Probably not unlike fighting and training."

"They can definitely have a focusing quality," I agreed. "You have to watch your opponent, dodge the move he's making, try to figure out what he'll do next. It's very engaging that way. And the consequences for not focusing, for not paying attention, are pretty severe."

I'd learned that lesson early on. Catcher had been the first person to train me, and he'd used flaming fireballs to keep me on my toes. I'd managed to avoid getting hit straight-on, but I'd been nicked by plenty of errant sparks. Lesson learned.

She smiled. "I don't know how you do it. Just"—she waved a hand—"get out there and fight." She leaned forward over the hands she'd linked on the table. "Don't you get scared? I just can't imagine the stuff you and Ethan and the rest of the guards have to face all the time."

"We're trained not to run," I said. "So when you feel that flight-or-fight instinct kicking in, you stay and you fight. And it's definitely easier now than it was in the beginning. More confidence, I guess. The more battles you fight, the easier it is to fight the next one. Like baking, you can develop the instincts for it."

"And I guess the perks are pretty good. Our Master is no slouch."

"No, he definitely is not. A pain in the ass sometimes, but definitely no slouch." I glanced at her. "Are you seeing anyone?"

"Not at the moment." She tucked a lock of dark hair behind

her ear. "I think I'm nearly over my 'I want to be alone' phase. It's been great, but times like this, I really wish I had the comfort."

I nodded. "I totally get that." My phone rang, and I checked the screen. It was a message from Luc, telling me Paige was waiting.

I rose, pushed in my chair. "I have to get back to work. I don't suppose you've got any fresh coffee in the kitchen?"

She cocked her head at me. "Got some studying to do?"

"Yeah," I said. "I actually do." And I smiled, because research was something I could very definitely do.

Or not.

I had a master's degree and nearly a Ph.D., since my study had been interrupted by my transition to vampire. I'd done my time in libraries and coffeehouses, with notebooks, pens, sticky notes, cups of coffee, and bottles of water.

And I felt completely stymied by alchemy.

Ethan found me in the library as sunrise neared. I sat at a table across from Paige in jeans and a long-sleeved Bears T-shirt ("Monsters of the Midway," one of my personal favorites). There was a spread of alchemy books on the tabletop and a notebook to my right, along with a fountain pen and the travel mug I'd borrowed from Margot and had to bribe the Librarian to let me bring in.

"You'll spill it," he'd said, barring the door.

"I won't spill it."

"They always say that. And then they spill it."

"It's got a lid," I insisted, holding it out to show him.

"And they spill it anyway," he said testily. Information, the Librarian was good with. Customer relations, not so much.

That had gone on for nearly ten minutes, and didn't stop until I'd promised to lend him a book on medieval lyric poetry still in my collection. The book was out of print, and he'd been searching for a copy, hoped I might have one. I hadn't opened it in a year, so it was an easy trade, although I did make him promise to put a "Donated by Merit" sticker in the front.

Paige and I both pulled off earphones when Ethan walked in.

He grinned. "Is this what grad school was like?"

I capped my fountain pen. "Only if you're going to ask me to grab something to eat, get a drink, and go hear this band, but then ditch me and enjoy a pretty good time with a blonde in the corner."

Paige snorted. She'd been energized by the work, but she'd been doing it for hours. There were blue shadows beneath her eyes, and she looked beyond vampirically pale. Not good for a sorcerer.

"That is very specific," Ethan said, "and doesn't really match my plan."

"Then it's not an exact comparison," I said.

"How's the work going?" Ethan asked.

We both looked at Paige.

"It's going," she said, gesturing to the poster and easel. "Would you like me to play Vanna White?"

"Please," Ethan said with a smile. He perched on the corner of the desk, hands clasped in his lap, as she rose.

"Just like words, alchemical symbols can be grouped into sentences." She pointed to the subsets of symbols, which she'd bracketed together. "I'm calling them phrases. Each phrase has between three and ten symbols, and each phrase makes up a part of the entire equation."

"For the purpose of?"

"One, telling the user exactly what to do—like a recipe. And two, actually igniting the magic. We think that's why it's written in a particular place instead of a spell book."

She pointed to three symbols. "The phrases contain the elemental building blocks of alchemy, like mercury, sulfur, and salt." She pointed to symbols of Jupiter and Saturn. "There are symbols for the time of year, the position of earth in the cosmos. And that's where the magic gets customized with the hieroglyphs—the sorcerer's tiny drawings. Some, we think, are supposed to be objects. References to the things actually used to make this magic work. But most are the actions—distillation, burning, and like that."

Ethan frowned, crossed his arms as he studied the board. "So magic will have to be made?"

"Correct," Paige said, gaze scanning the lines of symbols. "The magic isn't self-effectuating. The symbols are magical enough that erasing won't stop the magic, but not magical enough to kindle on their own. Don't think of them as paint on a canvas." She looked back at Ethan. "Think of them more like"—she paused, considering—"carvings in the fabric of the universe. You can wipe away the ink, the color, but that doesn't change the underlying magic that's already been wrought just by writing them."

Ethan frowned, considered. "What else?"

She nodded, tucked a lock of red hair behind her ear. "So, the weird thing is that the order of the symbols doesn't really make sense. We'll find a few symbols that do something, a phrase in the correct order, but then they go wonky again." She pointed to one of the phrases. "This, for example, this is a nullification equation."

"What does it nullify?" Ethan asked, head cocked.

"Whatever you want it to. It's like a magical verb. Particularly, a verb of subtraction. But it doesn't do anything without an object to nullify, which also has to be spelled out."

Ethan's gaze tracked to the next group of symbols. "The lion, the beaker, the—what is that? A waterfall? They're the objects?"

"Theoretically, yes." Paige pointed to the next phrase. "This is the troubling part—the time, the position. When and where the sorcerer is supposed to make all this happen. It's gibberish, alchemically speaking and astronomically speaking. The planets don't align that way." She looked at me. "It's taken us two hours to figure out we can't translate this phrase, and there are hundreds more phrases just like it in the equation—ones that don't make sense in context."

The soft sound of footsteps had us all looking up. The Librarian strode toward us in a collared shirt, his wavy hair sticking up in tufts. He reached us, looked protectively at Paige, then at Ethan.

"It's late," he said. "Any objection if I get her out of here? She could use a break."

Ethan checked his watch, looked surprised by the time. "Your work is very appreciated," he said, lifting his gaze to Paige. "And I think you've done plenty of it for the night."

"Good," she said, "because I'm beat." Right on cue, she yawned, cupping delicate fingers over her mouth. "Sorry. Long night."

"For all of us," Ethan said, gesturing to the door. "Get some rest. We'll close up the library."

There weren't many vampires who could pull off a suspicious look at their Master, but the Librarian managed it. "But, Sire . . ."

Ethan arched an eyebrow. "I'm fairly certain we can turn off the lights and close the door. We probably won't even allow Malik to test the sprinkler system."

The Librarian's expression was dour. "That's not funny."

Ethan just smiled. "Take a break. Have a drink. Get some rest."

Paige pushed back her chair. "Maybe I'll have some sort of brainstorm in a dream." Although the sun wouldn't affect her the way it did us, many other supernaturals slept during the day, as if they'd adapted to our schedule.

She glanced at us. "You're heading out, too?"

Ethan smiled. "As soon as we see that you're tucked away."

"In that case, we're out," the Librarian said, and led her to the door.

"I'm surprised he doesn't sleep on a cot in the back," I muttered when the door closed behind them.

Ethan grinned. "He requested it when we remodeled the House and added the library. He's very committed to his job."

"So's Margot, but I don't think she sleeps in the pantry." Not that that would be a bad way to go. "I didn't know the library wasn't original."

He frowned, gesturing to the space. "There was a room, more akin to a study than an actual library. The Librarian created the initial plan, coordinated the assemblage of our collection. I don't think he would be offended to hear me call it his life's passion. Well, other than Paige. He is a man in love."

I smiled. "She's the only one who gets to call him Arthur. That's sign enough."

He chuckled. "In the same way that you're the only one who gets to call me Ethan in that particular tone."

From the gleam in his eyes, I assumed he meant a seductive tone. "I better be. I hear anyone else is taking liberties, and we need to have a serious talk."

"You're the only one I allow to take liberties," he said, and the gleam in his eyes deepened.

There was something about this sexy, beautiful man in this sexy, beautiful library that made my mouth dry.

"Then I should take advantage," I said, and walked toward him, put my hands on his thighs.

I slid my hands from his lean thighs to his lean abdomen, felt his sharp intake of breath, the clench of muscles beneath my hands. His body was warm beneath my hands, seemed to radiate heat.

I lifted my gaze to his; the green of his eyes had deepened. He watched me with intent interest, and with the arousal we'd already halted twice tonight.

"I have plans," I said, adjusting my body against his. I tangled my hands in his hair, pulled his mouth toward mine, and sank in.

At other times, there might be kisses of love, of companionship, of solidarity. This was a kiss of banked passion, of heat, of promise. Ethan's throat grumbled possessively, predatorily, as he deepened the kiss, tilted his body toward mine.

He pulled back, stared at me with silvered eyes languid with desire. "We should take this upstairs."

I shook my head. "Here. Right here." Others had had their fun tonight. I figured I was due.

Ethan opened his mouth to argue but then closed it again and slyly. "Very well, then." He walked to the double doors, locked them with a loud metallic click that echoed across the room. When he stalked back, he picked me up, set me on the table, and stepped between my thighs. He was already rigid, already ready, and he moved a hand between our bodies to ensure that I was, too. He didn't have to worry. I closed my eyes, arched back against passion.

Sensation pummeled me, and the first golden arc of pleasure swept over me like a firestorm, igniting every nerve in my body. "*Ethan*," I cried, nails digging into his shoulders as I worked to keep my grip on him, on reality.

My head spinning, I focused on stripping him of clothing. His shirt, mine, hit the floor, were joined by pants, shoes. And then we were naked in the middle of the Cadogan library, his body lean and hard with muscle and desire. I put a hand on the flat of his abdomen, watched his defined muscles stiffen.

"You are beautiful," I said, lifting my gaze to him. His eyes were silver now, his fangs bared, his gorgeous face framed by hair that gleamed golden in the moonlight. To an unsuspecting mortal, he'd have been terrifying. But to a vampire, to *me*, he was the embodiment of life and energy and strength. He was passion and desire, the hunger that would never really be sated, the eternal craving.

He put his hands on my face, stared at me for a long moment before setting his mouth over mine, kissing me deeply. This time,

I moved a hand between our bodies, finding him and driving him further.

He braced a hand on the table, eased me back, and thrust into me with power that had me sucking in air. Then we moved together, illuminated by the shafts of moonlight that speared down from the room's high windows. Heat and magic flared again, and I arched my neck to him and felt the press and pinch of his fangs all the way to my core, as if he'd reached the very well of my soul to the love that bound us together.

Our movements became more frantic, more desperate, as we climbed higher, grew closer, breathed faster. His thrusts deepened and he pulled away from my neck, groaning as he reached his ascent.

The sound—deep and primal—sent me over the edge, and I followed him over the top.

For several minutes—or maybe a few hours; I wasn't really in a position to calculate—we lay together, naked and sweaty, on the top of the library table.

"He is going to lose his mind about this," Ethan said, humor in his voice.

There was no need to ask which "he" Ethan meant. "Probably so. You'll have to increase his budget."

"Trust me, Sentinel. He wants for nothing." Carefully, he climbed off the table, then offered a hand to help me up.

I had to sit on the edge of the table for the few seconds until my head stopped spinning. "I'm glad to hear it. It's one of my"—I couldn't help snorting—"favorite rooms in the House."

"Well, now, certainly."

Standing in front of the table, Ethan put his hands on his hips. And there, naked in his House and the library he'd built for it, he surveyed his demesne. "It's very freeing, standing here naked in my library."

"I imagine it would be. And you've earned it, given how much you apparently pay for it." I hopped off the table, but kept a hand on the edge just in case my knees wobbled, and began collecting my clothes.

"Oh, I've earned it," he said with a salacious grin. "Shall I earn it again?"

I put a hand on his chest. "I love you. I do. But we're twenty minutes from dawn, and I would kick you in the shin to get to a shower right now."

He shook his head. "And so our romance begins to fade, even before the afterglow has worn off."

I pulled on pants and a shirt, nodded toward the windows. "We don't get out of here soon, we're going to experience an entirely new variety of 'afterglow.' And we won't survive that one."

"Eternally romantic," Ethan said, but began pulling on his clothes.

When we'd dressed—or enough to make the trip up one flight of stairs and down the hallway—Ethan turned off the lights, and we left the library in darkness.

We left the books to rest, and went to find darkness of our own.

Chapter Eleven

BED OF ROSES

When I woke, I found Ethan standing near the desk, staring at me. His body was tensed like that of a soldier preparing for battle, his expression was ice-cold, and a chilly wash of magic had coated the air.

He lifted his hand, held up a small, slightly crumpled piece of paper.

Shit, I thought as recognition dawned.

"Sentinel." Every syllable was as crisp as his tone, each sound tipped with anger. "What, exactly, is this?"

It was the note from Reed, the one I'd crumpled and thrown into the trash—or thought I had. I must have missed. Ethan had seen it, picked it up, and definitely read it.

"And more to the point," he continued, taking a step forward, "why have I not seen it before?"

There was no way to avoid it now. "Reed slipped it into yesterday's paper, or had someone do it. He was just being an asshole, so I threw it away."

"He threatens you, and you *threw it away*?"

"He doesn't care about me, and you know it. Not any more

than he cares about any of us. But he loves drama, Ethan, and I'm sure he was hoping you'd give him some."

Ethan strode to me. "Have there been any others?"

"What? No. Of course not. Look, it doesn't mean anything. It's just more of the same. It's the game he plays."

With radiating fury, he moved back to the desk, threw the note onto it. "I can't believe you hid this from me."

I hadn't, not very well. But if anything, this conversation proved I'd been right to try. "He's baiting you, Ethan. And I'm not going to let that happen."

"He's threatening you. And I'm not going to let *that* happen!" He turned back to me. "Reed's going to be at a charity event tonight at the Chicago Botanic Garden. We're going. And we're going to have a word."

"No. Absolutely not. That's the last thing—" I stopped, realizing what he'd confessed. "Wait. How do you know where Adrien Reed is going to be tonight?"

"That's missing the point."

"No," I said, rising from the bed and walking toward him. "I think that's exactly the point. How do you know where he's going to be?"

Ethan's eyes glinted like stolen emeralds. "I have friends in high places, too."

My stomach sank, and I took a step backward. Took a step away from him. I only knew one other person he might have called who knew about charity events and hated Adrien Reed. "You called my father."

Ethan didn't respond.

"You called my father and asked him, what, to keep tabs on Reed? Do you have any idea how dangerous that is? To involve him in something like that? He's human, for God's sake, and he's already in Reed's sights. Did you put a target on his back?"

"I made a single phone call to your father, and I understand he made a single phone call in turn. Your father has his own connections, Merit, and he's eager to use them. He's a man with a lot of ego, and he's not happy about Towerline." He closed the distance between us. "But more important, Reed already got too close to this House and to you. I won't let it happen again."

"By putting my family in danger?"

He looked baffled. "First, I did not put your family in danger. And second, I will use whatever tools are available to me to keep you safe."

"And yet you're pissed at Gabriel," I said, shaking my head and walking to the other end of the room. When I reached the opposite wall, when space was a barrier between us, I looked back at him. "You're pissed at Gabriel because he withheld information. That's ironic."

"I suppose we're both guilty in that respect. And just as likely to apologize."

The room went quiet.

My anger banked. "You named me Sentinel. You should trust me to handle myself, to understand whether my father would be the best source. To let me make that decision."

"I do trust you. Implicitly. And I named you Sentinel because I knew what you could be. Who you could be. If I had it to do over again . . ."

It wasn't the first time he'd suggested naming me Sentinel was a mistake. But it was the first time I really believed he meant it.

"Your skills, your brains, your heart. The fact that you always want to do more and better—"

"Are because you named me Sentinel," I finished for him. "Because you gave me a position that let those parts of me grow and flourish."

"I don't disagree," Ethan said, stepping forward. "But none of that matters if Reed puts a target on you. I won't let that happen, Merit. Not when he's already proven he knows how to get to me." His eyes clouded with fury. He was thinking about the Imposter, about what he'd done to me and tried to do to Ethan.

"I can't be less than what I am," I said. "Not now. Not after all this time." Because, after all that time, after feeling for so long that I'd only been playing Sentinel, putting on a costume that wasn't entirely mine, I'd *become* her. I'd become the guardian and warrior he'd wanted me to be. It was too late for me to step back, to let others fight the battles I'd been trained for, that I was now eager to fight.

Maybe he should have been more careful in what he'd wished for.

"I know. And I can't, either. I'm going to the event," he said into the silence that followed his declaration, "and I'm going to talk to Adrien Reed because that's what needs to be done. Reed expects us to play his game—to react to the stimuli that he throws at us."

"You think he didn't anticipate this? That you'd see the note and call him out?"

"Maybe," Ethan said. "Probably. But I doubt he thinks we'll do it in a public place."

I didn't think that was true, not at all. But there wasn't a point in arguing with him. He'd go, even if he went without me. And I'd be damned if he did it without me.

"I want it on record that I don't think this is the right course."

His eyebrows lifted. I argued with him, sure, but that was ego and banter. It wasn't often that I told him his strategy was flat-out wrong.

"But that doesn't matter," I said. "Because I'm going with you regardless." And that was almost not the worst part. "What do I have to wear?"

"It's black tie. I'll find you something."

That was just what I was afraid of.

I guess it could have been called a gown, although that might have been generous. Couture, definitely. Edgy, certainly. But "gown" just didn't quite fit.

There were two pieces two it, both in the deep, rich black that Ethan preferred. The first was a stiff black romper—a heart-shaped sleeveless bodice that fit as snugly as a corset and ended in a pair of hot-pant-style shorts. They covered what they needed to cover, but just barely.

And that was where the second piece came in. It was a skirt made of layers of inky black silk, one of Ethan's favorite fabrics. It connected to the romper at the waist but was open in the front. When I stood still, it looked like I was wearing a sleeveless black ball gown. But when I moved, the silk split, revealing the shorts, my legs, and the black, strappy stiletto sandals Ethan had also provided.

I walked to the other end of the apartment, did the full catwalk toward the floor-length mirror on the way back, watched the skirt flare around and behind me as I moved. It was going to be hard to stay pissed at him in a "dress" that looked this good. It fit like a glove, made my legs look a million miles long, and even managed to pump up my slender curves.

I pulled my hair into a knot at the nape of my neck, added delicate pearl earrings that were part of my own family's legacy, and looked, as I often did when Ethan selected my ensemble, pretty fabulous.

He was an imperious ass, but he knew how to make an impact.

There were *whoops* of excitement coming from the open doors of the Ops Room.

When I looked in, Luc, tousled hair falling over his brow, was bent over the conference table. In front of him was a small bundle of paper folded into a triangle. Lindsey sat at the other end, elbows on the table, her fingers and index fingers arranged in a set of mock uprights. He balanced the tip of the triangle beneath one finger, then flicked.

While half a dozen guards looked on, waiting with bated breath, the paper football flew through the air, toward the uprights. The paper hit her right index finger, bounced, and hit the table, three inches short of the goal.

"It's no good! It's no good!" yelled Brody, a recent guard inductee, waving his long arms back and forth like an NFL ref. Lindsey stood up and high-fived Kelley and Juliet.

Luc raised his fists to the sky. *"No!"* he yelled dramatically. "I could have been a contender!"

On the Waterfront, I guessed silently. Luc was one for movie quotes.

Lindsey strutted up to him, chin jutted out with pride. "I believe you just got schooled," she said, poking a finger into his chest.

"Best two out of three?" he asked, wincing.

"Not on your life." She took his shoulders, turned him toward me. "You have other things to deal with."

Luc glanced at me, and what would have been a smile faded when he took in the dress and the shoes. And then he looked downright pissed . . . and maybe a little bit sympathetic.

"Damn," Kelley said, interrupting whatever tirade he'd been about to make.

"You look amazing," she said, fingering a bit of the skirt. "Is this Valentino?"

I hadn't even thought to look. "I don't know. But I'm sure it was expensive."

She snorted. "Uh, yeah. Very."

When she walked back to her station, Luc dropped his voice. "What the hell is this?"

"Complicated. Can I speak to you outside?"

Luc didn't look thrilled about the request. But he rose, followed me to the door, and closed it when we were outside again. And then he crossed his arms.

"You're getting pretty good at that Master-to-Peon expression," I said.

"I've been on the receiving end plenty of times. What the hell's he doing?"

No need to explain who "he" was.

"Long story short, Reed wrote a note to me to inflame Ethan, and it worked perfectly. Ethan wants to confront Reed at a charity thing tonight at the Botanic Garden."

He eyes flashed, and anger flooded the hallway on a wave of magic. "Excuse me?"

"You know what I know. I can't stop him, but I'll be damned if I'll let him go alone. And that's not all."

I told him about Ethan's call to my father, watched his face for a sign he knew about it. I didn't see it. Instead he looked surprised and a little appalled. "Not a good idea."

"No, it wasn't. But it's done now. Is there something we can do? Protection we can offer?"

"Do you think your father would take it?"

"I don't know. What about the human guards? Could we post a couple near his house?"

Luc put a hand on my arm. "Sentinel, considering how angry you are at Ethan for talking to your father without checking with you first, do you really think it's a good idea to put guards on your father without talking to *him* first?"

I curled my lip. "Don't try to use logic against me."

"Perish the thought. Look, why don't I talk to your grandfather, broach the issue with him? He might have a better sense of, let's say, the proprieties."

Some of the pressure in my chest loosened. "I'd appreciate it."

Luc nodded. "This screws my plan for you to help Paige with the alchemy tonight. We need to focus on translating it."

"You're preaching to the choir. Unfortunately, using that metaphor, Ethan's the bishop. He makes the rules, and I can't just let him go by himself."

"What do you think Reed's got in mind?"

"I don't know, but I'm sure he's got a plan. That's the kind of man he is. Even when we're aggressive, like with Hellriver, he's still two steps ahead of us."

"He's the bad guy; they usually are two steps ahead until they're caught."

"Yeah." I sighed. "I'm going to try to keep Ethan out of trouble."

"Do your best," he said. "And I'm glad you came to me, told me about it. I'm pissed he didn't, but he's one of the more stubborn among us."

"Stubborn barely scratches the surface," I said, thinking of the night before at Little Red. "Have you heard anything from Gabriel? From the Pack?"

Luc's expression darkened. "No, although we wouldn't necessarily. I guess that's Ethan's complaint. At this point, not hearing anything is probably best. Means they haven't declared war against us."

"They wouldn't do that."

Luc didn't look as convinced. "It wouldn't be the first instance of internecine warfare."

"I know. And I know Ethan's pissed, and Gabriel's probably pissed now, too. But they're both adults. They both want what's best for their people, and that can't be war with each other, Luc. It can't." My voice had become pleading.

"Let's hope not, Sentinel. Damn. What a night. Ethan's probably talking to Malik, but I'll throw myself onto that grenade if he hasn't."

Resigned, I nodded and began walking toward the door to the parking garage. But I glanced back at Luc. "Do me one more favor?"

"Anything, Merit."

"Call the lawyers, and get them ready."

The Botanic Garden had been—and still was—a beautiful place to visit. But I knew this trip wasn't going to go well, and the paths and gardens were still shadowed by my memories.

My mother had held my sister Charlotte's sixteenth birthday there. I'd been stuffed into a party dress and forced to join in. She was three years older, and I felt ugly and coltish beside her friends, who already knew their ways around makeup, clothes, and pretty hairstyles. I was already uncomfortable in starchy crinoline and a training bra. I felt even more so when matched against Charlotte's beautiful friends.

More recently, I'd walked there after Ethan's death, when I'd wanted solitude and solemnity. That hadn't fostered happy memories, either.

The park had closed a few hours ago. But the large black gates at the entrance were open, a man in a dark suit checking invitations and waving expensive cars into the park.

He waved us in, and Ethan pulled into a parking slot backward, the car facing the front entrance in case we needed to make a quick getaway.

"You look beautiful and formidable," Ethan said as he opened my door and offered a hand to help me out of the car.

"Let's hope the latter more than the former." Once out, I adjusted the skirt so it fell appropriately around my hips. Not that it wouldn't make an impression regardless, which was surely part of the reason Ethan had chosen it.

The deep black tuxedo he'd selected for himself certainly made an impression. He'd brushed back his hair, tucked it behind his ears, and looked very much the rich magnate. Which was true, to a point.

He didn't say anything, but offered me his arm, and when I slipped mine into it, we walked from the parking area to the main building, where a jazz ensemble played and Chicagoland's wealthiest humans sipped champagne.

Just inside the door, two women sat behind a table with LADIES AUXILIARY printed across the tablecloth. Ethan offered our names, and one of the women provided small silver pins in the shape of tulips. No sticker name tags or Sharpies for this crowd.

The other woman gestured toward the door. "You'll find the silent auction over there, cocktails and light snacks on the terrace. You're welcome to explore the park. The lights of Evening Island are on, and it's a lovely night for a walk."

"That it is," Ethan said with a smile, and handed me a pin as we walked inside. To the women and men who checked us out—or checked *him* out—he'd have looked cool and collected as he surveyed the room, evaluated his options. But I knew him better than most, and certainly well enough to recognize the tension in his shoulders, the low-level buzz of irritated magic around him.

"Do you see him?" he asked.

"No." But this vibe wasn't right for Adrien Reed. The crowd here was mostly young couples with young money. Louboutin rather than Chanel. It was different flash for different generations, but flash all the same. Reed liked ostentatious wealth—his palatial house was as baroque as it got—all gilding and velvet and dark wood. But this wasn't his particular brand of it.

"I don't think he'd be in here," I said. "You're sure he's coming?"

"I'm sure."

I wanted to hound him, to ask how my father had been sure, to get the details of the singular "phone call" he'd made. But this wasn't the time or the place.

"Champagne?" he asked as a waiter in black walked by with delicate flutes on a silver tray.

"No. I'd rather have my wits."

"Fair point," he said. "I think you're right, and he's not in here."

"I don't suppose that means you're ready to return to the House?" The question was rhetorical, I knew, but my tone was cutting.

"No," Ethan said, eyes flashing, a reminder that he hadn't forgotten his mission.

"Are you up for a walk?"

I'd have preferred Pumas to the heels I was currently wearing for that particular activity, but I knew what I'd gotten into.

"Why not?" I said, and we made our way through the crowd.

The Chicago Botanic Garden was actually composed of several themed gardens with weaving paths between. Evening Island was on the opposite side of the basin pond and was linked to other gardens by paths and bridges. We passed a rose garden and a small walled garden before reaching the meadow that surrounded the basin.

The night was lovely and crisp, and there were plenty of people out for a stroll. It wasn't often you could walk through the gardens after dark, which explained why so many people had donated a pretty penny for the opportunity. Unfortunately—or not—none of those people was Adrien Reed.

The lights on Evening Island made a glow, reflecting lights like stars across the dark water that surrounded it. On a different kind of night, with a different kind of purpose, it would have been incredibly romantic. The kind of spot I could imagine Ethan proposing in. He'd want some kind of production, had already hinted that he'd given thought to the how and where, although it certainly wouldn't be on the agenda tonight.

We crossed a wooden bridge, passed beneath budding willow trees, and stepped onto the island's footpath, took a moment to survey the humans who'd gathered there.

The first face I recognized didn't belong to Adrien Reed. It was even more familiar.

My father stood at a crossroads where two paths met, chatting with two silver-haired gentlemen, all three of them in tuxedos that probably cost more than most Chicagoans made in a month. My father was gesturing to the building across the water, probably waxing poetic about architecture or development, two of his favorite subjects.

He looked up, realized we'd arrived. "Excuse me," he said, and walked toward us. The expressions of the men he left mixed curiosity and hostility.

"Merit. Ethan."

"Have you seen him?" Ethan asked.

"Not yet. Although I was assured he planned to attend."

"Did it occur to you that gathering information about him might put you in danger?" I asked. My tone was as sharp with my father as it had been with Ethan.

"He's dangerous whether I'm here or not," my father said, straightening his jacket. "It's better for me if I'm here, where I can at least keep an eye on him. And, frankly, it's necessary."

"Because being on the outs with Adrien Reed could put you in a pinch," Ethan guessed.

"Financially and otherwise." My father slipped his hands into his pockets. "Pinch or not, you have to be careful what you do here among these people. They are wealthy, and they are powerful."

"As he's threatened Merit in my own home, I believe I'm entitled to a conversation."

My father's brows lifted, his gaze shifting to me. "What kind of threat?"

"A note promising victory at any cost," Ethan said. "I don't tell you that to alarm you, as Merit is safe in the House, but to make you aware. Reed continues to play a game, and he won't stop until he believes he's won. You heard about Caleb Franklin's death?"

That Ethan had to ask the question said he and my father weren't working together that closely. That helped, at least a little.

"The shifter who was murdered? The news said it was random violence."

"It wasn't," Ethan said. "We believe it's related to magical symbols we found near where he was killed. And we have reason to believe Reed is involved."

"That's the alchemy?"

Ethan nodded.

"Merit's grandfather mentioned that." My father looked out over the water, which rippled with the evening breeze, sending lights shimmering across its surface. "The more I think about Reed, the more I have trouble deciding whether he is guided by narcissism or insanity."

"The most successful evildoers are usually both," I said.

Another man rounded the corner, two short glasses in hand. It was my brother, Robert, who shared my mother's blond hair and pale green eyes. I wasn't close to my family, and my brother was no exception. I'd always felt like the odd one out, and certainly hadn't changed when I became a vampire.

Robert handed a glass to my father and took a sip of his own, which gave him a moment to look us over, pick his first volley.

When he lowered his drink again, he settled on "What are you doing here?"

"Good to see you, too, Robert." I kept my expression bland. "We were invited, just like everyone else. You remember Ethan?" I gestured between them.

Ethan offered a hand, and Robert shook it, but the act seemed distasteful. I was half surprised he didn't wipe off his palm.

Ethan looked nonplussed. But then again, Robert wasn't the target of his ire.

"This is an important night for Merit Properties, and an important event," Robert said primly. He was being groomed to take over the family business. And while my father had undoubtedly helped us during our last go-round with Reed, it didn't look as though his good faith would extend to Robert.

"And our being here risks that how?" Ethan asked, giving Robert a cool stare that would have iced over another man. But Robert was a Merit; the stubbornness was genetic.

"You tell me. Trouble seems to follow you everywhere you go."

"Ah, but we aren't the trouble. Through hatred and fear, it finds us." Ethan let his gaze slip away to the other faces around us.

"Look," Robert said. "Adrien Reed will be here, and I've been promised fifteen minutes to talk to him. He's an integral part of our development plan in this fiscal year and next."

I glanced at my father, saw his expression tighten. And I'd bet good money he hadn't told Robert the truth about Towerline, why he'd lost it to Reed.

"Your business concerns are not mine," Ethan said. "Your sister's concerns are."

Robert looked at me. "What concerns?"

"Reed isn't a fan of ours. He's decided we're his enemies, and he's taken a particular interest in Merit."

Ethan was being circumspect—a wise course, given Robert's apparent allegiances. Merit Properties was his lifeblood, his inheritance. I was the weird sister he suspected of inciting trouble and being overly dramatic.

"Then maybe spend a little less time trying to get news coverage," Robert muttered into his drink.

"Would you like to say that again, and aloud?" Ethan's eyes glittered. "Your convictions are wrong, but then I could at least say you had courage in them."

Robert rolled his eyes, but before he could open his mouth to spew more invective—or say something Ethan would definitely make him regret—my father put a hand on his elbow.

"Why don't we take a walk," my father suggested, "before we all say something we might regret?"

"Too late," Ethan said, watching them walk away. "It appears your father may no longer be a complete asshole, but your brother's keen on taking his place."

"High praise indeed."

"For a man who tried to sell his daughter to vampires, yes."

"We could leave," I said. "We could leave right now."

Ethan turned to face me, his expression fierce. "You heard what he said, what he believed, what others believe. Your father once believed you'd done something wrong; your brother still believes it. Despite all evidence, he believes Reed couldn't possibly be evil because he's rich, because he's powerful, because he has what others want. And that's bullshit. Adrien Reed will not stop until he is *stopped*. We will do our part in that."

When I looked away, he tipped my chin back to meet his eyes. "I know our tactics are different. I can live with that, because it's him. Because he will destroy this city if he can. And because it's you, and I will be damned if he hurts you to get to me."

I found I couldn't meet his eyes, and that made me unbearably sad.

And the man who stood metaphorically between us emerged from the darkness, his wife at his side.

"Well, well, well," said Adrien Reed. "Look what the cat dragged in."

CHAPTER TWELVE

PRIDE AND PREJUDICE AND VAMPIRES

Ethan turned his body to shield me as they stepped onto the path in front of us. I didn't like it, but I knew this was a battle he needed to fight. A battle he believed he needed to fight for me.

Reed looked coolly powerful in the dark tuxedo. His dark hair curled at the top of his collar, his goatee carrying more gray than his hair. He wore the same expression of arrogant conceit as he had in the *Tribune* photo.

Beside him, Sorcha wore a long column dress in her preferred color of emerald green, her thick blond hair pulled up into a complicated braid that wound around her head. Around her neck was a gold necklace in the shape of a serpent, the triangular head resting in the deep V between her breasts.

While Reed looked at us, Sorcha gazed at her phone, fingers tapping furiously. She looked up at the sound of Reed's voice, and her eyes widened at the sight of us. But then the emotion was gone, replaced by bored indifference, her attention back on her phone.

"Crashing a party isn't your usual style, but it does show your lack of character." Reed was playing his part, wearing the mask of cool and moneyed indifference. That mask was a lie; we'd seen the glimmer of excitement in his eyes at the possibility of murder, of destruction.

Ethan's smile was thin. "We were invited, as I'm sure you're aware."

"Beggars can't be choosers, I suppose. If you'll excuse us," Reed said, and made to step around Ethan. But Ethan moved in front of him, blocking the path.

"We'll have words, Reed. Now or later, but we'll have them."

"What could we possibly have to talk about, Mr. Sullivan?"

"The threat you've made against Merit. The danger you pose to this city."

Reed's eyes flashed with what looked like pleasure, but his voice stayed cool. "As usual, Ethan, I don't know what you're talking about. I find most supernaturals tend toward hyperbole."

Ethan cocked his head. "Then how about the death of Caleb Franklin, the alchemy written near Wrigley Field?"

"I have no idea who that is," Reed said casually, lifting a champagne glass to his lips. That was perhaps the most infuriating thing about Adrien Reed. He bluffed as well as any vampire.

"Ah," Ethan said, nodding. "So you'll play the mogul here, when surrounded by others who have money. Is that it? Afraid to let your true self show? Afraid they'll see you for what you really are?"

"And what, pray tell, is that?"

"A thug." Ethan dropped his gaze to Reed's tuxedo. "A common thug at that, in a suit of medium quality. I'm surprised at you, Adrien—that your taste doesn't run to something finer."

That arrow found its mark, slipping through Reed's armor. The monster flashed across his gray eyes. "You forget yourself."

"I don't, actually. I've remembered myself, and what my people stand for."

"Which is?"

"Chicago, mostly. I'm sure you know we've discovered something of yours. A club in Hellriver. La Douleur, I believe it was called?"

"I don't know it."

Ethan frowned. "Curious. You don't know Caleb Franklin, who was killed by one of your vampires. You don't know about the alchemy near Wrigley, and you don't know about a club run by one of your own people in a neighborhood where more of the same alchemy was located."

Ethan glanced at Sorcha. "For a man who professes to have his finger on the pulse of the city, your husband is surprisingly unaware of what his own people are doing."

She didn't react. No flush, no huff of surprise, no curse. She just kept staring at her phone.

While she seemed unaffected, Reed was annoyed, and angled his body in front of her. It also kept anyone else nearby from seeing his face.

"I am aware of everything," he said, that self-satisfied glint in his eyes. "From Robert Merit's financial desires to the very unfortunate tension that's developed between shifters and vampires."

"Tension you created."

"Actually, no. I didn't kill Caleb Franklin, nor did I order him killed. And if, hypothetically, I had any familiarity with the other matters you've mentioned, what of it? You could never prove it." Reed returned the condescending look Ethan had given him earlier. "They'd never believe you over me. I'm a pillar of Chicago. You are, quite literally, a parasite."

Reed shifted the momentum again. His anger now rising, Ethan's magic filled the air, his glamour potent, and my body unfortunately primed for it. My eyes silvered and my fangs descended in reaction to the glamour he spilled around Reed.

But it seemed to have no effect on Reed. "Glamour doesn't

affect me. Call it a side benefit of having . . . *powerful* . . . friends," he said, then glanced at me. "Considering the look on your girlfriend's face, seems like she could use a friend like that."

His tone was vulgar, obviously intended to incite Ethan, embarrass me. But I'd seen enough of Reed to be unsurprised. I glanced again at Sorcha, intrigued and baffled. If the comment bothered her, she didn't show it. Then again, Reed was manipulative, controlling. Maybe she was under his thumb, too.

Ethan dropped the glamour but bared his fangs. If he'd been wearing his katana, he'd probably have pulled that, too. "Stay away from her, and from the rest of my House."

But Reed was enjoying himself now. "Why should I? Your entire community is a mess, and that's just one sliver of our city. Do you know how many murders occurred in this city last year?"

"No, but I imagine you had a hand in most of them."

Reed shook his head. "Tsk-tsk, Ethan. I didn't, of course. And the answer is, too many. Chicago is, in your parlance, a disaster."

"And you're going to save it?"

"Not that it's your concern, but let's say I'm less troubled by the end result than the profitable middle. My job involves evaluating financial opportunity. Chicago has that in spades. Hypothetically speaking, a man with connections in both legitimate and illegitimate worlds would bring order and efficiency to a city that wastes time and resources on people who refuse to do their part."

My brain tripped back to Cyrius Lore and the conversation in his office, to the order he'd mentioned, Reed's "plan." Lore had believed Reed was a messiah. I wasn't sure if that was spin by Reed or naïveté by Lore, but it was wrong either way.

"So which is it?" Ethan asked. "Do you want the money or the power?"

Reed clucked his tongue. "You know better, Ethan. Money

and power are inseparable. Money begets power; power begets opportunity; and opportunity begets more money."

Reed should have that motto inscribed in his ouroboros, if it wasn't already. Probably explained why he called his organization the Circle.

"Power," Reed said, "is the only game worth winning."

Ethan went rigid. "Chicago isn't a prize for you to buy with dirty money."

"Don't be dramatic," Reed said. "This isn't Gotham, and you aren't some tragic superhero. This is the real world. People want money and power, so they respect money and power. I have both, so they respect me for it. And if you're smart, you'll heed it and walk away right now." He slid his reptilian gaze to me. "Before anyone gets hurt."

Ethan's magic flared again, this time with heat. "I've already told you once to stay away from her."

Ethan, he's baiting you.

Stay out of this. Even in my head, his voice was edgy, angry.

I wanted to drag him back, to push Reed away. But that wouldn't have helped anything. I wasn't sure there was anything we could do right now that wouldn't make things worse.

Reed couldn't have heard the byplay, but his gaze said he realized it was there. "Fortunately, you have no control over me. Which must irritate you greatly."

"What irritates me is your arrogance."

Reed smiled easily. "You want to hit me, don't you?"

Ethan's expression was grim. "More than anything else."

It was an obvious ploy. But Ethan would have known he was being baited, and wouldn't have cared.

"Then take your shot, vampire. I dare you."

Ethan stepped forward.

The air suddenly buzzed with steel and guns. Cops appeared at our sides, weapons drawn. "Step back!" said one of them to Ethan. "Step back, and get your hands in the air, very slowly."

Reed had cast the bait, and Ethan had taken a bite. Now we'd pay the price.

Ethan's jaw clenched with unmitigated fury, but he didn't move. "Whatever you may be, whomever you may have in your pocket, you are, at heart, a coward."

Reed shook his head ruefully, put a protective arm around Sorcha's waist. "As we expected, Officer, they continue to stalk and threaten my family."

"Hands in the goddamn air," the cop said again, tension rising as Ethan and Reed stared at each other.

I could see Ethan wanted to move. He wanted to ignore the cops, step forward, and give back some of the pain Reed had caused us. But that wouldn't have helped. It wouldn't have done anything but land us in even more trouble.

Step back, Ethan, I said. *Now.*

I will have my chance at him, Sentinel. For all that he has done to us, I will have my chance at him.

Not here, and not now.

It took Ethan a long moment to weigh justice against consequence, honor against action.

He is mine, Ethan said, but took a step back, lifted his hands into the air.

The cop stepped forward, pulled Ethan's arms behind him, forced him to his knees. A second cop did the same thing to me. I winced as I hit the ground hard, my bare knees scraping across the rough stone of the path. My arms were wrenched behind me, my wrists zip-tied together, because I was obviously a threat in a ball gown and stilettos.

"You should use two ties," Reed said. "I understand that's more effective on vampires."

The cop was last on the list of people I hoped to battle tonight. Reed, for being an unmitigated monster, was number one on the list. Sorcha, for just watching as the officers cuffed us, was second. And Ethan, whose stubborn ass had gotten us into this, fell in at third.

"We were, of course, prepared," Reed said as they pulled Ethan to his feet, hands cuffed behind him. "I was afraid you'd show up and cause a scene, so we requested the additional security. The CPD was happy to oblige." He looked at the officers. "If you've got them in hand, I'd like to get my wife to safety."

For the first time, the cops looked unsure of their steps. "We'll need to talk to you and your wife," said the one who'd cuffed Ethan. "Formalize the report."

"Of course. We'll just be in the main building. My wife becomes distressed by these two. I just want to get her away from them. I'm sure you understand."

"Well, all right," he said after a moment, gesturing to his partner. The other cop stepped aside so Reed and Sorcha could walk past him. The humans who'd gathered nearby to watch nodded as they walked by, offered supportive words.

"You disgust me," said the first cop as I was pulled to my feet. Then they escorted us in the same direction Reed and Sorcha had gone, past the same gauntlet of humans.

When we passed beneath an overhead light, the second cop happened to glance at me. "Oh, shit," he said, pulling me to a stop. "You don't know who they are?"

Ethan's cop looked at him, then back at me. "No. Should I?"

"These are those Cadogan vampires. The ones who are always in the news. I think one of 'em's related to a cop, too."

"Chuck Merit," I said, uttering the first words I'd said in many long minutes. And when Ethan and I were alone, they wouldn't be the last. "He's my grandfather."

The second cop shook his head ruefully. "I know Chuck Merit. He's a good guy. You doing this? Putting him in this position? That's a damn shame. You need to change your ways, ma'am. You need to get your shit together, and change your ways."

"I have my shit together," I muttered as we were led back toward the main building.

But right now that felt like a complete lie.

When we reached the visitors' center, they called my grandfather, agreed to wait until he arrived. He was the city's supernatural Ombudsman, after all. That put us squarely in his jurisdiction.

It took half an hour for him to arrive with Jeff in tow. No sign of Catcher, but Jeff and my grandfather looked irritated enough to fill Catcher's usual quota.

"I don't believe they need to be cuffed, gentlemen," my grandfather said. "It's your call, of course, but these two aren't violent. They may not be especially smart, but they aren't violent."

The cops looked at each other; then the first cop looked at my grandfather. "You'll vouch for them?"

"I will. She's my granddaughter, and he's her beloved. They both usually have more sense than this."

There was a pause before the cops reached some agreement, stepped forward, and cut the zip ties. My wounded arm sang with pain, and I rolled it to release some of the tension.

"Might I have a word with my granddaughter?" my grandfather asked, and the cops shared a glance and stepped away.

My grandfather stared down at us, the disappointment clear in his face.

I hadn't gotten in trouble much as a kid. I hated the feeling of it, the violation of trust, the sickening sense that I'd disappointed someone, the humiliation that came with having done something *wrong*. I hadn't been the type of child who handled it well.

I felt doubly sickened tonight by the fact that I'd disappointed the relative I trusted most of all, and that disappointment was compounded by anger at Ethan. I wasn't especially surprised, because I'd predicted right down the line *exactly* what would happen. But I was furious that my grandfather's reputation had been impugned, and that we'd put that look in his eyes. And Jeff didn't look so happy, either.

"Would you like to tell me exactly what happened here?"

"Words," Ethan said. "Only an exchange of words."

For the first time, Jeff spoke, and his tone wasn't any more pleasant than my grandfather's. "Nothing physical?"

"No," Ethan said ruefully. "I didn't get that far. The cops showed up first."

"He told them we were stalking and threatening him," I explained.

Jeff and my grandfather exchanged a glance.

"Reed's already called the CPD once," my grandfather said. "That adds credence to his contention this is a pattern of bad behavior." He looked at Ethan. "Did you come here specifically to piss him off? Specifically to get arrested? Because if that was your plan, I'd say you accomplished it."

"We had our reasons," Ethan said.

My grandfather lifted his eyebrows, waiting for an explanation.

"He sent her a note," Ethan finally said. "A threatening note."

"A direct threat?"

"Implicit."

My grandfather didn't roll his eyes, but that looked like a close call. "Goading you to act, just as you've done?"

"I did what I thought was best."

My grandfather sighed, patted Ethan's arm. "I don't doubt that, son, but there are times to fight, and times to wait. This was one of the latter."

There was something odd about my grandfather, a man in his seventies, referring to a four-hundred-year-old vampire as "son." But the dynamic worked.

"You know this is part of a bigger plan," Ethan insisted.

"I know what kind of man Reed is, and I'm not alone. There are others on the force—Detective Jacobs, for one—who agree with us, who understand. But, by God, you're playing right into his hands. You're proving the point he's apparently decided to make—that he's a businessman who's doing right by this city, and you're unstable monsters with a personal vendetta. You're too smart for antics like this, and I'd say the same thing about your trip to Hellriver last night."

"We wanted to get out before the CPD arrived," Ethan said.

My grandfather looked dubious. "While I'm sure that was part of the motivation, I doubt that was all of it."

Ethan had to know my grandfather was goading him to answer, but he obliged. "I was hoping Cyrius Lore would get away, tell Reed."

"You thought you'd provoke him to act."

"I want him to come at me." Ethan pushed his hands through his hair. "I want him to come at me like a man with some courage."

"And there's the fault in your logic," my grandfather said. "A man like Reed doesn't have courage, not in the way you mean. He has *soldiers*. He has men who fight his battles for him."

Ethan took a slow, heavy breath. "It was my call, not hers, and I take responsibility for it."

My grandfather nodded, acknowledging the admission, then looked at me. "You're unusually quiet."

Because I was seething with anger. But there was nothing to gain in airing that anger in front of Jeff and my grandfather.

I settled on "It's been a long night."

My grandfather watched me for a moment before nodding. He could probably read my face, understood Ethan and I would have words later.

"Did you find anything in Hellriver?" Ethan asked, bringing my grandfather's attention back to him.

"No. They'd cleared out the entire building other than a few pieces of furniture. If there was anything that tied the building to Reed, it was gone by the time we got there."

"Damn," Ethan said. "There'd been file boxes in the dock area. Dozens of them. Merit had suspected it was paperwork, maybe records of improper business dealings by Reed."

My grandfather's eyebrows lifted. "I don't suppose I need to tell you that we might have gotten to it if you'd phoned us earlier."

"You do not," Ethan said. "That was also my call."

"Next time," my grandfather said, "make better calls."

The cops walked back to us again. "Mr. Merit, we need to get these two to the station, get them processed. You know how it goes." The CPD might have given my grandfather some deference, but we were still criminals.

"I do," my grandfather said, then glanced at Ethan. "I'll warn Malik. And have them put the House on alert. Just in case."

We were driven to the nearest station in the back of a cruiser, processed, and separated, stuck in separate rooms for interviews.

My room was small, with a hard tile floor and a small table with four chairs. The wall beside the door was mirrored. Probably two-way glass so people in the hallway could look in on the woman in the fancy party dress who was mentally kicking her boyfriend.

I was a well-dressed cautionary tale.

I'd been sitting alone for fifteen minutes when the door opened. Instinctively, I sat up straight.

The woman who walked in was tall and slender with dark skin, wavy brown hair, and very serious brown eyes. She wore dark trousers, and a cream silk top beneath a fitted taupe blazer that curled into pleats across the bottom, showing long and elegant legs. There were pearls at her ears and throat, and a no-nonsense handbag on her arm. She set down the bag and a leather padfolio on the table, pulled out a chair for herself, and sat down.

"You're Merit." Her expression was as no-nonsense as the bag.

I nodded.

"I'm Jennifer Jacobs. Arthur Jacobs's daughter."

Arthur Jacobs was the CPD detective and ally my grandfather had mentioned. He'd actually been the cop who responded to Reed's previous call.

"Did he send you?" I asked.

"He asked me to check in on you, make sure you're all right. I'm an attorney," she said, checking her phone when it buzzed, then sliding it back into a slim pocket on the side of her purse. "Not your attorney. I'm not offering you representation, nor am I representing you with respect to any criminal complaint that Adrien Reed may file. I'm just doing my father a favor."

A favor, by her tone and lengthy disclaimer, that she wasn't thrilled about. But since she was here, I could be gracious.

"Then thanks to you both. It's nice to meet you, if under these circumstances."

Jennifer didn't respond, but took a good look at me, then linked her hands on the table.

"I'm going to tell you something, Merit," she said, her gaze direct. "My father is a good cop. A good father and a good cop. He doesn't need trouble."

I was getting tired of this speech. "We haven't brought him any trouble."

"All evidence to the contrary." She sat back in the chair, crossed one leg over the other. "He has some kind of affinity for supernaturals, probably because he's friends with Chuck Merit. He should be captain right now. Was close to it, until he began involving himself in supernatural affairs."

"In my eyes, that's something to respect him for."

"In my eyes, it's something that could get him killed."

And there it was. I sympathized, but I was sick of taking undeserved blame.

"We're not troublemakers, although our enemies enjoy painting us that way. They also enjoy targeting us because of who we are, because we're different. I have a great deal of respect for your father, because he understands that. I'm sorry you have to worry for him. I worry for my grandfather. But their involvement is their choice."

"You're frank," she said.

"I don't see the point of not being frank." My voice softened, considering what her family had recently been through. "I'm very sorry about your brother. I understand he was a wonderful young man."

Her brother, Brett, had been targeted by a serial killer whose latent crazy had been triggered by unrequited love.

Jennifer's expression tightened. "That should help you understand my concern."

"I understand it, but I didn't cause it, and I'm not sure what you think I could possibly do about it."

"Don't involve him in your troublemaking."

I linked my hands on the table, leaned forward. "Ms. Jacobs, I don't know you. I don't know your father very well, but like I said, I respect him. His intelligence, his sense of fairness, and his ability to think critically about supernaturals. I would suggest you spend a little less time accusing vampires and a little more time listening to what he actually has to say. Your attitude? It's exactly what he's fighting against."

Her eyes flashed. "I'm not concerned about your people. I'm concerned with mine, as they aren't immortal. Stay away from my father, and we won't have any problems."

She rose, slipping her handbag over her arm before grabbing the notebook. "I'll advise my father that conditions here are fine, and you're awaiting your attorney's arrival. That should fulfill my part of the bargain."

She walked to the door, glanced back. "Stay away from him."

And with that, she walked out.

Much like the flowers at the Botanic Garden, nourished by the warmth of spring, our list of enemies was growing.

Chapter Thirteen

FIRST, KILL ALL THE VAMPIRES

The House's lawyers arrived—a bevy of men and women in smart black suits (of course) who assured me everything would be fine.

They asked me to relay what had happened; four of them took notes while one asked the questions. They explained the process, promised I'd be out on bail in no time, and told me to sit tight, that they'd get the wheels of justice moving.

Having gotten my mandated meeting with counsel, I was then placed in a holding cell for supernaturals. Ethan was already there, sitting on a bench that cantilevered out of the wall. He jumped to his feet when I entered, checking me for injuries.

You're all right?

I'm fine, I said, taking a seat beside him on the bench. *Arthur Jacobs's daughter, Jennifer, came by to explain how unhappy she is that we're involving her father in supernatural affairs.*

His eyebrows lifted in surprise. *What?*

She's an attorney. He asked her to look in on us. She decided to take advantage of the situation.

I wasn't aware we controlled his behavior. His voice was flat as a windless sea.

I'm sure she realizes that. And yet . . .

And yet it's easier to blame the monster in front of you than the human with free will. I have apologies to make, Ethan said, *but they are not to her.*

I didn't disagree with that, and since he had plenty of apologizing to do to me, I wished him luck with it.

He was going to need it.

We waited another hour, sharing the cell with a drunk shifter who was snoring on the floor, the smell of cheap booze obvious even a few feet away, and two River nymphs with torn dresses and black eyes. River nymphs managed the ebb and flow of the Chicago River. They were petite and busty and favored high heels, short dresses, and candy-colored convertibles. Nymphs ran hot and cold, and not much in between. The heat probably explained the injuries. But whatever animosity had been between them faded when we walked in. At the sight of us, they huddled together, enemies bonding to dish about the disheveled vampires in party clothes.

At the end of that hour, hard-soled shoes clapped toward us. A female officer with pale skin and dark hair pulled into a messy bun pointed at us, then unlocked and slid open the barred door. "You're free to go."

"Bond was posted?" Ethan asked, rising and walking forward.

"No bond necessary. Mr. Reed isn't going to press charges."

Ethan's eyes narrowed with suspicion, but I wasn't surprised in the least. Reed couldn't torture us if we were locked away. He'd get more enjoyment from having us freed, forcing us to watch his ascendancy.

We signed some paperwork, picked up our personal effects, and headed outside. Jeff stood in front of the Audi, which he must have driven over from the Botanic Garden. Shifter or not, he was a stand-up man. And by his expression, still very irritated.

"You all right?" he asked, looking us over.

"We are," Ethan said. "Thank you for bringing the car, and for coming earlier. Especially considering . . ." Ethan didn't have to mention the item in consideration—the fact that we were currently fighting with Jeff's alpha.

Jeff nodded. "Pack's still a democracy. I didn't know about the Circle; obviously, I'd have mentioned it." He sounded mildly perturbed about the fact that he hadn't known. Understandable, since he'd been among the group of us who'd had to track it down.

"And I'm not saying I agree or disagree with Gabe," he added, lest we think he was completely on our side. He looked pointedly at Ethan. "Being a leader means making decisions that, in hindsight, look regrettable."

A smile was not appropriate, so I bit it back. Jeff was usually too agreeable for his alpha side to pop out, but it would be wrong to forget he was still, literally and figuratively, a tiger.

"It's worth saying again that we appreciate your help. And perhaps I should get Merit back to the car before she decides to leave with you."

"It's a close call," I agreed.

Jeff nodded, handed Ethan the keys.

"Do you need a ride?" Ethan asked.

Jeff glanced back at the car. "Even if I did, there's no room in the car for me. But no. Fallon's waiting." He gestured to a motorcycle parked a few stalls away. A petite figure in black leather and a matching helmet revved the bike with a flick of her wrist.

Jeff smiled, magic and love blooming in the air.

"I'll be in touch tomorrow about the alchemy," he said, shifting his attention back to me. "I've been talking to Paige."

It was another shot, and a completely fair one. Reed had distracted us, which was probably part of his plan.

"I'm also working on the safe-deposit box key. I'm about sixty percent through the first search of bank records but haven't found anything yet."

"Thank you," I said. "I plan to offer my help to Paige as soon as I get back to the House." And out of the dress and heels. What novelty there'd been had completely worn off.

"Where's Catcher tonight?" I asked. "It's unlike him to miss a chance to bitch at us."

Jeff nearly smiled, which was good enough for me. "He's following up with the Order again. Still trying to confirm they don't have any information about our alchemist. He made the trip to Milwaukee in person." He checked his watch. "Probably on his way back."

"Not the wisest move to induce a pissed-off sorcerer to travel to see you," Ethan said.

"No," Jeff said. "It wasn't. But then, you usually have better sense, too."

I snorted. "I think he sank your battleship."

"Maybe Reed is making everyone crazy," Ethan said.

"Speaking of which," I said, gesturing to the station, "did you know there are River nymphs in there?"

Jeff nodded. "We're letting them cool off. They won't press charges against each other, so they'll be released when they calm down."

"Already in process," I said. "They were gossiping about us when we left."

"Just doing our part," Ethan said. "Thank you again, Jeff. I'll try to get Merit back to Cadogan House without further trouble. And perhaps we could meet at dusk to discuss what we've all learned so far?"

Jeff nodded. "I'll tell Chuck, Catcher." He squeezed my hand before walking toward the bike, then climbed on the bike behind Fallon and put on the helmet she offered him. More engine revving, and they drove away.

"I believe I pissed off your knight in shining armor," Ethan said.

"Probably so," I said, and gathered up voluminous silk to slide into the passenger seat. The anger I'd pushed down began to bubble up again. "He's protective of me, and I got arrested, so . . ."

"Would you like me to say you told me so?"

"That won't change anything."

"No," Ethan said, closing the door. "It won't."

It was the first time we'd been alone together since we arrived at the Garden, and my first opportunity to vent. "You put my father and my grandfather in a hell of a position, and you put us right into Reed's hands. We made our reputation worse—and we're damn lucky there weren't paparazzi outside the station waiting to reveal our arrest to the world."

"He got under my skin."

"And that's no excuse. You have centuries more experience. You know better. You are better." Tears stung my eyes. "That was absolutely humiliating."

"He thinks he's invincible." His voice was measured, still edged with fury. "He thinks he's untouchable. None of that will change if we go along to get along. If we wait for someone else to do the dirty work. Nothing will change until someone calls him out." He looked at me. "If we don't do it, who will?"

"I don't disagree with you. But he's powerful, well protected, and very savvy." I looked at Ethan. "He plays games with people, Ethan. He did it with Celina. He did it with the vampire pretending to be Balthasar. That's who he is. He's a narcissist, an opportunist, and a criminal entrepreneur. But maybe most of all, he's a psychopath.

He likes to torture people, take advantage of their vulnerabilities. Their insecurities. We have to be smarter than that. We can't just play into his hands."

"I should have listened to you. I didn't, and I should have. I may be wise in the ways of supernaturals, but you're better with humans."

In fairness, I'd been one about four hundred years more recently than him.

"Now you're just kissing my ass," I said.

"I am trying my damnedest." He paused. "Is it working?"

"No."

He glanced at me, reached out to push a lock of hair behind my ear. "You know I lost my family once. You are my family now, Merit. I will not lose you."

"I still *have* a family, Ethan. They certainly aren't perfect, but I won't lose them to a man like Reed." I looked at him. "And I won't have them used."

I could practically see his frustration rising again. "It was one phone call," he said. "Your father owes you that much and more."

"That was my decision to make. Not yours."

"As you reminded Jennifer Jacobs, no one forced him to do as I asked."

I nearly punched him. Right then and there, I nearly plowed a fist into that gorgeous face for turning that around on me. Even if he was right.

Ethan started the car, backed onto the road. "Be angry with me if you must, Sentinel. I can bear it. But Adrien Reed will not lay a hand on you."

It was past midnight when we rolled back into the Cadogan garage.

Ethan went to his office to update Malik and Luc.

I went upstairs to update my ensemble. The gown had done its part, whatever that part might have been. I placed it on the bed, where laundry or dry-cleaning elves (or a vampire directed by Helen, more like) would attempt to clean and repair it.

I changed into jeans and a navy T-shirt with CADOGAN in white block letters across the front to head back to the library.

My phone beeped as I was closing the door. I found a message from Jonah: HEARD ABOUT ARREST. CALL IF YOU NEED TO. AND PHOTO NOT FAMILIAR.

Word of our near incarceration had apparently spread. Jonah hadn't been in a hurry to get back to me about the Rogue, and I hadn't thought to follow up. But I'd have to deal with him and the RG's baggage later.

I made it down the flight of stairs before my phone buzzed again, this time with a phone call. I pulled it out but didn't recognize the number. "This is Merit."

"Hi, Merit. It's Annabelle—the necromancer. You told me to call if I found something alchemical."

My heart began to pound with anticipation. "Hi, Annabelle. What did you find?"

"I'm not entirely sure. But you might want to get here sooner rather than later."

My phone beeped again, signaling the receipt of an image. I scanned the screen and the photograph she'd forwarded—and the dozens of alchemical symbols pictured there.

"We'll be right there," I promised.

Once again, the library would have to wait.

Ethan was Master of the House and one of the twelve members of America's reigning vampire council.

But there was nothing vaguely obedient—or even very polite—in the angry stares Luc and Malik sent him from their unified front in Ethan's office. They stood side by side, a wall of frustration matched against the Master who'd endangered himself. As much as they hated Reed, they were pissed at Ethan.

Ethan hadn't changed clothes, but he'd taken off the bow tie and jacket, unbuttoned the top of his shirt. The coiffing he'd done earlier had loosened its grip on his hair, and it waved like golden sunlight around his face, highlighting sharp cheekbones and firm mouth.

"We've taken a big enough hit tonight," Luc said. "You and Merit, particularly, don't need to take another risk by going out again."

"And there are supplicants in the foyer," Malik pointed out.

"There are," Ethan acknowledged. "And I will apologize to them personally. But we can't ignore another instance of alchemy. Especially since it seems what we have upstairs is only part of the story."

"You could send someone else," Luc pointed out.

Ethan shook his head. "Merit found the first alchemy, and she's familiar with the symbols. She has a rapport with Annabelle, and she can defend herself if the sorcerer shows up." He slid his gaze to me, over the invisible wall between us. "And she's not leaving without me.

"Yes, I let Reed provoke me, and he'll almost certainly try again. We can't stop that until we stop him. But if we stay here and put our heads in the sand—we also play into his hands. That's what has allowed him to gain as much power as he currently holds. That's what he's counting on."

Malik and Luc looked at each other, and then Luc slid his gaze to me. "Sentinel, your analysis?"

"As much as I hate to admit it, he's right."

"Not entirely flattering," Ethan murmured, rolling up one of his shirtsleeves.

"Wasn't meant to be," I assured him, the tension still heavy between us. I looked at Luc and Malik. "He knows how to provoke us, how to play with emotions. That's what he does. It's what he's good at."

"Balthasar," Malik said, and I nodded.

"Exactly. And yeah, he likes to wax poetical about the game we're playing, the chess match, whatever. He likes to screw with people. But we know he has a bigger plan. Lore admitted it. Reed admitted it, with all that messiah complex nonsense about saving Chicago. Whatever he has planned, we aren't the focus. I think moments like this—this drama he orchestrated at the Botanic Garden—they're part of his sideshow. He had CPD officers waiting for us. There's no way they'd have gotten there so quickly otherwise. But they weren't the main event, because we aren't the main event. The alchemy, the plan. That's the main event. That's why we have to go tonight, because that's what Reed cares about. That's what he's trying to distract us from. If we don't go, we help him win."

There was silence for a moment.

"That's not bad, Sentinel." Luc wiped a faux tear away. "I'm actually pretty proud."

"I had good teachers. But let's not get too cocky," I said, and pulled out my phone, handed it to Ethan. "Call my grandfather," I said, meeting his gaze. "Tell him where we're going. And then let's get this show on the road."

Wisely, he didn't argue.

Annabelle asked us to meet her at Mount Rider Cemetery, which was located on the city's far northwest side. My grandfather promised to meet us there—or to send Jeff or Catcher, depending on who could get there quickest. We gave her a heads-up in case we weren't the first to arrive, then climbed into the car again.

Unlike Longwood, with its chain-link fence and fallen headstones, Mount Rider was as much park as cemetery, its rolling hills landscaped and artfully dotted with trees, shrubs, and reflecting pools. The monuments were tall enough to be war memorials, with plenty of weeping angels and marble obelisks.

Annabelle was still in her car when we arrived, and there was no sign of Ombuddy yet. It took a good fifteen seconds—and an offered hand from Ethan—for her to unwedge herself from behind the steering wheel of her Subaru. "Three more weeks," she said, locking the door behind her. "Just three more weeks."

"Your first child?" Ethan asked.

"Second," she said, adjusting the long, drapey wrap she'd worn over a tank and long jersey-knit skirt. "Marley's a very precocious four right now. My husband, Cliff, stays at home with her. She is very eager to be a big sister, and he is very excited about having another little one in the house." She smiled. "I am excited about being able to stand up without assistance. But enough about me." She glanced around. "No Ombudsman?"

"Right here," said a voice behind us. Catcher jogged up, stuffing his car keys into the pocket of the dark-wash jeans he'd paired with a gray T-shirt. NO MAGIC? NO PROBLEM was written across the front. The Ombuddies were showing love for everyone.

"I parked on the other side of the block," he said, running a hand over his shorn head. "Didn't want too many cars parked in one spot, just in case. Catcher Bell," he said, extending a hand to Annabelle.

"Annabelle Shaw. You're the sorcerer."

"And you're the necromancer."

"All night long."

We chuckled. Supernatural inside joke.

"Heard you were dealing with the Order tonight," I said.

Catcher's lip curled. "They have the bureaucracy of a DMV office with one hundred percent less effectiveness."

"Any news about the sorcerer?" Ethan asked.

"Not from the Order. They maintain they have no knowledge of a sorcerer with expertise in alchemy, nor of alchemy being used in the city. And they're holding the line on Reed—that no union sorcerers work for him."

"Adrien Reed?" Annabelle asked. "Is he involved in this? With the alchemy?"

"We believe so," Ethan said. "But we're still trying to figure out the mechanics."

"And who the sorcerer is."

"Exactly," Ethan said with a nod.

"Sometimes I wish I was more involved in the city's supernatural communities," she said. "And sometimes I hear about nonsense like this and I'm glad I live under the radar."

"Stay sequestered," I recommended. "Unless there's a potluck."

And that reminded me: I needed to plan a potluck.

"Fair enough. Shall we?" she asked, and when we nodded, she walked to the cemetery's gate, used an enormous key on an equally enormous round key ring to unlock it.

We followed her inside and down another crushed-stone path.

"They never sleep as well when their memorials are disturbed," she said.

"Then by God," I said, trying to step as lightly as possible in her footsteps, "let's not do that."

We followed her over a low hill. Heavily pregnant or not, she moved like a sprite, walking under a copse where dew glimmered in the moonlight like fallen coins, and then stopping outside a small brick building.

"It used to be a maintenance facility," she said, stepping back onto the paved walkway that led to the front door. The glass in the windows and door had been painted white, not unlike the treatment at La Douleur. An open padlock hung from the door's handle. Annabelle pulled it off, pushed open the door, and flipped on the light switch just inside it.

"Welcome to Symboltown," she said, the room illuminated by a bare bulb that swung from the ceiling.

Its circle of light shifted back and forth across the square room, illuminating the symbols that had been drawn in black across the whitewashed walls.

"That's affirmative for alchemy," Catcher said, spinning in a slow circle to take it in.

"The scale is impressive," Annabelle said, hand on the small of her back, her gaze on the walls. "But I don't get the point of going to all this trouble. Alchemy seems more trouble than it's worth."

"Maybe this is magic that only alchemy can accomplish," I said, nearly skimming my fingers over the symbol for mercury until a hand gripped my arm.

I glanced up, found Ethan's hand there, his expression concerned. "You looked like you might dive right into it. Perhaps a step back, Sentinel."

I took the advice and made it a big step.

"Alchemy's not my bag," Catcher said. "But I see your point. This is a lot of symbols."

"Does any of this look familiar?" Ethan asked. "In the specific equations, I mean?"

I walked around the room, trying to find the starting point, settled on a symbol near the ceiling of the back wall where the symbols seemed a little bit larger than the others, as if he'd shrunk them slightly as he worked to fit them all in.

I followed the symbols as they moved down the wall, looking

for a pattern, part of the equation that might have matched the ones I'd seen while helping Paige. The symbols were basically the same—the primary symbols of the alchemical language, along with some of the same hieroglyphs we'd seen at Wrigley.

"It looks like the same set of symbols," I concluded, "but that doesn't really tell us anything, except that he's decided he needs them in a second place."

"Did you know alchemists sometimes put false symbols in their texts?" Annabelle asked. "I thought it would be a good idea to read up."

"Maybe that's why none of it makes sense," I said. "How are we supposed to tell the true from the false?"

"To do that," Catcher said, "we need to understand the context. That's what we're missing."

"Even if it takes him time to get the code together, Jeff's algorithm might still be the faster option. I mean, unless we find the sorcerer and can ask him."

Ethan glanced at Annabelle. "I don't suppose you've seen him?"

"Actually, I might have."

Catcher glanced back sharply. "You saw him? The sorcerer?"

She held up a hand, smiled apologetically. "I mean, sorry, I didn't see his face. So, I saw the light on in here for the first time maybe two or three weeks ago. At the time, I thought someone was doing some late maintenance work. Tonight's the first time I've actually been in here. But a few days ago—before I met Ethan and Merit—I noticed someone leaving."

"What did you see?" Ethan asked.

She closed her eyes, remembering. "Not a tall guy. Maybe five foot eight or nine? Not an especially big guy. On the leaner side. Wore a suit, I think. I mean, it was dark, so I'm not sure, but just from the shape of the clothing, looked like a suit."

"Did you see where he went?" Ethan asked.

"I didn't. This was before I met you, learned about the alchemy, so I wasn't on the lookout. He walked out of the cemetery, and I heard a car start a couple of minutes later. Once we did meet, and you mentioned you were looking for alchemy, I thought I'd better check it out. I expected to find some graffiti, maybe evidence teenagers had been drinking or getting high." She gestured to the walls. "Did not expect this."

Her phone rang—her ringtone Chopin's famous and haunting funeral march—and she checked the screen. "Appointment about a potential client." She put the phone away, looked up at us. "I'm sorry, but I need to go."

"Of course," Ethan said. "We can't thank you enough for your help. All things considered, I wouldn't mention what you've seen to anyone else. It's unlikely Reed would know you're involved, and it's safest to keep it that way."

The irony of his saying that wasn't lost on me. And from the heavy look he offered me, it wasn't lost on him, either.

"No argument there. If I see anything else, I'll let you know."

"Would you like an escort back to your car?" Catcher asked, and she just smiled.

"Thoughtful offer," she said, patting his arm. "But the night I can't take care of myself in a graveyard is the night I need to hang up my license." She turned and walked out the door.

I looked at Catcher. "I bet she and Mallory would get along really well."

"Merit, Sentinel of Cadogan House and magical matchmaker." Ethan smiled, probably grateful for the levity.

"I got Paige and the Librarian together," I pointed out.

Catcher pulled out his phone "Technically, Mallory got them together. Let's get this photographed for Jeff."

I nodded, pulled out my own phone.

"I'd like to meet at dusk," Ethan said, walking to one of the walls and staring at it, hands on his hips.

Catcher nodded. "Jeff mentioned it. You might try not irritating Adrien Reed in the meantime," he said, angling his phone to get a shot.

"Been holding that one in for a few hours?" I asked.

"I have."

"It's good advice," I said. "You should convince Ethan to take it."

"You might make the same suggestion to Reed," Ethan grumbled. "I suspect it won't be long before we hear from him again."

"Then we'll have to double our efforts," Catcher said.

"We may need to do more than that."

Catcher and Ethan both stopped, looked back at me.

"We've found symbols in two different parts of town. At a cursory glance, it looks like they're part of the same kind of magic." I looked at Catcher. "Chicago's a big town, and two sets isn't very many for magical purposes. If they really are connected, wouldn't we expect to see more than two?"

"Possibly," Catcher said. "But that would mean there are more sites out there. Potentially many more."

"Yeah," I said. "My point exactly."

Ethan looked at Catcher. "Maybe Chuck could ask the city's sups to keep an eye out, report in if they see anything?"

Catcher nodded. "I'll talk to him about it."

"So we know our sorcerer wore a suit," I said.

Ethan gestured to the tuxedo pants he still wore, the button-down shirt. "Many supernaturals wear suits."

I thought of the sup at La Douleur in the suit and fedora, the one who I thought had ratted us out to Cyrius. We didn't know if he was a sorcerer, but he'd known enough to want us out of the club. And he'd been a snazzy dresser.

"I know," I said. "I'm grasping at straws. Because other than his connection to Adrien Reed, we don't have anything."

"Dusk," Ethan said. "We'll work through the steps, and we'll figure this out. He won't be able to hide much longer."

Good. Because he'd been hidden long enough.

Chapter Fourteen

NEWSIES 2.0

Ethan and I returned to the House, stopped at the basement stairs.

"You're going to the Ops Room?" he asked.

I nodded. "You're going to meet with supplicants?"

"It's only fair."

We stood in silence for a moment. We were both afraid—afraid of losing something dear, afraid of what Adrien Reed wanted to take from us. That fear had blossomed into anger and frustration, and those emotions roiled between us, a barrier we hadn't yet crossed.

"I'm not sure what else I can say."

I looked up at Ethan. "Me, neither."

He looked down, nodded. "Then let's go about our work until we do know. I'll see you later." Without waiting for my response, he began to trot up the stairs.

When he'd disappeared, I pressed a hand against my stomach, which had tightened with nerves and fear.

Yet another reason to detest Adrien Reed.

I walked down the hall, but when I opened the Ops Room door, Lindsey shook her head.

"Nope, nope," she said, moving to bar the door with arms outstretched. "You have company upstairs."

I frowned at her. "Company? Who?"

"A very pissed-off sorceress."

Damn. "Paige? Because of the alchemy?"

"Paige is in the library. It's Mallory."

"Mallory?" I checked my watch. It was late, and I didn't have any idea why Mallory might be pissed off.

"And before you ask," Lindsey said, "no, I don't know what she wants, even with my wicked psychic powers." She released one of her arms, used it to shoo me. "Go upstairs, talk to her, and get her to knock off the bad juju. She's magically funking up the joint."

I wanted to argue but decided the fastest way to figure out what was up with Mallory was to actually go upstairs and ask her. Still, I felt a low sense of dread. I didn't know anything I'd done to piss her off, which raised other issues—did it have something to do with the shifters? My grandfather? Dark magic?

I hustled up the stairs, glanced around the foyer, saw no one but the supplicants in the foyer and a vampire at the desk.

The assault came from behind me. She popped out of the woodwork like a pixie, began slapping at me with fluttering, butterfly hands.

"Ow! What the hell, Mallory?" For a petite woman with plenty of magic at her disposal, she slapped pretty hard.

"Biggest thing to happen in either of our damn lives and you didn't even tell me!"

"I have no idea what you're talking about."

"Gabriel's prophecy," she said in a fierce, growling whisper.

I stopped, stared at her.

There weren't many who knew about it, and I hadn't told anyone other than Ethan, for obvious reasons, and Lindsey, and because she'd mostly guessed it.

"How did you—"

She crossed her arms. "Gabriel's angry at Ethan. I guess he let it slip to Jeff, and Jeff told me."

Supernaturals could not keep secrets to save their lives. "Does my grandfather know?"

"No. Jeff didn't even mean to tell me, and he swore me to secrecy."

I rubbed my temples, which were beginning to ache from the weight of too much drama. Or Mallory's psychic funk.

"Let's go for a walk outside," I said.

But Mallory just kept staring at me, and her eyes began to fill. "You didn't tell me."

Crap, I thought, and took her arm much more gently than she'd have taken mine.

"Let's go outside," I said, heading off another round of bruises, "and I'll tell you everything."

I walked her through the House and the cafeteria, which was filled with chattering vampires and the scents of meat and chilies. It was Tex-Mex night, a House favorite. Thankfully, the food kept their attention as we walked past.

I led Mallory outside to the House's enormous pool, a beautiful rectangle of sparkling water. I sat down on the concrete that surrounded it. Mallory sat in front of me, cross-legged.

She put a hand on her chest. "Is it because of the magic? Because you don't trust me? Because you don't want me to know that you're trying to get pregnant?"

The fear in her eyes was obvious.

"No," I said, and when she looked at me, I said it again. "*No.*

Big no, little no, no. We're not trying to get pregnant, and it doesn't have anything to do with you or trust. It doesn't have anything to do with anything, really. It's just—it may not ever happen. It's all very fuzzy and up in the air."

She frowned, then cast a quick and wary gaze at my crotch before lifting her gaze to mine again. "You're going to need to explain that. Jeff was vague on the details, and I'm not really sure I understand how pregnancy could be fuzzy or up in the air."

"Because it's a prophecy, not a pregnancy test. Gabriel thinks we'll have a child—me and Ethan. But that would basically be a miracle among miracles."

"Why?"

"Because no vampire child has ever been born."

She leaned back in surprise. "Ever?"

"Forever ever. Three known vampire conceptions in the entire history of the world. None made it to term."

Her expression fell. "Damn, Merit. Those are pretty shitty odds."

"They are. Which makes Gabriel's prediction that much more awesome, and that much more questionable. And, to add insult to injury, we have to go through some kind of test before it happens."

She frowned. "What kind of test?"

"I don't know. Something bad that we have to endure."

She snorted lightly. "Hasn't there already been plenty of that?"

"I had the same question. I don't know what it will be, or when, or if it's sitting out there around the corner just waiting for us."

Or were we already in the middle of it—this nightmare with Reed? Was this the nastiness we had to survive, individually and together?

"What?" she asked.

I shook my head, not wanting to talk about Ethan, but she thumped me on the shin. "*Ow*. You are violent tonight."

She grinned. "It's very effective. And if you don't spill, I'll do it again." To prove her point, she made a circle of her thumb and index finger, held them near my shinbone.

"Ethan and I are fighting. I think."

"That is just shocking, because you're both so easygoing."

"Sarcasm will get you nowhere."

"I disagree, but I'll skip the argument. Spill."

I sighed. "You know about the Botanic Garden?"

"I got the earful, yeah."

"He found out Reed was going to be there by calling my father, having him make a phone call or something, confirm Reed's attendance."

"*Hmmm,*" was all she said.

"Yeah."

Mallory pulled up her knees, wrapped her arms around them. "The territory near your father is tricky, tricky ground. On the one hand, yeah, he's an adult. Could have told Ethan to pound sand. And just making a phone call isn't necessarily risky."

"And on the other hand?"

"On the other hand, Ethan even potentially involving your father with Reed again? That's dicey."

"Yeah, it is. That's exactly what I said."

"Has he apologized?"

"In the way that he apologizes. 'I would do anything to protect you,'" I said, in a pretty good imitation.

Mallory nodded. "He gave you an alphapology."

"What now?"

"An alphapology. The apology made by the alpha male, which isn't really an apology, but more a reason for insane behavior. Catcher does it all the damn time. Drives me up the *wall.*"

"Alphapology," I repeated, kicking the tires. "Yeah. That's pretty much it. What do I do about it?"

"Depends on Darth Sullivan's particular brand of alpha. He knows you've got a rocky relationship with your family, but he also knows they matter to you. And frankly, Merit, at least some of his asinine behavior is because of Reed. Reed's a crazy asshole, and crazy breeds crazy. If Ethan gets to the point where he acknowledges the phone call was a mistake, you can carry on."

"And if he doesn't?"

"Then Darth Sullivan isn't the man I thought he was." She reached out, took my hand, squeezed it. "And he is that man, Merit. Look at it this way. If this is the testing, you know you'll get through it. Or at least through it enough to get knocked up," she said with a snort.

"That's not really funny."

"I know."

"You know, I'm kind of surprised Gabriel didn't mention this to you when you were tutoring with him."

"Gabriel's really weird about his prophecies. He doesn't like to talk about them." She frowned, as if considering her words. "I'm not even sure 'prophecy' gets to the heart of it, not really. The word makes it sound like he knows this independent piece of information—this bit of knowledge that's separate from him. But it doesn't work that way. Shifters are connected—to the earth, to the things living on it, to the kind of"—she waved her hands in the air—"universal timeline. The things they prophesize, that knowledge, is part of that interconnected timeline. Part of who they are."

"That's pretty deep."

"It sounds like horseshit," she said with a grin. "Like the nonsense I'd have spewed in my Grateful Dead and patchouli days."

"Those were very colorful days." Mallory had braided her hair, worn broomstick skirts, and stocked the fridge with Cherry Garcia. I hadn't complained about the last.

"They were something," she agreed. "But Gabriel's the real

deal. You've seen the Pack together. Hell, you saw Convocation. You know what they're like."

"Yeah. But I don't know if that makes me feel better or worse."

"I'd say, take the middle ground. Cautiously optimistic. Or optimistically cautious."

"My question is, how's it actually going to happen?"

"Well, Merit, Ethan will put his—"

I held up a hand. "I didn't mean literally. If no child of vampires has ever been carried to term, how are we going to beat those odds?"

"I don't know," she said, brow furrowed. "Something with magic?"

"That was my guess, but I still don't know how the mechanics would work."

"Tab A, slot B."

"This conversation has taken a weird turn."

"Yeah, but that's kind of our thing." She leaned forward, put a hand on my knee. "My God, do I want to see Ethan facing his first loaded diaper. And can you imagine him dealing with milk puke?"

"I think he'll be a good dad." A protective one, certainly. He had that gene in spades. "I mean, for a four-hundred-year-old pretentious Master vampire."

"Well, yeah. But that's his burden to bear, and we shouldn't hold it against him. You know what we need?" she asked suddenly. "A beach vacation before you're ankle-deep in poopy diapers. I mean, I know you can't sunbathe, but we can still do manicures. Pedicures. Eat plenty of fried fish and listen to Jimmy Buffett by moonlight."

"I've never listened to Jimmy Buffett in my life."

"I haven't, either. But I think that's what you do on the beach. While drinking a margarita. We'll call it a retreat! I'll write a grimoire of good and helpful magic, or work on SWOB stuff, and you can, I don't know, sharpen your sword."

"Is that what you think we do in our free time? Sharpen our swords?"

She grinned. "Yes. Literally and figuratively."

"You are incorrigible."

"I know." She sighed happily. "All the shit we've been through—all the shit *I've* been through—and I can still make lascivious jokes with the best of them. That's impressive, Merit. That's character. And I'm serious about the retreat idea. I might even let you bring Ethan for a night if you two make up. I bet he'd look fine in one of those tiny Speedos."

I grimaced. As far as I was concerned, no one looked good in them. But I imagined Ethan would look good emerging from the ocean, body drenched and trunks riding low on his hips, striding across the sand like Poseidon.

I cleared my throat. "If we make up, I'll talk to him."

Mallory grinned. "You were thinking about him naked, weren't you?"

"No. Maybe. Yes."

"Good," she said with a grin. "'Cause you got a baby to make. And I should get going. I need to run an errand. I'm going to buy a crucible, actually. I mean, technically it's part of an old ceramics kiln. But I figure it will do the trick."

According to the books the Librarian had provided, crucibles were a crucial part of alchemy. "Are you going to actually try a transmutation?"

"I haven't decided yet. I'm thinking it would be worthwhile to try out one of the subequations—one of the shorter alchemical phrases. I was thinking that will help us fill in some of the nonsensical spots. But I don't want to accidentally set Reed's big plan in motion."

"No argument from me there."

"You gonna work on the symbols?"

I checked my watch. I'd spent part of the night on the road, part in a ball gown, part in a jail cell, and part in a cemetery. There wasn't much darkness left. "I'll at least stop by the library, yeah. I haven't exactly been a very good assistant for Paige."

"Since you're usually the one doing the heavy lifting, I wouldn't feel too bad about that. You're working other angles."

I nodded. "And speaking of, Ethan wants to meet here at dusk to talk. We told Catcher earlier."

"Yeah, he texted me. We'll be here." She pushed to her feet, offered me a hand. And when she'd helped me lever myself up, she surrounded me with a hug.

"I love you, Merit. Just—maybe give me a call the next time an Apex shifter predicts you'll have a bouncing magic vampire baby?"

I could practically see her gears working. "Don't say vambaby. And you'll be the first Bell I call."

"Damn right I will."

We walked back to the House over soft, cool grass, fell into a companionable silence.

"It's Tex-Mex night in there, right?" she asked when we reached the patio.

"It is."

"You think there's any enchiladas? Maybe I could grab one to eat on the trip back? Catcher's on a kale and quinoa kick. It's horrible."

"I'm sorry to hear that, and I'm not sure. But we can ask."

Arm in arm, we walked into the sensual embrace of Tex-Mex night.

This time, Lindsey let me into the Ops Room. The fact that I'd brought guacamole probably hadn't hurt, since the guards fell on it like wolves.

Double-dipping wolves, as it turned out.

"About damn time you made it down here," Luc said.

"Sorry," I said, and tried to remembered what I'd been planning to report before I was interrupted by a sorcerer and banned by a fellow guard. "Mallory had a personal crisis. Needed to get it resolved so we could all get back to work."

I offered my phone, showed him the pictures we'd taken at Mount Rider. "Catcher took pictures, too. He's going to ask Jeff to work them into that algorithm. And Ethan wants to meet at dusk."

"I don't think Ethan's in a position to make any demands right now," Luc grouched, spearing a chip into the bowl.

"Yeah, well, I'm not going to be the one to tell him that. But you go right ahead."

Luc made a dubious grunt. "You told Catcher about the dusk meeting?"

"And Mallory."

Luc nodded. "I'll tell Paige and the Librarian."

"I was going to go to the library," I said, but when I checked the clock, I realized dawn was approaching. "But the night has wasted away again."

"I talked to Paige while you were gone, made your apologies." He ran a hand through his tousled curls. "Frankly, Sentinel, I don't think your being there would have made much of a difference. She's stuck, too. Said the equations still aren't making sense. At least you got a new location tonight. Not that that helps with the scope of our problem. Just increases it."

"I've asked Catcher to spread the word among the sups, have them alert us if someone finds more alchemy."

Luc nodded. "That's something, but Chicago's an enormous city."

"We need to tell the Houses."

"They've got the basics," he said. "Wouldn't have been fair to keep the information about the alchemy from them. But requesting they jump in? Yeah. I mean, they aren't Cadogan House—more Hufflepuff to our Gryffindor—but we could use the extra bodies."

I just stared at him. "Harry Potter? Really?"

"Those books are quality, Sentinel. You should read them."

He said it like he was the first person to discover the books, to realize they were good. I decided not to mention my first editions.

"I'll make a note of it," I said. "Oh, and Annabelle saw the sorcerer." I passed along the minimal details she'd been able to see, my curiosity about the man at La Douleur.

"Lots of vampires wear suits."

"I know. Ethan said the same thing." Suddenly exhausted, I rose. "I'm going upstairs."

"Get Ethan on the right track," Luc said. "You'll both feel a lot better."

"Bang his brains out," Lindsey offered helpfully from the other side of the room.

Luc shook his head. "Apologies, Sentinel. My girlfriend is crude."

"And you love it," she said.

From his wide smile, I guessed she was right.

"Good luck, Sentinel," Luc said. "Our wands are up for you."

I didn't think that quite sounded the way he'd meant it to.

When I walked into our apartments, Ethan stood at his bureau. If circumstances had been different, I'd have teased him about Mallory, the fact that she now knew about the maybe-baby. That would raise the specter of baby showers, cribs, and godparents, which would have flustered him to my amusement.

But that's not where we were. Not right then.

I took off my clothes, washed my face, and slid into pajamas. He did the same, sat down on his side of the bed just as I'd sat down on mine. The wall was invisible, but it was there. "They know of the meeting at dusk?"

"They do," I said, turning off the bedside light and slipping my feet under cool sheets.

"Good. Perhaps we can make progress. Perhaps we'll all feel better if we make progress."

I wasn't sure if he meant himself or me or both of us. Either way, the sun rose before I could ask the question.

Chapter Fifteen

DRY ERASE MAGIC

Our dusk meeting would actually begin an hour after dusk to give everyone time to get to Cadogan House. Preparations were well under way when I headed downstairs. Luc was updating the whiteboard while Margot set out bottles of water and a tray of snacks. Ethan talked with Malik near the bookshelves on the left-hand side of the room, away from the flurry of activity.

I joined them, dressed in leathers and black boots.

"Sentinel," Ethan said, a question in his eyes—*Are we still fighting?* Since we hadn't reached an accord, and he hadn't even lingered in the apartments long enough to say good evening, I couldn't see how the answer was anything but yes. But I wasn't going to drag everyone into it.

"Did Luc talk to you about inviting Morgan and Scott?" I asked Ethan.

"He did, and they'll be here. He also suggested we invite Gabriel."

Talk about fighting fire with fire. "And did you?"

"I put in a call," Malik said. "It hasn't yet been returned."

So Gabriel was angry, too. Reed was turning the city's supernaturals into a seething cauldron of frustration, Cadogan House included.

Malik's phone beeped, and he checked the screen, smiled. "Excuse me. I need to grab this. It's Aaliyah."

That was Malik's wife.

"Of course," Ethan said.

As Malik walked away, lifting the phone to his ear, Ethan settled his gaze on me. "Good evening."

"Good evening."

We managed that much, then just looked at each other.

"Your father called," Ethan said carefully. "He wanted to be sure you'd gotten home all right after the incident at the Garden. He also wanted to let us know that Reed asked Robert to submit a proposal to manage the Towerline building."

So Reed would own the building, and Merit Properties would manage it. That could be a very lucrative contract, if it was really about the money. But it undoubtedly wasn't. "He's trying to suck them in again. Reed and my family."

"To get to them, to you, and to me. Yes." Ethan studied me. "Your father wants a chance at him, Merit. He knows he's being used as a pawn, and he wants to help take Reed down."

I stiffened. "He's not equipped to go up against Reed. His best bet would be to tell Robert the truth."

"Which, as you know, would only tip off Reed and possibly incite him further."

"Damned if we do, damned if we don't. What did you tell him?"

Ethan paused, looked at me. "Nothing. Yet."

The most frustrating answer. It neither told me what he'd do nor agreed to keep my father out of it.

"You aren't making this easy," I said.

"War is never easy. A soldier knows that better than most."

I looked up at him, surprised by the grimness in his voice. "Is that what this is? War?" I was asking about both of us—about us and Reed, me and Ethan.

"Reed believes it is, so we will treat it as such."

And use the weapons at our disposal, I thought, whatever the consequences.

Luc walked toward us, and Ethan's gaze went cool again. "I think we're ready, or will be as soon as everyone arrives." He looked at me, took in the leathers I'd paired with dark mascara and cherry red lipstick. "Sentinel, I like that color on you." He winked. "Looking fierce."

"She looks fierce," Ethan said, "because she is."

Luc looked back and forth between us. "I feel like I don't want to know what's happening right now, so I'm going to just walk away and let you handle it." Luc did, backing up until he'd put enough distance between us.

"All right, Sentinel," Ethan said, "let's get to it."

Until we were ready to talk, there was nothing more to do.

Chicago's Supernatural Problem Solving Team was an assortment of humans, vampires, and shifters.

Malik and Paige had already taken seats at the conference table. My grandfather came in with Jeff, and Mallory and Catcher arrived behind them. My grandfather patted me on the back as he moved past, then stopped to help Jeff with another board of symbols.

Morgan Greer—broodingly handsome, with dark wavy hair that reached his shoulders and soulful dark blue eyes—came in, followed by Scott Grey. Scott was dark-haired and tall, with the build of an athlete and a soul patch beneath generous lips. Grey House had an athletic bent, signaled by his jeans and Grey House hockey-style jersey.

Surprisingly enough, he wasn't alone.

He'd brought Jonah, whose auburn hair was swept back from his face, framing sharp cheekbones and canny blue eyes. He wore a gray V-neck T-shirt, jeans, and boots.

Jonah scanned the room, found me still standing beside Ethan, let his gaze linger there for a moment. And then the moment passed, and he was moving to the table to sit beside his Master.

Was I on good terms with *any* of my partners right now?

Ethan gestured toward the table, and I walked to it and joined Lindsey to stand at the end of the table.

"Thank you all for coming," Ethan said. "The city has been presented with a magical threat that's uncertain but potentially large, so we thought it best to have everyone in a room together. Since we're all here, let's get started."

"One bit of news," Jeff said, raising his hand, and all eyes turned to him. "Cyrius Lore is dead."

Ethan's eyes flashed to me, bright with anger, heavy with guilt. Cyrius had been an enemy only briefly, and by making the connection between him and Reed, we'd sent him to his death.

"His body was dragged from the river this morning," my grandfather said. "He'd been killed by a vampire."

"The same one that killed Caleb Franklin," Catcher said, "based on the distance between the fangs."

"I didn't know that was a thing," I said. "Measuring the distance between the fangs to identify a culprit."

"Supernatural criminal forensics," Jeff said with a mirthless smile. "A growing field."

"I guess so."

"Sorry," Scott said, holding up a hand. "Who's Cyrius Lore?"

"He was the manager of La Douleur," Ethan said. "He's one of Reed's people, and La Douleur was one of Reed's places. He confessed to Merit and me that Reed was responsible for Caleb Franklin's death, and that Reed has something big planned that will 'bring order to the city' by taking control of it." Ethan mimicked justifiable air quotes.

There was lots of grumbling around the table.

"Reed must have decided Cyrius was a loose end," Catcher said, and my grandfather nodded.

"That would not be out of character for the Circle," he said.

"And what's his long game here?" Morgan asked. "Even if he gets control, what's the point of it?"

"Among other things," Ethan said, "financial opportunity. Controlling the city's coffers, awarding himself lucrative contracts, directing the allocation of resources. From what little he's said, he's somewhere near insane fascist on the political spectrum. Doesn't like supernaturals, doesn't like the poor. We suck away city resources."

Scott snorted. "He's clearly not looked at our property tax bills over the last few years."

"Or any of the other ways we contribute," Ethan agreed. "Maybe he's using Celina's neediness as his gauge. The point is, his motivations are personal, financial, political."

"How does the magic tie in?" Scott asked, his gaze on the boards.

"That's what we have to figure out," Ethan said, and nodded at Luc.

Luc stepped forward, used a laser pointer—and whoever had given him that toy deserved an ear boxing—to gesture at the Wrigleyville symbols on the board from the library.

"These were found on an El track pedestal near the body of Caleb Franklin. The symbols are alchemical in nature. They constitute phrases that, taken together, appear to make up one part of a larger equation."

"One part?" Scott asked.

"A local necromancer found another site yesterday." Luc gestured to one of the new boards Jeff had brought in, which showed a map of the city, stars where the symbols had been found.

"There are similar symbols on both, including some hand-drawn images that look like hieroglyphics, so odds are they were created by the same hand."

"Sorcerer?" Jonah asked, glancing at Catcher.

"Sorcerer," Catcher said with a nod. "The symbols have magic to them, but the artist's identity and origin are unknown. We've checked with the Order, and they don't have any known alchemical specialists in Chicago. For what that's worth," he added grumpily.

"We have a very general description and a penchant for alchemy," Ethan said. "We don't have a name."

"But we think the sorcerer belongs to Reed?" Scott asked.

Ethan nodded. "Based on what we know so far, including Cyrius's statements, yes."

"And the symbols themselves," Jonah said. "What do they mean? What's the purpose of all this magic?"

"Unfortunately, we have more questions than answers at the moment," Luc said. "Mallory and Paige have been working on translating, with Merit's able assistance. Paige, would you like to take over?"

"Sure," Paige said, rising from her chair and walking to the boards. She wore a green T-shirt and jeans, a simple outfit that made her eyes seem to glow against her pale skin and red hair. For all that, she looked nervous. She'd been an archivist locked away in Nebraska. Probably hadn't done many presentations.

She cleared her throat, took the laser pointer Luc handed her, tucked a lock of hair behind her ear.

"So," she said, gesturing to the boards. "What we have here is a complicated alchemical equation. Classic alchemical symbols mixed together with small hieroglyphs. We know what the alchemical symbols mean. We have best guesses about most of the hieroglyphs, but they're still guesses, and there are gaps in our knowledge.

"Theoretically, when you read all the symbols together, it should produce something that's both an instruction manual—do this thing at this time in this way—and a written spell." She linked her hands together. "Both the writing of it and the doing of it trigger the magic that's intended by the entire equation."

Morgan leaned forward, smiled. "Sorry, but for those of us who are completely green where magic is concerned, can you give us some context? I mean, you say 'alchemy,' and I assume you want to make gold out of lead."

There were general murmurs of agreement.

"Think of alchemy like chemistry or biology," Paige said. "A set of methods and principles used to organize our understanding of the world. At its heart is the belief you can manipulate matter to get closer to its true essence. And when you reach that true essence, the matter becomes a powerful, magical, and spiritual tool. It might make you healthier; it might make you stronger; it might make you immortal."

"Those all sound like things Reed would like," Morgan said.

"Agreed," she said. "But I don't think this sorcerer is working on what I'd call the 'traditional' alchemy problems. The philosopher's stone, turning lead into gold, whatever. The phrases—the smaller chunks within each equation—don't match those traditional equations. They're very contradictory." She pointed the laser at one of the lines. "For example, this phrase tells you to do something." Then she dropped it to the line below. "And this phrase tells you to do the opposite."

"What's your best guess about the purpose?" Ethan asked.

Paige looked back at the boards, considered. "Something big. Even the equations that have tried to produce a philosopher's stone aren't this complex, or this contradictory." She frowned. "Because of that, I don't see this being intended for one person. I mean, you want to make yourself blond, rich, immortal, whatever, you don't need this many lines of code, so to speak. I think it's intended for other people."

"What other people?" Ethan asked.

She looked back at us. "I don't know yet. But as large as the equation is, I'd say a number of them. Many, many people."

"I'm working on an algorithm," Jeff said. "A program that will automatically translate the symbols, make predictive guesses about the hieroglyphs, and give us best translation results."

"How far along are you?" my grandfather asked.

Jeff frowned. "About two-thirds? Need a few more hours to get the cipher right, and then I can compile the code, and we'll be ready to roll. Might need to do some contextual tweaking—like Mercury next to the sun instead of the moon means you need to hop on one foot or whatever—but we'll be close."

"Good," Ethan said. "We appreciate the work."

Jeff nodded.

"So Reed's got a sorcerer working some kind of big magic," Scott said, his gaze on the board. "Big magic that could affect a lot of people. But we don't know what the magic is yet, and we don't know how many people. And most of Chicago still thinks he hung the moon."

"And made it shine," Ethan said. "That's a fair summary."

"Then what can we do?" Scott asked.

"Be vigilant," Ethan said. "I can't stress that enough. He's looking for opportunities." He met my gaze. "He likes to use what he perceives as personal weaknesses against people. He's very intelligent, and he likes to manipulate."

"He's very egotistical," my grandfather said. "Likes to create a dramatic scene, but doesn't always think through the implications." He looked at Ethan, then me. "It turns out, the cops who arrested you at the Garden thought they were doing a favor for someone very powerful—putting away supernaturals who'd been stalking his family. They were, let's say, set on a better path."

"Thank you for that," Ethan said, and my grandfather nodded.

"The inaccuracies can be corrected," he said. "But that's the kind of manipulation we're dealing with."

"As for the magic," Luc said, "spread the word. Alert your vampires to the possibility of more symbol sites, and ask them to report anything they find."

"The odds of that seem pretty slim," Jonah said. "I mean, not that there are more sites, but that we'll randomly stumble across them." He glanced at me. "That's pretty much how you found the Wrigleyville symbols, right?"

"Almost exactly," I said.

"Maybe we can build something."

We all looked at Mallory, who was staring blankly at the open windows.

"What kind of something?" Catcher asked.

She blinked, looked at him. "I'm just talking this through, but a machine that would find the other sites? A magical radar, something that could send back a signal from concentrations of alchemy."

Catcher frowned, seemed to consider. "You're thinking about a receiver? Something to pick up the alchemical signals?" He paused. "Yeah. That might be possible. The sites would work like reflectors, if you could tune in to the alchemy's signal." He grabbed a notepad and pen from the center of the table, began scribbling.

"Is such a thing possible?" Ethan asked.

Mallory snorted. "Anything and everything is possible."

"Truer words," I murmured.

"Visibility could be a problem," Mallory said. "Actually being able to see where the symbols are, I mean. If they're spread out, we'll have line-of-sight problems."

"Maybe I could help with that," Jeff said.

"What are you thinking?" Catcher asked.

Jeff rubbed his temple absently. "Maybe I can align a program to the magic? So even if we can't see the locations' IRL, we can watch them on a screen? A three-dimensional map?"

IRL? Ethan asked silently.

In real life, I said. *As opposed to the lighthearted fantasy we're pretending to live in.*

"Yeah," Mallory said, nodding as she looked at Jeff and Catcher. "Yeah. That might actually work."

Ethan looked at Mallory. "There's no risk that this would harm you?"

His question was softly spoken. And it wasn't about doubt or lack of confidence in her, the fear that she'd use dark magic again, backslide into the hole she'd only so recently crawled out of. There was only concern for a woman who'd been his enemy, and who'd gained back enough trust to become his friend.

"No," she said, her voice calm and clear. And then she held out her hands.

Black magic, when she'd been using it, had chapped and cracked them. But they looked healthy and healed, each nail painted a different pastel shade, so they formed a long rainbow when she lined them up. Which made for a gorgeous effect.

"I wasn't asking—" Ethan began, but Mallory shook her head.

"I know," she said, meeting his gaze, chin up. "I was showing you. I owe you that much."

Ethan's expression stayed serious, and he nodded at her, something important, something weighty, passing between them. I had to bite my lip to keep quick, bright tears from welling. That he and

I weren't in sync right now didn't minimize the importance of the gesture, especially given the similarity between Reed's alchemy and Mallory's dark magic.

Catcher put an arm around his wife, pressed a kiss to her head.

"Well, then," Luc said. "That gives us a plan for the alchemy."

"And Reed?" Scott asked, rocking back in his chair. "What's the plan there?"

Ethan's gaze went flat. "His destruction and expulsion from the city of Chicago."

"So humble goals, then," Scott said.

"He won't stop," Ethan said. "This isn't a vendetta against me or my House. Reed doesn't care about anything other than his empire. We've seen that with Cadogan, we've seen it with Navarre, and now we've seen it with the unfortunate shifter who crossed his path."

"Then we won't let him," Morgan said, raising a bottle of water like a sword of allegiance. "It's about damn time we took back this city."

When details had been discussed and work assigned, supernaturals rose and dispersed. Some lingered and chatted; others left immediately.

Scott and Jonah were the first to go, which meant I didn't have to make awkward small talk while avoiding the real issue between us. Morgan followed, and then the guards went back to the Ops Room, and Paige returned to the library.

I checked with Jeff again about the safe-deposit box key. Still no dice after checking nearly three-quarters of the city's banks. Yes, it had been a long shot. We didn't even know if the key fit a box in Chicago. But we had to keep trying, had to do the work, even if it didn't seem to lead anywhere.

Margot brought in a care package for Mallory—a bag of junk

food apparently intended to make up for the "kale and quinoa" at the Bell house. While Catcher and Ethan chatted, Mallory shuffled through the bag of chips, popcorn, and cookies Margot had prepared like a woman preparing to wage her own Hunger Games.

"You have an entire chocolate drawer," I reminded her, thinking of the long bay of chocolate I'd collected when we were roommates.

"*Had* an entire chocolate drawer," she said.

My blood ran cold. "What do you mean, 'had'?"

"Quinoa," Mallory said by way of explanation. "He took the rest of it to the Ombudsman's office for the communal candy dish. It's all chia seeds and whole grains in there now."

"That bastard," I gritted out. In truth, I had only myself to blame for losing all that lovely chocolate. I should have taken it all with me when I moved into the House.

She cast a sly glance toward her husband. "I need to go sneak this into the car. Wanna go on a secret mission?"

"Candy-related missions are my favorite type," I said as she handed the loaded bag to me. I caught Ethan's glance on the way out the door. *I'll be right back.*

He nodded, slid his gaze back to Catcher.

With Mallory in the lead, car keys in hand and walking in a fast shuffle, we walked out of the House and through the gate. Catcher's sedan was parked right in front of the House.

I glanced at her, my brow cocked. "How'd he get this prime spot?"

"Said we were on an urgent mission. Which the guards bought, because it was the absolute truth."

"Did I mention I love your nail polish?" I asked.

"You did not, but thank you. Times like this, you gotta have a bright spot. You gotta have something to lighten the mood." She shrugged. "Catcher's homemade waffles and enormous dick usually do the trick. But a little paint and color never hurt."

I had no idea how to respond to that. Or what I could say that wouldn't encourage her to go into details. I decided on simple agreement. "Paint and color never hurt."

She popped open the car's trunk, moved aside a blanket, a spell book, and an enormous ceramic vessel the color of bone.

"Is that the crucible?" I asked, putting the bag in the trunk and smirking while she covered it with blankets.

"It is." She tucked in the bag like it was precious cargo. "I think I'm going to distill something. Try to make a salt, which doesn't really mean what you think it means." She sighed happily. "Oh, alchemy. You're so wonderfully wacky."

She might have appreciated the alchemy, but she wasn't nearly as careful with the ceramic crucible as she was with the bag of snacks.

"Mallory, you know I love you, but I wonder if going to this much trouble to keep some candy from Catcher is a bad plan."

"What he doesn't know won't kill him. I just need a new hiding place. I'm thinking a cabinet in the basement, but then the spiders might get in there." She wrinkled her nose. "I don't want to make light of this Reed situation, but honest to God, we have apocalypse-level spiders. Spiders big enough to operate motor vehicles. If the world ends, it will be because they've stolen tanks and challenged the president."

"Nope." I held up a hand. "Nope. Nope. I do not want to hear about revolutionary spiders."

"You truly don't," she said. Having secured her goodies, she slammed the trunk closed.

I turned to head back to the House . . . and that was when I saw him.

A lean man about forty yards down the sidewalk, looking up at the fence and stone behind it. Pale skin, thick hair. He wore jeans, dark shoes, a dark jacket, and a black skullcap.

It wasn't the first time I'd seen someone staring up at Cadogan. Gawkers and tourists visited all the time, as did paparazzi, hoping for a million-dollar shot. There were even tourist buses that carted humans down the street for a look.

The man shifted, situating his face in the light of the corner streetlamp and revealing the thick beard that made him all too recognizable.

He wasn't just an onlooker.

He was a vampire—the vampire who'd killed Caleb Franklin. The one who'd gotten away from me in Wrigleyville and was now standing in front of Cadogan House.

My heart began to race, my blood to pound with need, with *fight*. "Get in the House, Mallory."

"What?" Her smile faded, and she looked around, sensing my sudden caution.

"Get in the House, right now. Tell Ethan to close the gate and lock it down."

"Merit, I'm not—"

I looked at her, and whatever she'd seen in my eyes must have convinced her.

We might have started this journey together, unsure of our steps, unfamiliar with the kinds of darkness we'd come to see. But we knew it now—how to react, how to protect. Her gaze steeled, and she slid her glance slowly, casually, to the vampire who I didn't think had yet realized we were watching.

"He works for Reed," I said. "I'm going to approach him. He's going to run, and I'm going after him. I'm not going to stop until I get him."

Ethan would be pissed that I was doing exactly what I lectured him not to do—taking Reed's bait—but it couldn't be helped. I couldn't just let the vampire go. Not when we'd made a promise to Gabriel. And not when Caleb Franklin deserved better.

Fear crossed her eyes, but she put it away. "I'll tell Ethan," she said. "Go."

I turned toward him.

He turned, I think, because he'd noticed my movement. And it took only an instant for him to recognize me, to see. We looked at each other, just long enough for me to confirm that he was the vampire I'd wanted . . . and for him to confirm that it was time to go.

He smiled at me, and took off in a sprint, heading north.

I'd be damned if I lost him again.

With the House's gate clanking closed behind me, I followed him down Fifty-third toward the lake. He barreled past bars and twenty-four-hour restaurants where patrons still lingered, me in his wake.

All the while, I checked my pace, kept my gaze trained on his back, and wished to God I'd had my katana. But it was in the House, parked in our apartments, because I hadn't thought I'd need it in a meeting of friends.

I'd been half right.

He ran toward the Metra Station, then inside the lobby. A train had just arrived; people streamed through the station, trying to get outside. I lost him in the crowd, scanned heads and shoulders frantically to catch sight of him.

I just saw his skullcap as he jumped the turnstile, then headed up the long, jagged staircase that led to the platform. I hustled through the crowd and over the turnstile as people yelled behind me, promising to send Metra the fare. Humanity pressed back against me like a tsunami.

He slipped into the train heading north. I did the same, managing to get inside just before the doors closed, and found him standing alone inside the empty car.

There, in the cold light of the train, I got my first real look at the vampire who had killed Caleb Franklin.

He'd lost his skullcap in the bustle, and stood with his legs apart, braced like a captain on a ship. His hair was thick, straight, and brown, and it was pulled into a knot atop his head. His face was handsome. But there was a coldness in his expression, a deadness in his brown eyes.

And there was something familiar.

Memories flooded back, slicked over sudden and battling bursts of fear and fury.

Freshly cut grass, still wet with dew. His fingers, rough against tender skin. The sharp shock of pain as his fangs tore into skin, spilled blood. And the speed with which he'd abandoned me, his quarry, when Ethan and Malik found me, saved me, and made me immortal.

This was the vampire who'd killed Caleb Franklin . . . and the vampire who'd attacked me on the Quad one year ago.

Chapter Sixteen

MAKER'S MARK

Many times I'd wondered if this moment would ever come—if I'd ever look into the eyes of the man who'd tried to kill me, the vampire who'd changed my life forever.

We'd believed he'd been a Rogue, a vampire not affiliated with Cadogan, Grey, or Navarre. He didn't look vampirically familiar, for what that was worth.

Enough time had passed that I figured he was dead or gone, had left Chicago in order to avoid a run-in with me or Ethan. I hadn't expected that run-in would come on a northbound train a year after the attack.

But a year was a long time, and I wasn't the girl he'd found that first night. I was vampire. I was Cadogan Novitiate. I was Sentinel, and I knew how to push down fear. I braced my legs just as he'd done to keep myself upright against the swaying of the train, and I faced him, this man who'd tried to take my life, who seemed to value life so little.

"Hello, Merit," he said.

Stick to the facts, I told myself. We'd have only a few minutes before we reached the next stop. He might disappear, or humans might jump on, which wouldn't help matters. "Who are you?"

"You know who I am."

I swallowed hard against the bile that threatened to rise. "No, I know what you did to me and to Caleb Franklin. I'm pretty sure I know the why and for whom. But I don't know who you are."

In answer, he pulled a matte black dagger from a sheath beneath his T-shirt. His smile was slick and confident, and it made my skin crawl, sent a line of cold sweat down my back.

For the first time since I'd seen his face, I stopped thinking about *that* night, and started thinking about *this* one—the fact that I'd chased him onto an empty train. That he'd managed to lead me away from my House, my partners, my allies.

Reed couldn't have planned it better himself. Unless he *had* planned it himself.

What, exactly, was I going to do? What was my play? I'd survived the vampire's attacks. Was I going to kill him then and there for what he'd done to me? Did I even have the right?

I swallowed hard, made myself focus. "Once upon a time," I said, preparing to relive my darkest fairy tale, "you did Celina Desaulniers's bidding. You attacked me because she paid you. Who's paying you this time?"

He made a clucking sound. "Let's say this one is a freebie."

Something about the cockiness of his tone, the jocularity, spurred my anger.

And God, anger was so much better than fear.

"For Adrien Reed?"

His eyes tightened, just for a moment. Long enough to know I was on the right track—if the most dangerous one.

I might have been conflicted about the fight, but he wasn't. Blade at the ready, he moved toward me, began with a swipe of the knife that would have sliced my abdomen if I hadn't jumped back quickly enough.

While he reset, I remembered the dagger I'd stashed—as always—in my boot, and pivoted to keep him in front of me. He slashed out again, nimble and fast.

As the city blurred past the windows, I took the offensive, feinting to the right before dropping, slicing the dagger along his leg. I made contact, scraped metal against skin. Blood seeped through denim and plopped in heavy droplets onto the metal floor, scenting the air with the tang of fresh blood. If not the type I had any interest in.

The vampire roared, eyes silvering and fangs descending, and swiped at me again, and I rolled forward, switching our positions. I jumped onto the seats, turned back. His eyes were wild, angry.

I smiled at him, but there was nothing happy in the look. It was the smile of a predator preparing for battle, and it gratified me more than a little to see his eyes narrow, reassess.

The first time he'd attacked me as a human, after dark, and when my guard was down. The second time he'd had a gun and a Trans Am.

"Yeah, it's not nearly as much fun when the prey fights back, is it?" I tilted my head at him. "Does Reed still pay you if you lose?"

He growled, ran forward. And this time, in the full blush of blood fury, he was faster.

How much of him was in me? How much of his skill, his mind, had I absorbed when he ripped into my body?

I jumped again, catapulting over him when he struck out. But he grabbed the hem of my T-shirt, pulled me down on top of him. We hit the floor with a thud, and he snaked an arm around my waist, drawing me against his body. My dagger skittered away.

"Not so funny now, is it, Caroline?" His voice was as close as a lover's.

His glamour began to seep and sink into the air around us, heavy and cold as fog. His glamour wasn't like Ethan's. It didn't support, build up, elaborate on love. It would tear down, seep in, and infect.

I froze as panic slicked cold sweat over my skin, made my blood pound in my ears. I went back to that dark night, the wet grass, the same arm around me, teeth ripping, pain as hot and sharp as lightning.

He wanted me afraid. He wanted me cowering so he could finish his assignment and clear the black mark of his earlier failure.

"Celina paid me well and good," he said. "But Reed might pay me double. Depends on what I do, and how crazy it'll make that boyfriend of yours."

A small part of me—the shadow that carried the memories of the attack—wanted to let go, to ignore what was happening, to recede into a dark and safe part of my psyche. Into a cupboard of denial. That part of me was moved by fear and magic, which were powerful enemies. It was the same part his glamour called.

But that part of me hadn't held a sword, found a family, stood for her House. The rest of me was stronger, more experienced, and less afraid. I'd lost battles, and I'd won battles, and I knew the point wasn't the victory, but pulling yourself together and crawling your way back. That was life.

I might not have been immune to glamour any longer, but I certainly wasn't going to give in to it like this. Not to him. I pushed down the part of me that wanted to hide, locked it away where even the liquid spill of his magic couldn't reach it.

"Two things, asshole. First, anything Adrien Reed could do to you would pale—utterly pale—in comparison to the personal hell Ethan Sullivan will rain down on you if you so much as break one of my fingernails. And second, I don't need him or anyone else to fight my battles."

I slammed back an elbow that nailed his jaw with a satisfying crunch. The glamour fell away as he bellowed and raised hands to the blood streaming from his face. I took advantage, trying to slide away on the floor of the train, now slippery with sweat and blood, but he grabbed my ankle. I swore, kicked back as he crawled forward with bloodied teeth, and hoped he'd chewed off a piece of his own tongue.

He pulled me backward, sharp fingernails digging against my leathers. I turned onto my back, and he grinned victoriously, crawled over me.

"FYI, that was a ploy," I said with a smile, then buried my knee in his crotch—or tried to. He deflected with his knee, backhanded me hard enough to put stars behind my eyes. Quick karma for too much ego, I thought, hearing Catcher's training in my head.

"I don't miss," the Rogue said, but that wasn't going to be relevant. The train lurched, began to slow as it neared the next station.

"Considering I'm alive, you're about a year wrong."

When he grabbed the edge of a seat to keep from falling over as the train slowed, I took my chance, stuck pointed fingers in the crux of his elbow. He yelped, released his arm, floundered backward in the jarring train.

I climbed to my feet, head still ringing from his slap, and kicked him in the ribs, then slipped across the car to grab my dagger.

The train came to a stop, and the doors opened. We both looked up as a small girl in a polka-dotted shirt jumped inside, her black hair wound prettily into knots on each side of her head.

"Hurry up, Mama!" she yelled, glancing back through the doors at her mother, whose eyes had grown wide at the sight in the train—the bloody vampire on one side of the car, me on the other, the dagger in my hand, staring at him like an executioner ready to mete out punishment he'd long been owed.

The world stilled.

The Rogue waited for me, the child waited for her mother, and her mother stared at us with terror that locked her in place.

The child's eyes shifted to me, dropped to the dagger, then the bloody vampire.

I could have moved. I could have run forward, pierced his black heart. But in front of a child? Should I be the one to give her nightmares?

Unfortunately, that brief hesitation was just what he needed.

He jumped forward, his gaze on the child. Her mother realized what was happening, reached out to grab her daughter, but the vampire moved quicker. He snatched up the child, yanked her to his chest with an arm around her waist, held his knife to her throat. Her mother screamed, but before she could move, the train doors closed and the car lurched forward.

"Put her down," I demanded, the little girl screaming in the vampire's arms, her mother screaming on the platform, the passengers who'd come through the other door staring at both of us in confusion and horror.

"Make me," he said with a grin. "I'm going to walk out of here with her, and no one is going to stop me."

The train rumbled as it rushed toward the next station. I could feel the humans, fearing for the child, moving closer behind me. I held out a hand to stop them but kept my eyes on the Rogue.

"So you're a coward. All that trouble to get me alone, to take me out and finish your work, and you're going to walk away with a human shield? How do you think your boss is going to react to that? You think he'll be impressed?"

"Fuck you," he said, but he was smart enough to look alarmed. He'd know as well as I did, if not more, how violent Reed was, how manipulative, and how protective of his public reputation. Cyrius Lore was proof enough of that.

The girl was squirming in his arms, kicking against him, tears streaming down her face. My chest ached to reach out, touch and comfort. But her safety was entirely up to the Rogue, and I had to keep my focus on him—convince him to let her go, and move along.

Even if that meant I lost my chance at him.

"Actually," I said, "this probably helps us. I'm sure someone has called the cops, and I'd bet some of those humans behind me have phones, are recording or photographing this little interaction." Precisely because they were recording it, I didn't dare say Reed's name aloud. No one would believe he was involved without hard evidence, which I didn't have. And I wasn't going to set myself up for another arrest.

"Long story short," I continued, "your boss will see that you've failed, and we'll have that much more evidence to build the case against him, to put him away for a very long time. All that, of course, will happen after he takes care of you."

The vampire stared at me, a bead of sweat trickling down his nose. Rational thought could do that to a psychopath.

The train began to slow again, and he jerked his gaze to the doors, looking for a way out.

"Hand her to me, and you walk away," I said.

"I'm not an idiot," he said. "I hand her to you, and you kill me."

"Not in front of witnesses."

We pulled into the station, jerked to a stop. The door opened, and he hesitated, and then tossed the child at me like an unwanted rag doll.

I jumped, hit my knees, arms outstretched . . . and caught her. She wailed with terror, kicked out with pointy little knees and elbows, caught the cheek that sung with pain from his slap.

But she was safe.

People rushed into the train to travel, off the train to get away from the vampire. I climbed to my feet, the child still in my arms, and squeezed through them to the platform.

The vampire was gone.

I waited with half a dozen human witnesses at the platform for the CPD's inevitable arrival.

In the meantime, we learned Hailey Elizabeth Stanton was three and a half years old. She'd stopped crying, at least in part because the humans made funny faces to make her smile, and bribed her with bottles of water and pieces of candy when that failed. She wouldn't let me go, so she stayed at my hip, tiny fingers digging into my neck. While we waited she told me about her favorite "Poesy Pony Princess," which I presumed was a toy and not actually a royal horse. In these halcyon supernatural days, it was hard to be sure. Anyway, Hailey's pony was named Princess Margaret Hollywood Peony Stanton, and I was informed several times she did *not* go by "Maggie."

So of course I kept calling her that, and Hailey kept giggling.

Finally, CPD officers escorted the girl's frantic mother onto the train platform. I stood up, passed the child back to her.

"Mommy!" she said while her mother hugged her and checked her for injuries.

"Did you get him?" I asked one of the uniforms. The humans had relayed to the 911 dispatcher that the vampire had gotten away after using the child as a shield.

"No," he said. "Do you know who he is?"

"Kind of," I said, and gave them the story.

Correction: I gave them *part* of the story. I told them about Caleb Franklin, identified this vampire as the one who'd killed him.

I skipped the speculation about Reed and the fact that the Rogue was the vampire who'd first attacked me. Only a few knew the reason I'd become a vampire. Since most became vampires by choice—because they wanted immortality, to join a particular House, to escape a particular illness—the truth of my making was too personal to share, and theoretically could have put Ethan at risk. He'd technically changed me without my consent, even if he'd done it to save my life.

A CPD detective talked me through the details for twenty minutes, then stuck me in the back of a police cruiser for twenty more. When the door finally opened, it was my grandfather who met me, Jeff behind him.

Concern was etched in the lines of my grandfather's aging face, but his blue eyes were as bright as ever. "You're all right?"

I nodded. "I'm fine," I said, and took the hand he offered to help me out of the car.

His gaze focused on the blood on my hands, dots of it on my shirt.

"It's not mine. It was the Rogue's. You heard what happened?"

Jeff nodded. "We were at Cadogan. Ethan locked down the House, and Luc and Malik made him stay put, just in case. Then we waited for news. Photos and videos starting hitting the Web. You did a great job with him, Merit. With the kid."

Ethan would have been relieved to see the footage, and still livid that I'd left in the first place. That I'd done exactly what I'd told him not to do: I'd let my emotions take control, and I'd put myself in a situation that could have gone very, very badly.

"I couldn't agree more," my grandfather said, but his gaze was still wary, and I could feel my panic bubbling up. The fact that I'd held back from the rest of the officers.

"Merit?" he asked.

"He was the vampire who attacked me."

The words spilled out, faster than I'd meant them to.

I'd seen protectiveness in Ethan's eyes. The anger that showed in my grandfather's was pretty similar.

"From the Quad?"

I nodded. "I didn't recognize him the night Caleb was killed; I didn't see his face. It wasn't until we were on the train that I saw—" Bile rose, and I had to stop, close my eyes, wait for the nausea to pass.

"Here," Jeff said after a moment, offering me a cold bottle of water.

I nodded my silent thanks, pressed the bottle against the back of my neck. "Kind of hits you funny."

"It does," my grandfather said. "And it's completely understandable."

"You were fucking incredible."

Surprised by the curse and the tone, my grandfather and I both looked at Jeff.

His gaze was fierce.

"I mean it," he said. "You found out who he was, and you didn't back down. Hell, you fought him, and you were a total warrior."

"I was scared shitless."

He smiled. "That's because you have a brain in your head. You know how it goes, Merit. Fear doesn't stop a warrior. It pushes you further."

I reached out, squeezed his hand. "Thanks, Jeff."

"It's the absolute truth."

I nodded, made myself tell them the rest of it. "He basically confirmed Reed's pulling his strings. He wants to kill me, make Ethan crazy. Two birds, one stone. I didn't tell the cops—I don't want to make that situation worse. Too many people already think we have it in for Reed."

My grandfather nodded. "It was smart to be cautious. And you've told me. That's fine for now. You'll have to tell Ethan."

I just nodded.

"Mallory said it looked like the vampire was watching the House," Jeff said.

"Casing it, is my best bet. I don't think he planned to make a run at me tonight—probably because there were so many other people there. You guys and Scott and Morgan. He would have watched and waited."

And he still would watch and wait. Because nothing had been decided tonight. This had been the first round of a battle that had to continue. I'd see him again. He'd make another attempt.

"Am I done here?" I asked, glancing back at the uniforms. "I'd like to get back to the House." Away from here, from trains and cops and onlookers.

"You are," my grandfather said. "Would you like a ride?"

Normally, I'd have jumped at the offer, but I needed time to think. Time to process. A few minutes of solitude before I walked into Cadogan House, because God knew I wouldn't get it then. I'd have to talk. I'd have to report. I'd have to *tell*.

"Actually, I think I'd like to grab a cab if you don't mind."

My grandfather squeezed my arm. "There's nothing wrong with taking a few minutes to settle. You've earned it."

"Do you think that's safe?" Jeff asked.

"He's long gone," I said. "Too many cops around. And he won't try the House tonight. Not after this. He'll know we're watching."

"I don't disagree," my grandfather said.

"Let me get you a cab," Jeff said. "Least we can do is make sure you get in it safely." He walked to the curb, signaled for a cab, waited until one pulled up.

"You'll let me know when you get home?" my grandfather asked, and put up a hand to stop any grumbling. "I know you're a grown woman and can take care of yourself, but I'd appreciate it if you'd do me the favor tonight."

"I will," I promised, and gave him a hug, them climbed into the cab and pulled out my phone. I sent Ethan a simple message. I'M ON MY WAY.

I kept it short and simple, but I had little doubt he'd have plenty of things to say.

I had the cab drop me off at the corner. Even after the twenty minute ride, I was still procrastinating walking back in the front door.

I'd been a grad student. I could recognize procrastination a mile away.

Why stand outside the House? Why delay going back to the man who loved me? Because I felt so suddenly vulnerable. Stripped emotionally bare because the vampire who'd attacked me was back again. I felt like I was standing naked in a spotlight, blinded to the onlookers, knowing they were there.

And that wasn't all. I felt that I'd failed because I'd let him go. Yes, that had been to save the life of a child, but it still ate at me. He was still out there. And he wouldn't go away.

I could defend myself, sure. Would defend myself when we inevitably met again. But until then, there was waiting. There was feeling exposed.

That sent me back toward the House, toward the fence and the gate.

Tonight's guards were two human women I'd seen standing sentry before. One was tall and leggy, with pale skin and a crop of pale blond hair. The other was shorter and curvier, with a strong body and dark skin, her dark hair pulled into a tight bun.

"House is on alert," said Liv, the taller guard.

"Yeah," I said, looking up at the imposing stone structure. "That's my fault. Any problems?"

"Very quiet, actually," said Valerie, the shorter guard.

I nodded. "I should get inside. Stay safe out here."

They nodded, opened the gate just enough to allow me entrance. For the second time tonight, I listened to it work. Only this time, I was on the opposite side.

There were three supplicants in the foyer tonight—a man and two women. Their gazes flicked to me as I walked in, then back to the phones they watched to pass the time.

I nodded at the Novitiate who staffed the table as I passed, then walked to Ethan's office. I paused outside the open door for a moment, steeling my nerve, and walked inside.

Ethan stood in front of the windows, hands in the pockets of his black suit, back to me. Malik stood to his right, a sheaf of papers in his hands.

Both looked back as I walked in, took in the torn clothes, the blood. The magic that poured through the room was a heady cocktail of relief, anger, and Masterly irritation.

Ethan looked at Malik, who nodded at some unspoken command. Malik situated his papers, walked toward me. He paused when he reached the door.

"You're all right?"

I nodded. "Yeah. Thanks."

He nodded, left the room, and closed the door.

It took a solid minute for Ethan to say anything. And when he did, his voice was low and dangerous. "Would you like to explain what the hell you were doing, running off by yourself to chase a murderer? A man who's already shot you once? Who killed a shifter in cold blood?"

I'd been prepared for Ethan's anger. It was rooted in fear for my safety, and I could understand that. What Ethan feared, he would try to control.

But I found I wasn't at all interested in apologizing, in bearing the weight of his heavy emotions. Mine were burdensome enough. So much so that I didn't yet have the words to voice them.

Telling my grandfather and Jeff about this vampire, who he was to me—that was a report. Emotional, sure, but still just relaying the facts of what had happened, however hard it had been.

Telling Ethan was different. He and I were bound together eternally by this vampire, this careless monster who'd tried to kill me but hadn't succeeded precisely because of Ethan's intervention. Telling Ethan would be exposing myself all over again. Because he'd been there. He'd seen.

He knew.

So I played it off, kept my defenses in place until I was ready to release them. And if that pissed him off, so be it.

"I really wouldn't," I said. "And I don't like your tone."

An eyebrow arched and his anger rose, peppering the room with magic. "I don't much care if you like my tone, Merit. I'll be damned if you take chances with your life."

"Yes, I would like to have a drink," I said by way of answer, apropos of nothing. I walked to the bar, poured Scotch into a crystal glass, and took a heady sip. The liquid warmed through my chest, took just enough of the edge away.

I finished the glass, put it back on the shelf with a little too much force. As if that had been the last of my strength, I braced my hands and caught my breath.

Ethan's banked fury crested, broke across the room. "Just let me know when you're done making use of my office."

There was a bite in his voice, irritation that I was ignoring the chain of command, or maybe hurt that I was putting him off. I understood both, because both were true. But that didn't change anything.

Because I hadn't answered him, he'd moved closer. He might

have been angry—so very angry—but he loved me and had guessed that something was wrong. The magic in the room shifted from fury to concern.

"Merit," Ethan said, and this time the word held naked concern.

I closed my eyes. If I couldn't be vulnerable with Ethan—with my lover, my likely future husband, the future father of my child—who could I be vulnerable with?

CHAPTER SEVENTEEN

THE CLOSER YOU GET

I fisted my hands so they wouldn't shake, turned back to face him. He watched me the way a man might watch a caged panther. Cautiously, and with great care.

"Mallory probably told you I saw someone outside the House," I said.

"A vampire who worked for Adrien Reed," he bit off.

"The vampire who killed Caleb Franklin. He saw me coming, and he ran."

"And you followed him. Without backup, without weapon." *Without me*, I guessed, he'd left unspoken.

"If I'd waited or delayed, he'd have disappeared. I told Mallory to get inside, to lock the gate, and then I chased him to the train. You saw the rest?"

Ethan nodded, just once. "What there was to see." He watched me for a moment. "And what aren't you telling me?"

I gathered up courage, held it tightly. "He's not just the vampire who killed Caleb Franklin." I paused. "He's the vampire who attacked me in the Quad."

Ethan went very, very still. Fury and possessiveness flared

together in his magic, spun together in the room. "He's the one who attacked you."

I nodded. "I didn't recognize him at first. But when we were on the train, and the light was better—when I could see his face and, I don't know, sense something familiar in his scent or his magic—I knew it was him."

I shook my head. "I don't know his name. I *still* don't know his damn name." That seemed so important to me right now, so much that my voice trembled, and I shook my head, swallowed hard, as emotions rose.

The wave of anger crested, followed by a flood of sympathy. "Merit," he said, voice full of emotion, concern.

I just shook my head, held up a hand. I wasn't ready for sympathy yet.

"He works for Reed. He'd planned to get to me to throw you off. You're Reed's real target. He wants to hurt you. To manipulate you. That's who he is."

"Fuck Adrien Reed."

His voice was so sharp, so forceful, I had to look up at him again. His expression held the ferocity of a warrior, a man intent on destroying his enemies.

"Death cannot come soon enough for Adrien Reed, but beyond that, he is not important to me. The only thing that interests me about Reed is the risk he presents to my people, to you. I care about that very much."

It was very nearly an apology. Very nearly an acknowledgment that Reed had made him do regrettable things—including calling my father.

"What is Reed's connection to the Rogue?" he asked, before I could bring up that subject. Which was probably best for both of us. And still, he kept me talking. Kept me reporting on facts, rather than slipping back into fear.

"It has to be Celina."

"How?" he asked.

"She paid the vampire to kill me. She's been in debt to Reed for years; he was financing her lifestyle. Maybe she got the money from Reed, and that's how he found out about the Rogue. Or maybe Reed wasn't just the source of the money. He's a kingpin. Maybe he supplied the assassin, too. Although, if that's the case, why wait so long to throw him back in my face?"

Ethan's gaze darkened, probably as he thought of Balthasar. "Reed is a man who knows how to bide his time."

I nodded. "He loves the dramatic. No, it would be more accurate to say he loves an emotional mind-fuck. And he has, by God, succeeded. I feel like it's happened all over again. Like I'm starting from square one. I feel—like everything is in the wrong place."

"Oh, Merit," Ethan said. He reached for my hands, ignored my attempts to shake him off, and drew me up and against him. He embraced me, wrapping his arms around my body as if he might force out the rest of the world, or protect me from the sharper edges of it.

I buried my face in his chest, allowing the tears I'd been holding back for hours to finally begin to stream.

"I let him go," I said when I reached the ugliest part of the tears. "I fucking let him go. And I hate myself for that."

"You are entitled to your emotions, but that is undeservedly harsh. You saved a child, Merit."

"I let him go." I looked up at him. "Three times, Ethan. Three times he's hurt me and walked away from it. When is he going to receive justice? When is he forced to pay the price?"

"I don't know, Merit. I don't know if you'll get justice or if he will." He pulled back enough to look at me. "You are not a child, and you know the world is not fair. You've had your share of unfairness, and got a stark reminder of that tonight. But I swear to you, Merit—I swear it on my life, my House, and my soul—he will *never* touch you again."

I was suddenly so, so tired. "He'll try. He will try, and Reed will try. He'll take a shot at you, or at me, or at my father."

The remembrance of my father—of my lingering battle with Ethan—made me look away. But Ethan took my chin between two fingers, forced me to meet his gaze.

His eyes were narrowed, his brow furrowed, as he looked down at me. "We'll have this out, too, while we're dealing with everything else. Your father has been cruel to you so many times over. Why has a phone call become a wall between us?"

"Because maybe he's changed."

The words came out, words I didn't even know I'd been holding in.

I hadn't been angry at Ethan. Not really.

I'd been *afraid*.

I made myself meet Ethan's gaze. "I guess I hoped Towerline had changed him. That it was a sign that he was accepting me for who I was, understanding that he'd have to deal with me on my terms, not on his. That we could have a different kind of relationship. That something could begin. And if Reed puts a target on him, if Reed takes him out . . ."

"Then I'd have taken away that new family," Ethan said, and cupped my face in his hands. "I am so sorry, Merit. I didn't mean to risk him. I meant only to protect you, because you're the closest thing to family I've known in four hundred years. You are my miracle."

His arms banded around me as I sobbed again.

"In the future," he said after a time, when my tears had subsided, "I will talk to you before involving—even potentially—your family."

"Thank you." I cleared my throat. "Thank you for that. You must have been angry and worried tonight, and I'm sorry for that."

"I was worried," Ethan agreed. "And I was angry. You inspire both emotions, Merit, and not infrequently." There was a hint of amusement around his mouth.

"I'm sorry," I said again. "But I'd do it again."

He looked down at me, eyes burning bright. "Oh, would you?"

I could feel the fear seeping away, as if his being near—and our being on the same page again—had siphoned it out of me, wicked it away. And as the fear receded, the bravado came back.

God, I loved the bravado.

"I love you, Ethan, and I love this city. And however much I fought it, I love this goddamn House. It's part of me, and I'm part of it. I'm not going to stand here and watch a man tear down everything that you've built. I'm not. And if that means I have to chase another man who threatens this House, or apologize to you more than I like, so be it. I don't want that, but I can live with it. Because I can't live without you."

Silence fell.

"Well," he said after a full minute had passed, "you're not leaving me with much room to yell at you."

"That was part of the plan," I said with a watery laugh. "Fear is what Reed uses against us. For Celina, fear that she would be average. For you, fear that you would become a monster like Balthasar, that I'd be hurt. And for me, fear that I will be that vulnerable human all over again."

"It is his gift," Ethan agreed ruefully. "To find those tender spots and press into them. Fear, my Sentinel, is inevitable. It is one of our more important instincts. It keeps us alive. Fighting through the fear is a choice. That's the choice you've made since that April night one year ago. That's the choice you'll continue to make, because that's what's inside you. I love you, and I believe in you, more than I have ever believed in anyone. And it is absolutely terrifying."

I thought that might have been the nicest thing he'd ever said to me. I put my hands on his cheeks, pulled his head down to mine, and kissed him. "I love you, Ethan."

"I love you, Merit." He smiled. "And now it feels like the world is righting. Would this be an opportune time for me to point out that, despite your having berated me yesterday, you did exactly what you scolded me for doing?"

He was right, so I let him get away with it. "You mean I let Reed bait me? I ran headlong into danger probably orchestrated by Reed, even if I ruined his plan a little by forcing his asset into play a little earlier than he'd probably intended? Yeah, I know." And then I played a card of my own. "I guess you could say I pulled a Darth Sullivan."

He knew about the nickname but clearly didn't like it, given the curl of his upper lip.

"If it makes you feel better, you can tell me your nickname for me."

"That would spoil all the fun." He sighed, put his arms around me again. "We may fight again, Sentinel. We may rail at each other until the sun breaches the sky. But the truth is this. I love you. And I found you once, that April night. I will always look for you, and I will always find you. And as for your monster, we'll find him together," Ethan said, pressing a final kiss to my forehead. "We'll go downstairs, we'll talk to Luc, and we'll find him. And one way or the other, we'll find Reed, too. And then may God have mercy on his soul."

I cleaned up and washed tears from my face and blood from my hands, and we walked downstairs to the Ops Room. Luc and Lindsey rose when we darkened the doorway, hurried toward us.

"Is everything all right?" Lindsey asked. "Malik didn't give us the details, just that you were back and seemed to be in one piece."

"I believe 'all right' is relative," Ethan said. "Why don't we sit down and talk about it?"

"My House is your House," Luc said, and moved back to his seat at the table. "And we're glad you're home, Sentinel."

Right now there was nowhere else I'd rather have been.

When Kelley, Juliet, Lindsey, Luc, and Ethan had gathered at the conference table, I gave them the story of my encounter with the Rogue, such as it was. From contact to chase, to his use of a human as hostage and shield, to the Rogue's escape into the night.

Luc knew the circumstances of how I'd been attacked, made a vampire, as did other key players in the House—including Malik, since he'd been there. I'd figured word had still spread—vampires liked gossip as much as humans—but from the sympathetic look on Kelley's face, I guessed I'd been wrong about that.

"As far as I'm aware," I finished up, "the CPD hasn't found him."

"He'd have gone underground," Kelley said, flicking back a lock of straight, dark hair over her shoulder. "To wherever rats scurry and hide." She looked at me, and there was strength and solidarity in her gaze.

"Yeah," I said. "Agreed."

Luc linked his hands on the table, leaned forward, his gaze solemn. "You think he'll try again?"

"I know he will. Especially if this is prompted by Reed."

"Then we'll find him first," Kelley said.

"It might be worth talking to Noah again," Lindsey said. "At least you'll have a description to give him now."

"We'll do you one better," Luc said. "Keiji," he called to one of the temps at the bank of computers. "Can you scan the Internet videos of the fight, see if you can get a clear shot of our perp, enhance and distribute the images?"

Keiji looked back, nodded once, his eyes sharpening with interest in the task. "On it, boss."

Luc nodded, looked back at me. "The video wasn't great, but should be clear enough to get a rough image."

"Send the image to the Chicago Houses," Ethan said. "Put them on alert."

Luc nodded.

"Thank you for the help," I said. "I need to know his name. I'd feel better somehow if I knew his name."

Juliet smiled, serious hard blue eyes a contrast to her delicate features. "Knowing the name of your enemy is important. Names define us as individuals, and in relation to each other. They"—she paused, looking for the right phrase—"set the boundaries of who we are. If you can give this guy a name, you give him a boundary. It gives him less power, and gives you more."

Since "Merit" was actually my last name, and I didn't use my first name for personal and family reasons, I understood the notion of names defining us.

"We'll put the pictures in your box," Luc said. "Did the child's mother say if she wanted to press charges?"

"She told the CPD she didn't want to," I said. "He didn't know her or her child, and she didn't want to give him any more information by pursuing it. I told them I didn't want to pursue it, either."

"At least not officially," Luc suggested, and I nodded.

"And Reed?" he asked.

"If the vampire was telling the truth," Ethan said, "and we have no reason to believe he wasn't, this isn't inconsistent with what Reed's done before."

"He uses the personal," I agreed. "He used Balthasar against Ethan, he used money against Celina, and he's used the Rogue for me, which is another hit at Ethan. He'll try again," I added.

"Then we'll stop him before he does," Luc said. "And if we don't, he's yours."

"Although you may have to battle Gabriel for him," Ethan said lightly. "This vampire has a long list of very powerful enemies."

"The way my luck with him is going, Gabe might have a better shot," I muttered, in a moment of self-pity.

"You should tell her about Calamity Jane," Lindsey said to Luc.

I glanced from her to Luc. "Who's Calamity Jane?"

"Long story very short," he said, "she was a woman from my dry and dusty and tumbleweed-ridden past." Luc had been a cowboy in his human life.

"She was a thief, an assassin, and a general ne'er-do-well," Lindsey said with a smile. "Accused of fourteen murders that the county was aware of. And she escaped from him four separate times."

Four was definitely larger than three. If not by a lot.

"'Escaped' is a tough word," Luc said. "I prefer to say she 'evaded incarceration.' But yeah, four times."

"How'd you finally get her?"

He smiled. "With help from the dirt and dust and tumbleweeds. She rolled into Dodge City wanting, of all things, a hot bath. I caught her while she was performing her ablutions," he said, eyebrows winging up.

"Is the moral of that story that it's safest to avoid good hygiene?" Ethan asked.

"Har-har, Sire. Har-har. The moral of the story is to always keep going! Ever forward! Forward progress! You can do it! And all that other motivational shit." Luc looked at me, a gleam in his eye. "And if you can catch 'em with their pants down, they tend to be a little more amenable."

Words of wisdom.

* * *

Following Lindsey's suggestion, I e-mailed Jonah, asked for a meeting with Noah the next evening at the RG headquarters to talk about the Rogue vampire.

When this evening drew to a close and we were secure in our Hyde Park tower, Ethan carefully removed my clothes, used hands and words to soothe and seduce.

This was about need as much as the library had been, but of a different variety. This was about partnership as much as touch. About tenderness as much as passion. And about comfort as much as satisfaction. Every movement was slow and languid, every word tender. His mouth was soft against mine, then against the rest of my body, and pleasure rose and crested in waves that cleared violence from my mind.

We rode those waves together, bodies linked and hearts finally reunited. Love wasn't a battle, and it wasn't a war. It was a partnership, with missteps and miracles and all the rest of it.

When we were both sated and languid, Ethan lay naked beside me, his head on my abdomen. I ran my fingers through his hair as he traced a fingertip across my still-heated skin.

"Do you remember, Sentinel, the first words you ever said to me?"

I grimaced. "No. But I bet they were rude." I hadn't been a fan of Ethan Sullivan the first time I walked into Cadogan House.

"Oh, it was." His eyes glinted like shards of green glass. "Your life had changed, and you were furious at me. You said you hadn't given me permission to change you."

"Which, in fairness to me, was accurate." I paused, remembering my seething dislike for the Master of my new House. "I didn't like you very much."

"No, you didn't. But then you came to your senses, realized you were wrong."

I tugged on a lock of his hair. "Don't push your luck. It took some pretty good campaigning on your part."

"Thank you for not calling it begging."

I grinned. "I was going to, but changed my mind at the last minute."

"Because it would have been cruel."

"But a really good play on my part. I'd have gotten a lot of points for that."

"Are we keeping score?"

"Yes. Redeemable for Mallocakes." They were my favorite chocolate snack cake, although I hadn't had one in a few weeks. Not since the Night of a Thousand Mallocakes. Which was why I was willing to give them to Ethan.

"I have no interest in your Mallocakes."

"I'm going to hope that's not a euphemism."

"It isn't, obviously." He lowered his mouth to my stomach, nipped playfully.

"I remember the first words you ever said to me," I said. "It was the night I was attacked. You had your arm around me, there on the grass, and you told me to be still."

He rose onto his elbows and stared at me. I'd never told him that I'd remembered that much of it, of what had happened, and what he'd said. But those words—those two small and impossibly huge words—still had the same power.

"You remember that."

I nodded. "I think that's important, Ethan. I think that matters. I don't remember anything *he* said or did, just the pain he caused, that he ran away like a coward." Like he always seemed to do. "But I remember what you said to me. Those two words were, I guess, an incantation."

He balanced his head on his curled fist, reached up to brush hair from my face. "I remember how pale you'd been, and how lovely. I was afraid we'd been too late. But we weren't. And you grew angry, and then you grew to accept who you were."

"And you grew to accept who I was. Except for those times you're still overprotective."

"I'll never stop being overprotective. Not because I don't believe in you, or trust you. But because that's who I am. That's what being a Master is all about."

"And yet you named me Sentinel. The one person whose job is to argue with you."

"Not just argue," he said with a grin. "Although it often seems that way."

Taking a ploy from Mallory, I thumped him on the ear.

"Ow," he said with a laugh, and pulled his earlobe. "It's about checks and balances, Merit. The point of all this is that we've changed. We've grown and evolved since the night I met you, and the night you met me." He put a hand on my stomach. "And someday, we'll have a child. A family. That won't be easy—having a child, having a vampire child, and having the first vampire child. But we'll manage it."

"How, exactly, do you think that's going to happen?"

He shifted into Master vampire. Mouth slightly quirked in a grin, one eyebrow arched imperiously as he looked back at me. "I'm fairly certain you know exactly how it happens, Sentinel."

What was it with people and the conception jokes? "You know I didn't mean that. I meant, you know"—I circled a finger toward my lower half—"the unproven mechanics of vampire gestation. To not put too fine a point on it, what's going to keep him or her in there?"

His face went utterly serious. "Sentinel, I honestly do not know." He pressed his lips to warm skin. "Shall we try to let nature take its course?"

Chapter Eighteen

SALEM'S FIRE

Jonah's message was waiting the next evening, a single question mark that somehow managed to query and chastise at the same time.

It was so easy to have opinions, and so much harder to actually do things. Which was one thing I planned on talking to the RG about.

I offered a time that would give me a chance to get dressed, changed, and fed. I still felt low after the past night's battle, despite the good that being on the same page with Ethan had done.

After grabbing a breakfast wrap in the cafeteria with Lindsey and Juliet, I stopped by Ethan's office. He, Malik, and Luc were chatting when I walked in.

"Did I miss a meeting?" I asked.

"No," Ethan said, Malik and Luc splitting apart to let me join their circle. "We were reviewing the photographs of last night's perpetrator."

Ethan extended the portrait-sized color photograph to me, and I could feel him watching my reaction.

Luc had been right last night. The video was grainy, but it was definitely him. The brooding eyes, the beard, the muscles.

"Yeah." I looked at Ethan first, nodded just a little to assure him that I was okay. "Recognizable enough. Does he look familiar to either of you?"

"Not to me," Malik said. "Not as a Novitiate or an attacker. It was dark that night, and he moved quickly."

"No dice for me, either," Luc said.

"Nor me," Ethan said. "You're going to talk to Noah?"

"I'm working on a meet, yeah. Can I borrow the photograph?"

"Take it," Luc said. "I've printed a few more, and we've alerted the Houses. We'll also run it against the database of Housed vampires, just in case. It's always possible he was a Housed vampire once upon a time and left."

"Not unlike Caleb Franklin, who was an official Pack member once upon a time," I said. "Thank you again."

"Think nothing of it," Luc said. "He threatens you, he threatens the House." He patted my arm. "You're one of us, Sentinel. For better or worse."

"Some nights I presume it definitely feels worse," Malik said sympathetically, then glanced at Ethan. "I'm going to get back to fielding calls."

"And I'm going back to the Ops Room." Luc put a collegial arm around Malik's shoulder. "Hey, did I ever tell you about Calamity Jane?" he asked as they walked to the door.

I looked back at Ethan. "I'm shocked I hadn't heard that story before now. Seems like he enjoys telling it."

"It's in the rotation," Ethan agreed.

"What calls is Malik fielding?"

"Press," Ethan said, and walked to his desk, then behind it. There was a stack of papers there, and the light on his phone was blinking fiercely. "The *Tribune*, the *Sun-Times*, the *Chicago World Weekly*."

The first two were legit. The *Chicago World Weekly* was the city's gossip paper.

"Who reads the *Weekly*?" I asked, taking the paper from the stack. I was in the color photograph on the front page, Hailey Stanton in my arms. VAMPIRE SAVIOR? was the headline.

"Not the worst headline I've ever read," I said. "Overblown, but generally positive." It had been a crappy week for vampires, but a pretty good week for vampire press.

"It's not bad," Ethan agreed. "The print media are generally positive. The Internet is the usual mix of praise, condescension, idiocy, and trolls." He glanced at his computer. "And, at last check, four marriage proposals for my Sentinel."

My mood brightened, and I leaned toward the desk, trying to see around to the screen. "Really? Any good candidates?"

"I don't find that amusing."

"I don't find fake proposals amusing." I grinned and spread my hands. "And yet here we are."

Ethan's gaze went so immediately sly that my heart skipped a beat in anticipation.

"At any rate," he said, smiling as he looked at the screen again, "there are several requests for statements, for interviews, for information about the perpetrator and the reason you chased him."

"They'll find out sooner or later who he is and what he did."

"They may," Ethan agreed. "You don't have to talk about that unless you want to; Malik won't respond to any questions in that regard. But at the risk of sounding overly strategic, should you decide to discuss it, it would help build the case against Reed."

I nodded. "I've thought about that. Depends on whether we need it or not. Problem is, I'm relatively small dice. He has too much goodwill in the city, even if he didn't come by it honestly. If we're going to bring him down—and by God we're going to bring him down—it will have to be big. We need a break, and soon." We also needed allies, I thought, and glanced at Ethan with speculation. "Have you talked to Gabriel?"

"I haven't."

I guessed that meant Gabriel hadn't called him, and he hadn't reached out. Since we weren't fighting (at the moment), I opted to poke the bear. "And do you think you should?"

"That's a bit passive-aggressive for you."

"I learned the technique from Meredith Merit, mistress of passive-aggressive." That was my mother.

My phone beeped, and I checked the screen. FIFTEEN MINUTES, was the entire message from Jonah, and it took me a moment to grasp the meaning. I had fifteen minutes to get to the meet with Noah, and since Jonah hadn't specified a location, the meeting place would be the Chicago Lighthouse, not far from Navy Pier.

There was no way I'd make it from Hyde Park to Navy Pier in fifteen minutes, much less over the breakwater I'd have to climb to get into the lighthouse.

They were setting me up to be late, which was a remarkably petty thing to do. Was Jonah that pissed, or was this punishment for my not having bowed to the RG's demands?

Not that it mattered. I'd asked for information, and this was his offer. I didn't have a lot of choice.

I looked at Ethan. "I don't suppose you could get me downtown in fifteen minutes?"

He smiled with masculine enjoyment. "Let's find out."

It took him eighteen minutes and, by my count, fourteen seconds. That was no fault of Ethan or the car. The LSD was a nightmare, as it had been all week.

Ethan didn't know exactly where the RG was located, but due to the spying of one of his former flames, he knew it was near Navy Pier. I was perfectly fine with his ignorance of the details. That was need-to-know information, and not even my lover and the Master of Cadogan House needed to know it.

"Just drop me off here," I said as he pulled the car to a stop in front of the pier.

"I can walk you in."

"I have to draw a line somewhere. Might as well be in front of Bubba Gump Shrimp." I leaned over and kissed him hard on the lips. "Don't follow me."

"I would do no such thing."

"You absolutely would, partly because you're curious, and partly because you enjoy vampire lording."

"I do not lord." Ethan bit off each word.

"Oh, you lord," I said. "That's why we call you Sire and obey your every whim and command."

His eyes sparked, light passing through peridot. "I am but a common soldier."

I snorted. That had been an insult leveled at me by that same former flame. "Yeah, pal. Me, too." I climbed out of his luxury vampire lording car, closed the door, and leaned in through the window.

"How will you get home?" he asked.

"Taxi," I said. "I'll message you when I'm on my way. And if we're lucky, I'll bring information with me."

"Good luck," he said, his expression utterly serious now. "And take care."

"I'll do my best," I promised, then watched the car speed away.

I looked back at the lake, the broken shoal that led to the lighthouse. I was going to need all the luck I could get.

Unless you had a boat, traversing the barrier of rocks and riprap that made up the harbor's protective wall was the only way to get to the RG's HQ. Jonah had once hinted that the RG had just such a vessel, but they certainly weren't sending it for me.

The breakwater was several hundred yards long, and it took

precious time to make my way across it, which certainly wasn't going to help with my punctuality problem. The trip wasn't an easy one. The hulking chunks of concrete were meant to keep the harbor safe, not provide a walking path. To the contrary—anyone making the attempt would have been thwarted pretty easily.

The lighthouse itself was called a "spark plug," a shout-out to its slightly stumpy shape. I climbed the rusty ladder that led to the main platform, wiped my dirty hands on my pants, and walked around to the red door that led inside.

I waited for a moment before knocking, gathering up the self-righteousness I was going to need if there was going to be any headway. Knocking making me suddenly self-conscious (and not just because I'd be facing the partner I'd seen only once in a matter of weeks), I straightened the hem of my jacket.

They made me wait for a solid two minutes before opening the door.

Jonah greeted me, wearing jeans and a dark Henley shirt, his hair tucked behind his ears. "Come in," he said, and stepped aside.

I walked into the room, which was heavy on the brass, nautical accents, and 1970s décor. Half a dozen vampires were in the room, and none of them looked pleased to see me. I didn't recognize many. RG members weren't in the same place at the same time very often.

I did recognize the man at the small table on the other side of the room—tall and thin, with pale skin, dark hair, and enormous, fuzzy sideburns. Horace had been a soldier in the Civil War. His girlfriend, a petite woman with dark skin and a cloud of dark hair, walked into the room, moved to stand beside him.

It was common—hell, maybe even expected—for RG partners to date. That was another bit of tension between me and Jonah.

I'd seen Horace's girlfriend a couple of times but still hadn't learned her name. From the expression on her face, which wasn't exactly friendly, I guessed I wouldn't be learning it tonight.

"You're late," said a voice from an interior doorway.

I glanced back. Noah Beck, broad-shouldered, with pale skin and shaggy brown hair, his eyes bright blue, walked into the room. He wore a Midnight High School T-shirt, dark blue with a white spider icon across the front. All RG members got T-shirts for the faux high school; we wore them in the rare times we appeared together in public to help identify one another.

Noah walked to the table, put a hip on the edge, crossed his hands in front of him. The other vampires gathered around him, like a posse coming together to battle a common enemy. Jonah stayed closer to me, but positioned so that I stood between him and the rest of the guards. Symbolic enough that I wondered if he'd done it on purpose.

The room quickly filled with magic, and none of it friendly.

"I was at the House," I said. "I came as soon as I got your message." I let my flat voice point out the obvious—I could only get here so quickly.

"We haven't seen you around much," Noah said. "Except in the papers, of course."

"Then you know I've been busy," I said, then glanced at Jonah. "And I haven't been invited."

"And what brings you here tonight?" Noah asked.

"A threat. I take it you've heard what happened last night?"

"Your very public battle with another vampire?" Noah asked. "Yes. Hard to avoid."

I ignored the tone. "I don't know his name. But he's the one who killed the shifter in Wrigleyville. Caleb Franklin."

Jonah frowned, his expression all business now. He might have been angry with me, but Grey House was in Wrigleyville, which meant Wrigleyville was his territory, and Franklin's death was a concern.

"He's also the vampire who attacked me the night Ethan made me a vampire. He's the *reason* Ethan made me a vampire."

The lighthouse went quiet again.

"You were attacked," Jonah said. I guessed word hadn't spread to him, either.

I looked at him, met his concerned gaze. "At U of C. Celina hired him to kill me. He made the attempt, but Ethan and Malik happened upon us, and he ran away."

Jonah's eyes widened with realization. "You were one of the women Celina tried to kill."

I nodded. "Yeah. She didn't succeed." Quite the contrary; I'd killed her in former Mayor Seth Tate's office.

"There'd been no sign of the Rogue since he attacked me," I said. "Not that I'm aware of, anyway."

"Until he killed Caleb Franklin," Noah said, and I nodded.

"We didn't see his face that night. We gave chase, but he had a car, got away. Last night, he was standing outside Cadogan House."

"He ran," Noah said, "and you gave chase again."

I nodded. "I knew he was Franklin's killer. I didn't realize until we got on the train that he'd been my near assassin, too."

"You're certain it was him?"

I looked at Noah. "Without a doubt." I zipped open my jacket, and when the vampires jumped, I slowly removed the photograph, handed it to Noah. "We got this from the video. Celina told us the vampire she'd hired had been a Rogue, but we didn't have any details. Do you know him?"

Noah looked at the photograph, then handed it to Jonah, who'd stepped forward to take it.

"I don't know him," Noah said. "I heard the rumors a Rogue

had been involved with Celina's murders, but never any specific leads. When Celina was arrested, the story went quiet."

"You're the head of Chicago's Rogue vampires. Wouldn't you be in the best position to know him?"

"I'm a spokesman, if that. Vampires go Rogue because they don't want to be Housed. And for many, it means they don't want to be tracked. Is it possible I'd know him? Yes. But I don't."

Jonah handed the photograph back to me. "I don't know him, either."

"He's working for Reed," I said, and gave them the details about Reed, the alchemy, and his plan.

I let my gaze slip to the other vampires in the room, who still watched me with some suspicion. But there was, at least, more curiosity now than there'd been when I opened the door.

"Have you seen anything like that? The alchemy? Magical symbols in a room, on a wall?"

No one spoke, raised, a hand, indicated they had any idea what I was talking about.

"Reed is well connected—politically, economically, supernaturally. And whatever he's cooking up—whatever this alchemy is for—is going to be big. Dangerously big. We could use your help."

"You want *our* help?" A female vamp I didn't know stepped into the doorway from which Noah had entered, crossed her arms. She was tall and thin, with straight, dark hair, tan skin, and wide brown eyes. "That's rich. You won't do our work, but you'll ask us for a favor?"

It didn't bother me that they thought ill of me, as it didn't come as a surprise. It didn't even bother me when she walked toward us, stood protectively by Jonah. But it did bother me that she—and the rest of them—had so entirely missed the point.

"I do your work," I said, and it only just occurred to me that

that was what had bothered me about the RG all along. "*Cadogan House* does your work. We watch out for the vampires in this city, deal with the nasties that keep cropping up, and handle the human fallout. You don't."

"We're a secret organization," Noah said.

"Of which we're all well aware," I said. "But you aren't even requesting private access to Cadogan House to attend meetings. You aren't offering to contribute anonymously. You aren't offering to contribute at all. Instead you're stuck on this idea that I'm the enemy. Why would you think you have anything to worry about?"

"Morgan and Celina," Horace and his girlfriend said simultaneously.

"You know what she's done with the Circle," he said.

"Celina's debts to Reed have nothing to do with Morgan; he was innocent." Or close enough for my purposes, anyway. "She was indebted to the Circle for millions. Had been for years. Morgan didn't even know about it until it was too late. But I'll bet you knew something, and yet you did nothing about it."

The woman had the grace to look a little chagrined. "That's more complicated than it sounds."

"Oh, I'm aware of how complicated it is," I said, anger starting to build, "because Cadogan House ended up in the middle of it. Cadogan House *always* ends up in the middle of it, and even when we've done absolutely nothing wrong."

I took an aggressive step forward, could feel them growing restless. "By contrast, *nothing* is exactly what you do. You want to fix the bad guys? Fine. But you should also be willing to help the good guys. Which we are."

"So you say." Horace's expression wasn't friendly.

"Damn right I say. And I'd be happy to go a round with anyone who says different." I looked at Noah, decided that if he was putting me on the spot, I could put him on the spot, too. "Why did you invite me to join the Red Guard if you didn't trust me?"

"He was dead when we invited you," Noah said.

Silence fell over the room like a curse. Noah's voice was flat. I didn't think he'd meant to be cruel, even if the statement was crude. But more important, it was wrong.

"No," I said. "He was *alive* when you invited me. I said yes when he was gone, because I couldn't possibly have betrayed his confidence then. There was no risk to me that way. He wasn't dead the first time I came to the lighthouse, or any of the other times since then that Cadogan House has stepped up."

I put my hands on my hips. I hadn't meant to come here and begin a tirade, but I found I couldn't stop. I was too frustrated by inaction, by apathy, by their treating every issue as someone else's problem.

"When the GP came knocking at our door, when the cops came knocking at our door, when Adrien Reed came knocking at our door, you weren't there. So don't give me bullshit about how you're on the side of vampires against the oppressors. You pick and choose your battles. And you know what? I think you've decided Ethan and I are one of those battles because you think that battle's actually winnable. I think you know the Red Guard is useless, that if you demonstrate you can control me, control Cadogan House, you can show you have balls. But that's bullshit. The only thing you get out of it is pissing off the people who have worked themselves to death—literally—to clean up the messes you've been ignoring."

"Looks like Sullivan's creating his own mess," the tall woman said. "He's making a spectacle of himself with Reed."

"Going to the Garden wasn't the best idea," I agreed. "Reed threatened me, wanted to get a reaction out of Ethan, and he did.

Ethan knows it was a mistake, but the arrest was a complete sham. They'd spent maybe ten minutes talking. It was a show of power by Reed, because that's the kind of guy he is. That's why we need to be united. That's why it's crucial." And it was a damn pity I couldn't say that to Ethan and Gabriel right then. But one step at a time.

The woman opened her mouth to speak again, but I held up a hand. "No. I'm not done. I'm sure you've had plenty of conversations about me, and this is my chance to speak my piece. Here's the question you have to ask yourselves: Are you going to keep wasting your time on me, on Ethan, when there are enemies out there with plans to bring the city to its knees? Instead of joining us, instead of helping fight, are you going to keep debating whether I'm the enemy? Here's a tip: I'm not."

"Big words," someone muttered.

"Damn right they are," I said. "And not easy ones. You've seen what Cadogan has gone through. I'm not saying it will be easy. But that's not why the RG was founded, was it? To do what's easiest?"

I didn't wait for a response, but walked to the door, glanced back. I centered my gaze on Jonah, let it linger there. His eyes, crystalline blue, showed absolutely nothing.

"When you're ready to get to work," I said to him, "you know where to find me."

And I walked out.

I stared out the windows of the taxi that sped toward Hyde Park. The driver kept checking his rearview mirror, and he'd made it plain he was in a hurry to get me the hell out of his car.

"I could drop you off at the university," he said for the third time.

"You'll drop me off at the House, or I'll call the city and tell them you refused a fare to a vampire."

I didn't think that was illegal; civil rights for vampires hadn't exactly caught on. But he blanched, and kept driving.

Sometimes you took the victory where you could find it.

I slammed into the House in the mood for a fight, was momentarily disappointed Ethan and I had made up. A good, screaming yell-fest would have worked out some of my anger. The next best thing, I decided, would be a good bout of exercise. I could go for a run or get in a little time of my own in the training room, maybe practicing the ballet Berna had mentioned.

But Mallory intercepted me in the hallway. She wore cropped jeans rolled up above her ankles, sneakers, and over a fitted shirt, a stained canvas tunic that looked like something kindergarteners wore to protect their clothes while finger-painting. Her hair was parted to the side, the wider part braided in front, the braid tucked behind her ear. "First of all, Catcher told me about the Rogue, which completely sucks. But it looks like you kicked his ass."

"Not enough to bring him down permanently."

"One step at a time," she said. "Second, I have something to show you. Ethan said you were on your way back to the House." She gestured for me to follow her. "You need to come outside."

"Mallory, I don't have time for—"

"Come outside," she said again. "Ethan, Malik, and Paige are already out there, and it's work-related, I promise. I've got a little something in the crucible."

That wasn't an offer I thought I should refuse.

They'd set up in the House's fancy barbecue, an enormous brick structure that was as much outdoor kitchen as grill. I recognized Mallory's crucible, the slightly pitted and char-marked surface. It had survived the trip back to Wicker Park. I wondered if Margot's snacks had fared as well.

Paige stood in front of the brick counter, looking at a book open beside the crucible, a basket on the brick patio at her feet.

Ethan and Malik stood a few yards away, presumably out of the danger zone. Both had their arms crossed as they watched the proceedings warily.

"What's going on, exactly?" I asked as I joined them, and Mallory joined Paige in front of the barbecue.

"We've picked out a testable portion of the alchemy," Paige said, putting drops of clear liquid in the crucible with a dropper.

"And why are you testing it here?"

"Because it needs testing," Mallory said. "And we don't want to burn down Wicker Park."

I glanced at Ethan. "So you're going to let her burn down Cadogan House?"

"I'm not going to burn anything down," Mallory said, looking back with a grin. "It's just, the houses in Wicker Park are really close together, so if anything did go wrong—*which it won't*—it would spread quickly. Here, there's plenty of room. Besides, I have Paige as my partner in crime."

"I don't have nearly as much practical experience," she said. "More of the book stuff. So this is good practice for me."

"I'm not sure that inspires confidence," Ethan murmured.

"No, it does not," Malik agreed.

"And what, exactly, will you be doing?" I asked.

"We're increasing the resonance of rosemary," Paige said, holding the crucible still as Mallory glopped green paste into it, stirred it with a wooden spoon.

"Elaborate, please," Malik said.

"Alchemists were really committed to the idea that everything in its basic form was a little bit crappy," Paige said. "But if you worked hard enough, you could raise something to its true potential."

"Like all the work we've put into Merit over the last year?" Malik asked with a wink.

"Like that," Mallory said, with an answering grin. "Pretty much anything organic—especially plants and people—have that quality. A lot of alchemy is about distilling things down to their essence—to the purity inside them. And if you can do that, if you can get, I don't know, rosemary, down to its true, unadulterated essence, its resonance changes, and it develops these healing properties. You ingest those, and you get closer to your own real essence, spiritually and physically, to a change in your own resonance."

"Alchemy is really weird," I said.

"Completely bonkers," Paige agreed.

"How does resonance—this test of it—relate to the symbols we've found?" Ethan asked.

"This is what we're calling a 'pattern test,'" Mallory said. "The actual equations are set up in phrases that, so far, don't stand on their own. In order words, we haven't been able to find one excerpt that we can run as an experiment. It would be like mixing one part of a recipe—let's say baking soda and flour—and expecting to get cookies out of it. That one step is useless on its own."

"We're looking for confirmation we're translating correctly," Paige said. "Even if we can't yet translate the entire thing, we'll know we've translated correctly certain parts of it."

Mallory nodded. "It will help me calibrate the machine. We want to find this alchemy. I need to be certain I'm looking for this alchemy. Otherwise we're going to end up with a machine that tags, I don't know, coffee drinkers in Chicago or something."

"Which would be useless," I said. "Especially in the Loop."

"And Wicker Park!" Mallory said. "There's a whole-bean, shade-grown, cage-free coffeehouse on every corner now."

"I didn't realize beans required cages," Ethan said.

"Neither did I," Mallory said. "Now hush and let me work."

"I guess she's giving you orders now," I said to Ethan with a smile.

"I guess she is," Ethan said as they turned to their work, putting material in the crucible, arranging components on the top of the patio.

Paige and Mallory looked happy and very compatible working together. Paige's height and red hair matched interestingly with Mallory's petite stature and blue locks. Mallory moved quickly, efficiently, as she prepared the work. Paige's movements were more deliberate. For two sorcerers on the right side of the law, they hadn't spent much time together. Maybe a friendship could blossom. If so, I'd take credit for that, too.

"How was the meeting?" Ethan asked.

In response, I growled.

"I guess that means we'll discuss it later."

"That would probably be best."

"All right," Mallory said as Paige handed her a box of matches. "Let's do this."

When Mallory snapped the match against the side of the box, Malik, Ethan, and I took a simultaneous step backward. As she dropped it into the crucible, Paige took a step backward, too. Mallory stayed exactly where she was, watching and waiting for something to happen.

The crucible rattled once. Then again. And then it began to vibrate as if someone had flipped a switch.

"Ladies and gentlemen, we have alchemy." Mallory put her hands on her hips, and her smile was as sly as a vampire's. "That's resonance."

We clapped politely, and Malik leaned in. "Is anyone else disappointed there wasn't a pretty blue or green explosion?"

It was as if he'd made a wish.

There was a whistle, like a teapot at the ready, and a small blue spark popped out of the crucible, burst like a tiny firework.

Malik nodded. "Nice."

A second spark popped, and then a third, all in shades of blue, all shattering in the air like tiny crystals. But it took only a moment for those few pretty sparks to grow bigger, faster, and more explosive. Daubs of blue flame began to shower from the crucible, whistling like an Independence Day celebration.

Paige squeaked, darted away from the showering fire. Mallory just stood there, hands on her hips, and stared at it like a woman contemplating the cosmos.

After a moment, when the sparks had died down, she patted at a spark in her hair. "And that's why we didn't do it in Wicker Park."

Chapter Nineteen

OLD WOUNDS

Mallory concluded they hadn't distilled the plant's "salt" as much as they'd needed to before running the experiment. But otherwise it was a success. They cleaned up the mess and put out the residual sparks, and Mallory headed home to work on the machine.

The rest of us went back inside, found vampires streaming toward the cafeteria. Margot had prepared an all-American dinner: hot dogs with the appropriate Chicago trimmings, hand-cut fries, milk shakes. Meals like that were always more popular than the fancy French things she was just as capable of cooking.

Ethan and I grabbed food, but took it back to the office to talk through status while we ate. Ethan no longer ate his hot dog with a fork off undoubtedly expensive China, and he'd striped it with neon relish and added sport peppers, which brought it closer to a proper Chicago dog. I was getting through.

"Would you like to tell me about your RG visit?" he asked, taking a bite.

"Nothing changed," I said. "That's really all there is to say. We're at an impasse."

"Odd. You'd think meeting atop the Navy Pier Ferris wheel would make for a happy occasion."

I started to say something, then looked at him. "Are you trying to guess where the meetings are?"

"I would do no such thing."

"You completely would. But, seriously, the Ferris wheel?"

He formed a box with his fingers. "I believe it has cars."

I just shook my head. "How have you lived here so long without a ride on the Ferris wheel?"

"I'm a vampire," he said, as if that was the obvious explanation.

I just sighed.

"Did they recognize the Rogue?"

"No. No one recognized him, and no one had seen any alchemy. They don't seem naive to the possibility Reed's our villain, but they don't seem terribly interested in doing anything about it, either. I gave them a speech about how we're the allies, not the enemies, and then walked out and left them to think about it."

Ethan smiled, attacked his dog. "There may be a Master in you yet."

"Don't even joke about that. I know you have to look at bank statements and spreadsheets."

"There's nothing like the beauty of a good P-and-L statement."

"I'll take your word for it."

There was a knock on the threshold, and we both looked up.

Jonah stood in the doorway.

Assuming he was there for me, I wiped my mouth with a napkin, rose. "Hey. Is everything all right?"

"Yeah. I'm sorry to interrupt your dinner. Could we talk? Merit, I mean."

I blinked. I hadn't expected to see him here, much less to pose anything in the form of a question. I'd expected yelling, angry text messages, demands that I return the Midnight High T-shirts and medal I'd received when I was inducted. But asking me to talk? That was a new one.

"Sure," I said, and glanced at Ethan, got his nod.

I took a final drink of milk shake, pushed my chair under the table again. "Don't eat my fries while I'm gone."

"Finders keepers," he muttered, and snatched one from my plate.

"Sorry to interrupt your dinner," Jonah said as we walked down the hall toward the front of the House. I wasn't in the mood for another session of Confessions in the Garden, so I opted for the smaller of the House's two front parlors. It was a cozy room, with a wall of bookshelves, a couch, and a few chairs. It was also empty of vampires, since most of the Novitiates who lived in the House were in the cafeteria chowing down.

I took a seat in an armchair. He took the one across from me.

"No problem. I'm surprised you're here, after . . ."

He nodded, looked at his hands, rubbed them together. Was he nervous? "To tell you the truth, I am, too," he said. "Listen, about the lighthouse—"

"Yeah, I'm sorry about that."

He gazed up at me, eyes bright. "Don't be sorry. You were absolutely right. And you said something that people have been thinking for a while now. The world is different than it was when the RG was created, and we haven't really adapted." He paused, seeming to consider. "Historically, the good vampires were the ones who didn't make trouble. Who kept their heads down. The bad vampires didn't. They drew attention to themselves."

"That's a very pre-Celina attitude," I said, since she'd been the one to out our existence to the rest of the world.

"Exactly. And it's where they still are. For a long time, it worked. When our focus was staying quiet and safe, it totally worked. But you're right. It doesn't work anymore. It's time we change."

He looked up at me. "It's going to be hard for some to adapt. Some will be afraid, and some will probably leave the RG. But I don't think we have a choice."

"We?" I asked, very deliberately.

The question must have made him antsy, because he rose, walked to the bookshelves, putting space between us.

"You still think I'm a traitor to the cause," I said. "Because I won't spy on him."

He ran a hand through his auburn locks. "No. It's more complicated than that. And not really complicated at all."

Silence descended while he looked everywhere but at me. And I just stared at him, baffled. Finally, after a good two minutes had passed, Jonah cleared his throat again and looked at me with stormy blue eyes. "I handled the request poorly—asking you to watch Ethan, to report on Ethan—because I still have feelings for you."

I stared at him. "You . . . what?"

"Yeah," he said with a sad little shrug. "I haven't been able to shake it."

I was staggered. Flattered, absolutely—who wouldn't be?—but also staggered. I'd been with Ethan for virtually our entire partnership, and Jonah knew how I'd felt. I hadn't done anything to encourage him, at least as far as I was aware, but that didn't really make me feel any better.

"I'm sorry," I said. "That really sucks."

He threw his head back and laughed until he was wiping tears from his eyes. "Sorry," he said. "Cathartic laugh." And then he shook it off. "Yeah. Unrequited feelings are never fun. I guess that's why your refusal to report about the House felt like a betrayal. Not because you picked Ethan, or not just anyway. But because I lost out on the piece of you that should have been mine—our RG partnership. He won that, too. And it pissed me off."

He looked back at me, smiled sadly. "I just, I don't know, feel a connection. Which you don't share."

"I'm sorry you've been hurt by that."

Another half laugh. "I'm not sure 'hurt' captures the real poetic desperation of unrequited love. Which, if I'm honest with myself, is part of the draw. Oh, the poignancy of wanting someone you can't have."

This time, I smiled, too. "Maybe you could find someone a little more emotionally available?"

Jonah snorted. "I can't even ask if you have a sister, since I took her to prom."

"Oh my God, I forgot about that. Small world. And, I mean, her husband wouldn't appreciate me trying to get you together again."

On the other hand, that didn't mean I didn't have ideas. And if fixing Jonah up would ease the tension between us, I was more than happy to help. In fact, hadn't someone just told me she was ready to date again?

"How do you feel about food?"

He glanced at me, eyebrows lifted. "Is that a trick question?"

"Nope. Completely earnest."

He lifted a shoulder. "I mean, I like food."

That worked for me. Now I just had to talk to my new target.

"So what do we do now?" I asked. "I mean about the RG."

One hand on his hip, another on the bookshelf, fingers tapping, he frowned as he contemplated. "I think I should go back to the RG, present them with a specific plan. I think it's harder to imagine themselves as crusaders. But if we give them a task, and they begin to see their new role that way, it might help."

"You up for working on some alchemy?"

He smiled, and some of the old humor was back in his eyes. "I am. I've got permission from Scott."

"Good. Because there's a lot of work to do. Confusing, confusing work."

"I'm willing to learn. I'm glad we had a chance to talk about all this. To clear the air."

That clear air was fractured by the huge sound of metallic wrenching.

"The front gate," I said, and had just pivoted into the foyer when the blast blew in the front door.

Sometime later, I blinked. Once, then twice, until the two images of the foyer's coffered ceiling above me combined into one again.

I was on my back on the floor, eyes stinging from dust and smoke, my ears ringing from the concussion of noise. I pushed myself up on my elbows, ribs aching on my right side. Jonah lay across my legs, facedown, arms sprawled. He'd turned his body toward mine as the wall of hot air hit us, and the blast had hit him full-on, throwing us both across the foyer until we'd nearly hit the staircase.

I lifted my gaze. The front doors were broken and splintered on the floor, the walls around them cracked and crumbling, smoke pouring into the House. There'd been a vase of flowers on the round table in the center of the foyer. The table was in splinters, the vase shattered, the flowers scattered across the floor among pieces of the door and spilled water.

Since no one else had come out to investigate, I guessed I'd been out for only a few seconds.

As carefully as I could manage, I rolled Jonah onto his back. There was a large cut across his forehead, streaming blood and sending magic into the air. Jonah and I had complementary magic, uniquely compatible. My body, wounded and eager, wanted that blood so badly my hands began to shake.

"No," I muttered, grabbing a piece of cloth from the floor, probably part of the foyer table's cover, and pressed it to the laceration.

I tapped his cheeks. "Jonah! Jonah! Wake up!" And when he didn't, I put fingers on the pulse point in his wrist. He had a pulse, but it was slow.

Shots began to ring out, bullets whizzing through the front of the House with the speed of an automatic weapon. I ducked, covering him with my body, lowered my lips to his ear. "If you die, I will personally kick your ass."

The bullets kept coming, spinning through the hallway to splinter the wood of the stairs, the plaster and art on the opposite wall.

There was a break in the noise, probably as guns were reloaded. Help would come soon. But in the meantime, I had to get him out of here. Wincing as pain shot through my torso, I grabbed him under the arms, pulled him into the parlor.

Merit!

Thank God for psychic connections. *I'm all right,* I told Ethan, the fear in his voice keen. *I'm in the parlor. Front door's gone. I think they hit it with a grenade, and they're still firing. Jonah's down; he shielded me. I've dragged him into the front parlor. Too much smoke to see the perps, but this kind of fight doesn't seem like Reed. Open the arsenal, Ethan. We're going to need it.*

Covering fire en route, Sentinel. Keep your head down.

On that. There wasn't much else I could do. Not with Jonah unconscious. Bullets wouldn't kill me, but I could dodge them. He couldn't, and I wasn't about to leave him alone.

A bullet zinged through the wall over my head, and I ducked again, covering Jonah as plaster filled the air.

I reached up, pulled down a blanket from the sofa, flipped it over his body. That would at least keep dust out of his eyes and mouth. I belly-crawled across the floor to the far end of the window, used the end of the couch as a shield to raise up.

There was a Humvee in the front yard, the hook and winch on the front still attached to a mangled piece of the front gate.

The human guards who'd been at the gate were on the ground beside one of the giant brick pillars. They were blood streaked, but had weapons in hand, and were shooting the enemy combatants who'd taken positions around the Humvee.

The guards wouldn't have let someone winch off the gate without a fight. They must have been targeted first, wounded or moved aside, and then the winch was hooked up. And then the Humvee came through, probably lobbed a grenade at the front door.

"You sons of bitches!" A man with broad shoulders, dark skin, and a shaved head pointed an enormous gun at the House. "You goddamn bloodsucking assholes! You wanna fuck with us? We will destroy you."

Angry magic buzzed through the air like an upended hornets' nest.

It wasn't Adrien Reed, or his sorcerer, or his vampire.

It was a shifter.

Claxons sounded as the House went on full alert. Two figures in black moved through the lobby. Guards, although they moved so quickly I couldn't tell who. Others would go around the back, and temps would be stationed on the roof. Luc hadn't skimped on the response plans.

Ethan darted into the room with a belted sword, another in hand, and a handgun. Vampires didn't usually use guns. But then again, sups didn't usually come at the House with an army's worth of weapons.

He hit the floor beside Jonah, took his pulse. "Knocked out?"

"I think so. I haven't been able to wake him." I swallowed down the ball of emotions that rose suddenly to my throat. "He moved in front of me when they blasted the door."

"Looks like he took a good blow to the head," Ethan said, lifting the cloth I'd placed on the wound. "Concussion, I'd bet. I wish Delia was here."

"She's not?"

"At the hospital. She's en route, and we have other vampires trained as medics. But she's the best."

I had no reason to argue with that. "They're shifters, Ethan. Shifters who are totally pissed off about something."

He turned to me, stared. "Shifters. Pissed about Caleb Franklin? That was nearly a week ago."

"I don't know. I just know the guy who looks to be calling the shots is a shifter, and he's pissed."

A vampire I'd seen around the House but didn't know personally—a man with tan skin and black hair—dodged into the room, a medical kit in hand, and fell to his knees beside Jonah.

"Unconscious," Ethan said. "Head wound."

"On it, Sire," the vampire said, opening his kit and arranging his tools.

"Thank you, Ramón. Take care."

"Always. You, too, Sire."

Ethan nodded, looked back at me, handed me a katana. I unsheathed it, took in the beautifully engraved blade, glanced back at him.

"One of yours?"

"Peter Cadogan's," Ethan said. "Luc brought it up from the

arsenal." Because mine was still in our apartments; I hadn't taken it with me to the lighthouse. "Seems appropriate our Sentinel bear it to protect the House." Ethan rose, offered me a hand, pressed a hard kiss to my lips. "Let's get it done."

The air was thick with blood, with smoke, with magic. Sirens were closing in, and house and car alarms were sounding up and down the street.

A shifter rushed toward me, damp footsteps on grass. I pivoted, turned, sliced with the katana. He crumpled to the ground, screaming as he held an arm against the laceration across his abdomen. The air filled with the powerful scent of shifter's blood. My predatory instincts kicked into overdrive, wanting that blood, *craving* it. Once again, this wasn't the time or the place.

Another man came charging at me in a bruised leather jacket covered in NAC and motorcycle club patches. He had a bowie knife, its blade down as though he meant to take me with a single thrust.

I had two questions: Why were NAC shifters attacking us, and where the hell was Gabriel?

"Fucking vampires! We know what you did!"

"We didn't do anything!" I yelled back, using the spine of my katana to block his strike. The spine caught in one of the notches in the serrated blade, and I twisted the sword, yanking it out of his hand and sending it flying through the air. It hit the ground fifteen feet away. The shifter gave one quick glance at his lost weapon before deciding hand-to-hand would be just as effective.

"You're trying to kill us! Trying to take us out!" Light flashed as magic surrounded him, ensconced him. And when it cleared, I was facing an enormous ruddy-colored wolf. His hackles were raised, and his massive yellow teeth dripped saliva.

Now I began to sweat. I was skilled at fighting two-legged creatures. I didn't exactly have the skill set for a wolf, even if I could get over the emotional baggage of intentionally hurting an animal.

When he leaped at me again, my hesitancy disappeared. I was a predator, too, with a mighty fine survival instinct.

I spun to dodge him, brought my sword around low, catching the tip of the blade on the back of one of his paws. He yelped and stumbled. Light flashed and magic spun around him again, and then he was in human form, naked and screaming at the gaping and bloody wound in his left Achilles tendon.

That was why shifters so often fought in their human forms. A shift into animal form would heal any injuries they'd suffered as humans, but the magic didn't work in reverse.

"Maybe think before you attack next time," I murmured. My store of sympathy was tapped out.

"Sentinel!" Juliet screamed, and I glanced back just in time to dodge the enormous fist aimed at my head. I hit the ground, rolled, came up again with my katana in front of me. It was the shifter who'd screamed and aimed the automatic weapon at the House.

"Thanks!" I yelled out to Juliet. She'd brought a handgun to this particular fight, fired neat shots into the shoulder of the first female shifter I'd seen tonight. They were the shifter version of unicorns—public sightings were rare, especially in battle.

I looked back to my enemy, who eyed me with loathing that seemed to radiate off him.

"You think you're better than we are? You think you have the right?"

"Only in this particular instance," I said as he punched again with his right fist. I dodged, but he grazed my sore shoulder, sending a shock of hot pain all the way to my toes. I went into a crouch, aimed an elbow into his stomach when he moved over me. The shifter grunted, stumbled back a few feet before regaining his footing.

He must not have expected much from me, because the fact that he hadn't knocked me out seemed to infuriate him. He came at me again like a linebacker, hands out and ready to move me back across the line.

Both hands on the katana's handle, I sliced diagonally, leaving a stripe of blood across both hands. He howled, fisted his hands so blood ran down his wrists, and aimed an uppercut at my jaw. I turned the blade to the side, whipped the steel against his flank, and when he was a step beyond me, kicked the back of his knee so he hit the ground.

He rolled to get up again, but I was faster. I put a boot on his chest and the katana's point at the throbbing pulse in his neck.

I'd had it there for only a moment when a voice rang clear behind me.

"Kitten, I'm going to have to ask you to move that sword."

Gabriel Keene had walked into our war zone.

I glanced back at what had remained of the gate, found my grandfather assembling and organizing CPD teams. Luc was also there, his shirt ripped and bloodied, pointing to spots where the House had been attacked, where the shifter had tried to destroy us. They'd let Gabriel in. But why?

Before I could even think to warn Ethan, he flew across the yard, slammed Gabriel to the ground.

"You son of a bitch!"

They rolled once, then twice, before Ethan flipped him over, pounded a fist into Gabriel's jaw. Gabriel's forearm deflected some of the blow, but not much of it. Ethan's fist still knocked pretty hard, sending Gabe's head flying back. Gabriel roared, as much in insult as pain, and kicked up, sending Ethan flying into the grass ten feet away.

Ethan wasn't deterred. He scrambled to his feet, made another run at Gabriel, who'd climbed to his feet again.

The shifter on the ground tried to take advantage of the chaos, slowly lifting his head, probably hoping he could roll out from under my katana.

I snapped my gaze back to him, pressed the point farther into his neck. "I can see you moving, moron. And given what you've done to our House, I doubt running to Gabriel is going to help you much."

"This is the second goddamn time your people have attacked our House!" Ethan said, touching the back of his hand to his face, drawing back blood. "This time, you're going to pay for it."

"Hold on a goddamn minute," Gabriel said, rising and spitting blood. "I didn't authorize this attack or request it. I don't know what the fuck it's about."

"Look at my House, Keene! Look what your people have done!" Ethan stepped toe-to-toe, and there was war—and worse—in his eyes. "She was in the front room, Gabriel. The front goddamn room. And if you had hurt her, a split lip would be the least of your concerns."

Gabriel changed tactics, raised his hands. "All right," he said. "All right. I didn't know anything about this. Your Sentinel, who looks to be healthy at the moment, has a sword pointed at one of my soldiers. Can we ask him what the hell this is about?"

I nodded toward the shifter. "He had the gun, was screaming about vampires taking out shifters."

"May I?" Gabriel asked, and I glanced back at Ethan for the all-clear.

When Ethan nodded, I lifted the katana.

That made the shifter brave. "*Bitch,*" he said, and would have crawled to his feet had Gabriel not put a boot in his balls. His face turned green; he turned to his side, moaning.

"His name's Kane," Gabriel said, crouching in front of him. "What the fuck have you done, Kane?" Every word was bitten off like a bitter pill.

"They're killing us."

Gabriel's eyebrows lifted. "Caleb Franklin wasn't killed by this House."

"Killer was a Rogue, paid by Cadogan." Kane squeezed his eyes shut, probably as pain rolled through him. "Same Rogue did Kyle Farr tonight."

"Farr's dead?"

"Fucked up," Kane said, opening eyes that had gone watery with pain. "Vampire fucked him up."

"We paid no Rogue, or anyone else, to harm anyone," Ethan said. And yet we knew a Rogue who'd murdered, and probably wouldn't feel much reluctance about lying.

"What did the vampire look like?" Ethan asked.

Kane moved to sit up, huffing through his teeth. "You know what he looks like. He's one of yours. He said so."

"*Kane,*" Gabriel said. A request, an order.

"White. Dark hair. Lean. Muscles." He moved a hand across his jaw. "And had a beard. Big, thick beard."

CHAPTER TWENTY

FACTS OF WAR

Gabriel let CPD corral the shifters into a corner of the yard. They lay facedown, hands on their heads, while Catcher, my grandfather, the SWAT team members watched them. The SWAT men and women had weapons in hand, and they looked as though they were daring the shifters to move.

There'd been seventeen of them. They'd come to the House in the Humvee on the lawn, two more parked outside it. It had taken two vehicles to pull off the gate—proving that no system was foolproof.

The House looked like an apocalypse had rolled through. The entryway was a disaster. The front doors were gone, and most of the front windows had been blown out. The stone was pock-marked with bullets. It hadn't looked this bad since the last time the shifters attacked us. That had been Adam Keene's doing. And for that and other sins, he hadn't lived to talk about it.

Gabriel Keene would have much to answer for.

Kane had been gathered up, deposited on the other side of the lawn away from his friends or minions, whoever he'd gotten to follow his crusade.

Ethan and I stood around him, katanas unsheathed and at our

sides. Gabriel stood in front of him, his anger unmasked, hot waves of furious magic spilling through the yard like an angry tsunami.

"We were at Bill's Eat Place," Kane said.

"Where's Bill's Eat Place?" Ethan asked.

"What does it matter?" Kane asked, frustration ringing in his voice. I imagined from his perspective we were ignoring the obvious.

Gabriel crouched in front of him. "I told you to answer whatever questions he asked you. You don't answer his questions, and I'll turn your ass over to Sullivan and his Sentinel right now, and let them decide what to do with you."

Kane turned his brown eyes on me. I let my eyes silver and my fangs descend, and showed them off.

"Wrigleyville," he said. "It's in Wrigleyville." He looked back at Gabriel, as if that might make the horrifying specter of me disappear. "We were having drinks, and Kyle Farr and me went out to the alley to piss. We finished up, and I'm going back inside. I look back, and Farr's squinting at people down the alley a little ways. Sups. They start walking toward us—vampire and another guy—I didn't get a good look at him.

"Kyle starts walking down the alley toward them. I'm thinking he's going to confront them, and I'm up for some action. They get closer. I can see the vamp, but the man hangs back, stays in the shadows. Then he whispers something, does some abracadabra. Draws this symbol in the air, and it glows like neon."

"What kind of symbol?" Ethan asked.

Kane shrugged. "Nothing I recognized. Some kind of shapes. Square or triangle or something? I don't know. Anyway, soon as he did that, Farr got this faraway look in his eyes. And then he starts *whaling* on me. I'm like, what the hell, man? I give him a punch of my own, but he just keeps coming. And the entire time, the vamp and sorcerer—I'm figuring that's what he is at this point—they're just standing there with this symbol just glowing. And every time the sorcerer moves a finger, Farr does something else. He just keeps coming and coming and wailing on me."

Gabriel shook his head. "That's not possible."

Kane pulled down his shoulder, showed a jagged wound that I hadn't put there. "Absolutely possible. Absolutely *happened*."

I felt the sharp shock of Ethan's magic. He'd been under the control of a sorcerer once—brought back to life by Mallory when she'd been under the influence of black magic. She'd tried, and failed, to make him a familiar, but the magic had left a temporary link between them, one that allowed her to work through him and feel her emotions. This sorcerer was using alchemy, but the power sounded just as disturbing.

"Anyway, Kyle keeps coming and coming, and I finally get him on the ground. By this time, Twitch has come out of the bar, and Rick, and all those guys. They see Farr on the ground and these sups down the alley, and I say, let's get these guys. The vampire says he also took out Franklin and we can thank Cadogan House because they paid for both."

Gabriel worked his jaw in obvious frustration. "And did he say why Cadogan House would pay him to kill a shifter?"

Kane slid his gaze to Ethan. "Because Sullivan wants control of the city, and he's proving to you that he's in charge."

And wasn't that ironic, coming from Reed's minion?

"Where's Farr?" Gabe asked.

Kane finally looked regretful. "Don't know. That symbol disappeared, and so did they. When we looked back, he was gone."

They disappeared him? Ethan asked silently.

Or convinced him to walk away, I said. *Or worse, convinced him to go with them*.

"And so you came here," Gabriel said. "With Humvees and automatic weapons."

"We protect our own."

Gabriel sighed. "I'm sure you believe you were protecting the Pack, Kane. Unfortunately, you're protecting it from the wrong people. You got played."

"No, but they said—"

"And they were lying. The vampire you saw is the one who killed Franklin, but Cadogan House didn't do it."

"They were there when it happened."

"They were there *after* it happened because they'd been going to a goddamn night game. And instead of leaving our man where he was, they chased the vampire and got shot in the process."

Kane looked suspiciously from Ethan to me. I almost showed him my bullet wound, but decided I wasn't going to justify my existence to a man so ready to believe the worst of us.

"But the vampire said—"

"You got played," Gabriel said again. "You attacked innocents who've been trying to find Caleb's killer. And when you had a chance to take him down, you were dazzled by magic and let him go."

Kane deflated like a balloon, like all the piss and vinegar and righteousness leaked out of him at once.

"Haul him up," Gabriel said to Fallon and Eli Keene; Gabriel had called them into action, probably because he knew they were trustworthy. "Put him with the others." There was sympathy and disappointment and anger in his voice.

They escorted Kane to the holding area for the other shifters, stepping over broken and bloody pavement to get there.

"Tell me the rest of it," Gabriel said, watching his men. Ethan glanced at me, nodded. This was my story to tell.

"We think Reed has two main players—the sorcerer and the vampire. We don't have an ID for the sorcerer. We believe the vampire's a Rogue"—I paused—"and we know he's the Rogue who attacked me the night I became a vampire."

Gabriel went very still. "Last night—your fight on the train. That was him."

I nodded.

"You're all right?"

I nodded. "I'll do."

He watched me for a long, silent moment. "I told you, when he killed Caleb, that I wanted him. I'd say you've got a claim, too."

I nodded. I could admit I wanted my chance at the Rogue.

Our deal done, Gabe looked at Ethan again. "And we don't know anything about the sorcerer?"

"He belongs to Reed," Ethan began, "knows alchemy, and doesn't like to be seen."

"And apparently has the ability to control a shifter, to make him fight like a damn marionette."

"Is Kane trustworthy?" Ethan asked.

Gabriel made a rough and ragged sound. "I wouldn't have said no before tonight. But what kind of judge am I now?" He put his hands on his head, turned around, and looked back at the House. "We've wrought destruction here tonight." He glanced back at Ethan. "But there may be worse coming. It was alchemy? What he saw?"

"The symbol the sorcerer drew could have been alchemical. But there's nothing we've translated so far about controlling shifters."

Ethan glanced at me for confirmation, and I nodded. "Nothing in the parts we've been able to translate. But we're still missing some glyphs."

"It may not just be shifters," Gabriel said. "He's not known to have any specific animus against us. We may have been the unlucky ones they've tested this on. The rollout may be larger."

"But the purpose might be the same," I said. "Not just controlling supernaturals, but using them to fight." Just as they had with Farr.

"You're talking about an army," Gabe said. "A supernatural one."

"We don't know how long he's had this in the works," I said. "But he knows we've been watching him, and that he's been connected to the Circle. He wants control of the city. Supposedly wants to bring order to it. More likely, he wants to unify his kingdoms. The Circle's got plenty of guns and money. Supernaturals would make a fine army."

Ethan glanced at Gabe. "At the risk of minimizing what he's done to my House, if Kane's retelling the story accurately, I don't entirely blame him. This is as disturbing as it gets."

"Yeah," Gabe said. "For you, for us, for the city." He glanced back at his shifters. "I'm not going to object to their arrest. A little prison time might knock some sense into them."

Ethan nodded. "You, of course, still owe us."

"Acknowledged," Gabriel said, teeth gritted.

"You can start by arranging medical care for the human guards and preparing the House for dawn." Ethan checked his watch. "We don't have much time."

"Then I'll need to get on that, Your Highness." Gabe's tone was flat, and frustrated magic seemed to swim around him as he gestured for Fallon. "And I can now worry about the shifter I'm missing and the possibility a man with an unbridled ego has figured out some kind of charm to control us. Helluva goddamn night," he said, then gestured toward the damage to the House. "Reed wants to hurt sups, or make us look bad in the press, he couldn't have planned this better."

"Who says he didn't?" I said.

Ethan and Gabriel looked at me.

"I'm not saying he finagled getting your people to the bar, but the sorcerer and vampire were smart enough—and had authority enough—to take advantage of the situation they found themselves in. They play with the shifter, and then they turn the heat onto us. That keeps us from working on the alchemy, getting closer."

"It's a distinct possibility," Ethan agreed with a nod.

Gabriel ran a hand through his tousled waves, which glinted gold under the House's security lights. Even at night, even in darkness, Gabriel seemed touched by the sun.

"Actually," Ethan said with resignation, "there is something that will make us slightly more even." He pulled from his pocket Caleb Franklin's key.

About damn time, I thought.

"What's that?"

"A safe-deposit box key we found when we searched Franklin's house."

Gabriel's jaw clenched. "You didn't mention that when you came to the bar. When you came to the bar," Gabriel said again, "and berated me for withholding information."

"So now you've proven you're both assholes," I said.

They both, very slowly, turned their heads to look at me again.

"Assholes whom I respect immensely," I said, holding up my hands. "But still assholes. And that's not an insult to either one of you. Sometimes you're assholes because you have to be. Because that's what's required, and better you be the asshole than risk the people you're supposed to protect."

They both watched me for a minute, as if unsure whether to yell at me or not. Finally, Gabriel relented. "What bank?"

"We don't know," Ethan said, then paused before identifying the man who was investigating that. "Jeff's looking into it."

"Sneaky," Gabriel said. "I knew he continued to work with you, and didn't object to that. I didn't know it was about this."

My grandfather walked toward us. "They'd like to begin escorting the shifters out to the supernatural facility."

The city had renovated a former ceramics factory into a prison for supernaturals, given their special needs (like darkness) and abilities (like glamour). Had Ethan and I been formally charged, we'd probably have ended up there.

"Do what you need to do," Gabriel said. "They've got punishment coming to them, and this might knock sense into their damn heads."

"We'll give you the origin story later," Ethan said to my grandfather. "I know you'll want the details."

"I would. The disagreement, let's call it, is done for now?" he asked, looking between Apex and Master.

"It is," they agreed.

"Good. We don't need infighting right now. Not when we're all on the cusp."

"Truer words," Gabe said, then pulled out his phone. "I'll call a contractor. I've got friends with connections. I'll be sure that they have someone here at sunrise to begin the repairs."

"I'd appreciate that," Ethan said. "As to Reed, he's planning something big, and the alchemy is part of it. Farr, or what happened to him, could be, too. You want in—the investigation, the fight—you're in."

Gabriel nodded. "You keep me informed, and I'll keep you informed."

And that, I thought, was as much an apology as he was going to give.

"What a mess," I said when Gabriel walked back to Fallon and Eli, began to talk about strategy.

"It's the inherent danger of shifters," Ethan said, "and one of the reasons they prefer to live away from humans. They're as much wild creature as human. They're strong, potentially violent, often unpredictable."

"And sometimes amazingly loyal," I said as Jeff helped a limping Juliet into the House.

"Indeed, Sentinel. Indeed."

Mallory walked down the sidewalk, mouth agape and a large duffel bag in hand, weighted down in the middle by something relatively small and obviously heavy.

"What the hell?" she asked when she reached us, her gaze still tripping around the destruction.

"Confused shifters," I said, so we could skip the longer play-by-play. "A shifter was manipulated by magic, and his friends blamed us."

"I haven't heard from Catcher yet, so I didn't know. Damn, you guys."

"Yeah," I said. "It's a disaster. And there's something else. The shifter went postal because someone played puppet master with a shifter near the Wrigleyville symbols."

Mallory opened her mouth, closed it again. "Say what, now?"

"You know what we know. Apparently made the controlled shifter beat the crap out of a fellow Pack member while the sorcerer played composer." I waved a hand back and forth like conducting an orchestra.

"Holy shit," Mallory said. "That's . . . not good."

"We're agreed on that," Ethan said.

"How did they make it work? Magically, I mean."

"The shifter said the sorcerer drew a symbol in the air," I said. "He couldn't ID the symbol, but it was glowing shapes of some kind."

She looked at the ground, processed. "So it was alchemy. And Paige had it right—the alchemy is about affecting other people." She scratched her forehead thoughtfully. "But I just don't see that reflected in the parts we've translated. I'm going to have to think about this. In the meantime, would you like some good news?"

"God, yes," Ethan said.

"The machine's ready. The alchemical detector—that's what I'm calling it. We just need to make sure Jeff's done with his part, and we're ready to deploy. We just need some height."

Ethan glanced back, lifted his gaze to the House. "I believe I know a place."

We waited until the situation at the House was stable. Until the human guards had been cared for and shifters had covered the broken windows with plywood, installed a make-do door and make-do gate, and stood guard outside both. They'd stay until the House was secure again. Architecturally, anyway.

We also waited until Scott and the Grey House physician were let through the barrier, could tend to Jonah. Ramón had kept an eye on him during the fracas, monitoring him until the battle was over.

"Concussion," the doctor said, but frowned. "I don't like that he's unconscious, but it's not uncommon with a good knock to the head. Let's get him someplace safe and stable, and I'll monitor him from there."

I pressed a very platonic kiss to Jonah's cheek and watched as they drove him away.

Getting all that arranged put us on the House's narrow widow's walk only an hour before dawn. It was a narrow space accessible through the attic and a window to the roof and bounded by a wrought-iron rail.

Cadogan House was the tallest building on the street, which at least meant there weren't too many line-of-sight issues. The city unfolded around us, a blanket of orange and white lights, buildings tall and short. And to the east, the lake spread like dark, rich ink, virtually untouched by artificial light. It looked as if the world simply stopped.

"Damn," Jeff said. "You forget how beautiful it is when you

only see it from down there. When you only see the anger and petty squabbles."

"Speaking of which, let's try to fix this one," Catcher said.

"I think that's a hint that my husband is eager to get this show on the road."

"Husband" still hit my ear wrong.

Mallory, Catcher, and Jeff began to prepare their magic. Beside me, Ethan kept his gaze on the city. *I would give it to you if I could, Sentinel. And all of it in peace.*

I smiled and held out a hand. *Let's go see if we can make a little of that happen.*

A few feet away, Mallory pulled off the satchel she'd worn diagonally across her chest and spread it open. She put both hands inside, very carefully lifted out what looked like a spinning spice rack, and placed it on the ground. There were jars in about a third of the slots, and the middle of the older had been carved out, a small porcelain crucible placed inside. A small, square mirror was mounted on a bracket above it.

Silence followed.

Ethan and I cocked our heads at it.

"Huh," I said.

"Pretty sweet, isn't it?"

"It's not what I expected."

Mallory moved the bag out of the way. "It's not the shimmy in the magic, it's the magic in the shimmy. Right, honey?"

"Put that on a T-shirt," Catcher said, crouching beside her.

Jeff pulled a tablet from his backpack, began scrambling fingers over the screen. He might not have been vampire—we couldn't all be so lucky—but his fingers were faster than any I'd ever seen.

Good for Fallon, I thought cheekily.

"How, exactly, will this work?" Ethan asked, peering over my shoulder.

"With unicorn farts and happy wishes," Catcher said, adjusting the gadget's glass cylinders. Alchemical symbols were inscribed in the wood around the bottles and crucible.

"Oh, good," Ethan said. "I was concerned we weren't adequately addressing our energy needs by ignoring the unicorn farts."

"At least you've kept your sense of humor," Mallory said, expression tight with concentration. When they'd adjusted the bottles, she adjusted the mirror, then stood up again.

Catcher did the same. "This will detect alchemical resonance."

Mallory nodded. "We've created the appropriate mix of salts and mercury, added the necessary symbology. We just have to quicken the magic. You ready?" she asked Jeff.

"Calibrating," he said. "Nearly there." With a final tap, he rolled his shoulders and moved to stand behind the machine, aiming the tablet at it. "Ready."

"We're going to do Wrigley first," Catcher said. "We know where those symbols are, so it'll be a good test." At Mallory's nod, he struck a match in the dark. The smell of sulfur singed the air. As Mallory closed her eyes to whisper quiet words, he dropped the match into the crucible.

There was a pop and the hiss of fire meeting fuel, and a pale beam of smoky light shot from the crucible, bounced off the mirror above it, and shot north. It faded as it moved away from us, and disappeared completely when a building interrupted our line of sight. Probably for the best—we didn't need to field phone calls about laser beams over Chicago.

"Here," Jeff said, and we gathered around him. He'd pulled up the three-dimensional map of the city. The light was green on the tablet, and it speared north from Cadogan House to Wrigleyville.

"Nice," Mallory said, offering her husband a high five. But his gaze was stuck to the screen. The beam of light didn't stop when it reached Wrigleyville. It flared and refracted, flying out on another trajectory until it stopped and flared again, hitting another hot spot.

And it didn't stop. The light kept flaring, refracting, traveling again until the program had traced a dozen hot spots across the city. Nearly to Skokie to the north, nearly to Calumet City to the south, and from the lake to Hellriver in the west. There'd been more symbols in Hellriver, and we'd missed them, not that we'd known to look.

The hot spots and the line between them formed their own alchemical symbol—a circle inside a diamond inside a square, all of which was surrounded by another circle.

"There are so many of them," Jeff said quietly.

Ethan stood silently and stoically beside me, concern flaring as he looked at what seemed an obvious threat to his city, his vampires.

"Holy Batman Jesus," Mallory murmured, staring at the screen, then the city, then back again. Then she looked at me. "That's why the code doesn't make sense—even when we can translate the symbols. You read it in the *round*. A little bit from each hot spot, one hot spot after another, in order."

I looked down at the symbol again, imagined reading one line of alchemy after another across the symbol before starting back at the beginning and reading through the second line.

"*Oh,*" I said. "Yes. That's why the phrases seem contradictory. Because they are, at least within each block of text." I looked back at Ethan. "If we can get images of all the hot spots, we can improve the odds of actually getting the thing translated."

"Then we'll make it happen," he said. "What's the significance of the symbol?"

"It's called the *Quinta Essentia*," Catcher said. "The square represents mankind. The inner circle represents earth. The outer circle is the universe, which represents the higher resonance. The diamond is the mechanism through which you reach the resonance."

"Increasing the resonance," Mallory said. "That's got to be part of the equation."

Catcher looked at her. "What are you thinking?"

"I don't know," she said. "Let me play it out." She paced to the other end of the widow's walk, looked over the city for a moment, arms crossed and cardigan pulled tight against the chilly breeze.

"Can you send a screenshot of the symbol to Gabriel?" I asked while she paced. "It might be the symbol Kane saw."

Jeff nodded, looked down at the tablet. "On that."

Mallory walked back to us. "The nullification part of the equation—that's the part that's been bothering me. I couldn't figure out why the sorcerer would want to nullify something about himself. I hadn't thought about what we know now—that the alchemy is intended to affect other people. And I think that's true of the nullification term, too."

"Who is it nullifying?" Catcher asked with a frown.

"Us. Our free will."

We stared at her.

"I don't understand," Ethan said. "Even vampire glamour can't conquer free will."

"Not alone," Mallory said. "But we aren't talking about just a vampire."

"We're talking about a vampire and a sorcerer," Catcher said, voice low and heavy with concern. "And they're working in concert."

"Exactly," she said. "We'll have to check this against the actual code, but what if the alchemy, I guess, twists the vampire's glamour together with the sorcerer's magic? Like, I don't know, braiding steel cables together to make them stronger, or something."

"And that's where the nullification comes in," Ethan said. "To boost the effect of their magic by eliminating our defenses."

The mood went understandably morose. Who wouldn't be worried about that? I thought of that moment on the train when the Rogue's glamour had sought out the part of me that was soft and fragile as a nestling. It had been vulnerability stacked atop vulnerability. That exposure twisted and magnified was terrifying. Added to whatever warped activities he actually wanted us to do? Exponentially worse.

"All right," Ethan said, the words piercing through the fear-laden magic that swirled with the winds across the roof. "There is no point in fear. That's what Reed would prefer. We figure a way forward. And I am open to ideas."

I couldn't look away from the pulsing symbol that surrounded an enormous segment of the city. "I don't know if ideas are going to help us."

I felt Ethan's gaze on me. "Sentinel?"

"Look at the symbol," I said, looking back at them. "All the hot spots have been drawn. All the alchemy's in place. He just has to kindle the magic."

The fact that neither Mallory nor Catcher argued with that didn't improve the mood.

"We need a countermagic," he said. "Since we can't just erase the symbols, the magic needs to be literally reversed."

"And that means we need to know the entire equation," Mallory said, glancing at Jeff. "If we have images of all the hot spots, could you plug them into the algorithm you've been working on? Come up with a final code?"

"It's possible," Jeff said. "But it wouldn't be fast. I've got the skeleton of the program under way, but it's not done yet. I'm missing variables—the symbols we haven't yet been able to decipher."

Catcher looked at Mallory, nodded. "We'll get to work on a countermagic. I just hope we have enough time."

Chapter Twenty-One

EASEL LIKE SUNDAY MORNING

Dawn came and went, and dusk followed again. I checked on Jonah, was assured by Scott that he was awake, if not yet at a hundred percent. That was, at least, part of the weight off my shoulders.

Kane thought the QE was the symbol he'd seen. That pretty much confirmed our controlling-sups theory, and it was terrifying to have gotten that right. Catcher and Mallory would work on a countermagic. We just had to hope we had time to finalize it.

Jeff had given us a list of the locations Mallory had pegged as *Quinta Essentia*—QE—hot spots. Gabriel volunteered shifters to visit the spots, take photographs. Malik coordinated joint shifter and guard teams, and they'd been sent across the city to gather the rest of the images, which I was helping Paige translate as they came in. Luc coordinated extra security for the House; since the defenses had been breached, it wasn't hard to imagine Reed would take advantage and take a shot at us.

Paige and I sat at the library table that was starting to become a second home to me. Of the dozen sites, information about two of them had come in. We'd gathered every easel and whiteboard in the House and the three nearest office supply stores. After bargaining with the Librarian to move some tables around (Paige took that one), we used the easels to create a mock-up of the QE. That way, we could post the boards on the easels in their relative positions and in the correct order.

We stared at them, walked around them, brainstormed near them, trying to figure out the symbols we were missing—the ones that would give us the keys to the whole thing.

My phone rang, Jeff's image on the screen. I answered it, but not until after I'd gazed around shiftily for the Librarian. I didn't think he'd want me talking on the phone in the library, but no harm if he hadn't seen it.

"Merit," I said. Quietly, just in case.

"I found the bank."

"The bank?" I asked absently, head tilted as I tried to understand the transition from one set of symbols to the next.

"For the safe-deposit box key."

I stopped moving. "No shit?"

"No shit. It's for a box at Chicago Security Bank and Trust. The key is a really old-fashioned shape. They don't use them much anymore, and I found people complaining about it on a forum online."

"You are a genius!"

"I try. And it turns out, Gabriel Keene is a co-owner of the account."

Now, that was interesting. "And was Gabe aware of that fact?"

"I mean, I only—*cough, cough*—received this private bank information anonymously." Of course he had. "But there's no signature card on file, at least as far as I can tell from what the anonymous informant passed along." He said each word carefully, like the FBI was listening in. Which probably wasn't impossible.

"There's one more thing," Jeff said. "The account was set up only a couple of days before Caleb was killed."

My blood chilled, and my magic must have, too, because Paige looked back at me.

"He got a safe-deposit box, put Gabe's name on it, hid the key, and was killed," I said, working through the timeline. "His death might not have been some spur-of-the-moment thing."

"Yeah," Jeff said darkly. "That's what I was thinking. You should get down there."

I checked the clock. "It's late. What time does the bank close?"

"We're in luck. They run special summer hours two nights a week. This is one of those nights."

I was already rising. "You'll talk to Gabe?"

"Already done," Jeff said. "I'm still programming. He'll meet you there."

Ethan and I met Gabriel at the bank, and we snuck in right under the wire. A woman in khakis and a bright polo—CSB&T embroidered in white on the pocket—was putting keys in the lock when we arrived.

"You're closing?" Gabriel asked.

"Nope!" she said with a smile. "You've got ten minutes. I'm just locking the side door here."

"We'd actually like to open a safe-deposit box," Gabriel said. "I just found out I was named as an owner, but I'm not certain what's in it."

She smiled. "Of course. You have a key and identification?"

"I do." Gabriel pulled out his wallet—black leather on a silver chain—slid out his ID, handed it and the key to the woman.

"I'll just check this," she said, and gestured us to follow her. She walked behind a desk, sat down in a rolling chair, and began to type.

"All right," she said after a moment, handing the items back to him. She opened a drawer, pulled out a second key on a long silk cord, and rose again. "Just follow me, please."

Easy enough, Ethan said silently.

The deposit boxes were in a long vault behind a barred door, open since we were still, technically, there during business hours. The woman walked to a row of boxes about halfway down the right-hand wall, slid her key into one of the two slots, gestured for Gabriel to do the same.

When the tumblers moved, she pulled open the small door, then took out the long black box. She slid out a tray built cleverly into the wall, and put the box on top of it.

"You only have five minutes," she said, glancing at her watch, "but you're welcome to visit again tomorrow if you need more time."

"We can do it in five," Gabriel said, and waited until she'd left before opening the box.

Gabriel pulled out a single folded piece of paper. Without a word, but with an eyebrow arched, he opened it . . . then handed it to me.

On the piece of torn paper, hastily scribbled, was a list of alchemical symbols.

"Damn," I whispered, staring at the slanted writing when he offered it to me. "It's a cipher."

"You're sure?" Ethan's voice, for the first time in days, held a note of hope.

"Yeah. I'm sure." I held it out so they could both see it, pointed to the first column of scribbles. "These are the icons—the hieroglyphs that are specific to the sorcerer—and what they mean."

Which meant Caleb Franklin had either found the list or translated the hieroglyphs and put them in a safe-deposit box Gabriel could access.

"Why a safe-deposit box?" Ethan asked. "Why not just tell you what was going on?"

"He tried," Gabriel said, his words heavy with guilt.

We both looked at him.

"He called me the night before he was killed. I didn't call him back. Meant to, but got occupied with other things." He paused, shook his head. "No, that's not honest. I put it off, because I thought he'd offer more excuses and justifications, and I didn't want to hear them. But that's not what he was offering. He learned what Reed was going to do, or some of it, and he wanted to stop it. And they killed him for it."

"He probably tried to intervene at Wrigleyville," Ethan said. "Prevent them from finishing the alchemy."

Gabriel nodded. "And instead they finished him."

"I'm going to take pictures," I said, pulling out my phone. "I'll send them to Paige and Mallory, let them get started. And copy Jeff," I added, "because we aren't going to need that algorithm now. We can do a straight translation."

This was a big break, and all because I'd tried to think like a shifter at Caleb's house. Lesson learned there.

"Good," Ethan said. "Because we're running out of time."

"Caleb," Gabriel said as we walked out of the vault again. "They took him out, because they thought he'd destroy their plan. Little did they know he'd already sown the seeds, and they blossomed anyway."

"He has left a legacy," Ethan said. "Let's try to make good on it."

My phone rang just as we hit the sidewalk and the bank locked its doors behind us.

I pulled it out, found Jeff's number on the screen.

"Did you see it?" He asked the question before I even managed to say hello.

"See what?" I said, holding up a hand to get Ethan and Gabe to stop beside me.

"The watermark on the paper you sent me."

I stopped on the sidewalk, pulled out the paper I'd wrapped in Ethan's handkerchief, just in case.

"Bottom left-hand corner," Jeff said. "I figured you didn't see it—or feel it—or you would have mentioned it."

I held up the paper, with its tight, slanted writing, to the streetlight. Sure enough, in the bottom corner, was the leading edge of a circular watermark—a spot where the paper had been lightly embossed. It looked like a company seal, and not just for any company.

I couldn't read the entire seal, but the portion I could see was clear enough. The letters EED INDUSTR were visible, along with the tip of a building.

"Holy shit," I murmured.

"Yeah," Jeff said. "That list is on Reed Industries paper. Reed would probably say Caleb Franklin stole it, but then he'd have to explain how Caleb got access to his offices, which opens up a can of worms. In any event, combined with the alchemy, Chuck thinks it's enough for a warrant for Reed's office."

I threw a victorious fist in the air. "Damn good job, Jeff."

"It's teamwork," he said. "And it's Caleb Franklin. This is because of him. And now he has a legacy."

It was the least we could do for him.

Luc was waiting in the basement when we walked into the House again. We were actually running pretty high, so the dour expression on his face wiped the smiles off ours.

"What's wrong?" Ethan asked, and Luc slid his gaze to me.

"We found him."

Ethan looked puzzled, but I knew exactly who he'd meant. "The Rogue?"

Luc nodded, handed me a sheet of paper. Pale skin. Short

brown hair. Brown eyes. No beard when this was taken. MCDONALD HOUSE was printed across the top of the page. LOGAN HILL was printed across the bottom.

"Logan Hill," I said. "He was in McDonald House." McDonald was based in Boston, and one of the oldest Houses in the U.S. Second only to Navarre, if I remembered correctly. It looked like the database search had been successful after all.

Luc nodded. "Matched the eyes. I don't know if he goes by that name now. Almost certainly not. But once upon a time, he did."

"Why'd he leave McDonald?" Ethan asked.

"Insubordination. I talked to Will." That would be Will McDonald, Master of the eponymous House. "He said Hill wasn't a team player. Lots of skill, but lots of ego that ultimately didn't work well in the House system."

"Caleb Franklin and his killer," I said. "Both supernatural misfits, and both fell in with Adrien Reed. It's like he's a magnet for sociopaths."

"Yeah," Luc said. "We just need to find his sorcerer. I know this isn't much, but I wanted you to know that he has an identity now. A name. A file with NAVR, which we will be updating."

I gave the picture one last look and handed it back to Luc. "Thank you. I appreciate it."

He nodded, and Ethan put an arm around me.

"It seems like all this is going to come to a head pretty soon," Luc said. "We may not find him by then—this Logan. But sooner or later, we'll find him."

I doubted we'd have to wait that long. He'd probably find us first. But for now, we had bigger concerns.

"Put him on the back burner," I said. "We have bigger news."

"Oh?" Luc glanced between us.

"We have a cipher for the rest of the alchemy—the symbols we couldn't translate. And the cipher was on Reed Industries stationery, which my grandfather thinks is enough for a warrant for Reed."

Luc whistled. "Productive trip."

"Damn straight," I said. "I'm going to go upstairs, help Paige to finish the translation."

"Do that," Ethan said. "It's that, or lose Chicago . . . and possibly ourselves."

Two hours later, Paige and I stood in the library in identical poses: legs spread, arms crossed, chins down. The shifter-vampire teams had delivered the rest of the symbols from the QE's tangents, and we'd arranged all the posters on their respective easels and marked them up with Caleb's cipher. When we'd marked everything up, we took more photographs, sent them to Mallory and Catcher for the countermagic, and then walked the entire QE like a labyrinth, trying to ferret out from the magic the details of Reed's plan.

We weren't comforted.

"There's nothing that suggests this is limited to shifters," Paige said, squinting as she leaned in to look at one of the panels in the inner circle. She touched a finger on one of the symbols Caleb had decoded, which looked like an asterisk with a circle around it. It actually meant "magic" and, when paired with the skeleton icon, seemed to refer to those of us who possessed magic or were magical, whatever the form or degree.

"And I don't want anyone poking around in my brain," she added, standing straight again.

"Me, neither," I said, and purposefully made myself put away the fact that Logan had already tried.

As far as the mechanics went, Mallory had been right on. The equation moved from one panel to the next, back and forth in a way that mirrored the magic of a sorcerer (illustrated by the drawing of a crucible) against that of the vampire (a crescent moon). Like the layers of glass in a camera lens, we thought the mirroring focused and magnified the magic. And when coupled with the waves of nullification would basically substitute the evildoers' will for the supernaturals'.

It was terrifyingly creative.

The library door opened, and we both glanced back. Ethan walked in. His expression was too neutral for me to gauge his mood, but his magic was all over the place.

"Your grandfather just reported in. Detective Jacobs got a judge and got a warrant for Reed's downtown offices. They're preparing to execute it right now. He also called Nick Breckenridge, advised him of the search. He'll be in place if they collect anything."

Nick Breckenridge was a family friend, and a very well-respected journalist in Chicago. He had a Pulitzer for his investigative journalism, and would do a thorough job with Reed.

"They'll collect something," I said. "I don't know what, and I don't know how much, but Reed's too arrogant not to have something about the Circle close at hand. He thinks he's invincible. That will have made him sloppy." I frowned at Ethan. "That's good news, so why do you look unhappy?"

"If Reed doesn't already know, he'll find out. That may accelerate whatever else he has planned."

"That's a risk," I agreed. "That's why everyone is doing their part."

He looked at the easels. "And how are you doing?"

"Good on the magic," Paige put in. "Dire on the results."

Ethan crossed his arms, expression transitioning to Masterly concentration. "And how does it work?"

Paige gave him the summary. "It's very clever," she concluded. "And narcissistic, and a smidge sociopathic. But very clever."

"That sounds about right. Will it work?"

"Kyle Farr is evidence it already worked," she said. "But on a smaller scale. We figured the symbol had to have a purpose—some reason to use that much magic, that much energy, for it to just be a laser light show."

Ethan slid his hands into his pockets and regarded us with Masterly suspicion. "Why do I feel like you're preparing me for something?"

"Because we are," Paige said. "We think it's a boundary. Or, maybe more accurately, a net."

"A net . . . ," Ethan began, then trailed off as realization struck him. "For the supernaturals in its border. The magic is supposed to reach all the supernaturals within its territory?"

Paige nodded.

"That's hundreds of square miles," he said. "And if the QE works the way the sorcerer's sample with Kyle Farr did, he'll control every sup in that area?"

"Yeah," Paige said with a nod. "If you weren't scared before, you should be now."

We left Paige to call Mallory and coordinate on the countermagic while we worked in the Ops Room on the House's response to the more general threat of Adrien Reed.

That Jeff, Catcher, and Mallory were walking in the front door when we reached the first floor—and that they'd come to the House together without even a warning phone call—didn't ease my concerns.

"What's happened?" Ethan asked, apparently of the same mind.

"A lieutenant in Vice, one of the men on the Circle task force, got a wild hair," Catcher said. "He learned about the document pull, decided this was the time to come down on the Circle and on Reed. His team raided Reed's home about an hour ago."

"How did that happen?" Ethan asked.

"There was a leak, probably an informant in the department or the judge's office that issued the warrant. We aren't sure; Jacobs is looking into it. Anyway, Reed's lawyers met them at the door, but by the time they made it inside, the Reeds were gone."

"He'll escalate," Ethan said. "He'd been waiting for the right time to move. This is probably it."

Catcher nodded, and his expression was bleak. "That's why we're here. The Vice guys were going through Reed's house when a group of River trolls—two men and two women—showed up. There was a shoot-out. Four cops were killed, and all four of the trolls."

They were the fruitarians we'd discussed a few days ago, large men and women who lived primarily beneath the bascule bridges that crossed the Chicago River.

"Jesus," Ethan muttered, low and sorrowful.

There was pounding on the stairs, and Luc raced into the front room, magic flurrying around him. He stopped when he reached us, and his expression was as cheerless as Catcher's.

"The raid?" Luc asked.

Catcher nodded.

"We just heard on the scanner," Luc said. "They'd kept the radios off during the op."

"They wanted to keep it quiet in case Reed had informants inside the CPD," Catcher said. "It didn't seem to matter much."

"This was probably a one-off," Mallory said. "Kyle Farr, but with trolls. We'd know if he'd started the big magic. But he won't wait much longer."

"Did Paige catch you? Talk to you about the net?"

"The net?" Luc asked.

"We think the QE is a boundary for the magic," Ethan said. "Or, if you prefer, a trap for everyone within it."

Luc's eyes widened. Understandably.

"We can't let this happen," I said. "We can't let him take us all over." I could feel the rising panic, and I ignored it, wouldn't let it rise again. I wouldn't let his glamour happen again.

"We won't," Mallory said, and pulled a plastic bag of what looked like braided friendship bracelets out of the messenger bag she'd canted over one shoulder.

"We haven't had time to finish the countermagic. We're working on it—and there are supplies in the car. We can finish it on-site. But I was able to make a few of these. They're shielded," she said, handing one to Catcher, to Ethan, then looked at me. "Wear your apotrope. It should keep them out of your head. It's probably a better shield than these"—she lifted up her right wrist to show the bracelet she wore—"but they're all I had time to prepare."

The apotrope was a bracelet with a raven-engraved charm Mallory had bought in what she called Chicago's "Scandinavian District," magicked for good luck. I'd used it to keep Faux Balthasar out of my head. Made sense it would work here, too. I'd have to remember to grab it.

"We thank you for the effort," Ethan said, sliding on a neon pink and green bracelet. He held it up against his immaculate white button-down. "How does it look?"

"Oh so fashionable," Catcher said, sliding on a navy and red one.

Mallory offered the bag of bracelets to Luc. "I don't have enough for everyone in the House," she said. "But at least everybody on the ops team can have one."

"Appreciated," Luc said with a nod. "When we figure out what we can do, we'll hand them out."

"Paige can ward the rest of the House," Mallory said. "Although that means she'll have to stay here."

"Might be best to limit the number of supernaturals running

around out there," Ethan said. "Does it matter how many supernaturals are here?"

She shook her head. "No. The ward will be on the physical structure. You could fill it to the rafters with vampires, and the ward won't become any less effective."

"Then we'll load it up," Ethan said, and looked at Luc. "Call Morgan, Scott. Explain, and tell them they can send their vampires here or out of the net." He looked at Mallory. "Will that be enough? If they're outside the symbol's boundaries?"

"Give me a buffer," she said. "A few hundred yards outside the symbol should do it."

Ethan nodded. "We'll call it a mile to be safe." He looked back at Luc. "Call Gabriel, too, and update him. Same offer for the Pack."

Luc scowled. "There are already shifters on the door and the gate. The House won't be happy about more coming here."

"It's unlikely Gabriel will accept the offer," Ethan said. "But we make the offer because it's the right thing to do. It's easy to be an asshole." He smiled, but there wasn't much happiness in it. "And harder to do the right thing. We do it anyway."

"Aye, aye, boss. We'll get some bracelets to the men on the gate."

Ethan looked at Catcher. "The nymphs? The fairies?"

The city's mercenary fairies weren't exactly our allies anymore. All the more reason to ensure that they weren't suited up as soldiers for Reed.

"We've gotten the word out. Told the Order, too. And Annabelle."

"Good," Ethan said. "There will be some we can't reach. But the fewer supernaturals we give him to work with, the better off we'll be." He looked at Mallory. "How will he work this?"

Mallory squeezed her eyes closed, kneaded her forehead with her fingertips. "This is a big operation that's going to need a lot of power. We're talking about, what, a few thousand supernaturals within the net? The magic has to be powerful enough to affect them all, or it's not much good. A sorcerer carries power innately. But this is exponentially larger than one person."

"So, how will he do it?" Ethan asked.

"If it was me," Mallory said, opening her eyes again, "I'd either have a generator, or I'd tie right into the grid, maybe with a transformer that turns electrical power into magical power. And I'd put it as close to the middle of the QE as I could. That makes the spreading of the magic more efficient."

"So downtown," Catcher said.

Mallory nodded. "If it was me. And he'd want high ground, too. Taller than Cadogan House."

Ethan looked at me. "Any sense of where he'd go? A building that he'd want to use for this?"

There was, of course, one building that he'd wanted most of all—the one he'd wrenched from my father.

I looked at Ethan. "Towerline. We'd thought Reed had wanted it for his portfolio. Maybe that hadn't been the only reason."

Ethan looked at Luc. "Assemble everyone. We won't lose anyone else on my watch. We take Reed down, and we do it tonight."

CHAPTER TWENTY-TWO

IDENTITY

Mallory studied the translated equation, then helped Paige set the wards on the House. When it was protected, or as well as it could be, the city's supernatural leaders were called, and we prepared for battle.

By the time we gathered in the conference room, we were leather-clad and katana-wielding. Ethan wore a black moto-style leather jacket over dark jeans and boots, his hair pulled back with a leather cord. I'd added my apotrope to my ensemble.

Lindsey, Kelley, and Juliet were also dressed in leathers. Luc and Malik would remain at the House—Luc to keep it safe, and Malik to keep it under control. As Ethan's Second, he'd be in charge of the House in Ethan's absence—and the hundreds of vampires who'd come here to escape the magic.

Malik joined us, as did Paige and the Librarian, Catcher and Mallory, Gabriel, Eli, Jeff, and Fallon. Jonah walked into the room with Scott, which filled me with relief. I rose, met them at the door, could feel Ethan's gaze on both of us. But since Jonah had jumped out in front of me and probably saved my life, he could bear a little jealousy.

"How are you feeling?" I asked.

"Not bad," he said with a smile. "Thanks for dragging me out of the line of fire."

"Thanks for taking the hit for me." I smiled up at him. "And don't ever do it again."

"I'll make a note."

I stepped aside so they could walk to the table, was surprised to see Morgan walk in behind them. He was as leather-clad as the rest of us, a yellow katana belted at his waist. And his expression was fierce.

He found Ethan. Morgan, the dark-haired Master of the nation's oldest vampire House, matched against Ethan, the blond-haired Master of the city's most active House. A former boyfriend matched against my forever love, and a vampire who'd been too human matched against one who, until recently, hadn't been quite human enough. It was interesting how things had changed.

"I hadn't expected you to fight," Ethan said, extending a hand.

"You don't mean that as an insult," Morgan said, "but it's embarrassing all the same. I should have been fighting a long time ago, against Reed and otherwise. Better late than never, I hope."

Ethan nodded. "You're here now. That counts."

"I hope so." Morgan glanced at me, smiled with disarmingly boyish charm. "I've seen Merit fight. She can avenge me if I go down."

"Let's hope no one needs avenging," Ethan said.

"We're ready," Luc said when he and Jeff had finagled a small projector in the center of the table that shot an image onto a screen that descended at the far end of the conference table. Luc dimmed the lights.

A map of the Loop that showed Towerline—or its currently skeletal frame—and the surrounding blocks was projected on one half of the screen. Jeff's projection of the QE filled the other.

"This is the *Quinta Essentia*," Ethan said as heads turned to look at the symbol. "I don't want to spend too much time on the magical details. Suffice it to say we believe Adrien Reed, his sorcerer, and his vampire, who's been identified as Logan Hill, a Rogue, have been working on a complex alchemical equation. That equation is intended to provide one or all of them control of every supernatural within the boundaries."

"Control," Scott repeated, incredulous.

"Control," Ethan confirmed. "They've manipulated a shifter and, as of earlier tonight, several trolls. They're dead," he said, and glanced at Gabriel. "Your shifter?"

Gabriel just shook his head. "No sign of him."

"So he could still be under Reed's control," Ethan said.

"What's his long game here?" Scott asked. "He can't have imagined this would work out well—that people wouldn't notice what he was doing."

"I believe Reed expected we'd take much, much longer to figure out what he's doing. We literally stumbled onto the Wrigleyville symbols."

Mallory nodded. "If we hadn't figured out the what and where of the magic, he'd be doing all this right now, only without police surrounding the building. We'd fall to his control, and he would have a supernatural army, and we would be none the wiser. And with that magical army, with that power, humans would be hard-pressed to argue with him."

Ethan paused to let that sink in.

"If the QE is kindled, we're all at risk," he said. "The House is warded. All supernaturals are invited to shelter here. Mallory will have wearable countermagics for anyone on the go team."

"How, exactly, does the magic work?" Morgan asked, leaning forward and linking his hands on the table. "And how can we use it against them?"

Ethan nodded at Mallory, who stepped forward. "The alchemy

utilizes, combines, the sorcerer's magic and the vampire's magic. That's where the control arises."

"So we can just take out one of them?" Morgan asked.

Mallory shook her head. "It's not that simple, unfortunately. Their magic gives effect to the QE, yes. But once the QE is on, it's on. Taking them out won't affect anything; that's part of the fail-safe they've built into the alchemy. Ditto erasing the symbols," she said, glancing at Paige, who nodded. "The only way out is backward. We have to use a countermagic—literally reverse the magic to remove its effect."

"And you can do that?" Scott asked.

"We can," Mallory said, looking at Catcher with adoration and pride. "They've got a vampire and a sorcerer. We've got three sorcerers. I say we win."

I couldn't help smiling despite the circumstances.

"Where do you need to be?" Ethan asked.

"On the ground."

Catcher nodded, gestured to Jeff, and the picture switched to the street view, and a shot of the Loop I'd never seen before—almost completely devoid of people.

"The CPD's cordoned off a two-block radius around the construction site," Catcher said. "Chuck and Arthur Jacobs are coordinating from the ground."

"I want to be here," Mallory said, pointing to the plaza in front of the building. "I think this is the best place to set the countermagic—draw the reverse QBE. And then we'll kindle the magic, begin to reverse theirs."

"You'll be in full view of the public," Malik said quietly. "If they see you do this, they'll know what you are, and what you can do."

The public knew a lot about supernaturals. But they hadn't yet learned about sorcerers.

Mallory looked at Catcher, squeezed his hand, then looked

back at Malik. "We know. On the one hand, it can't be helped. And on the other hand, it's about damn time."

"And their magic?" Scott asked. "What's their HQ?"

Luc switched the image to photographs of the building's current "roof." It was a square of concrete, one of the building's previous upper floors, surrounded by the steel framework that remained around it. The photos showed several figures moving around a large black structure that was partially hidden by a cloth. Probably a drop cloth to keep it covered until they were ready to go.

"It's the sixty-eighth floor," Catcher said, stepping forward. "They've got two construction elevators that go all the way to the top. The CPD confirmed by drone that there are six figures on the floor, but they shot it down before they could confirm their identities."

"It's most likely Reed, Logan, the sorcerer, and supernaturals to keep them safe," Ethan said.

"And possibly Sorcha," I said. "She's always at his side."

Ethan glanced at me. "You think he'd bring her into this?"

"I don't think either of them cares about the difference between legal and illegal, danger and safety. He's clearly crossed a line here—that division between his public and private personas—and may want to make a show of it for her."

"Maybe she's involved in it," Morgan said.

"We haven't seen any evidence of that," I said, and flipped through my memories of her. Bored or vacant or typing on her phone.

"So potentially the four of them," Ethan said, "and at least three supernaturals."

"With heavy weaponry," Catcher added. "He'll have borrowed from the Circle's cache."

"Oh, good," Scott said. "Because this wasn't already an enormous cluster fuck."

"No argument there," Ethan said. "He'll control any sups within the boundaries who aren't otherwise protected. They'll come at us, irrespective of their desire or their alliances, because the Circle wills it."

I wondered if my immunity from glamour would have given me any protection. Not that it mattered now.

"What do we do about them?" Morgan asked. "We can't take them out."

"Chuck's working with the CPD on that," Catcher said. "They've been developing some small-batch tranq weapons. We're hoping we can use those, since these sups won't have been fighting through any fault of their own."

"You have enough for the entire team?" Jonah asked.

"I'm waiting for word," Catcher said.

"And speaking of the team," Ethan said, "we propose Catcher and Mallory, Jeff, Gabriel, Eli, Fallon, Morgan, Merit, and I go downtown." He looked at Scott and Jonah. "Bringing the sups here will protect them, but if Reed figures that, he may split his troops and attack here. I'd appreciate it if you'd work with Luc and Malik to protect the House."

Scott drummed his fingers on the table while he considered, then nodded. "I'll have my vampires come here." He glanced at Malik and Luc and nodded. "We'll do what we can to keep everyone here and safe."

"Appreciated," Ethan said, then looked at Gabriel. "You have any bodies you want to spare?"

"The countermagic work on shifters?"

Mallory nodded. "Yep. Anything that meets a magical threshold."

"Then if you've got enough, I can offer a few more. They'll stay outside on the grounds. They don't need to be in the House. Not after what they've done. The rest of them will stay outside the QE."

Ethan nodded. "Then we leave now. Basement in fifteen, and we'll arrange transportation." He looked at all of us like a general surveying his troops. "This isn't our war, nor is it a war we want to fight. But it is a war all the same. Reed would control us, obliterate us as creatures with free will in order to achieve his ambitions. We must not allow that to happen. We *will* not allow that to happen."

We scattered, colleagues clustering together to make plans, arrangements. I drank a bottle of blood—like an athlete preparing for battle. When I returned to the foyer, Ethan and Malik stood together, Ethan's hands on Malik's face.

Ethan whispered something, Malik's eyes flared with concern. It wasn't difficult to guess the nature of Ethan's words. This was the last communion of a soldier and his family before war. It was a promise by Malik to care for the House, a confirmation by Ethan that he knew Malik would protect and serve it, and a good-bye for both of them.

I'd seen this scene before, and each time it moved me; I had to look away to keep tears from blooming.

"Sentinel," Malik said, walking toward me when their discussion was complete. "Good luck. Take care of yourself and our Master."

"He's the first thing on my mind," I promised. I embraced him, then Luc.

"You got this, Sentinel. Go kick their asses."

"I fully intend to."

There was one particular vampire on my mind.

CPD had cordoned the blocks around Towerline with police tape and crowd barriers. Officers in riot gear were stationed every few yards, and people were stacked ten deep behind them, cameras raised high above the crowd to catch photos and video. They probably weren't entirely sure what was going to happen, but they figured it would be exciting.

Magic filled the air like the tingle of electricity before a thunderstorm. The entire city was waiting for something to happen. And Reed was working to ensure that it did.

The plaza was empty of people, but figures moved inside the building's two-story atrium, which had already been surrounded by glass. Maybe that had been a strategic decision, too.

We walked toward the cordoned area, were waved in by my grandfather, who stood with Detective Jacobs in the middle of a V formed by two canted police cars in the northbound lane of Michigan Avenue. My father stood with them in a Merit Properties windbreaker against the spring chill, and his expression was utterly dour. I had an extra twinge of guilt about both of them. Fathers and daughters were a complicated thing.

My grandfather greeted us, then introduced the rest of the team to the several officers he was working with. But for him and Jacobs, they were also dressed in riot gear—dark shirts, dark pants, boots, protective vests, and plenty of communications equipment. They were not messing around.

How much blood would have to be shed to satisfy Reed's ego?

"They're still on the top floor, as far as we can tell," Jacobs said. "Sups in the lobby with automatic weapons."

"I'm surprised they haven't been more aggressive," Ethan said.

Morgan's gaze tracked the moving shadows. "We're tools to him. He'll think of them as assets, and he won't want to waste them until his plan's completely in place."

Jacobs nodded. "Our thought as well. We move toward the building, and he'll attack."

"That's why we go in first," Ethan said, and the cops around us went quiet, looked back at us.

"You aren't qualified for that," said a man in SWAT gear, but it sounded more like a question than an accusation.

"We are," Ethan said. "All of us are combat-trained in some manner or other, and all of us are experienced in dealing with supernaturals. We've also been shielded against the magic. Oh, and some of us are immortal."

His tone was dry; he didn't intend to give up his chance to fight Reed.

"Look," Catcher said. "We're not trying to step on anyone's territory. But Reed's brought this battle to supernaturals. For better or worse, we're the ones best equipped to do the fighting. We take care of the magic on the ground, and we send in a team to bring Reed out."

"The goal is to limit fatalities," the SWAT guy said.

"That's our goal as well," Catcher said.

Jacobs held out his hands as sorcerer and cop edged closer together in the rising tension. "This is my task force and my call. The sups are better equipped to deal with magic, and they won't be sensitive to the vampire's glamour. We would be. They go in, neutralize. We extract."

"For what it's worth," my father put in, "it was *my* building. They say they can handle it, we let them handle it."

It had taken twenty-eight years to get even that much approbation from my father. I wasn't sure if that made it feel better or worse.

"There's something else," my grandfather said, and looked at my father.

"Robert's meeting with Reed was tonight," he said.

My body went cold, but my heart just pounded further.

"Elizabeth called a little while ago," my father continued. "Asked if I'd heard from him yet because it was late. I hadn't."

"We're working from the assumption he's in the building with Reed," my grandfather said. "Reed would see him as an asset, so I don't think he'd hurt Robert."

"We'll find him," Ethan said confidently, looking between two generations of Merit men, and promising protection for a third. "We'll find him, and we'll get him out of there."

Fear wanted to bubble up and strangle me, but that was a luxury I couldn't afford. Especially now that the magic in the air was increasing—the buzz of anticipation growing. There were gasps in the crowd. We looked up, followed the crowd's gazes, and stared at the green lines that were beginning to spread across the city like lines of infection. Where Mallory's magic had been nearly invisible, light as smoke, this was a sickly, radioactive green.

"We're out of time," Mallory said, slinging off the backpack she and Catcher had filled with countermagic essentials. "We need to get to work."

"What do you need?" my grandfather said.

"Room to work," Catcher said. "And when the doors open and the shooting starts, we wouldn't mind some cover."

"When should we move?" Ethan asked.

"Let Mallory get the symbol drawn before you rush in," Catcher said. "We don't want him to react too quickly or feel like he has to rush things. He's dealing with a lot of power up there; one wrong move, and Towerline ends up in pieces on the ground."

"Do try to avoid that if you can," my father said, but his voice was kind.

"We'll do our best," Mallory promised, then looked at us. "It won't be immediate—the magic, I mean. We've got to draw the marker, build the salt, kindle the magic, then work some more symbols to kindle the reversal. That's when the countermagic will begin to take effect."

"How long?" Jacobs asked.

"Not quick," she said. "There are thousands of lines of code—of symbols—that make up their equation. It's like a cassette tape—it will take the magic time to rewind."

Catcher looked at his watch. "Let's mark the time—it's nearly midnight, right? I'm going to aim for that."

We checked our watches, confirmed the time. And when that was done, my grandfather nodded. "We'll keep you safe while you do it." He looked at Ethan. "And upstairs?"

"You've got the tranqs?"

In answer, the SWAT guy pulled out an enormous hard case, popped the latches. Inside a nest of gray foam were a dozen small silver tubes a little larger than a roll of quarters, with one end tilted ninety degrees. He popped the cap off the end, pointed to an orange button on the side. "You need skin-to-skin contact. Hold the dispensing end against skin—doesn't matter where—and press the button to engage the tranq. You'll get results in two or three seconds."

"How many doses per weapon?"

"Only three," he said, and handed them out. I tucked mine into the pocket of my jacket. "These are still in R and D, and it's the best we could do on short notice."

"We're happy to take them off your hands," Ethan said. "That's potentially thirty-six fewer fatalities."

God willing, it would be enough.

"We go in," Ethan said. "Make our way to the elevators, put down everyone that we can. We go upstairs, and we contain."

The SWAT guy—who I realized hadn't bothered to introduce himself to us—nodded.

Thunder rolled threateningly as energy spread above us, and we all looked up. The sky was clear of clouds, but tentacles of magic flowed like rivulets across the lines that made up the QE.

"He's screwing up the ionosphere," Mallory muttered. "What a douche."

"For that and many other reasons," Ethan said.

Backpack in one hand, Mallory turned to me, wrapped her free arm around my neck, squeezed. "Be careful up there," she whispered.

"Be careful down here," I said, squeezing her back.

I released her to Catcher. Linking hands, they walked to the curb, and the division between concrete and granite. They blew out a breath and did the thing all heroes must do—they took that terrifying first step.

Mallory walked in front of Catcher, and she seemed impossibly delicate walking into the empty square, Towerline rising like the body of a dark and long-forgotten cryptid in front of her.

A cadre of cops stepped behind them, watched while Catcher and Mallory looked up at the building, then the square, gauging the best location. When Catcher nodded to them, pointed, they moved to form a line between the sorcerers and the building.

She looked at them for a moment, as if adjusting to the possibility their bodies were her shield, then pulled out a thick crayon from her pocket and began to drew a white line, then another, until she'd sketched onto the granite a kind of *Bizarro World* QE, with the symbols in a different order.

When she was done, she nodded at Catcher, who joined her at the boundary. Together, they stepped carefully inside the middle square. While he held her backpack, she unzipped and unloaded what I'd recognized as an Alchemy Starter Pack—glass bottle, her crucible, a box of matches, a notebook, and an assortment of herbs.

For five minutes they worked, combining materials and pressing them into the crucible, drawing small symbols in the square, and reading words from the notebook. Occasionally, one or both of them looked up at the tentacular magic that flowed above us. The air buzzed with it, so even the steady-looking uniformed cops glanced around, shifted on their feet.

Catcher pulled a match from the box, looked at Mallory, waiting for her nod. When he got it, he flicked it against the box and dropped it into the crucible. Lightning or magic or some combination of both cracked down the building like an explosion, shattering the new columns of windows and sending glass shooting down over us. We ducked as glass rained down.

All hell broke loose.

There was no time to wonder whether their magic was working. The tower's doors burst open, and supernaturals ran forward.

"Fallon, Jeff," Ethan called out, and we unsheathed our katanas. "Stay with Mallory and Catcher! Keep them safe!"

And we rushed forward.

Chapter Twenty-Three

A Soul Inspired

Reed had anticipated an attack, and he'd been prepared for it. Maybe by using the individual magic the sorcerer had worked on Kyle Farr, Reed had collected the supernaturals who came out to meet us. There were dozens of them. Shifters, vampires, River trolls, the similar-looking mercenary fairies who'd once guarded our door, River nymphs, and a very tall, willowy creature I'd never seen before.

A dryad, Ethan said silently, as if sensing my confusion. That was a kind of tree nymph, if I remembered my *Canon*. She had the look—skin that was nearly gray beneath her pale green, Grecian-style dress, hair that was silvery green, and long arms that ended in reedy, pointed fingers.

As if the opening of the doors had unleashed power as well as creatures, magic seemed to pour out of the building. It was intrusive magic, biting and terrible magic that felt like alien fingers pinching, grasping, looking for literal and metaphorical access into our psyches. The bracelet kept the magic out of my head—and I was ridiculously grateful for that—but it didn't mute the disturbing sensation of it.

The dryad reached me first, swinging her long arms as fluidly as waving branches but as sharp as whips. I dropped and rolled to avoid being snapped by one, came up on the other side, and swept my katana back. I'd slicked a cut across her arm. It seeped green and put the scent of crushed leaves into the air. She made a horrible, windy sound of pain, lashed her arm out again. I'd prepared to drop again, but she adjusted her trajectory at the last minute and caught my ankle.

I hit the ground on my back but shifted my weight and hopped back to my feet just as she moved closer, tried to swipe again. This time, I grabbed her arm; her skin was rough, but it moved in my hand like an eel, which was weirdly disconcerting. I grabbed the dispenser from my belt, pressed it to her arm.

With a scream, she ripped her arm away, leaving ropelike burns on my palm. She stumbled back once, and then her silvery green eyes rolled up and she fell to the ground like a felled tree.

That tranq was damn effective. The fact that the CPD had made it just for sups was probably worth some thought, but not tonight. Tonight was for magic.

"One down," I said, glancing over the plaza. "A dozen to go."

Ethan was a few yards away, battling two vampires with slashing katana moves that had him nearly blurring with movement. His opponents were fast, too, at least Strong Phys in the scale of vampire power rankings. But being controlled made them clumsier than they would have been if they'd been fighting on their own.

I don't see why you get to have all the fun, I said silently, and ran toward him, stepping to one of his opponents as he executed a gorgeous butterfly kick that had the vampire flipping backward.

They fought in silence, I realized. No cursing, no groans of pain, not even grunts of effort—like the ones tennis players made when returning hard plays. There were still sounds—the sharp *ping* of metal against metal, the *shush* of fabric, the *crunch* of glass underfoot. But they didn't speak at all.

The second vampire lunged for me. I used a side kick to shift his weight. He stumbled to the side but regained his balance and came back at me with silvered eyes and descended fangs. He thrust the katana downward; I used the spine of my sword to deflect, push it away.

Got him, Ethan said, moving forward and slapping the plunger onto the vampire's back. A pause, and then he crumpled to the ground like a puppet whose strings had been cut.

Spoilsport, I said, but my cheeky smile was interrupted by an avalanche of screams.

"Everybody take cover!"

I instinctively looked back at the sound of Catcher's voice, found him running toward us, eyes on the balustrade that separated the plaza from the canal that contained Chicago River.

I followed his gaze. One of the River nymphs stood in front of the wall, her hands lifted toward the river—and the wall of water she'd raised over the river, and apparently planned to drop over the plaza.

"Oh, shit." Ethan's voice was a horrible whisper.

"I got it!" Catcher said, and moved toward it, raising two hands, palms out, to face the wall of water that was still growing, towering over the petite nymph who'd lifted it dozens of feet over her head. The wind blew fiercely, sending a mist across the plaza, which glittered with glass, and threatening to drown us all with the surge.

Power crackled around Catcher as he gathered up magic, building a transparent wall that sparked with energy. Slowly, as sweat crossed his brow, he began to push it forward, a sea wall against the tsunami the nymph was threatening.

Their gazes locked on each other, their expressions fierce with determination. They moved toward each other, the wall of water shivering above the nymph as if with anticipation of falling, of covering the earth again. But she was so focused on Catcher that she didn't see Morgan move around behind her. He watched her and Catcher, gauged the right moment, and moved forward, tagging her with the tranq.

She dropped, and the water—now forty feet high—hovered above the plaza.

Sweat popping across his brow, Catcher took one step forward, then another, blue sparks flying around his hands as the water shivered, lifted. He sucked in a breath, as if gathering up his resources, then gave the water a final shove.

Loud as a train, the water flew back toward the river, but unevenly, rushing across the Michigan Avenue Bridge—pushing CPD cruisers into one another with another mighty *crash*—before falling back to the river again.

Catcher fell to his knees, body limp with exhaustion. That was the downside of being a sorcerer; you had to recharge.

"Hey," I said, running toward him and crouching in front of him. "You all right?"

"Took a lot out of me."

"Yeah, saving a few thousand people can do that. That was a pretty good Moses routine—you know, parting the waters and all."

He looked up at me, a half smile on his face. "Are you making a joke at a time like this?"

"Catcher Bell," I said, offering a hand and helping him climb to his feet, "if you can't make a joke at a time like this, what's the point of living?"

"I guess."

"Are you going to be able to help Mallory? I could call Paige, get her out here."

"I can manage it," he said, testy as ever. "Paige has to stay on the House ward."

"In that case," I said, and pulled the slightly squashed PowerBar from my pocket, handed it to him, "you'll need this more than me."

Catcher accepted it, looked at me with a warm smile. "Did you bring a battle snack?"

Since he'd already ripped open the package and bit in, I decided it wasn't worth the trouble to respond.

Ethan ran toward us as a different magical pas de deux occurred behind him—the QE and the countermagic battled for control, the green tendrils in the sky waving erratically as power fought power.

"We've got a path toward the building," Ethan said.

"Then use it," Catcher said with a nod, stuffing the wrapper in his jeans as he ran back toward Mallory. "And thanks for the battle snack!"

"Which are a brilliant idea!" I yelled back as Ethan rounded up the troops to head inside.

"Get to the elevators!" he called out, waiting until the rest of the team had acknowledged the order. Stairs would have been cooler, but that was the tricky part about having to battle on the top floor of a would-be high-rise.

We made it into the building—Gabriel bringing up the rear in his wolf form—just as another bolt of magic flashed outside the building. It hit the pavement like Thor's hammer, putting a crater in the plaza as big as a car, and sending shrapnel into the air.

Down! Ethan said, covering me as shards of granite crashed against the glass, burst through to litter the lobby floor.

As if sensing us, the supernaturals who remained outside began to run toward the lobby. Magic flashed again as Gabriel shifted from gray wolf to naked and sun-kissed human. Eli tossed him a backpack, probably filled with clothes.

"Get to the elevators!" Gabriel said, pointing to the bank of them. "Reed's sorcerer is fighting the countermagic. You don't do this now, he'll take down the goddamn building and everyone in it!"

"We got this," Eli said, a curl falling over a gash on his forehead.

"Let's go while we can," Morgan said, and with a nod from Ethan, we ran for the construction elevators and slipped into a car.

We'd decided to take the elevator to the floor beneath Reed and the others.

There was only red steel mesh between us and the sky as the crude digital display ticked off one floor after another. The wind blew ferociously through the car, which made the ride bumpy and my knees a little shaky.

Ethan pushed a hand through hair dampened by exertion and magic. He glanced at me. "You all right?"

"I'm fine," I said as I stood in an elevator between two Master vampires who'd both been affected negatively by Adrien Reed.

As we rose into the air, anticipation began to build again. Logan Hill would be on the roof; he had to be. He was part of the alchemy, part of the magic, part of the Circle.

I would have my time with Logan Hill. I would have my reckoning.

I also would have to keep a better check on my emotions, because both men turned their heads to look at me. I kept my gaze on the elevator doors.

"Sentinel?" Ethan asked.

"I'm fine," I said again. And I was; I had my game face on.

The elevator slowed, then came to a gentle stop as it reached our destination. We took battle positions once again, just in case they were waiting for us.

"Ready," Ethan murmured as the elevator buzzed its warning and the mesh door slid open.

The floor was empty—an expanse of concrete bounded by steel pillars—except for the broken body on the floor. I went cold as ice and rushed forward, fell to my knees beside my brother.

"Robert! Oh, damn, Robert!" It took all the bravery I had to reach out and touch him, to gauge whether the man who'd chased me as a child was still alive. His skin was cold and clammy, and vibrated with power. Something magical, maybe. Something the sorcerer had done to him.

Morgan moved beside me, checked Robert's pupils. They were tiny black pinpricks.

"Magic," he diagnosed. "Probably to drop him, keep him out of the way. But not kill him," he added, checking Robert's pulse, "because he's a tool, too, just like the rest of us."

Magic cracked again, flashing brilliantly across the hallway and sending a green sheen across the tall bank of windows opposite the elevator. The concrete beneath our feet shook as if a hurricane raged outside, then stilled just as silently. It hadn't broken, but the sound of glass tinkling to the stone plaza below filled the air like music.

"I can get him out of here," Morgan said. "But you'll have to go forward alone."

I looked back at Ethan, found his gaze on mine, green and intent. Neither of us was masochistic enough to want war, but we wanted the men who stood on the other side of that door, and we wanted them badly. And when push came to shove, there was no one else I'd rather go through the door with.

"Take care of him," I said to Morgan, then pressed a kiss to my brother's cheek and climbed to my feet again, looked at the ladder beside the construction elevator that led to the building's top floor.

"Ready?" Ethan asked.

"Always." Anticipation began to drain away, replaced by pure adrenaline and luminous anger. I felt as if I glowed with it—although that could have been the magical battle taking place around us.

I took the ladder first, climbed silently upward, one rung at a time, until I was high enough to just peek through the hole. The action was taking place on the other side of the floor. There was a man watching on the elevator—he'd have heard it moving upward—but he hadn't realized we'd stopped on the floor below.

There was an enormous utility box to my left. Probably some kind of HVAC unit.

Silently, I climbed forward into powerfully swirling winds and the scent of bitter magic and slipped behind the unit.

Come up and to the left, I told Ethan. *Behind the utility box.*

This isn't the time for a romantic tryst, Sentinel.

You're hilarious. And there's a man to your right, so be quiet.

Ethan's head popped up. He watched the man for a moment, and when he was certain of the man's inattention, he joined me in a crouch.

You're ready? he asked, and I nodded. *In that case, we go out on three. One—two—three!*

We jumped forward and were greeted by a shifter, a man in a Cubs jersey who looked exhausted and unkempt, and who came at us with raised fists and blank eyes.

"Kyle Farr!" I guessed, and drew his attention to me.

He growled, leaped forward. But he was obviously tired, had probably been under Reed's control since he'd disappeared. He missed me, and when I threw out a foot to trip him, he hit the roof on his knees. Ethan took his chance, moved forward, and depressed the tranq to Farr's arm. His eyes closed, and he drooped.

I climbed over his body, moved to stand next to Ethan. *Ready?* he said.

Ready, I agreed, and we moved cautiously forward.

There, in the middle of the roof, was an enormous metal sculpture. It was probably ten feet across, at least as tall. It was built like a tree—if the tree had been built from metal scraped from the bowels of the earth and blackened by fire, every branch sharpened and honed to a point. It was hollow in the middle, and green smoke and magic poured out of what I guessed was a crucible. That smoke rose and twisted and seemed to take form above us.

And there in front of the crucible stood Sorcha and Adrien Reed.

He wore a black suit that would have befit a presidential candidate.

Sorcha stood beside him in her signature color, an emerald green sleeveless jumpsuit with a formed and fitted bodice in bias-cut emerald silk, with an enormous, structural ruffle over one shoulder. On her left biceps was a four-inch-long gold scarab atop a gold cuff. And atop her head was a cannily perched fedora in matching green, a satin ribbon around the brim. Magic swirled around her in pale green tendrils that matched those in the sky. Three of them danced together in her cupped palm.

"*Son of a bitch,*" Ethan and I muttered simultaneously.

Our sorcerer was a sorcer*ess*. And a damn stylish one.

Sorcha Reed had been the "man" at La Douleur, the "man" Annabelle had seen at the cemetery. The sup we'd seen at La Douleur—the one I believed had ratted us out—had been relatively small of stature. But because of the suit, the fedora, I'd assumed the sup had been a man. I hadn't even considered the possibility that she—or any other woman—had been Reed's sorcerer. And in retrospect, I couldn't have been more stupid. Who else would Reed have trusted so completely with his master plan, with the magic he figured would give him control of the city? Who else would he have allowed into the inner circle?

This wasn't the vacuous Sorcha I'd seen at Reed's side. This was the woman I'd seen peeking through—working busily on her phone, surprised that we'd shown up at the Botanic Garden but seemingly excited by the fact that we'd been arrested.

Tonight, she showed poise and power, and her eyes shone as coldly as Reed's.

"Oh, look," she said blandly, with an eyebrow arch that nearly rivaled Ethan's. "They've made their way up."

If her tone was any indication, she didn't think we posed much of a threat.

"And they're staring," she said to Reed. "Yes, I know what you're thinking. You're surprised. Most are, but then, that's the point.

"I was born into a family not unlike yours," Sorcha continued, apparently eager to offer up a soliloquy. "Older, and more genteel, of course. From Salem, originally," she said with a widening grin. "But when I discovered my magic, they made me shut it down, made me reject my true nature. And then I became a debutante, like I was a horse to be shown off." Her gaze slipped to her husband. "And then I met Adrien. He has his games, his pleasures, and I have mine." Her eyes shone with purpose. "I've turned the system on its head."

"You're biding your time," I said. "You play the perfect wife, help Reed establish his legit connections. And when he's powerful enough, has control of enough, you can both rule the kingdom."

She clapped her hands together, condescension in her expression and her movements. "Bravo, Caroline Evelyn Merit." Her gaze skipped to Ethan. "I see you've adopted a similar plan."

Anger pierced me, the fact that she believed I'd used Ethan in some kind of rebellion against my family. The recognition that she probably knew better—that she was baiting me just as Reed liked to do—kept me in my place.

"We have a countermagic," Ethan said, getting us back to the point. "Your alchemy is being unraveled as we speak, and the CPD is waiting for you below. Your bluff has been called, Reed. It's time to step away from the table."

"You misunderstand," Reed said. "Your magic's failing." He gestured to the airspace above us, where the QE still hung in the sky. It did look more stable than it had seemed before we came up here, but I refused to believe Mallory and Catcher weren't beating it back, reversing the magic they'd created. I believed in her as much as I believed in anyone. And good had to win sometimes.

"It's your sorcerer against mine," Reed said, "and mine wins every time. She's exquisitely powerful." He slid his hands into his pockets, just casually enough to rankle. "I assume the magic's effect on you has been dampened by those trinkets you're wearing. A clever, if unsophisticated, measure. Not that it will matter. We appreciate a good game, but our magic is winning. When we have Chicagoland's vampires—and everyone else—under our control, you'll become nothing more than rounding errors in our empire."

He doesn't know about the House, I told Ethan. *About the ward.*

And let's keep it that way, he said.

"And, of course," Reed continued, because the man loved to hear himself talk, "we have a vampire." He looked back at me, and his gaze crept over my body like a spider. "I understand you're acquainted."

I would have lunged for him, if Ethan hadn't held me back.

Reed's smile widened. "As I expected. That had been a bit of luck. I hadn't known Logan when he was in Celina's employ. And wasn't it fortuitous that we met again, and he told me of his exploits?"

It was too late for fear. I'd already done that. "He's failed to kill me three times. I'd say I have the upper hand there."

"And speaking of the upper hand . . . ," she said. Her gaze slipped to my left just as I heard Ethan's warning in my head.

He came out of nowhere, slamming me to the floor and covering me with his weight. And then his hands were around my neck, squeezing.

"Fourth time's a charm," he said.

I tried to suck in air, kicked to dislodge him, but he kept his seat, kept his weight forward, his big fingers pressing, pushing. His eyes stayed flat and brown, a man for whom killing had become routine, just another task to check off the list.

My eyes sought Ethan, looked for hope and help, and found him frozen in front of Sorcha, a hand outstretched as if he'd moved toward me. His cheeks looked faintly blue, and his body shivered. It was the same magic she'd used on Robert, some cheat not reached by the bracelet Mallory had provided. It wouldn't have, I thought. Those were geared to the alchemy, to the magic. Sorcha had used old-fashioned magic, probably of the dark variety. I had no respect for a woman who cheated her way out of a fight.

And worse, if Logan killed me, she'd kill Ethan. There wasn't a doubt in my mind. She'd probably let him suffer first. Let him mourn before taking his life.

I was our best hope. Which meant I had to get out of Logan's grasp. I stopped struggling, went momentarily still, and felt his grip loosen in what he believed was victory. Chest heaving, he sat back.

I took my chance. I grabbed his neck with my hand, pushed fingers into the tender skin just beneath his jaw. He sputtered, tried to move away. I scissored my legs to push him off me, jumped to my feet, and snatched up the sword I'd dropped when he slammed me to the ground.

Logan coughed, rose to his feet, pulled a dagger from his waistband. "I've always wanted to fight you with a katana."

I didn't let myself think about Ethan, and kept the smile on my face. "Same here, my friend. Let's make it happen."

I struck first, slicing to the left with a double-handled strike. He blocked the strike with his dagger, but the blow unbalanced him. He hadn't been prepared for my being aggressive. Good. That was a strategy I enjoyed.

I didn't give him time to think twice. I kicked back, nailing him in the kidney. He stayed on his feet, caught the tip of his dagger on the back of my calf. But adrenaline had numbed me to pain. I stepped into the kick and pivoted, aiming a punch from the left at his unguarded head. He dodged, the shot glancing off his chin. But his head still popped back, and when I kicked him in the stomach, he hit the roof.

And then I was on his chest, one foot propped at his side, my knee in his abdomen, my katana across his neck.

And as he looked up at me, surprise in his gaze, I pulled out the aspen stake I'd slipped into my waistband before leaving the House.

It was one of the stakes Jeff had given me for protection shortly after we met—and if stabbed through the heart, it was one of the surefire ways to kill a vampire.

Logan lifted his eyebrows. "So that's how it's gonna be? I gave you immortality, and you want to send me to hell?"

My voice was hard. "You gave me nothing. You took, or tried to. Turns out, you weren't very good at it."

I held my katana in one hand, the stake in the other, poised above his heart. My hand shook with need, with hatred, with the fear of having this man, this monster, haunt me for the rest of my life.

He did this. Caused all of it. He was the prime mover, the reason I was a vampire, and the reason my family had been endangered as a result. He'd hurt my brother, injured my friends, and apparently had no qualms about using his magic to make us puppets, to turn us into minions in the sociopathic kingdom he probably believed he'd rule with Reed.

I wanted him dead. I wanted Logan Hill—his name, his magic, his essence, his existence—erased from the earth by my hand. I wanted to plunge the stake into his heart, and see him turn to ash. Because this was his fault.

But even so . . . nothing I could do would change any of that. Nothing I could do with the stake in my hand, nothing that his death would accomplish. I would still be alive, a vampire. Caleb Franklin would still be dead, as would the other girls Logan had killed at Celina's command.

I understood justice, but if he died by my hand, if he died like this, it would haunt me forever. I didn't deserve that. And neither did he.

Gabriel had acknowledged that I had a claim on Logan Hill's life. I wasn't the only one now, and probably wouldn't be the last. But I got to decide how to play my chit.

"Logan Hill," I said, staring into those malicious eyes. "You aren't worth any more of my goddamn time."

I reared back and plunged the stake into his thigh. Blood spilled, hit the roof, and spread in a pool beneath him. I stood up as he howled in pain, screaming as he wrenched himself up, gripped the stake, tried to pull it from his leg.

Yeah, that had been small of me. But damn, did it feel good. "Now we're even, you raging asshole."

"You bitch!" he said, spittle at the corner of his mouth as pain racked him. "You fucking bitch."

I leaned down, smiled at him. "Bitch or not, I just kicked your ass."

And then, because we had bigger battles to fight, I tranq'd him.

I stood up and turned back to look at Sorcha and Adrien. She stood proudly in front of her creation, an amused smile on her face.

"That was entertaining," she said, "if less entertaining than it might have been if you'd actually killed him. And why didn't you?" She cocked her head to the side like she honestly couldn't fathom why I wouldn't have killed him.

"I could tell you, but then I'd have to kill you."

Her grin widened. "Doubtful," she said as magic crackled above us. She glanced at the sky, eyes narrowed like she was reading portents there. And she didn't seem to like what she saw.

She looked at Reed. "Can we get them out of the way?"

"As you wish," Reed said, his gaze on the sky. At one time, he'd relished the idea that he was playing a game with us. But not now; we weren't important anymore. The magic, the QE, and the control it would give him—those were the important things. He wanted control, was waiting for the magic to snap into place. That hadn't happened yet . . . but whatever Mallory and Catcher were doing, it also hadn't erased the green smears of magic from the sky. Was it going to work?

Sorcha looked back at me and grinned, and then threw out a hand. Magic—a bright green sphere of it—launched toward me.

I didn't want any part of that.

I lifted my katana, turning the blade flat, and aimed. The mirrored surface deflected the shot, sent it spinning toward the building, bursting out a chunk of the concrete wall. I was glad that hadn't been me.

She made a frustrated noise, tossed another ball, then another. I spun the sword, the blade catching the light of her alchemical machine before deflecting both shots. One spun off the roof and burst into sparks in midair. The other skidded across the roof, leaving a ten-foot-long char line as it burned out.

"Dull, dull, dull," she said, and turned her malicious gaze to Ethan. She lifted her hands, fingers canted to aim, and let magic fly.

I raced toward him, using every ounce of speed I could muster, dove in front of him, and braced myself for impact.

But the shot burst into crystalline sparks of magic.

On the floor, and not missing any chunks, I looked back.

Mallory stepped off the elevator, her blue hair blowing around her head. Catcher must have been minding the magic downstairs, which was fine by me. I wasn't sure I'd ever been so glad to see her.

She walked forward, surveyed the roof, the machine. And her gaze momentarily widened with surprise as she took in Sorcha before spreading into a smile.

"Should have figured it was you," she said, looking over Sorcha's outfit. "The magic's as overdone as the fashion."

The shot struck home. "You don't know what you're talking about. You're a worthless little hack." She pointed to the sky with a delicate and manicured finger. "You've already lost."

Mallory walked forward. Petite and blue-haired, in a stained shirt and jeans, she faced down Sorcha, tall and lithe and wearing a jumpsuit that probably cost more than Mallory had ever made in a month. They were an unlikely pair, which I guessed was part of the point.

"Actually," Mallory said, "that's not true. Our countermagic has stunted yours. Unfortunately, because your raggedy-ass alchemy was ten times more complicated than it needed to be, the entire situation has locked up."

Sorcha looked absolutely confounded by the possibility.

"Long story short," Mallory said, "we blue-screened your magic, bitch. And in order to break this little tie"—she turned her gaze to the metal tree—"I'm going to need to go to the source."

Sorcha's expression didn't change, but she moved to stand in front of her creation. "If you'd like to test your mettle, let's do it."

Mallory dipped her chin, her eyes fierce. "Bring it."

Now magic filled not just the sky, but the air, as Mallory and Sorcha launched volleys against each other. I shifted to stand in front of Ethan, katana in front of me in case I needed to shield him from the shots of magic, or in case Reed became suddenly interested in what was happening around him.

But they'd all but forgotten we were there. While Reed

watched the city and the sky, Sorcha fought back with one flaming ball after another, and the grin on her face never wavered.

She underestimated Mallory, who'd mixed up the direction of her volleys, but each had moved Sorcha a few inches away from the machine, until she was completely clear of it.

"No!" Sorcha screamed as Mallory gathered up her reserves until a flaming blue ball of magic floated above her hand. And, with a windup as good as any major league pitcher's, threw it toward the tree.

For a split second, nothing happened—no sound, no movement, as if the tree had absorbed the magic and hadn't been affected by it.

Sorcha grinned, but she'd celebrated too early.

Because then there was a deafening groan of metal on metal, and the tree burst down the middle. Light and magic poured upward like a volcano, spreading a thousand feet into the sky and casting blue-green light across the city. We could hear the screams of humans below, afraid the apocalypse had finally befallen their city. The magic that rushed from the machine grew louder, faster, until the tree was vibrating with it.

"Down!" Mallory said, an order the Bells were getting good at delivering tonight. I wrapped an arm around Ethan's head, squeezed my eyes closed.

The explosion felt as if the sun had settled onto the roof, and shook the building so hard I nearly lost my footing and was afraid it would crumble to the ground beneath us.

Shrapnel flew across the roof, stabbing into the walls and showering over the sides of the roof. As rock and metal shards rained down around us, I looked up. The sky was clear and dark, the lines of the QE gone.

Freed from the magic Sorcha had wrought, Ethan stumbled forward. I caught him, waited until he'd blinked confusion from his eyes.

"You're all right?" I asked, helping him find his footing again.

"I'm fine." He lifted a hand to my face. "You're all right?"

I thought of Logan, of the decision I'd made. "I will be."

We were interrupted by screams of frustration.

"No!" Reed shrieked, staring at the remains of the machine that his money had built, and which had ultimately failed him.

He walked to Sorcha, cracked a hand across her face. "What have you done? What have you done? You've ruined everything!"

Ethan growled and, before I could stop him, moved toward Reed with the gaze of a very pissed-off alpha male.

Mallory pulled Sorcha away from the fray, her cheek flaming red from Reed's violence, and kept her still with the threat of magic that percolated in her hand.

As Ethan approached him, Reed looked gratifyingly unsure of his steps. I decided Ethan needed to handle him, and it didn't take him long. Adrien Reed was a man who'd gained power through others' work: others' misery, others' criminality, others' fights. When push came to shove, and he had no minions to protect him or magic to back him up, the facade crumbled.

He offered Ethan a couple of testing jabs, but those seemed to be for form. And when Ethan used a right cross—one of his favorite moves—Reed hit the deck.

"And that," Mallory said, "is how we do it in Chicago."

My grandfather found me standing over Logan, Ethan standing over Reed, and Mallory standing over Sorcha Reed. We probably all looked happier than we should have been. Well, Mallory and I. Ethan still looked disappointed that Reed hadn't put up more of a fight, had proven to be the coward we'd suspected.

We walked out of what remained of Towerline's lobby to screams and applause. In the madness and chaos, humans had encroached on the CPD's barricades. They'd been kept off the plaza, but they filled Michigan Avenue and celebrated as if the Cubs had won another pennant.

I could understand the enthusiasm.

They probably didn't understand what they'd seen, or what we'd done. That we'd been protecting ourselves as much as them. But they understood victory, and that we'd been victorious against the magic that had threatened to tear their city apart.

The plaza looked miserable, scattered with steel and glass and broken granite. Reed and Sorcha screamed obscenities as officers escorted them from the building to the car. Logan's tranq must have worn off, as he shot me nasty looks, so I waved back pleasantly. I wouldn't be afraid of him anymore.

"You know," my grandfather said as he joined us, "I don't think the Reeds are going to enjoy prison. I don't think they'll find it up to their standards."

"No," Ethan said with a grin, "I suspect you're right."

"Robert?" I asked.

"Hospital," my grandfather said. "He stabilized when the Reeds went down."

Relief rushed me. "Thank God."

My grandfather nodded. "Morgan saw him out, fought back a few monsters to keep him safe."

"He's got good instincts," Ethan said. "Only gets into trouble when he ignores them."

My grandfather looked around at the destruction. "And isn't that true of all of us?"

Then he shifted his gaze back to us, smiled. "You did good tonight, kids. Good by Chicago, good by your family, good by your House. I'm proud of both of you."

The weight of disappointing him dissipated, replaced by the warm glow of approval. "Thanks, Grandpa," I said, and, when he pointed to his cheek, leaned forward to press a kiss there.

"I'm going to get the paperwork started," he said, then glanced back at the building and whistled. "And attempt to mollify your father."

"Actually, Chuck, you might want to wait for a moment."

I looked back at Ethan, surprised at the comment, and found him staring at me, his gaze utterly serious.

"Are you all right?"

"I am," he said. "More right than I've been in many, many years." He put his hands on my face. "You are the bravest person I have ever known."

"You aren't so bad yourself," I said with a grin, but Ethan's expression stayed serious.

"What?" I asked, afraid for a moment that he'd been hurt or someone else had. "What's wrong?"

"Nothing," he said, his thumb tracing a line across my cheek as he stared down at me. "I am precisely where I should be."

And there, in the middle of the broken plaza, Ethan Sullivan went down on one knee. He stared up at me with eyes wide with love and pride and masculine satisfaction. He held out a hand, and I put my fingers in his palm.

The crowd of humans—thousands strong—who realized what he was doing roared with excitement. Cameras and cell phones began to flash around us.

"*Holy shit!*" I heard Mallory cry out somewhere behind us, but I couldn't bring myself to look away from the warrior in front of me.

I put my free hand against my chest as if that would stop my throbbing heart from bursting through it. That didn't stop the shaking of my fingers.

"You're all right?" Ethan asked, glancing up at me with obvious amusement at my reaction. "I can stop if you'd like."

I grinned at him. "No, you go ahead. I mean, you're already down there."

"Very well," he said, and the crowd went silent as they strained to hear him.

"Caroline Evelyn Merit, you have changed my life completely. You've made it large and happier, and you have given me love and laughter. Perhaps most of all, you have reminded me what it means to be human. I've looked for four centuries to find you. I cannot fathom a world without you in it. Without your heart, and without your honor. Merit, my Sentinel and my love, will you marry me?"

He was stubborn and arrogant, domineering and imperious. He was brave and honorable, and he was mine. There was no one else. Had never really been anyone else, even before I knew he'd been waiting for me. And if I said yes, there would never be.

"Of course I will."

The crowd erupted again with screams and hoots and applause as Ethan Sullivan, my former enemy, jumped to his feet and kissed me deeply, winding his hands into my hair.

"I love you," he said, pulling back to gaze down at me. "I love you."

"I love you, too." I cleared my throat. "At the risk of asking an ungracious question . . . ," I began, when he smiled down at me, and I smiled back.

"Don't worry, Sentinel. There's a ring. I just hadn't anticipated there'd be a moment quite this perfect." He let his gaze slip across the crowd that watched and cheered around us. "Or a location."

Forever, he said silently, just for me. *And for an eternity after that.*

Forever, I agreed.

Epilogue

TROMPE L'OEIL

Green had been her signature color. Orange most definitely was not. But it was oh so satisfying to see Sorcha and Adrien Reed stripped of expensive clothes and jewelry.

Sorcha was now known as the "Chicago Witch," and her treatment only slightly warmer than her ancestors' treatment in Salem likely had been.

The raid of Reed's office had been accidentally successful, at least after the fact. While there, a very nervous admin confessed to the CPD that Reed had moved computers and files into the Community Safety Center—the very outpost he'd created to coordinate public safety—only the week before. He'd probably thought no one would question files stored in a facility dedicated to the public welfare.

Once again, he'd underestimated us.

Nick Breckenridge had broken the story of Reed's criminal involvement. The Reeds had been stripped of their friends, their positions, and the sycophantic devotion they believed they were entitled to. I'd grinned hugely at the photograph of the two of them in their ill-fitting jumpsuits, hair uncoiffed and Botox (or magic) fading, shuffling along with legs and hands chained together. Logan Hill had been behind them, looking decidedly unhappy about the turn of events.

The trio was now in the same prison that held Regan and Seth Tate and a handful of shifters. And since Seth was technically on our side, he promised they wouldn't have access to magic for a very long time.

Robert was healing physically but had a long way to go emotionally. Rather than admitting he'd been played by the Reeds, he'd decided the story, the charges, the magic were part of a conspiracy. He was an intelligent man, and I had to hope he'd come around. But my father's prejudices—which, ironically, he'd mostly grown out of—had infected Robert.

He'd refused to see me, had even declined to attend the dinner Ethan and I had had with my parents to celebrate my birthday. It hadn't been the most relaxing evening—they were still my parents, after all—and Robert's absence had been obvious. Elizabeth had come, made apologies, but the stiffness in her smile showed she also wasn't quite sure of me, or of us.

Ethan said he had another surprise, so when we'd climbed back into his car after an evening with more "foams" and "mousses" than should ever have been together on a single plate, he demanded I wear a blindfold "so as not to spoil the surprise."

The request was odd enough in itself, but the fact that he'd had one was rather intriguing. I was learning all sorts of things about my Masterly fiancé.

And I was still getting used to calling him that.

Ethan drove the car north; I could tell the direction from the scent of the lake to our right and the quiet of the dark water. The sounds of the city on our left extended only so far. But when we left Lake Shore and headed into the city, I lost my sense of direction. He turned enough times that I thought we might be going in circles, which seemed more surreptitious than necessary considering the fact that I couldn't see at all.

"Could I at least get a hint?"

As if sensing he had me on the hook, he took a moment to answer. "I need to return something."

I chuckled. "I hope you're not thinking about returning me."

"No," he said with a smile I could hear. "I've long since ripped your tags off."

"Har-har."

After a few more quiet minutes, the car slowed and pulled to a stop. "A moment, Sentinel."

The weight in the car shifted, and the door shut. A moment later, my door opened and he touched my arm. "I'm here, Sentinel. Let me help you out."

I put my hand in his, turned to put my feet on the ground, and stood. I took in a breath, trying to scent out where I was, but got nothing unusual. "Time to take this off?"

"Not yet," he said, closing the car door, and situating himself on my right-hand side, tucking my arm into his. "A bit farther to go first. Just hold on to me."

Not having a better choice—I'd long ago decided to trust him—I took careful steps, one hand wrapped around his biceps, the other out and feeling for any obstacles in my way. That was how I knew we'd passed through a door and traveled down a hallway before emerging into a larger room. A few more steps, and he came to a stop.

"I'm going to take the blindfold off now."

I nodded while he unknotted the silk, then blinked when he revealed only darkness.

There was a buzz of sound . . . and then the lights came on.

"Dear God," I said, eyes wide and staring. We weren't in a room, big or otherwise.

We were in the middle of Wrigley Field.

I turned in a long, slow circle.

Because my last try had gone so horribly wrong, I hadn't actually been inside Wrigley since becoming a vampire. I hadn't seen the bleachers, the scoreboard, the Wrigley rooftops where fans outside the stadium watched the games. None of it since I'd gotten fangs, which didn't explain why I was here now.

I looked back at Ethan, found his gaze on me, his expression indecipherable. "What are we doing here?"

"Last week, Logan took this from you—this experience at Wrigley. But I took this from you more generally one year ago when I made you a vampire. I took from you things that you won't get back, including afternoon baseball." Ethan took my hand. "So I mean to give you back what I can."

Realization struck me. "The night we went to Wrigley," I said. "You'd meant to propose."

"Yes."

I thought back to that night. "That's why everyone was gathered in your office. It wasn't a 'feel better' celebration. It was supposed to have been an engagement party."

"You should have gotten a ring; instead you were shot. Unexpected metal, either way, but I thought you still deserved a gathering."

I smiled at him. "Or you didn't want to waste the champagne."

"I'm not a troglodyte; it was very good champagne."

I didn't try to rein in my adoring grin. "You were going to propose to me at a Cubs game, and you had an engagement party planned. Ethan Sullivan, that nearly makes up for your centuries of imperiousness."

"It's neither the first time nor the last time I've been romantic, Sentinel. Much like Liam Neeson, I have certain . . . skills."

He even got the pause right; Luc would have been proud.

"Color me convinced. Ahem. At the risk of sounding ungrateful, what, exactly, did you have planned?"

"A proposal on the big screen."

"No!" I whined, dropping my forehead to his chest. I loved big-screen sports proposals. And it would have been even better now; the new Cubs screen was enormous.

"You'll note that even though I was not able to reschedule the screen, I did, in fact, give you Wrigley Field. And then there's this." Ethan Sullivan pulled a small burgundy box from his pocket.

I probably looked like a kid on Christmas staring down at it.

Ethan chuckled. "I assume from the awestruck expression on your face that you'd like to see what's inside?"

"I mean, you went to all the trouble, so . . ."

Ethan flicked it open.

Nestled on a bed of burgundy satin sat a glorious double-diamond ring. The band, so delicate it looked like diamonds had been threaded together on silver string, spiraled around two round diamonds.

It was a *toi et-moi* ring. The phrase meant "you and me"—symbolized by the gemstones. Napoleon had given Josephine one. I knew, because I'd researched it for my dissertation before I was made a vampire.

"Damn, Sullivan."

"I do my research," Ethan said, sliding the ring from its box. He took my left hand in his free one, slid the ring onto the fourth finger. "Now it's official."

He drew me toward him, kissed me good and hard.

"And now," he said, pulling back and glancing behind me, "we celebrate."

He turned me around.

Ethan had given me diamonds, Wrigley Field . . . and my family. My grandfather. Mallory and Catcher. Jeff and Fallon. Luc and Lindsey. Margot and Malik. They rushed forward with bottles of Veuve Clicquot and glasses, and threw glittering handfuls of silver confetti that danced in the light. There was a small table in the grass covered with a Cubs cloth and dotted with snacks.

A man who'd already given me immortality, who'd sacrificed his life to save mine, who'd stood for me and challenged me . . . and on occasion made me utterly and completely crazy, had thrown me a party in Wrigley Field.

Sentinel? Are you all right? You look a bit wan.

I looked back at him, drank in the golden hair and gemlike eyes. He was my recent past, and my eternal future. *I've never been better. Unless you also happened to grab me one of those Cubs flashlights?*

He rolled his eyes.

Mallory flat-out ran toward us and wrapped her arms around me. "You're getting married! You're getting married!" She squeezed me tight, her voice a squeak of excitement. She pulled back, her arms on mine. "And not just married. You're getting married to *Darth Sullivan*!"

"I am," I said, most of the air squeezed from my lungs by her exuberance, but I managed to hug her back nonetheless.

"I knew from the moment you two met, you'd either kill each other or get married. I guess you chose the latter."

I glanced at Ethan, who was chatting with Catcher, golden hair framing his face like a beautiful, young god. And, more important, who'd understood me when I faced the kind of decision that changes you. "I'm not sure I had a choice," I said.

"All right," Catcher said, after a moment, gently turning her away. "Let's let the rest of them get in here." He leaned forward and pressed a kiss to my cheek. "Congratulations, Merit."

"Thank you," I said with a smile as my grandfather moved toward me, wrapped his arms around me.

"I'm so happy for you, baby girl."

"Thank you, Grandpa. I'm happy for me, too."

My grandfather offered Ethan a handshake. "I'm not just losing a granddaughter," he said. "I'm gaining a grandvampire."

"That's a very positive outlook," Ethan said. "And it's appreciated."

"I'm very happy for both of you," he said with a smile, then held out a hand.

Jeff walked over, enveloped me in an enormous hug. "Congrats, Merit."

I squeezed back. "Thank you, Jeff." When he pulled back, I grinned at him. "When do I get to start harassing you about proposing to Fallon?"

He just smiled. "A man has his secrets, Merit. Oh, hey, look who's here!"

We looked back, found Gabriel and his wife, Tanya, walking onto the field. She was delicately pretty compared to his rugged maleness, with brown hair and blue eyes, her cheeks flushed pink, her lips generous and smiling.

Gabe's son, Connor, was in his arms, chewing on a plastic giraffe I'd seen before. He was a beautiful little boy, nearly a year old now, with his mother's dark hair and blue eyes. He was the prince of the North American Central Pack, and even as a child, he seemed to glow with potential.

"Very interesting," I said as Gabriel scanned the crowd, walked toward us. Ethan stepped beside me, which I didn't think was a coincidence.

"I understand congratulations are in order," he said, offering Ethan a hand. The other vampires in the hall had gone quiet as they watched the interaction, just in case there was still bad blood. Ethan took it, and they shook heartily.

Gabe turned to me, pressed a kiss to my cheek. "Congratulations, Kitten. Berna sends her warmest regards."

"You sure about that?" I asked.

Tanya offered a tall, cylindrical paper bag that smelled like yeast and sugar. "*Korovai,*" she said. "It's a traditional Ukrainian wedding bread. She's happy you're engaged, but she's irritated about something to do with ballet."

"Berna enjoys her opinions," Gabriel said with a grin. "It's like a hobby for her."

"Well, it smells amazing," Ethan said, accepting the bread. "Please thank her for us. And please, help yourself to some champagne."

"Can't say no to that," Gabriel said with a grin, and escorted Tanya toward the snack table.

And as I glanced around, I realized my grandfather had stepped away, had his ear to his phone. Ethan, catching the direction of my gaze, looked, too. And soon enough, everyone was watching him, expressions tense.

When my grandfather put the phone away, he glanced at us. "At the risk of ruining the party—" he began, but Ethan shook his head.

"Please, go ahead. Say what needs to be said."

"A judge offered bail to Sorcha and Adrien Reed."

There were curses and disgusted looks throughout the group. Fistfuls of angry magic replaced the confetti that had sparkled through the air.

"You are freaking *kidding* me," Mallory said.

"Unfortunately not," my grandfather said. "Nick has pointed out the particular judge was mentioned in Reed's papers. He was a supporter. But that lack of ethics isn't the biggest news. The Reeds were driven home a few hours ago with monitoring devices. They were tampered with, which sent an alert to the CPD."

We shifted nervously, waiting for the rest of it.

"Adrien Reed is dead. Killed, it appears, by his own hand. Sorcha Reed is gone. Their accounts have been cleaned out."

Ethan closed his eyes ruefully.

"She killed him," I said, and all eyes turned to me. "Her plan—her long-term plan to get free—to become queen, failed. Killing him, taking the money, running. She'd have considered that a consolation prize." It didn't fit with the Sorcha I'd seen on Reed's arm, but it fit with the one I'd seen at Towerline.

"We'll see what the evidence says," my grandfather said. But there was a flatness to his voice that indicated he didn't disagree.

"What if she comes back?" Mallory asked.

"Then we'll deal with it," Catcher interjected, putting an arm around her. "Just as we've dealt with everything else."

"And we'll help," Ethan said, and looked around the crowd, got nods from his vampires, from the shifters.

"All for one and one for all?" Catcher asked.

"All for Chicago," Ethan amended. "Because that's what this is really about. Not vampire, not shifter, not sorcerer, not human. A man and a woman who believed they were entitled to more than they'd earned and were willing to use people to get it." His eyes sparked like fire. "She tries something here again, and she'll see how hard Chicagoans will fight."

And until then, I thought, as he took my hand and squeezed, we had each other. And we'd try to make the best of it.

Turn the page for an preview of the first novel in
Chloe Neill's exciting Devil's Isle series:

The Veil

CHAPTER ONE

The French Quarter was thinking about war again.

Booms echoed across the neighborhood, vibrating windows and shaking the shelves at Royal Mercantile—the finest purveyor of dehydrated meals in New Orleans.

And antique walking sticks. We were flush with antique walking sticks.

I sat at the store's front counter, working on a brass owl that topped one of them. The owl's head was supposed to turn when you pushed a button on the handle, but the mechanism was broken. I'd taken apart the tiny brass pieces and found the problem—one of the small toothy gears had become misaligned. I just needed to slip it back into place.

I adjusted the magnifying glass over the owl, its jointed brass wings spread to reveal its inner mechanisms. I had a thin screwdriver in one hand, a pair of watchmaking tweezers in the other. To get the gear in place, I had to push one spring down and another up in that very small space.

I liked tinkering with the store's antiques, to puzzle through broken parts and sticky locks. It was satisfying to make something work that hadn't before. And since the demand for fancy French sideboards and secretaries wasn't exactly high these days, there was plenty of inventory to pick from.

I nibbled on my bottom lip as I moved the pieces, carefully adjusting the tension so the gear could slip in. I had to get the gear into the back compartment, between the rods, and into place between the springs. Just a smidge to the right, and . . .

Boom.

I jumped, the sound of another round of fireworks shuddering me back to the store—and the gear that now floated in the air beside me, bobbing a foot off the counter's surface.

"Damn," I muttered, heart tripping.

I'd moved it with my mind, with the telekinetic magic I wasn't supposed to have. At least, not unless I wanted a lifetime prison sentence.

I let go of the magic, and the gear dropped, hit the counter, bounced onto the floor.

My heart now pounding in my chest, the fingers on both hands crossed superstitiously, I hopped off the stool and hurried to the front door to check the box mounted on the building across the street. It was a monitor with a camera on top, triggered when the amount of magic in the air rose above background levels—like when a Sensitive accidentally moved a gear.

I'd gotten lucky; the light was still red. I must not have done enough to trigger it, at least from this distance. I was still in the clear—for now. But damn, that had been close. I hadn't even known I'd been using magic.

Boom.

Already pumped with nervous energy, I jumped again.

"Good lord," I said, pushing the door open and stepping outside onto the threshold between the store's bay windows, where MERCANTILE was mosaicked in tidy blue capitals.

It was mid-October, and the heat and humidity still formed a miserable blanket across the French Quarter. Royal Street was nearly empty of people.

The war had knocked down half the buildings in the Quarter, which gave me a clear view of the back part of the neighborhood and the Mississippi River, which bordered it. Figures moved along the riverbank, testing fireworks for the finale of the festivities. The air smelled like sparks and flame, and wisps of white smoke drifted across the twilight sky.

It wasn't the first time we'd seen smoke over the Quarter.

On an equally sweltering day in October seven years ago, the Veil—the barrier that separated humans from a world of magic we hadn't even known existed—was shattered by the Paranormals who'd lived in what we now called the Beyond.

They wanted our world, and they didn't have a problem eradicating us in the process. They spilled through the fracture, bringing death and destruction—and changing everything: Magic was now real and measurable and a scientific fact.

I was seventeen when the Veil, which ran roughly along the ninetieth line of longitude, straight north through the heart of NOLA, had splintered. That made New Orleans, where I'd been born and raised, ground zero.

My dad had owned Royal Mercantile when it was still an antiques store, selling French furniture, priceless art, and very expensive jewelry. (And, of course, the walking sticks. So many damn walking sticks.) When the war started, I'd helped him transition the store by adding MREs, water, and other supplies to the inventory.

War had spread through southern Louisiana, and then north, east, and west through Alabama, Mississippi, Tennessee, Arkansas, and the eastern half of Texas. The conflict had destroyed so much of the South, leaving acres of scarred land and burned, lonely cities. It had taken a year of fighting to stop the bloodshed and close the Veil again. By that time, the military had been spread so thin that civilians often fought alongside the troops.

Unfortunately, he hadn't lived to see the Veil close again. The store became mine and I moved into the small apartment on the third floor. We hadn't lived there together—he didn't want to spend every hour of his life in the same building, he'd said. But the store and building were now my only links to him, so I didn't hesitate. I missed him terribly.

When the war was done, Containment—the military unit that managed the war and the Paranormals—had tried to scrub New Orleans not only of magic but of voodoo, Marie Laveau, ghost tours, and even literary vampires. They'd convinced Congress to pass the so-called Magic Act, banning magic inside and outside the war zone, what we called the Zone. (Technically, it was the MIGECC Act: Measure for the Illegality of Glamour and Enchantment in Conflict Communities. But that didn't have the same ring to it.)

The war had flattened half of Fabourg Marigny, a neighborhood next door to the French Quarter, and Containment took advantage. They'd shoved every remaining Para they could find into the neighborhood and built a wall to keep them there.

Officially, it was called the District.

We called it Devil's Isle, after a square in the Marigny where criminals had once been hanged. And if Containment learned I had magic, I'd be imprisoned there with the rest of them.

They had good reason to be wary. Most humans weren't affected by magic; if it was an infection, an illness, they were immune. But a small percentage of the population didn't have that immunity. We were sensitive to the energy from the Beyond. That hadn't been a problem before the Veil was opened; the magic that came through was minimal—enough for magic tricks and illusions but not much else. But the scarred Veil wasn't as strong; magic still seeped through the rip where it had been sewn back together. Sensitives weren't physically equipped to handle the magic that poured through.

Magic wasn't a problem for Paras. In the Beyond, they'd bathed in the magic day in and day out, but that magic had an outlet—their bodies became canvases for the power. Some had wings; some had horns or fangs.

Sensitives couldn't process magic that way. Instead, we just kept absorbing more and more magic, until we lost ourselves completely. Until we became wraiths, pale and dangerous shadows of the humans we'd once been, our lives devoted to seeking out more magic, filling that horrible need.

I'd learned eight months ago that I was a Sensitive, part of that unlucky percentage. I'd been in the store's second-floor storage room, moving a large, star-shaped sign to a better spot. (Along with walking sticks, my dad had loved big antique gas station signs. The sticks, at least, were easier to store.) I'd tripped on a knot in the old oak floor and stumbled backward, falling flat on my back. And I'd watched in slow motion as the hundred-pound sign—and one of its sharp metallic points—fell toward me.

I hadn't had time to move, to roll away, or even to throw up an arm and block the rusty spike of steel, which was aimed at the spot between my eyes. But I did have a split second to object, to curse the fact that I'd lived through war only to be impaled by a damn gas station sign that should have been rusting on a barn in the middle of nowhere.

"No, damn it!" I'd screamed out the words with every ounce of air in my lungs, with my eyes squeezed shut like a total coward.

And nothing had happened.

Lips pursed, I'd slitted one eye open to find the metal tip hovering two inches above my face. I'd held my breath, shaking with adrenaline and sweating with fear, for a full minute before I gathered up the nerve to move.

I'd counted to five, then dodged and rolled away. The star's point hit the floor, tunneling in. There was still a two-inch-deep notch in the wood.

I hadn't wanted the star to impale me—and it hadn't. I'd used magic I hadn't known I'd had—Sensitivity I hadn't known I possessed—to stop the thing in its tracks.

I'd gotten lucky then, too: The magic monitor hadn't been triggered, and I'd kept my store . . . and my freedom.

Another boom sounded, pulling me through memory to my spot on the sidewalk. I jumped, cursed under my breath.

"I think you're good, guys!" I yelled. Not that I was close enough for them to hear me, or that they'd care. This was War Night. Excess was the entire point.

Six years before, the Second Battle of New Orleans had raged across the city. (The first NOLA battle, during the War of 1812, had been very human. At least as far as we were aware.) It had been one of the last battles of the war and one of the biggest.

Tonight we'd celebrate our survival with colors, feathers, brass bands, and plenty of booze. It would be loud, crazy, and amazing. Assuming I could manage not to get arrested before the fun started . . .

"You finally losing it, Claire?"

I glanced back and found a man, tall and leanly muscled, standing behind me. Antoine Lafayette Gunnar Landreau, one of my best friends, looked unwilted by the heat.

His dark brown, wavy hair was perfectly rakish, and his smile was adorably crooked, the usual gleam in his deep-set hazel eyes. Tonight, he wore slim dark pants and a sleeveless shirt that showed off his well-toned arms—and the intricate but temporary paintings that stained his skin.

"Hey, Gunnar." We exchanged cheek kisses. I cursed when another *boom* sounded, followed by the sparkle of gold stars in the air.

I smiled despite myself. "Damn it. Now they're just showing off."

"Good thing you're getting into the spirit," he said with a grin. "Happy War Night."

"Happy War Night, smarty-pants. Let me check your ink."

Gunnar obliged, stretching out his arms so I could get a closer view. New Orleans was a city of traditions, and War Night had its own: the long parade, the fireworks, the spiked punch we simply called "Drink" because the ingredients depended on what was available. And since the beginning, when there was nothing but mud and ash, painting the body to remember the fallen. Making a living memorial of those of us who'd survived.

The intricate scene on Gunnar's left arm showed survivors celebrating in front of the Cabildo, waving a purple flag bearing four gold fleurs-de-lis—the official postwar flag of New Orleans. The other arm showed the concrete and stone sculpture of wings near Talisheek in St. Tammany Parish, which memorialized one of the deadliest battles of the war, and the spot where thousands of Paras had entered our world.

The realism lifted goose bumps on my arms. "Seriously amazing."

"Just trying to do War Night proud. And Aunt Reenie."

"God bless her," I said of Gunnar's late and lamented aunt, who'd been a great lover of War Night, rich as Croesus, and, according to Gunnar's mother, "not quite there."

"God bless her," he agreed.

"Let's get the party started," I said. "You want something to drink?"

"Always the hostess. I don't suppose there's any tea?"

"I think there's a little bit left," I said, opening the door and gesturing him in.

Gunnar was a sucker for sweet tea, a rarity now that sugar was a luxury in New Orleans. That was another lingering effect of war. Magic was powerful stuff, and it wasn't meant to be in our world. Nothing would grow in soil scarred by magic, so war had devastated the Zone's farms. And since there were still rumors of bands of Paras in rural areas who'd escaped the Containment roundup and preyed on humans, there weren't many businesses eager to ship in the goods that wouldn't grow here.

There'd been a mass exodus of folks out of the cities with major fighting—New Orleans, Baton Rouge, Mobile—about three weeks after the war started, when it began to look as though we weren't equipped to fight Paras, even on our own soil.

There were plenty of people who still asked why we stayed in the Zone, why we put up with scarcity, with the threat of wraith and Para attacks, with Containment on every corner, with Devil's Isle looming behind us.

Some folks stayed because they didn't have a better choice, because somebody had to take care of those who couldn't leave. Some stayed because they didn't have resources to leave, anywhere to go, or anyone to go to. And some stayed because they'd been through hard times before—when there'd been no electricity, no comforts, and too much grief—and the city was worth saving again. Some stayed because if we left, that would be the end of New Orleans, Little Rock, Memphis, and Nashville. Of the culture, the food, the traditions. Of the family members who existed only in our memories, who tied us to the land.

And some folks stayed because they had no choice at all. Containment coordinated the exodus. And when everyone who'd wanted to get out was out, they started controlling access to the Zone's borders, hoping to keep the Paras and fighting contained.

No, staying in the Zone wasn't easy. But for a lot of us—certainly for me—it was the only option. I'd rather make do in New Orleans than be rich anywhere else.

We'd tried to make the best of it. In the Quarter, we'd solved the scorched-earth problem by planting things in containers with "clean" soil. I had a lemon tree and a tomato plant in the courtyard behind the store, and I got more fruit and produce from the small roof garden shared by a few of us who still lived in the Quarter. We'd taken over the terrace that had once been a fancy pool and cabana at the abandoned Florissant Hotel, turned it into a community garden. Containment had done the same thing at the former Marriott to provide supplies for the agents.

War made people creative about their survival.

Owning one of the few stores left in the Quarter also had some advantages. Because so many of my customers were Containment personnel, I'd been able to get goods from the military convoys that crossed the Zone. It also helped that Gunnar worked for Devil's Isle's Commandant. Of course, that had unfortunate personal implications, too. Gunnar didn't know about my magic, and I had no intention of telling him. That would be bad for both of us.

Gunnar followed me inside to the small curtained area behind the front counter. It was the building's "kitchen," and held a small blue refrigerator that had lived (thank God) long past its prime, a gas stove, an old farmhouse sink, and a few stingy cabinets.

I sighed with relief at the burst of cold air from the fridge. Gunnar moved beside me, and we stood in front of it for a moment, savoring the chill.

"All right. Let's not waste the cold while we've got it." Consistent power was another rarity in the Zone. Magic and electricity didn't mix, which made the electrical system unstable. Keeping the lights on and the city dry were constant battles.

Considering that, it made sense to finish the tea while it was still good and cold. I grabbed the cut-glass pitcher and poured the rest of the tea into two plastic hurricane cups.

The pitcher had come with the store; the cups were my contribution.

Gunnar sipped, closed his eyes in obvious pleasure. "You could steal a man's heart with this."

I took a drink, nodded. "It's good, but it hasn't done much heart stealing so far." My last go-round hadn't been successful. Rainier Beaulieu had been tall, dark, and handsome. Unfortunately, when he told me I was the "only one," he'd forgotten to mention "right now."

I'd been in a lull since that little mistake. The Zone wasn't usually a draw for the young and eligible.

Gunnar grinned. "It's War Night. Everything could change."

That was the best part of it: Anything seemed possible. "My fingers are crossed. Feel free to keep an eye out."

"I love playing your wingman."

"I can wing my own men. You're just the scout. How are the crowds?"

"Emboldened by the heat," Gunnar said with a grin. "And embiggening. It's gonna be a helluva night out there."

"War Night always is," I said, but knew exactly what he meant. New Orleans could never be accused of shyness, and War Night would be no exception.

He glanced at the wall clock. "Tadji's meeting us at the start. How much longer till you close up?"

Tadji Dupre was the third in our friendship trio. "Fifteen minutes if I keep her open until six."

"Be a rebel," he said. "Close early."

Funds were hard to come by these days, and I wasn't one to turn down even fifteen minutes of business. On the other hand, I probably wouldn't be missing big sales tonight. People would be thinking about jazz and booze, not dried fruit and duct tape.

Some of that jazz bloomed outside, and we walked back into the front room, drawn by the music.

Half a dozen men in brilliantly colored suits, the fabric and elaborate headpieces covered in feathers and beading, filled the sidewalk. They were the Vanguard, New Orleanians who'd served in the war and organized the first War Night parade six years ago. A few had been the feathered performers known as Mardi Gras Indians, and they'd brought some of those traditions into this celebration.

One of members stopped, tapped a dark fist against the window. I grinned back at Tony Mercier, a silver whistle between his teeth, a black patch covering the eye he'd lost in the Second Battle. Tony had fought with the Niners from the Ninth Ward. And now he was the Vanguard's Big Chief.

He pointed down the street, signaling their destination, and then back at me. That message was obvious: They were heading to the starting line, and it was time for me to join them.

"I'm leaving soon!" I called out, and waved them on. They shuffled down the sidewalk, followed by a second line band that grooved to notes wrought through worn brass. A tuba marked the beat, a trombone and trumpet pushed the rhythm and melody, and half a dozen men, women, and children with tambourines, silver whistles, and homemade drums danced behind them.

The song, the instruments, and the parade were bittersweet reminders of life before the Veil had opened. But they were also reminders of what made New Orleans so amazing: its creativity, its traditions, its willingness to band together and face down a common enemy.

I rejected the idea that I was part of that common enemy. And besides, tonight wasn't about fear or regret. Tonight was about life, about experience, about celebration.

"All right," I said, grinning at Gunnar. "Lock the door. Let the good times roll."

"Laissez les bon temps rouler," he agreed.

Chloe Neill, author of the Chicagoland Vampires novels (*Dark Debt*, *Blood Games*, *Wild Things*), the Dark Elite novels (*Charmfall*, *Hexbound*, *Firespell*), and the Devil's Isle novels (*The Veil*), was born and raised in the South but now makes her home in the Midwest—justclose enough to Cadogan House and St. Sophia's to keep an eye on things. When not transcribing Merit's, Lily's, and Claire's adventures, she bakes, works, and scours the Internet for good recipes and great graphic design. Chloe also maintains her sanity by spending time with her boys—her favorite landscape photographer (her husband), and their dogs, Baxter and Scout. (Both she and the photographer understand the dogs are in charge.)

CONNECT ONLINE

chloeneill.com

facebook.com/ authorchloeneill

twitter.com/ chloeneill